CRITICAL DOUBT

Off the Grid: FBI Series #7

BARBARA FREETHY

BARBARA
FREETHY
—BOOKS—

Fog City Publishing

PRAISE FOR BARBARA FREETHY

"A fabulous, page-turning combination of romance and intrigue. Fans of Nora Roberts and Elizabeth Lowell will love this book." — *NYT Bestselling Author Kristin Hannah on Golden Lies*

"PERILOUS TRUST is a non-stop thriller that seamlessly melds jaw-dropping suspense with sizzling romance. Readers will be breathless in anticipation as this fast-paced and enthralling love story goes in unforeseeable directions." — *USA Today HEA Blog*

"Barbara Freethy's first book PERILOUS TRUST in her OFF THE GRID series is an emotional, action packed, crime drama that keeps you on the edge of your seat...I'm exhausted after reading this but in a good way. 5 Stars!" — *Booklovers Anonymous*

"Powerful and absorbing...sheer hold-your-breath suspense." — *NYT Bestselling Author Karen Robards on Don't Say A Word*

"I loved this story from start to finish. Right from the start of PERILOUS TRUST, the tension sets in. Goodness, my heart was starting to beat a little fast by the end of the prologue! I found myself staying up late finishing this book, and that is something I don't normally do." — *My Book Filled Life Blog*

"Freethy is at the top of her form. Fans of Nora Roberts will find a similar tone here, framed in Freethy's own spare, elegant style." — *Contra Costa Times on Summer Secrets*

"Freethy hits the ground running as she kicks off another winning romantic suspense series...Freethy is at her prime with a superb combo of engaging characters and gripping plot." — *Publishers' Weekly on Silent Run*

PRAISE FOR BARBARA FREETHY

"Barbara Freethy is a master storyteller with a gift for spinning tales about ordinary people in extraordinary situations and drawing readers into their lives." — *Romance Reviews Today*

"Freethy (Silent Fall) has a gift for creating complex, appealing characters and emotionally involving, often suspenseful, sometimes magical stories." — *Library Journal on Suddenly One Summer*

Freethy hits the ground running as she kicks off another winning romantic suspense series...Freethy is at her prime with a superb combo of engaging characters and gripping plot." — *Publishers' Weekly on Silent Run*

"Grab a drink, find a comfortable reading nook, and get immersed in this fast paced, realistic, romantic thriller! 5 STARS!" *Perrin – Goodreads on Elusive Promise*

"If you love nail-biting suspense and heartbreaking emotion, Silent Run belongs on the top of your to-be-bought list. I could not turn the pages fast enough." — *NYT Bestselling Author Mariah Stewart*

"Words cannot explain how phenomenal this book was. The characters are so believable and relatable. The twists and turns keep you on the edge of your seat and flying through the pages. This is one book you should be desperate to read." *Caroline - Goodreads on Ruthless Cross*

"Hooked me from the start and kept me turning pages throughout all the twists and turns. Silent Run is powerful romantic intrigue at its best." — *NYT Bestselling Author JoAnn Ross*

CRITICAL DOUBT
Off the Grid: FBI Series #7

For more information on Barbara Freethy's books, visit her website:
www.barbarafreethy.com

CHAPTER ONE

ONLY THE GOOD DIE YOUNG...

The phrase went around in Ryker's head as he walked into the church auditorium Monday afternoon for the celebration of life honoring Lieutenant Paul Hawkins, dead at the age of thirty-two. He'd stood in the back of the church during the funeral, hidden in the shadows, exactly the way he liked it, but now he had to face the widow of one of his best friends. He had to acknowledge that Paul was gone—another one of his brothers had fallen.

Paul hadn't died in combat like Leo and Carlos; he'd passed away after a freak fall from the roof of a house, where he'd downed too many shots of tequila in an attempt to escape the demons that had been chasing him and every one of their seven-member Army ranger unit, including himself...

The past nine months had been hell, ever since a mission had led his team into a deadly ambush. Two had died, three had been injured, and while two had escaped without physical wounds, they hadn't escaped psychological injury. In less than an hour, his team had been shattered. They would never do another mission again. Not one of them was still in the army. They had either left by choice or been forced out through death and medical restrictions.

For him, it had not been a choice to leave the service, but his physical injuries had been too severe to continue to serve as a Ranger and he'd wanted to do nothing else, so his military career that had started at West Point and lasted another twelve years was over.

But the deaths weren't over.

The repercussions from that deadly ambush were still rolling, and today they were being felt by Abby Hawkins, a thirty-year-old woman and her seven-year-old son, Tyler. They stood by a table draped in the American flag, a gold urn in the center containing the ashes of a man who had not only been a soldier but also a husband and a father.

Abby had long, reddish-brown hair that hung like curtains on either side of her face. Every now and then, she seemed to duck behind those curtains to take a second for herself. But then she had to come back out, fake a smile, listen to whatever words of condolence were coming her way. Tyler was at her side, a freckle-faced, ginger-haired kid, who looked as unhappy as anyone Ryker had ever seen. Abby's parents were nearby, also appearing strained and emotional.

There wasn't anyone present from Paul's family. His mom had died when he was three, and his father, who had also been a military man, had passed away seven years ago. Since then, Abby's family had become Paul's family, and he'd said many times how grateful he was for them.

There were two men in uniform speaking to Abby now. The older man with the silver-gray hair, friendly face, and easygoing manner was Colonel Bill Vance, who Ryker and his team had served under in Afghanistan. Vance had been a mentor to Paul—to all of them. Next to Vance was Sergeant James Lofgren, a medic who had been attached to their unit, and had been one of the first to treat their injuries that fateful night.

Ryker struggled to breathe. Seeing Vance and Lofgren was taking him back to a place he didn't want to go. He forced himself to look away. But as his gaze moved across the room, it caught on a memorial photo display and another man he hadn't seen in a long time—Todd Davis. Todd had been part of their seven-member team and had been Paul's best friend. Todd wasn't in uniform today. He'd left the army months ago, and today he wore an ill-fitting dark suit that hung loosely on his lean frame. His dirty-blond hair looked like it could have used a comb, and he didn't appear to have shaved in a couple of days. He looked terrible and confused, shaking his head every other second in bewilderment, as he drank a beer and stared at a large photo of their ranger team.

Ryker's gut churned. He didn't want to look at that picture. He didn't want to be reminded of all who were lost. In fact, he didn't really want to talk to Todd, but he had to. He needed to find out what had happened to Paul, why he had been drinking so much, why he had gone on the roof, why he had fallen to his death when he'd been as surefooted as anyone Ryker had ever known.

His gaze swept the room once more as he wondered where the other members of his unit were. Hank and Mason should be here, too, but he hadn't seen them in the church. *Why weren't they in attendance?* If he could drag himself back into the world, so could they.

Frowning, he looked back at Abby. She squatted down to talk to a little girl. He could see her trying to smile, but the pain was evident on her face. He wished he could do something to change what she was going through, but he had nothing to offer but the same empty words of solace she was getting from everyone else.

Abby would want more from him. He'd been the leader of the team, and he'd let everyone down, not just the day of the ambush but ever since then. He hadn't spoken to Paul in probably eight months. Instead, he'd isolated himself on the Chesapeake Bay, living as far away from people and noise as he possibly could, because every tiny sound threatened to trigger the bells in his head that were relentless in their torturous sound.

The doctor said it was PTSD. There didn't seem to be a phys-ical reason for the bells to ring, but they did, and he never knew when the debilitating sounds would overwhelm his brain and make him feel like he was losing his mind.

Even now, he felt the sounds beginning to build. Hushed conversations seemed incredibly loud. Heels hitting the hard floor

made him cringe. Anxiety rose within him, bringing anger and
despair with it.

He'd once been proud of his fearlessness, but now fear seemed
to come from every shadow, every corner, and he couldn't seem to
stop the physical reactions. When someone jostled him from
behind, and he spun around, his defensive reflexes jumped into
overdrive. He raised his hands, prepared to strike. He could have
snapped the woman's neck in one second. Thankfully, he did not.

She gave him a startled look as she stepped back. Concern
flashed in her eyes as she probably read the murderous intent in his
gaze. But that worry was then followed by shock.

The same surprise ran through his head. He dropped his hands,
his confused brain trying to make sense of the beautiful woman in
front of him.

Was it her? Could it be her? It seemed unimaginable.

He'd last seen her in a hotel room on a hot summer night in
Doha five years ago. He'd been on leave, celebrating a successful
mission and taking some well-deserved days of rest. She'd been on
a layover, stopping in Doha after a USO show in Kuwait. He'd
taken one look at her stunning face and body and knew he had to
have her.

When she'd let him buy her a drink, he'd felt like his ride on top
of the world was going for another spin, especially when she'd
suggested no names, no promises and no regrets. He couldn't
believe his luck. He'd met the perfect woman.

One drink had turned into two, then three. They'd danced til
midnight, each step fanning the sparks between them, and then
made their way upstairs to his hotel room. It had been a night he'd
never forgotten. And surprisingly he'd had more than a few regrets
when he'd woken up to find her gone. He'd wished then he'd gotten
her name. In fact, he'd tried to find her after that, but no one
seemed to know who she was. He'd started thinking of her as a
beautiful dream.

But she was real, and she was here in Dobbs, Georgia, at the
funeral of one of his fallen teammates. *What the hell?*

Her gaze clung to his, and he saw the same unraveling of

memories in her striking light-green eyes. Her blonde hair had been shorter five year ago, barely reaching her shoulders. Now it fell halfway down her back in long, thick waves. She wasn't wearing a skimpy minidress today, but in her somber black dress, he could still see the curves of her body, the same curves that his hands and body remembered so very well.

"You," she murmured.

"You remember."

She licked her lips. "Yes, but it's been a long time."

"What are you doing here?"

"I'm here for my friend—for Abby." She tipped her head toward Paul's widow.

"You're friends with Paul's wife?" he asked, surprised again.

"Since we were kids. I spent most of my childhood in Dobbs."

"I had no idea."

She drew in a breath. "I know who you are. Abby showed me a photo of Paul's team two years ago, and you were in it. I had no idea you knew Paul when we…"

"Slept together?" he finished when her voice drifted away.

"Well, I don't recall us doing much sleeping, but yes. You're Ryker Stone."

"And you're way ahead of me. What's your name?"

"Savannah."

"Savannah," he echoed. "I guess that fits you, being a Georgia girl and all. But I thought you were from Texas, like the other dancers."

Her gaze shifted, and a flush spread across her cheeks. "I wasn't one of the dancers."

"You weren't? I don't understand. You lied to me?" More surprise ran through him. The perfect woman on the perfect night was starting to look not so perfect.

"I didn't lie. You assumed I was with the other entertainers. I just didn't tell you I wasn't."

"Why?"

"Does it matter?"

"I think it does. Why lie? What were you doing in Doha that night if you weren't with the show?"

"I don't want to get into all that now. Excuse me."

Before he could protest, she was gone—again. His lips tightened at her abrupt departure as more questions ran through his mind. *Why had she let him assume she was someone she wasn't?* Now he was more than a little curious to know exactly who she was.

But as Savannah moved across the room, he thought it might be just as well that she was gone. He wasn't the man she'd slept with. Maybe he didn't need her to see who he was now.

He did wonder if Savannah had told Abby she'd slept with him. She'd said she'd become aware of his identity two years earlier. *If Savannah had told Abby about their night, wouldn't Abby have told Paul? Wouldn't Paul have come after him, demanding to know what had happened, why he'd messed around with his wife's friend?* But Paul had never said a word. And as far as he knew, the only person on his team who even knew about the beautiful blonde in Doha had been Carlos, who'd been on leave with him.

Just thinking about his favorite wingman brought another wave of sadness. Carlos had died in the ambush, along with Leo Romano. He still hadn't come to terms with their deaths. Now he had to find a way to make peace with Paul's passing, and that didn't seem possible.

But he had to start somewhere and that meant talking to Abby. He hadn't spoken to her in probably three years, not since the team had been moved from Fort Benning, which was an hour away, to Fort Lewis in Washington State. Abby hadn't wanted to make the move, because Tyler had been sick, and she needed to be close to her family, close to Tyler's doctors. Paul hadn't wanted her to stay behind, but he knew that he'd be gone more than he was home anyway, and it was better for Tyler and Abby to stay in Georgia.

It was probably better now, too, because Abby and Tyler had a support system that they would need even more now that Paul was gone.

Drawing in a breath, Ryker knew he couldn't keep stalling. But as he took a step in Abby's direction, he saw Savannah grab Abby's hand and pull her toward the side door of the auditorium.

Savannah told everyone in the near vicinity that Abby needed a minute. And then they slipped outside.

He let out a breath of relief. He needed a minute, too. Maybe more than one.

"I can't do this," Abby whispered to Savannah, as they stepped onto the quiet patio. "It's too much."

"Just breathe," Savannah told her, forcing herself to take a few deep breaths as well. She was happy that they had the patio to themselves.

She'd been expecting the funeral to be difficult but running into Ryker had only made things worse. She'd thought he might show up, but she hadn't let that stop her from coming. Abby needed her, and she owed Abby more than she could ever repay.

"I should go back inside," Abby said, with a guilty gleam in her eyes. "My mother will be very upset with me for walking out like that."

"She'll get over it. No one is going anywhere. You're entitled to take a little time for yourself."

"It does feel better out here."

"You're not too cold?" It was February, with the temp in the low sixties, and at half-past four, the sun was already starting to slip past the trees.

"I don't mind the crisp air. It makes it easier to breathe. I feel like a coward, Savannah, hiding out here. I need to be stronger."

"You're doing great. The service was lovely. The reception is very nice. There's food and alcohol, and everyone knows each other. It's all going just as it should."

"It's good to have you here, Savannah. I wasn't sure you'd make it. I know you're busy with work."

"Work will be there when I get back to it. You're like my sister; you know that."

"And you're mine. But speaking of family…"

She saw the troubled look in Abby's eyes. "You don't have to say it. I know my father is probably coming."

"He said he was. I didn't see him in the church, but he sent me a note of condolence and said he'd be attending the funeral. He was friends with Paul's father, and I guess he feels an obligation to pay his respects."

"He's big on obligation when it comes to his fellow soldiers. And besides being friends with Paul's father, he liked Paul a lot. He always said Paul was one of his best students at sniper school."

"Paul had a lot of respect for him, too, even though I told him what a shithead your dad had been to you."

"I appreciate that, but I never wanted you or Paul to take sides."

"I know. I always thought it was a little crazy that Paul could be such a good sniper, which required him to be still, patient, unemotional, detached…he was never that guy at home. He was always moving a mile a minute. He was warm and funny, and he got emotional when he saw a stray dog in the neighborhood."

She smiled at that memory. "I remember when you had four dogs, because Paul couldn't stop rescuing them."

"And then Tyler's allergies kicked in, and we had to find them all good homes." Abby sighed. "Paul was a good guy."

"Of course he was." She wondered why there seemed to be doubt in Abby's eyes. "Am I missing something?"

"It's just that Paul's emotions went haywire after he was injured, after he realized he couldn't go back to his team, because he had nerve damage in his hand and arm. He didn't know what to do with himself."

"It's difficult for a lot of soldiers to start over, especially when the choice isn't theirs."

"I tried to be understanding; I really did. But it wasn't enough." Abby teared up. "Damn, you'd think I'd be done crying by now."

Savannah dug into her bag and pulled out a pack of tissues. "I came prepared."

Abby wiped her eyes. "Thanks."

"Is there anything else I can do to help?"

"Turn back time."

"I wish I could. I still don't understand how it happened." She regretted her words as soon as she said them, because more anguish entered Abby's eyes.

"I'm pretty sure it's my fault."

"Your fault? That's impossible."

"My mom blames me. I've seen it in other people's eyes, too."

She was shocked at Abby's words. "Why would your mother hold you responsible for Paul drinking too much and falling off a roof he shouldn't have been on in the first place?"

"I kicked Paul out three weeks ago, Savannah. He wasn't just visiting Todd that night; he was living there."

"I had no idea. I know you said you'd been having some problems since Paul came home, but I didn't realize they were that bad. Why didn't you tell me?"

"I was hoping Paul and I could fix things, but he's been different since he left the army. I almost wish he'd been able to stay in, which is crazy, considering how many times I prayed for him to get out. But he wasn't the same man. He was moody and angry, jealous and paranoid."

"It sounds like he needed help."

"Which he wouldn't get. I asked him to go to counseling with me, and he refused. I said I'd be fine if he went on his own, if he was worried about me being there, but he wasn't happy with that idea, either. He was drinking from morning 'til night. He was barely coherent in the evenings. He literally passed out at the dinner table one night. He fell head-first into the mac and cheese. He scared Tyler. My little boy ran out of the room crying. I had to drag Paul into the bedroom that night. He was so out of it. And the next day he didn't remember a thing. But I remembered."

"I'm so sorry," she whispered, feeling an overwhelming wave of sympathy.

"That's when I told him he had to leave. He had to get sober and get help. I thought I was protecting Tyler, but maybe I was too harsh. Paul served his country. He was a hero. He saved lives, and I kicked him out."

"You were protecting your son."

"Or was I just protecting myself?"

"No, you were doing what you had to do for both of you. What happened after he left?"

"He seemed to get a little better. He said he would see a doctor and that he was cutting back on the alcohol. I let him visit with Tyler a few times, and it went well. I thought that staying with Todd was good, too. Because Todd was in Paul's unit. He was part of the ambush. Paul could be himself with Todd. And Todd needed the connection, too; that's why he moved here from Jacksonville two months ago. They grounded each other. They were better together."

She'd met Todd once at a birthday party, and had thought he was a good guy, a little too hyper for her, but fun to be around. "What did Todd think about Paul's behavior?"

"He was worried, too, but he kept saying Paul would work his way out of it, that he loved me and Tyler, and he'd find his way back. I wanted to believe him. But now he'll never come home."

"Oh, Abby, this is so messed up. But you are not to blame for Paul's drinking or his fall."

"I'm glad you don't think so, but I know other people do."

"That's their problem, not yours. You and Paul were the only ones in your marriage. It was between you two."

Abby stared back at her, with her heart in her eyes. "I just worry that maybe it wasn't exactly an accident. I know that's also being gossiped about. Like maybe he didn't fall—maybe he jumped."

"Is there any evidence of that? Was Todd there when Paul fell?"

"No. He was asleep. He woke up when he heard Paul land on the trash cans. He ran outside and found him. Todd said…" Abby drew in a shaky breath. "He said his neck was broken and he was dead. There was no coming back."

"Oh, God," she whispered, putting a hand to her mouth.

"I wasn't home that night. I was in Atlanta with Tyler and some friends. By the time Todd got a hold of me and I got back here, Paul's body was already in the morgue."

She was horrified at the details. "I'm so sorry, Abby."

"Everyone says I should be glad he didn't suffer, that he probably never knew what happened, but I know. I can't forget it."

"Of course you can't."

"Paul's blood alcohol was twice the legal limit. He was very drunk, Savannah. It would have been easy for him to fall."

She nodded, wishing she knew what to say.

"I better go inside, Savannah."

"Are you sure you're ready?"

"I have to be. Oh, one other thing," Abby continued. "Your cousin Josie may also show up. I know you don't talk to her, but she came back to Dobbs a few months ago, and she's in all my social female groups. We've become friends. I think she's changed since she was such a jealous bitch to you. But I hope you don't think I'm betraying you."

She was touched that Abby even had the bandwidth to worry about that. "You're not betraying me. And you don't have to avoid her. If you're friends now, great. It doesn't matter to me."

"Good, then I won't feel guilty about that."

"You shouldn't be feeling guilty about anything."

"These days, guilt seems to be my middle name."

"Well, we're going to change that."

"Are you coming in?"

"I'll be inside in a minute. I just need to make a quick call." After Abby left, she let out a breath, not bothering to get her phone from her bag. She didn't have a call to make; she just needed to get her head together. The details of Paul's death, the last few weeks of his life, the problems in the marriage were all much worse than she'd realized. Now she was the one feeling guilty for not having kept up with Abby's life. But she would do better now. She would do everything she could to get Abby through this.

She just wanted the memorial to be over, so she wouldn't have anyone else to worry about but Abby. But at the moment, she was still dreading the idea of running into her father or her cousin and having to deal with old family business. And then there was Ryker...

She hadn't yet let herself think about him, but as she stood in the cooling, late afternoon air, she felt a rush of warmth as his image filled her head. She wasn't seeing the man who had looked like he wanted to kill her a few minutes ago, but rather the guy in the hotel bar with the compelling brown eyes, scruffy beard, and sexy mouth. He'd given her a confident, I'm-on-top-of-the-world smile and asked her to join him for a drink, and there was no way she could have said no. Because that night, that moment in her life, she'd felt completely adrift, lost between one world and the next, and she'd wanted a third option, an escape, a time-out from the pressures of trying to decide her life. Ryker had given her exactly what she needed in so many ways.

It hadn't been easy to leave his bed before dawn. A big part of her had wanted to stay, to talk, to share names and stories, to have breakfast, maybe lunch, perhaps even another night. But they were ships passing in the night. He was going one way; she was going the other. So, she'd left and for some reason doing that, taking that action, actually made everything else fall into place.

It might have just been a one-night stand for Ryker, but for her it had been a lot more. In some small way, she'd taken back some of her power, and she'd been able to make the hard choices that had been dogging her for a long time.

She'd never thought she'd see him again. Actually, that wasn't completely true. When she'd realized he was friends with Paul, she'd thought there was a chance their paths might intersect once more, but she'd never imagined it would be like this, on a very, very sad day.

Ryker had looked awful, a shadow of himself. He'd lost weight. He was paler than he had been, but it was in his eyes that she'd really seen the change. There had been sadness, anger, grief, and, strangely enough, uncertainty. He'd probably been the cockiest man in the bar the night they'd met, and she'd found his confidence inspiring. But today it felt like he was the one who was adrift.

She knew he'd been injured in the ambush and that he'd had to leave the army. He'd lost two friends—make that three now. He was definitely no longer on top of the world, and a part of her wished she could do something about that. But her focus had to be on Abby and Tyler. Ryker would have to deal with his issues on his own.

In reality, they barely knew each other. He had his life and she had hers. They couldn't go back in time and recreate that magical night. It needed to just stay a happy memory.

As she turned to go back inside, she froze, her happy memory materializing in front of her in a very real, very physical way. Ryker might be a shadow of his former self, but he still made her heart beat faster.

"I was just on my way in," she said, even though he hadn't asked what she was doing.

"Before you go, let's talk."

"Why?"

"Why not?" he countered.

"I'm here for Abby."

"But Abby isn't here, and you are. She can do without you for a couple of minutes."

"I don't want to talk about that night."

"Then let's talk about now. You said you weren't a dancer. What do you do, Savannah? Who are you?"

She stared back at him, not sure why she was hesitating. She was proud of herself. She was living her own life and no one else's. "I'm a special agent with the FBI."

His jaw dropped and wonder entered his eyes. "Well, I was not expecting that. You're serious?"

"Do you want me to show you my badge?"

"Were you FBI the night we met?"

"No. I was a soldier. I was on leave from my job in Army intelligence in Kuwait."

More surprise ran through his eyes. "Why did you let me think you were one of the dancers?"

She thought about that. The answer was really very simple, and it was a pattern she'd lived too many times in her life. "You wanted me to be one of those women. I gave you what you wanted."

He gave her a thoughtful look. "What about what you wanted?"

"I got what I wanted, Ryker. We had a good time. I didn't have any regrets. Did you?"

"Only one. I wished I'd gotten your name. I would have liked to see you again."

"I suspect you only wanted to see me again, because I left before you did. You like to control the timeline."

"Possibly," he admitted. "Why did you run away?"

"I didn't run away. The night was over. That's all we'd promised each other."

"It could have been more than that."

"But it wasn't." She paused. "You look like you've had a rough year, Ryker. Abby told me you were injured and that you couldn't go back to active duty. I'm sorry."

A shadow fell over his eyes. "I'm fine now."

She wondered about that. There was no visible sign of injury but there was something about the way he moved that felt a little stiff and not like the powerful, athletic man she'd met five years ago. "What do you do for work?"

"I run fishing charters on the Chesapeake Bay. That's where I live now."

"That sounds relaxing."

He shrugged. "I suppose. It's quiet. I need that."

"You—the life of the party—now likes quiet?"

Something passed through his gaze. "You have no idea how much I appreciate silence."

His words were odd. "What does that mean?"

"Nothing. You should go find Abby."

Now that he wanted her to leave, she felt inclined to stay. "When you first saw me, you had a deadly look in your eyes, as if you thought I was going to attack you."

He gave her an awkward nod. "Sorry about that. I'm a little on edge."

"Are you okay, Ryker? I know this must be awful for you. Paul considered every man on his team his brother. I loved him, too, but I didn't spend as much time with him as you did."

He gazed back at her, a look of pain in his dark eyes. "It's worse than awful. But it is what it is."

She glanced toward the church as the door opened, and Todd Davis stepped onto the patio. Todd's expression turned grim as he realized he wasn't alone. She could feel the tension in Ryker's body as he met Todd's gaze. She didn't know what was between them, but she had a feeling these two men had a lot to discuss, and she did not need to be in the middle of any more drama. "I'll let you and Todd talk."

"You don't have to leave."

"It's fine. I need to get back to Abby." As she moved past Todd, she gave him a brief smile. "I'm so sorry," she said.

He gave her a tight nod, his eyes strained. "Me, too. I'm glad you're here for Abby, Savannah. She needs you."

"Then I better get inside."

When she walked into the auditorium, she realized the crowd had grown. While some people had missed the service, they had come for the reception. And one of those people was a tall, older man in an army dress uniform. He had a strong build, and an imposing presence. His light-brown hair was now peppered with gray, but he looked every bit as stern and intimidating as he always had.

She felt a turbulent mix of emotions: love, hate, and everything in between. For the last five years, she'd been able to keep her past and her present apart, but they were getting closer by the minute.

CHAPTER TWO

RYKER STARED at Todd as he slowly made his way across the patio, each step appearing more reluctant than the last. Apparently, Todd wasn't that interested in talking to him, either. He was probably angry. He had a right to be.

"Didn't think you'd show up," Todd said, as he paused in front of him. He pulled out a cigarette and lighter, his hand shaking as he lit the flame.

Todd looked as bad as Ryker felt. His eyes were bloodshot, and the smell of smoke coming off his clothes told Ryker this wasn't Todd's first cigarette of the day. He'd also lost at least twenty pounds since he'd seen him last.

"You all right?" he asked.

"How could I be?" Todd returned, pain in his voice, anger in his brown eyes. "Paul's dead."

"How the hell did it happen?" He couldn't help voicing aloud the question that had been going through his head ever since he'd heard the news. "Paul gets drunk and decides to go up on the roof? Why?"

"Because he was messed up. Not that you would care."

"I do care."

"You have a hell of a way of showing it." Todd took a long

drag and blew smoke into the cold afternoon air. "Paul was drinking too much. He was destroyed after Abby kicked him out, not that he was much better before that."

"Abby kicked him out? When?"

"Three weeks ago."

"Why?"

"Because he'd become a raging alcoholic. He couldn't find his feet, Ryker. He was completely lost. He felt worthless. His family life was just as bad. He didn't fit in with Abby and Tyler anymore. They were a solid unit, and they didn't need him. They were used to him being gone. He was even jealous of Abby's friend Colin, saying he'd be a better husband to Abby and father to Tyler. I told him that wasn't true, but Paul started thinking Abby would be better off without him."

"Damn. I had no idea."

"How would you know? You haven't returned a call or a text in nine months."

He had no defense, and he didn't think Todd would tolerate any excuse he tried to make. *Why should he?* He'd let them down—all of them.

"When did you move here? I thought you were in Jacksonville with your mom," he said.

"I was, but her Alzheimer's worsened, and she didn't know me anymore. It got too depressing to visit her, and with Paul having rough times, I decided to move to Dobbs. I've been working with a private security firm out of Atlanta. When I'm not on assignment, I'm here. I tried to get Paul to come on board with the firm. They have some jobs that don't require field work, but he said he wasn't a desk guy and he'd have to figure something else out."

"I can understand that," he muttered.

"I heard you're a fisherman now."

"Yes."

"And you're living on a boat?"

"It's great. No commute."

"Sounds boring as shit."

"Boring works for me."

"It never used to."

"Well, it does now."

"How did we end up like this?" Todd muttered, giving him a look of confusion. "We were the best of the best, Ryker. We were changing the world. And then it all blew up—literally." He paused. "I keep thinking about our last mission. We had bad intel, but where did it come from? Did someone sell us out? Was it just an honest mistake? Or did one of us screw up?"

"I've been asking the same questions, not that it matters anymore. We can't change what happened."

"Carlos and Leo should be alive. You, Paul, and Mason shouldn't have been injured, shouldn't have been tossed out the way you were. That's one reason why I quit. I couldn't stand how you all were treated. Hank felt the same way."

He didn't know what to say. Todd's anger was ramping up, and maybe that was a good thing. Perhaps it was the only way he could deal with the immense guilt and blame that he was feeling.

Ryker was angry, too, on so many different levels. But he couldn't even get to the heart of his anger, much less let it out. It would probably be healthier if he could, because it felt like it was eating him alive.

"I'm glad the sun is going down," Todd said, sweeping his hand toward the horizon. "It shouldn't be sunny on this horrific day."

He followed Todd's gaze. The church sat atop a hill and from their vantage point they could see the wild Dobbs River that was swollen from the winter rains. The water rushed over boulders, disappearing between thick pine trees, as it moved downstream, where the tributary would eventually dump into the Chattahoochee River.

He'd spent a couple of years in Georgia, when he was stationed at Fort Benning, and while he hadn't been to Dobbs before, he had missed the beauty of the area: the gentle, rolling hills, the acres of farmland, and the neighborhoods where there was a real sense of community. Most of that community was in the church auditorium today. At least Abby had support here.

Todd tossed his cigarette butt on the patio and ground it out with his heel. "What's going on with you, Ryker? I know you've had your own shit to deal with, but why did you disappear?"

He shrugged, not wanting to get into it. "I'm sorry I wasn't there for Paul."

"Or for anyone. You were our leader. You know what happens when the leader goes down? Someone else steps up. Someone a lot less worthy. But the team has to follow, because without the team, what is there?"

His gaze narrowed at Todd's rambling words. "What are you talking about? There's no team. There's no leader."

Todd straightened. "You're right. I don't know what I'm talking about. I haven't slept since Paul went off the roof."

"That's understandable."

"If you ever want to leave the fish, you could always work with my company. I know you have physical limitations with your knee, but your brain is sharp, and you were one of the best tacticians and strategists I've ever seen."

"Thanks, but I'm fine with where I am." He wasn't anywhere close to fine, which was why he couldn't consider Todd's offer. The damn bells tortured him constantly. The only way he could sleep was to live alone on his boat. Hell, the only way he could get through the day was to see as few people as possible. The fishing charters were great, because his charter guests had to be quiet so as not to scare the fish. They had no idea that the silence was more for him than the fish.

"Yeah, sure. I figured."

"Is Mason or Hank coming today?"

"Mason is sick. Hank is out of town."

He didn't know if he felt relieved or unhappy that the other two men from his unit would not be showing up. But he knew one thing. If they were here, there would only be more questions that he didn't want to answer. Clearing his throat, he decided to change the subject. "So, do you know the woman you passed on your way out here?"

"You mean Savannah? Yeah, she's Abby's friend. She's a looker, isn't she?"

"What do you know about her?"

"Not much. I met her a couple years ago at a party. She's a former beauty queen. Abby grew up with her, but I think she lives in California now. She's stunning, but I would never hit on her."

"Why is that?"

"Her last name, dude."

"What's her last name?"

Todd gave him a surprised look. "Kane. As in Colonel Henry Kane."

"Seriously?" He could not believe that Savannah was the daughter of Colonel Kane. The grim-faced, hard-assed colonel had been on him every day of sniper school and beyond that. He'd never found much to like about the man, except for the fact that he'd been extremely good at his job. But the colonel had no compassion, no heart; he was cold as ice.

And the very hot, impulsive, free-spirited Savannah was his daughter? He shook his head in bemusement.

Todd glanced at his watch. "I can't do this," he said.

"Do what?"

"Be at this damned funeral that should not be happening. What did we do it all for, Ryker?"

"We did it for our country," he said automatically, although the words felt hollow in the face of Todd's emotion.

"And what has our country done for us?" Todd asked bitterly.

"It doesn't matter. We didn't choose to fight because we were going to get something back. That's not why we did it."

Todd stared back at him. "Even if that's not why we did it, we deserve more. Look at our team. Three are dead. The rest of us are scarred in one way or another. It's not right."

He could see that Todd was getting more agitated by the minute. Paul's death had clearly pushed him over the edge. "If you want to get out of here, I'll go with you. We'll get a drink. We'll talk."

"No. I don't think you and I speak the same language anymore."

"Todd, come on."

"It's fine. Don't worry about it, Ryker. You have your life. I have mine. They don't ever have to cross again."

"I'm worried about you, Todd."

"I'll survive. It's what I do. Other people die, other people get hurt, but not me. I'm not the one who takes the bullet. I'm the one who narrowly escapes."

"That's a good thing."

"Not when my friends are dying in front of me. Someone needs to pay, Ryker. Someone needs to be held responsible." He paused. "I have to leave. I need to be alone. I'm sure you can understand that."

He definitely could not argue with that need.

"Just tell Abby I'm sorry, okay?" Todd asked, desperation in his eyes. "Tell her I'm sorry about Paul, about everything. Maybe in the long run, she'll be better off."

He frowned. "Don't say that. Don't go, Todd. You shouldn't be on your own now." He was more than a little worried about Todd's state of mind.

"I have to leave, Ryker. I have to make this right. I have to find a way to change things."

"Change what?" he asked in confusion.

"You'll see."

"See what? You cannot leave like this, Todd."

"I'm fine. I know what I need to do, and it doesn't involve you. Don't follow me, Ryker. You could have helped if you wanted to, but you didn't. I don't need you now. No one does. Go back to your boat. Hang out with the fish. Maybe you'll end up better than the rest of us."

His gut churned as Todd stormed down the path to the parking lot. Todd had always been wired more tightly than the rest of them. But he'd never seemed so out of control, so filled with anger and rage. Maybe guilt was driving that anger. Todd was holding himself responsible for Paul's death.

Perhaps Paul's death was on him, too. In isolating himself, he'd let everyone down. He'd left them all without a leader. But there had been no team left to lead. And every time he'd stepped even a few feet outside of his quiet, his brain had gone haywire, the bells churning as if to alert him to something. But he didn't know what that something was.

Well, it was too late now. He couldn't change what had happened. He'd just go inside and pay his respects to Abby and then go back to his silence.

Although, as he headed into the church, it occurred to him that he hadn't heard the bells once during Todd's tirade. That seemed odd. But he should just be grateful that he'd finally been able to hear a friend. He could do better. He had to do better. Paul was gone. But there was still Todd, Mason, Hank…he could reach out to them. He could make sure they were okay, or he could get them help for whatever pain they were in. No one else needed to die.

———

Seeing her dad was always a painful experience. Savannah took a quick breath as her father's gaze settled on her. Then he excused himself from the conversation he was in and crossed the room. She mentally steeled herself to be ready for criticism or coldness. He never had anything else to offer. She'd tried in so many ways over so many years to find a way to connect with him, but nothing had ever worked. If anything, their relationship had gone in the opposite direction of love. Now, it felt a lot closer to hate.

"This must be a cold day in hell," he drawled. "Isn't that when you said you'd be back to Georgia?"

She hated the fact that in spite of her three-inch heels, her dad still towered over her like the giant he'd always been in her head and in her life.

"It feels like a day in hell with Paul gone. Abby is my friend. I came to support her."

Her father didn't comment as he flipped some imaginary piece of lint off the sleeve of his uniform. His medals had once made her the proudest girl on earth. Later, they'd just been a reminder of the life he'd chosen to live far away from her, even when they'd only been miles apart.

"I'm going to talk to Abby," she said when he remained silent.

"Wait."

His sharp command gave her pause. "Why? Do you have something to say to me? Because I'm not really interested in this awkward moment we're having."

A gleam flickered in his eyes. It almost felt like approval, but that was a foolish thought.

She'd been searching for her dad's approval most of her life, and she'd never gotten it. Now, she no longer needed it. She'd finally stopped trying to hold on to a relationship that had never been what she wanted and never would be.

"You still working for the bureau?" he asked. "Or did you quit that, like you quit everything else?"

"You know, we don't need to talk. Good things don't happen when we speak."

He frowned. "I shouldn't have said that."

She was shocked at his words. "That might be a first. An apology. And, yes, I'm still working for the bureau."

"I'm glad you're settled."

"Settled? I didn't settle for my job; I chose it."

"I just meant I'm glad you're sticking to something."

"Why would you care? It's not like you've ever worried about me."

"That's not true, Savannah. I've worried about you a lot over the years. I know I made some mistakes, but I tried to do right by you."

She was completely enraged by his comment. She told herself to calm down. Getting into a fight with him wasn't worth it. But she couldn't stop the words from bursting out. "Is that the story you tell yourself? Come on, Dad. Even you can't believe that lie. You got rid of me as soon as you could."

"I didn't get rid of you." Shadows filled his eyes. "I just didn't know what to do with you after your mom passed. And my career took me away for long periods of time. It made sense for you to live with your aunt and uncle."

"I was thirteen years old. You made me leave my home, my friends, my school—you."

"It was the best place for you to go. And you got to grow up with your cousin, with a family. It wasn't bad. They treated you well. You just couldn't let yourself be happy. You always had to make trouble for everyone. I know you were probably trying to get my attention, but that wasn't the way to do it."

"There was no way to do it," she said wearily. "And this conversation is pointless. Let's say good-bye."

He stared back at her with irritation, but then, her dad preferred to be the one who called the shots, who started conversations and ended them when he was done. "I didn't come here to fight with you."

"Whatever."

"Wait," he said again, his jaw tightening.

"What now?"

He took a moment to answer. "You look like your mom today. Seeing you…it's like seeing her. She wasn't much older than you are now when she passed."

As pain entered his eyes, she softened a little. Her father might not have loved her, but he had loved her mother. She'd never doubted that. "I'm glad I look like her. It's all I have left."

"She was always better with you than I was. You two had your own secret language."

"We would have shared it with you, if you'd wanted to share."

"I didn't know how to do that. And after she died, I knew I wouldn't be a good father to you. You needed a woman in your life. Stephanie was good to you."

"But she wasn't one of my parents. It wasn't her job to raise me. It was yours. You always speak about duty, but where was your duty to me?"

"I did my duty. I made sure you had what you needed."

"As long as what I needed wasn't love."

"Are you going to carry this grudge forever?"

"It feels like it." When he didn't answer, she realized his attention had wandered away from her. Why was she surprised? Following his gaze, she realized he was now looking at Ryker.

She hadn't considered until just now that they would know each other. Ryker had gone through Fort Benning's sniper school and been stationed there for several years. Of course he would know her father.

But there was no love in her father's eyes for Ryker. In fact, the anger he usually reserved for her seemed to be flowing in Ryker's direction.

Ryker hesitated, and then headed straight toward them.

Damn! The last person she wanted to know about her no-name, one-night stand was her very self-righteous father, for whom the lines of good and bad were very well-defined, at least when it came to her behavior.

"Colonel Kane," Ryker said, giving her father a respectful nod.

"Captain Stone."

Tension bristled between the two men, and Savannah didn't know why. It wasn't about her, that was for sure. *So what was it?* While she didn't get along with her father, most of the soldiers who worked with him thought he was amazing.

To her shock and amazement, her father blinked first, and with a muttered excuse, he walked away.

"What was that about?" she asked Ryker. "What's between you and my father?"

"That's a long story. Why didn't you tell me you were Colonel Kane's daughter?"

"I didn't even tell you my name. Why would I tell you who my father is?"

"I'm not talking about five years ago; I'm talking about fifteen minutes ago."

"I didn't think about it. I haven't been his daughter since I was thirteen years old."

Confusion entered his eyes. "What does that mean?"

"It doesn't matter. I came here for Abby. I don't need to deal with you or my father. You are both in my past."

She'd barely finished speaking when she heard a loud squeal of tires followed by a shockingly loud, reverberating crash that silenced the crowd.

She instinctively ran toward the door. Ryker was right on her heels. She headed toward the parking lot, the crowd streaming behind her. Smoke was rising from below, but she couldn't see the road yet. She took off her heels, running barefoot down the long, winding drive. Ryker kept pace with her, and while his long-legged gait was somewhat stiff and awkward, he still made it to the road first.

They stopped in horror, realizing that a car had crashed through the guardrail and flipped into the rushing Dobbs River. The vehicle was sinking fast as the water moved it downstream.

Abby came up next to her, screaming Todd's name.

Todd? It was his car? A sickening feeling ran through her.

Ryker stripped off his coat and kicked off his shoes. Before she could say a word, he jumped off the bridge and into the water, a drop of at least twelve feet. Two other men in uniform did the same. Her father called 911. Other men rushed down the riverbank, hoping to grab Todd when he came up for air.

"This can't be happening," Abby said, her shoulders shaking, as she put a hand to her mouth. "Not Todd, too."

She put her arm around her friend, wishing she could say Todd would be okay, but she didn't know if that was true. She was also worried for the men who had gone in after him. The car had completely disappeared now, and the rescuers as well as the vehicle were all being swept downstream.

She felt a rush of fear as a crazy thought ran through her. She didn't want to lose Ryker, even though he wasn't hers to lose.

CHAPTER THREE

TODD WASN'T in the car.

It had taken what felt like forever for Ryker to catch up to the vehicle in the fast-running current. He was down at least five feet now, but new hope ran through him as he held on to the open door, searching the car for some sign of Todd, but he was nowhere in sight. The airbag had deployed; the driver's side door had been open. Todd must have gotten out. He had to be swimming. Hell, he could be on shore by now.

With his lungs bursting, Ryker let go of the car door and kicked his way back to the surface. He gulped in air as he came out of the water, and then swore as his body hit a sharp rock. The current pulled him ruthlessly around a large boulder. He didn't try to fight the current. He was on the same ride as Todd. And he had a better chance of finding him if he just rode it out as far as he could.

Turning his head one way, then the other, he saw another man crawling out of the river. It was James Lofgren, and he was alone. Another man was a hundred yards farther down the river. He was talking to a cop, pointing toward the water. Clearly, he hadn't found Todd, either.

A police car and fire truck were racing down the road above the river. More cars followed, with people jumping out at every point, scrambling down the bank to the shoreline. A couple of them waved to him.

He gave a thumbs-up, letting them know he was okay. He was at least a mile downstream now, the river winding its way through tall trees that cast dark, despairing shadows all around him. And then he heard a helicopter, and new hope soared. Maybe they'd have a better chance of seeing Todd from that vantage point.

Another quarter mile down the river, and his body was beginning to chill; his arms and legs were tiring, reminding him that he wasn't even close to the physical shape he'd once been in. He didn't want to leave the river. He didn't want to abandon Todd. But as his leg rammed against a jagged rock, a sharp pain stabbed his knee. Then the water pulled him down, washing over his head, cutting off his breath.

He fought to get back to the surface and when he came back up, he made a wild grab for a low-hanging tree branch. He caught it and hung on, managing to swing his legs out of the water and onto a nearby boulder. He crawled over the rocks to get to the shore.

He walked along the river for another hundred yards until he could go no farther. The sun was almost completely cut off by the trees now, and there was nothing but darkness ahead. He couldn't stand the thought of Todd dying like this. He'd made it through a decade of action including the violent ambush that had taken the lives of Carlos and Leo. This damn river couldn't take his life. He had to be all right.

But Todd had been enraged when he left the church. He'd been agitated, on edge. *Had he been driving too fast? Had he missed the turn at the end of the drive? Had another car come down the road and he'd made too quick of an adjustment and gone through the guardrail?*

The questions ran around in his head, including one that he didn't want to hear. But it kept getting louder. *Had Todd deliberately driven off the road and into the river?*

He'd been distraught over Paul's death. He'd held himself responsible. *And what had he said when he was leaving?* That he knew what he had to do. But that didn't mean he had to kill himself. It had to have been an accident.

He shouldn't have let Todd leave. He should have made him stay, made him talk. But he hadn't. As the guilt swelled within him, the bells began to clang. He put his hands over his ears as the torturous sounds began to scream. His breath came too fast. His heart pounded against his chest and the pain in his head was almost debilitating.

The rushing river turned into a terrifying, horrifying symphony of clanging noises that didn't go together, like instruments hitting the wrong notes, nails on a chalkboard, every awful sound, ending always with a clanging bell.

The bells had been haunting him for months, stealing a bit more of his sanity with every awful sound.

"Stop," he yelled. "Just stop, dammit."

"Okay, I'll stop," a voice said.

It took him a second to realize the voice wasn't inside his head. The bells slowly receded as he stared into Savannah's worried face. Her eyes were so clear, a beautiful light-green with gold flecks that seemed bright in the gathering darkness. Those eyes had haunted him, too, for a very long time.

"Ryker?" she queried, as she came closer. "Are you all right?"

"I'm fine."

She didn't believe him, but he couldn't change that. He didn't know what he'd said, what she'd heard, but there was worry in her eyes. But her worry shouldn't be for him. "Has anyone found Todd?" he asked.

"Not yet."

"He wasn't in the car."

Her expression turned grim. "I heard that. The police, search and rescue, the fire department...everyone is searching for Todd. They'll find him. Hopefully, before he hits the rapids. They start about three miles downstream."

"Not that far," he said with fear.

"He's a strong guy. He can fight the current. You did."

"It was getting rough. And if he was injured...he could have become disoriented. He could have gotten trapped in the rocks, the trees."

"No one is giving up hope."

He wished he could say the same. In the past, he'd never been one to give up hope. He'd never looked at any problem as insurmountable, but that was before his team had been wiped out, and he'd almost died.

"Can I give you a ride back to your car?" she asked.

"What are you doing down here anyway? I thought you didn't want anything to do with me."

"The police are busy looking for Todd. But they were worried when you didn't get out of the water. I told them I'd look for you. I almost didn't see you down here. I was afraid..." Her voice trailed off. "Anyway, it's getting dark. I have your shoes and your suit jacket in the car. We should go."

"Okay," he said, becoming aware of the cold seeping into his bones.

As they walked down the bank, she said, "Did you notice if the airbags were deployed in Todd's car?"

"They were."

"Any sign of blood or clothing torn on the door?"

"Not that I could see. Do you have more information on what happened?"

"There were skid marks coming down the end of the church driveway but nothing directly in front of the guardrail."

"He tried to stop, but then he didn't?"

"It was an odd pattern," she admitted. "I don't know if there was another vehicle that he might have swerved to avoid. He could have accelerated and then overshot the turn. I'm just speculating. The accident investigation will go through every possible scenario. Or Todd will tell us what happened when he's found."

"I heard him crash through the rail. You heard that, too, didn't you?" He hated that he couldn't trust his own brain.

"Yes. I heard the brakes and the crash."

"Who's running the operation?"

"Chief Ed Tanner. I spoke to him at the crash site. He's a

former Marine. He'll do a thorough investigation. He'll want to get answers for a fellow soldier."

"He won't be alone. I'm not leaving Dobbs until I know what happened, or until we find Todd." He blew out a breath. "I shouldn't have let him leave the church. He was shredded by guilt over what happened to Paul."

"Abby told me that Todd was feeling that way, but she doesn't blame him. She said Paul was out of control. I didn't realize things were so bad. I haven't been the best friend to Abby."

"If you're going to feel guilty, you'll be in a long line."

"You, too?"

"Yes."

She nodded. "Well, you might not have stopped Todd from leaving, but you did jump into the river trying to save him. That's something."

"Too little too late."

"Well, if you're staying in town, you should come to Abby's house. She was headed there when I left. Chief Tanner said he'd come by her place with an update as soon as he has one. A lot of the people from the funeral will be waiting there as well."

The last thing he wanted to do was face Abby, who probably harbored as much anger and resentment toward him as Todd had expressed. But he wasn't leaving town until Todd was found, so it was her house or the police station. "All right."

As he followed Savannah up the rocky and somewhat steep hillside to the road, he felt pain in his knee, and had a feeling the rocks had done a little more damage. But he didn't regret going into the water. Todd would have done the same for him. They'd always had each other's backs.

Savannah scampered up the hill with an ease he envied and then gave him a thoughtful look as she waited by her car. "Are you hurt, Ryker?"

"Old wounds."

"Not so old. There's blood on your pants."

He glanced down at his knee, realizing for the first time that his slacks were ripped. "I didn't notice, but I hit the rocks a few times."

"Even more reason to get you to Abby's house. She'll have a first aid kit."

"It's nothing."

She opened the passenger-side door and handed him his shoes. He put them on as she walked around the car to get behind the wheel.

"I'm going to get the seat wet," he said, as he slid his arms into his coat, grateful for the warmth.

"It will dry. Don't worry about it." She started the car. "I was impressed with how fast you jumped into that beast of a river. You didn't hesitate for one second."

"I wasn't trained to hesitate."

"Do you miss the army?" she asked, as she drove down the road.

"I miss a lot of things. The army is only one of them." He paused, glancing over at her. "I can't believe you were a soldier when I met you."

"I was actually deciding what I wanted to do that night—stay in or get out. The next morning, I knew the answer."

"It came to you while we were having sex? And here I thought I had all your attention."

"You did have my attention," she admitted, giving him a quick look. "The answer didn't come during the night. It was the next morning. When I left your room and went down to the lobby, I ran into the dance troupe, and I was thinking about how you'd thought I was one of them. I realized that I'd once again tried to be the person that someone else wanted me to be. I couldn't do it anymore. So, I quit."

"Who wanted you to be a soldier? Or can I guess? It was your father—Colonel Kane."

"I did become a soldier for him. I thought it would help us connect, but it didn't."

He wanted to keep talking to her about her past, but they were nearing the site where Todd's car had plunged into the river. There was yellow caution tape across the gap in the rail now, and a police officer was talking to an older couple on the side of the road.

"Can you pull over?" he asked. "I want to take another look."

"Sure." She pulled into a turnout near the driveway leading up to the church. Then they got out of the car and walked down the road. Not a single car passed them coming in either direction. It definitely wasn't a busy traffic area.

When they reached the spot where Todd's car had gone over the side, he looked for clues, but as Savannah had said earlier, there wasn't much to see. There were no skid marks near the crash site, and beyond the church on the hill, there was nothing on the two-lane road in either direction for at least a mile or two. Which meant there were no traffic cameras or security cameras of any kind that might have been able to capture the accident.

The police officer came over to speak to them. He was a young, dark-haired guy, who didn't appear to be more than twenty-five, if that. "Hey, Savannah, you need to get back in your car," he told them. "The chief wants me to keep this area clear until we can complete our investigation. I know you're a big-time federal agent now, but Chief Tanner told me specifically not to let anyone hang out here, including you."

"I understand that, Ben," Savannah said. "This is Ryker Stone. He's a friend of Todd's—the man whose car went into the river. We're not going to touch anything. You don't mind if we just look, do you?"

"Well, I guess not," the officer said.

"What's the latest on the search efforts?" he asked.

"They'll look as long as they can, but rain is supposed to start within the half hour. The helicopter will probably have to land soon if the wind picks up."

Every word that came out of Ben's mouth made Ryker's stomach turn. "You can't call off the search," he protested, knowing that they could do just that and probably would.

"It's not my call. Chief Tanner will decide when to bring everyone in, but they'll go as long as they can. We all want to find Todd. I actually played a pickup basketball game with Todd and Paul a few weeks ago." Ben's lips drew into a tight line. "I can't believe Paul is dead, and now this…"

As Ben finished speaking, another police car pulled up, and an older, stocky man exited the vehicle, not looking at all happy.

"What's going on here?" he demanded. "Savannah, I told you to stay out of this. Dobbs is my town, and I run the investigation."

"Yes, you made that clear, Chief Tanner," she said evenly.

Ryker wasn't sure why the chief was so angry with Savannah, but his focus was on getting information, so he stepped in front of her and said, "I'm Ryker Stone. I went into the river after Todd. I found the car, but there was no one inside."

"Yes, yes, I saw you in the water. My officers yelled at you to get out, but you went right past them."

"I didn't hear them, and I got out as soon as I could. Has there been any sighting of Todd?"

"No. But we're doing everything we can. I'm Chief Ed Tanner. I'll do everything I can to bring this soldier home. However, the weather is turning, and with the winds picking up, we'll have to bring the chopper down. My office is setting up a volunteer search party for first light. We'll get as many bodies out as we can. You're welcome to join."

"Of course." He was just afraid that the morning would be too late.

"If there was another vehicle involved, one of the cameras in town might have picked it up coming down the road around the time of the accident," Savannah interjected. "I know you have a small department. I'd like to offer my resources."

"There's nothing to indicate there was another vehicle involved. It looks like Mr. Davis lost control of his vehicle on the hill and crashed into the river. Might have been faulty brakes or human error. Several witnesses told me he was extremely agitated at the funeral. We'll know more when we pull the car out, but that probably won't be until tomorrow. I told Abby I'd update her with any news. If you want to wait somewhere, wait there. I'm sure she could use your support."

"We're heading there now," Savannah said.

The chief tipped his head and then he and Officer Wickham stepped away to have a private conversation.

They walked back to Savannah's car in silence.

"Should we go to Abby's now?" Savannah asked, as they got into the vehicle.

"My rental car is in the church lot. I should get it."

"Okay." As Savannah drove him up the hill, he said, "I couldn't help noticing there was no love lost between you and the chief. Is that just him being territorial?"

"Partly. But he's also friends with my dad, and he thinks I'm a major screwup."

"Why would he think that?"

"He apparently can't forget I was a rebellious teenager. I wound up in his jail one night when I was sixteen."

"What happened?"

She pulled up next to his car, which was one of only three left in the lot. "It's a long story."

"So, give me the short version."

"You're not in a hurry to get to Abby's?"

"I don't think there's going to be any new information for a while, and I'm curious. How did you end up in jail?"

"Well, I was angry because I found out my boyfriend was cheating on me. I got drunk with a girlfriend. We had just learned how to make tequila sunrises, and I was definitely seeing red. We walked down the street to get some ice cream, and I saw my boyfriend buying this other girl a double scoop of chocolate, and I went a little crazy. I hurled a rock at his car, but I missed. Unfortunately, the rock went right through the window of a patrol car that was just pulling into the lot, and it was driven by the chief. I was taken to jail, where I spent the night."

"Ouch. That was bad luck."

"All my luck was bad then."

"You stayed the whole night in jail? Your dad didn't bail you out?"

"I wasn't living with my father at the time; I was with my aunt and uncle."

"Why?"

"You have a lot of questions, Ryker."

"Because every time you open your mouth, I find out something new about you." He paused. "You said before your dad stopped being a father when you were thirteen. Care to elaborate?"

"That's when my mother died. My father was overseas at the time. He came back on emergency leave for a few days and during that time, he decided I should live with my aunt and uncle. I thought it would be temporary, but it turned out to be permanent. He was too busy to have a daughter. He thought I'd be better off with his sister's family."

"Was he wrong?"

She thought about that. "Not in every way. But I'd lost my mother, and it felt like my dad had abandoned me, too. I had to learn how to be part of someone else's family. I tried to fit in, because I thought if I didn't, they might throw me out, too."

"Was getting drunk and throwing rocks your idea of fitting in?" he asked dryly.

"That was years later. When I first moved in, I did everything I could to be what my aunt wanted me to be. I even agreed to the beauty pageants, because that's what my aunt and cousin loved to do. I was Miss Georgia when I was eighteen." She paused. "You may not have slept with a dancer, but you did sleep with a beauty queen. Feel better?"

"To be honest, I have no idea how I feel about you."

"Fair enough."

He slid out of the car and then looked back at her. "I want to hear more of the Savannah Kane story some time."

"I can't imagine why. I'm not the woman you slept with, Ryker. She's gone. She's never coming back."

Her words hit him in a much more profound way than she'd probably intended. "I'm not the man you slept with, either. He's also never coming back."

She stared back at him, conflicting emotions in her gaze. "I—I don't know what to say."

"There's nothing to say. I'll follow you to Abby's house."

"All right." She seemed relieved to move away from the very personal conversation they'd just gotten into, and he should be relieved as well. There was no going back. Getting to know Savannah was pointless. And he certainly didn't need her to get to know him, not now, not in the state he was in. As soon as Todd was found, he'd be on his way back to his boat, to his solo existence, to the quiet that kept him from going insane.

CHAPTER FOUR

SAVANNAH'S HEART was beating way too fast, and it didn't just have to do with the horrifying events of the last few hours. Being with Ryker again was more than a little unnerving. She didn't know what to make of his renewed interest in her, but she did know that nothing would come of it. She certainly wasn't going to sleep with him again. She couldn't go back in time and recapture that moment, that incredible memory. It wouldn't be the same. It would only end in disappointment. She needed to keep her gaze on the horizon, to only look forward. That was where her future was. And that future didn't include another night with Ryker, even though she had to admit he was as sexy and attractive as ever.

But there was another dimension to him now that she didn't quite understand. Maybe it had always been there, or perhaps it had come with the accident that had taken him out of the army, away from the job he loved. He walked and ran with a bit of a limp, but he'd jumped into the river with no thought to his safety, and he'd been strong enough to battle the currents for several miles. He obviously had some physical limitations, but she suspected the psychological wounds went deeper.

When she'd found him at the river, he'd shouted at her to stop. Only, she didn't think he'd been talking to her. He'd been lost in his head. He'd given her a tortured, haunted look that had shaken her to the core. The man she'd been with had been charming and fun, reckless and bold, with an infectious confidence. That night, he'd made her realize that the power was in her hands. She could change her life. She could be who she was and not who everyone else wanted her to be.

But that night was five years ago.

This night was only about Todd and Abby. She needed to keep her focus on the present.

Picking up her phone, she punched in a number. Flynn MacKenzie's voice came over the line a moment later. Flynn ran the special task force to which she was assigned. But he was more than her boss, he was also her friend. They'd met at Quantico five years ago when they were in training, and since then they'd been through a lot together. There were few people she trusted more than him.

"How's it going?" Flynn asked. "Is your friend all right?"

"She's hanging in there, but there's been a development. I'm not going to be back tomorrow."

"What's happened?"

"After the funeral, Paul's best friend ran his car off the road and into the river. He's now missing. I can't leave Abby with this going on. It's too much."

"Of course you can't leave. Is he alive?"

"I don't know. They found the car and he wasn't in it, but the river is running high and fast. He's an ex-soldier. He's strong. He could survive, I think. I hope."

"I hope so, too. Take as much time as you need."

"Thanks. I might also need your help at some point. This is a small town, and the local cops don't have a lot of resources."

"Whatever you need, Savannah, just ask."

"I'm not sure yet. The chief is marking his territory, and I'm definitely on the outs with him. We have a personal history. But I'm still hoping he'll work with me to get answers."

"What answers? I thought it was an accident."

"It's possible there was another vehicle involved. I don't know.

Something feels off about it to me, Flynn." She paused, unable to put her finger on her uncertainty, but it was definitely there.

"I've never known your gut to be wrong, so follow it."

She appreciated his confidence in her. It was nice to be reminded that in her current life people did actually respect her.

"Although," he continued, "it sounds like you'll be spending more time in your hometown, and that's never your favorite thing to do. Have you seen your father yet?"

"Yes. We had an awkward and cold conversation—like always. Hopefully, there won't be another one. But, at the moment, he's the least of my concerns."

"Let me know if you need help. I can always fly out there."

"You can't fly out here. Isn't Callie's birthday on Friday? Isn't there some big, romantic proposal in the works?" she teased.

"I'm not sure I should do it on her birthday. She might expect it," Flynn said. "I like to keep her on her toes."

She smiled at the note of love in his voice. Flynn had finally found his match a few months earlier, and it was nice to see them moving forward in their lives. "I'm sure you will keep her on her toes no matter what you do, because unpredictable is your middle name."

"Actually, I think that might be your middle name, Savannah. You're never who anyone thinks you are."

"My secret weapon."

"Use it wisely."

"I'll be in touch." She ended the call as she drove down Abby's block. The driveway and street were crowded with vehicles, but she squeezed into a spot a few houses down from Abby's. She got out of the car and waited for Ryker, who had to park a bit farther away.

As he approached, unwanted tingles shot down her spine, and she told herself to get a grip. The man smelled like the river. His clothes were soggy and wrinkled. She should not be thinking he was attractive, but she was…

His dark hair was wavy and damp, and despite his now more noticeable limp, he was still compelling with his dark eyes, absurdly long lashes, and full, sexy mouth. This was not the time or the place to have those kinds of feelings, but her body wasn't as up to speed on that fact as her brain.

"Looks like the crowd from the church is here now," he murmured, not appearing happy about that.

"Hopefully not everyone." She didn't want to deal with her father right now.

As they approached Abby's front steps, she realized she was going to have to deal with her dad again. He was with Colonel Bill Vance, his long-time friend, and someone who had always been very nice to her. Even now, Colonel Vance was giving her a warm smile, while her father wore his usual stoic, emotionless expression.

"Savannah. I saw you at the church, but I didn't get a chance to speak to you," Colonel Vance said. "How are you?"

"Hanging in there."

"It's a sad situation," he said, his smile dimming. As his gaze moved past her to Ryker, he suddenly straightened. "Stone. I didn't see you there. I'm sorry about all of this. I heard you went into the river after Davis. I would have expected nothing less."

"Colonel," Ryker said, as they shook hands. "It's good to see you again. Unfortunately, I was unsuccessful in finding Todd and bringing him back to safety."

"You did your best. I'm sure of that. James is inside. He's kicking himself hard, too. But this isn't on you or James. It was a tragic accident."

"We should go," her father interrupted. "We have a dinner meeting."

Savannah couldn't believe her dad wasn't even going to acknowledge her, but he was already walking away.

Colonel Vance gave her an apologetic smile, then lingered behind while her father strode down the street to his car. "You look like your mother, Savannah. Your dad misses her more every time he sees you."

"Well, that isn't very often."

"I keep telling him he needs to work things out with you. I don't think he knows how."

"It doesn't matter. You should go. He doesn't like to wait."

"I don't worry too much about what your dad wants," Vance said with a smile. "But take care of yourselves—both of you."

As Vance left, Ryker said, "Your dad is an asshole."

"I can't argue that. I'm glad he's gone. Hopefully, I won't have to see him again any time soon." She turned toward the house. "Let's find Abby."

The front door was unlocked, so she walked in. The two-story, Craftsman-style home was decorated in warm, cozy chaos, lots of family photographs around, paperbacks and kids' books on the tables as well as numerous quilts on the walls or on the couches and chairs as Abby was a big quilter.

There were three couples and two teenagers in the living room, some of whom looked familiar, but no one she knew well enough to stop and say hello to. They moved down the hall to the kitchen and family room, where another dozen people were milling about. Abby saw them immediately and rushed across the room.

"Did you find Todd?" she asked Ryker.

"No, I'm sorry," he said heavily.

Abby's hopeful gaze turned bleak. "This can't be happening. I can't tell Tyler that Todd is gone, too. I can't do it."

"Where is Tyler?" she asked.

"My parents took him to their house. Tyler knows Todd was in an accident, but nothing else," Abby replied. "I just don't understand why no one has found him yet. You jumped into the river so fast, Ryker, as did James and Daniel." She tipped her head to the men, standing by the fireplace.

"I guess it wasn't fast enough," he said. "But Todd got out of the car. I have to hope he's in the woods somewhere and just hasn't found his way back."

Despite Ryker's words, Savannah didn't think he was feeling that optimistic. Nor was she. Every minute made the situation worse.

"Anyone need a drink?" Colin Barkley asked, as he joined them.

Colin had grown up with them in Dobbs, although he'd been two years older. He was now a high school teacher in Ridgeview, a bigger city about fifteen miles away, but his parents and sister still lived in Dobbs, and he spent a lot of time there. Actually, he spent a lot of time with Abby. He'd been a very good friend to her over the years. When Paul was deployed, Colin had helped Abby with all the things Paul used to do—getting the oil in the car changed, replacing a smoke detector, giving her endless rides to the hospital when Tyler had gone through a serious illness a few years earlier.

"I brought everything over from the reception," Colin added. "There's plenty of beer and wine."

"I wouldn't mind a beer," Ryker said.

"I'd like something, too," she said. "I'll come to the kitchen with you." She actually wanted a few minutes to talk to Colin more than she wanted a drink, so it was a good opportunity to get both. Before she left, she turned to Abby. "Ryker cut his leg on the rocks. Do you still have a first aid kit?"

"Of course. It's upstairs. Come with me, Ryker. I'll get you fixed up."

"It's really nothing," he said. "I don't need anything."

"Don't be silly. You were in the river. Let's get those cuts cleaned up."

As Abby took Ryker upstairs, Savannah followed Colin over to the ice chest on the kitchen counter.

He pulled out two beers, popped the top on one, and handed it to her. "What did you want to talk to me about?"

She smiled at the knowing gleam in his eyes. Colin was the kind of guy who could be counted on to be steady when the rest of the world was rocking. While she'd never been as close to him as Abby had, she'd liked him, and she'd always felt better knowing that Colin was nearby if Abby needed him.

"Did you know that Paul had moved out?" she asked.

His smile faded. "Yes, Abby told me. She was very conflicted, but he was not in a good place, Savannah."

"That's what everyone keeps saying. I wish Abby would have said something to me."

"She was hoping Paul would be back before people knew he was gone. She thought she was handing out some tough love, and that he'd get help, and they'd get back together. But he kept drinking even after he'd left." Colin paused. "He needed to be out of the house, Savannah. His temper was on a hair-trigger. He was yelling so much that Tyler was starting to feel anxious. I understand that his anger was directed as much at himself as everyone else, but that didn't change what was happening."

"Why was he angry with himself?"

"He blamed himself for the deaths of the men on his team. He felt responsible for the ambush, at least that's what he told me. He was also angry that he couldn't go back to his job. He wanted to get justice by taking down the terrorists who killed his brothers."

She wondered if Ryker felt that way, too. "That makes sense, but he loved Abby and Tyler so much. I can't believe he was willing to let them go."

"He changed over the years. He was a warrior first, a husband and father second. Abby saw his injury as kind of a lucky break. He would recover, but he wouldn't go back to the army. She'd never tell you that, of course."

"No, she wouldn't."

"But Paul was devastated. He didn't know what to do if he couldn't fight. Instead of being there for Abby, being the support she needed, he became another weight on her shoulders. And she was tired. When Tyler got sick two years ago, it was all on her. All the doctors' visits, the hospital stays. When he got better, there were the bills. She's still underwater on money. I think that was stressing out Paul, too, because he wanted to support her, but he didn't know what to do."

"I wish she would have reached out to me. I could have lent her some money."

"She's proud. I offered to help a number of times; she always turned me down. I know her parents paid for some things when she was desperate, but that also irritated Paul. He felt like he wasn't providing for her. That made him angry."

She took a sip of her beer as she thought about what he'd said. "What about Todd? Was he able to help Paul?"

"He was trying, but you can't help people who don't want to be helped. I know he feels badly about it."

"And now we have another accident that doesn't make sense. How on earth did Todd drive his car into the river?"

Colin gave her a troubled look. "I sure hope he didn't have a moment of temporary insanity."

"Is that what people are thinking? That it was deliberate?"

"There's a lot of whispering going on. The cops said he tried to brake, so why would he do that if he wanted to drive into the river?"

She couldn't help wondering if the odd pattern of skid marks simply revealed Todd's indecision. He could have been speeding, then braked in a panic, then decided to end it all and put his foot back on the gas. But that didn't explain where he was now. She took another long drink. "This is all so wrong, Colin. They're both too young to be dead. They survived war. How do they die in Dobbs, Georgia, four days apart, from freak accidents?"

"When you figure that out, let me know. Do you want to take this beer to your friend?"

"Ryker isn't my friend," she said defensively.

"Oh, sorry. It seemed like you two knew each other."

"We met once years ago, but we're not friends." She knew she was over-explaining, but she couldn't seem to stop herself.

"Well, he seems like a good guy. He went into the river to save his friend."

"It was very heroic," she admitted. "And I will take him that beer."

"Good."

"I haven't had a chance to ask how you are. Are you still dating that nurse in Ridgeview?"

"No, that ended several months ago."

"I'm sorry."

"Don't be. The spark wasn't there. What about you? Any lucky guys in your life?"

"I don't think any of the guys who have been in my life have actually considered themselves lucky."

"Don't be self-deprecating. You know how pretty you are."

"Maybe I have some good features, but that doesn't make me great at relationships. Anyway, I'm single, and I'm fine with it. I have the kind of job that takes me away for weeks at a time."

"I never ever thought you'd end up in law enforcement. When we were in high school, you were a troublemaker. If you saw a rule, you just had to break it."

"I have grown up, Colin."

He smiled. "I suspect you still break a few rules."

"Only the stupid ones," she returned with a grin, then she headed upstairs.

She found Ryker and Abby in the master bedroom. His pant leg was pushed up over his knee and Abby was applying a large gauze bandage to his new scrapes, but it couldn't hide the fact that there was a patchwork of deep scars running down his shin and around his calf.

"That's good," he said, as Abby finished, quickly shoving down his pants leg.

"I hope so," Abby said. "You might need a tetanus shot."

"I'm up to date. Don't worry about me."

As Abby stood up and took her first-aid kit into the bathroom, Savannah handed him a beer.

"Thanks." He took a swig, and then got to his feet.

"I'd like to offer you some dry clothes," Abby said, returning to the room. "Unless it would feel weird to wear something of Paul's. But he still has clothes in the closet. I kept thinking he'd come back for them…"

"It's not weird, but I'm fine. I'm dry now," Ryker returned.

"If you're sure." Abby paused. "I'm going to take a minute up here, so I'll see y'all downstairs."

"Do you want me to stay with you?" she asked, worried about the strain in her friend's eyes.

"Honestly, Savannah, I just need a little quiet, a few minutes."

"Okay." She followed Ryker out of the room and closed the door behind her. "I'm worried about her."

"She's a strong woman."

"But she's under a lot of pressure. Dealing with Paul's death was difficult enough. Now, she has to worry about Todd."

He nodded. "It's rough. Do you know where Todd lives?"

"Yes. Abby said he was renting a house a few miles from here, the old Thatcher place by the river."

"Can you give me the address? I want to check it out. I can't just wait around here and do nothing."

She liked the idea of being proactive. "I'll go with you."

"Can't get enough of my company?" he asked.

"That's exactly it," she said dryly. "But I'd also like to check out his house, see if there's anything to see."

Ryker stared back at her. "There won't be a good-bye note, Savannah. Todd didn't kill himself. This wasn't suicide."

She met his gaze. "I hope you're right."

CHAPTER FIVE

TODD LIVED in a two-story ranch-style house on a large lot that was thick with trees. While the homes were modest in this neighborhood, each one sat on at least a half-acre. As Ryker got out of his car, he appreciated the quiet. The bells in his head were silent for the moment. He hoped that would last.

Savannah was waiting for him at the front door, and he was surprised to see her slip a key into the lock.

"I thought we were going to have to break in," he said.

"I grabbed the key from Abby's kitchen drawer on my way out. Actually, I didn't know which one it was," she said, holding up the large key ring. "She has all her neighbors and friends' keys on this thing. But I got lucky. The second one worked."

He shook his head at the thick key ring. "Looks like she could get into a lot of houses in town."

"And they could get into hers. That's how it is in Dobbs. It's one very big dysfunctional family."

As she turned the knob and opened the door, he wondered if the police had already come by. But with their limited resources busy with search and rescue, and Chief Tanner being so convinced it was a simple motor vehicle accident, he doubted checking out Todd's house was a top priority.

He followed Savannah inside. The wood-paneled walls, dark hardwood floors, and the comfortable but mismatched furniture in the living area felt very masculine. As his gaze narrowed on the large, tall mug on the coffee table, the cigarette butts in the ashtray and the piles of sports magazines, he could feel Todd's presence. The feeling was so strong, he had to believe that Todd was coming back, that the house was waiting for him for a reason.

Savannah wandered around the living room, pausing to look at the framed football jersey signed by Mark Brunell, former quarter-back for the Jacksonville Jaguars.

"Todd's favorite team," he said, moving next to her. "He grew up in Jacksonville. His dad had season tickets when he was a kid. They went to every home game, until his dad passed on. Then it was just him and his mother. But she started losing her mind a few years ago, and Todd told me earlier that she doesn't recognize him anymore."

"Abby said that's why he moved to Dobbs."

Turning away from the jersey, he moved toward the stairs while Savannah wandered into the kitchen. There were two bedrooms on the second floor. In both rooms, the king-sized beds were unmade. Seeing jeans on the floor of one room, and a shirt tossed on the bed of the other, once again brought forth a wave of disbelief. *How could they both be gone just like that?*

It didn't feel like either one had planned to leave, had decided today or four days ago that that day would be their last one on earth. Everything felt off, like a mistake had been made, like he was trapped in a nightmare. In fact, that almost made more sense than anything else. Maybe he was dreaming.

But as Savannah came into the bedroom, he knew it was all too real.

"What do you think?" she asked quietly.

"It looks normal. It feels like they'll be back any minute."

"Todd only left a few hours ago, and the heat is on. The house hasn't had time to get stale."

"No, it hasn't." He folded his arms across his chest.

"I didn't see any obvious notes in the living room or kitchen. Anything in here?"

"I haven't gone through the dresser drawers or looked that closely."

"If either one had left a note, it would be easy to find. It would be in a place where we would see it."

"They weren't quitters, Savannah. They were warriors. They fought to the end. They didn't care how tough it was. They didn't give up. Believe me, I went through a lot of extremely tense situations with both of them. They didn't crack. Not when a lot of people would have."

"Sometimes the personal battles are harder to fight, especially when you're not with your team anymore."

"Well, I don't think they killed themselves. You can believe what you want."

"Okay," she said evenly. "I haven't actually formed an opinion; I'm still gathering facts."

"Is that what they teach you in the FBI?" He could hear the edge in his voice, and he saw the flash of annoyance enter Savannah's eyes.

"You sound like you want to pick a fight, Ryker, but I'm not interested in being your sparring partner." She turned on her heel and walked out.

He followed her down the stairs and into the living room. "You're right," he said, as she moved toward the front door.

She stopped at his words, slowly turning around, an expectant gleam in her pretty eyes.

"I am itching for a fight," he added. "I want to hit something. I want to blow something up. I want to burn something down. I want to put my anger somewhere, because it's eating me up."

Compassion filled her gaze. "I feel the same way. Abby and I go way back, and Paul was like a big brother to me. I didn't know Todd that well, but I'm in pain for my friend and for the loss of two men who should not have died like this."

"I get it. You care. I care. It's not a contest. It just sucks." He took a breath as he gazed around the room. "Everything has sucked for the last nine months."

"I saw the scars on your leg. What happened?"

"I blew out my knee, messed up some tendons, took some shrapnel. It's been a long recovery process."

"I'm sorry, Ryker."

"It is what it is."

"Abby said Paul wouldn't tell her what happened that night."

"Our mission was classified."

"It must have been important."

"And it was a failure in more ways than I can count. We lost two men that day and now two more are gone. There are only three of us left." He couldn't quite come to grips with that fact.

"You could have lost your life today, too, jumping into the river the way you did."

"Well, I survived." He thought about what Todd had said at the church. "It's ironic. One of the last things Todd said to me was that he was the one who always survived and sometimes he couldn't take it." As soon as he finished speaking, he realized he'd just reinforced what she was already thinking. "But Todd didn't mean that literally. I should have stopped him from leaving the church. But he was pissed off at me for not keeping in touch with him, and I let him go."

"You didn't know what was going to happen. Don't add another weight of blame to your shoulders; too much will crush you."

"Easier said than done."

"What else did Todd say to you?"

"If you're thinking he gave me some clue…"

"Just wondering what the conversation was about."

"He talked about Paul's problems, his drinking, his feeling of worthlessness. He complained about my lack of engagement with them. He thought I abandoned them. He wasn't wrong. I've been in my own head for a long time." He let out a breath. "And then he started ranting about the army."

"What do you mean?"

"He wanted to know what it was all for, how we'd ended up where we are. He felt like the army owed us more than we got."

"Do you feel that way, too?"

"Not really. I could understand where he was coming from, but we all knew the risks. We took them willingly. I said that, and he told me we didn't speak the same language anymore. That's when he told me he needed to be alone. He was definitely angry when he headed to the car. But he wasn't despondent. He was worked up." He paused, running a hand through his hair, realizing he was fighting a losing battle. "I actually don't know why I'm trying to convince you that Todd wasn't suicidal, when I have no idea if he was. Or if Paul was. His fall was bizarre, too."

"Well, hopefully, Todd will be found, and you'll be able to talk to him." She took a breath. "I should get back to Abby. Do you want me to help you find a place to stay? There are some hotels in Ridgeview; it's not that far. I suspect the two inns in Dobbs are full because of the funeral. I know Abby has some out-of-town friends who came in for the service."

"I don't need a hotel; I'm going to stay here."

Her brows shot up in surprise. "Here? Won't that be…strange?"

"I don't care. I need to be here. This is where they were both living. If there's a clue to what happened to them, to their state of mind, it's probably in this house. Besides that, if Todd does make it out of that river, I want to be here for him."

"I'm sure he'd appreciate that."

"I'm not so sure, but I'll be here anyway."

"I guess I'll talk to you later then."

"Let me give you my number," he said. "If you hear anything, call me."

"I will." She handed him her phone so he could put in his number. She then texted him, so he'd have her contact information as well.

He walked onto the porch with her, feeling a little reluctant to let her go. But she needed to be with Abby, and he needed to figure out what had been going on with Paul and Todd. He didn't know how long he had before the bells started ringing again.

Savannah thought about Ryker all the way back to Abby's house. She hadn't had much time to come to grips with his sudden reappearance in her life, and now it didn't appear that either one of them would be leaving Dobbs any time soon.

Ryker would stay until there was news of Todd, and she would stay until she felt Abby could manage without her. Although, it felt a little self-aggrandizing to think that Abby couldn't manage without her. She'd been running her life and Tyler's for years. Even when Paul was alive, he hadn't been around that much. Abby had been the one to keep the family going, and she'd keep on doing that.

But it was different now, because Paul wouldn't be coming home. There was no light at the end of the tunnel for Abby. This was her life now. She was a single mother. Her husband was gone. The big worry Abby had had every time her husband was deployed had come to fruition.

At least Abby had her parents nearby and plenty of friends. As much as Savannah had rebelled against the constraints of the small town, she knew that Abby would be surrounded with love, and that was what mattered.

When she returned to Abby's house, she found her friend alone in the kitchen, making a fresh pot of coffee.

"Where is everyone?" she asked. "I didn't think you'd be on your own."

"I asked them to leave. I just couldn't talk anymore."

"We don't have to talk, either."

"No, you're fine. You know me, Savannah. I don't have to pretend with you. Do you want coffee? I'm making a fresh pot. As exhausted as I am, I don't want to sleep until there's news about Todd."

"I'd love some." She set her bag on the counter. "Why don't you sit, and I'll make it?"

"It's fine. I like doing something normal. Are you hungry? There's so much food here; I need to donate some of it."

She slid onto a stool and grabbed a chocolate chip cookie off a plate. "These look good."

"There are casseroles in the fridge if you want something more substantial."

"I'm not that hungry."

"Where is Ryker? Did he go home?"

"No, he's at Todd's house. He's going to stay there until there's word or Todd comes back. I took your key to let him in; I hope that's not a problem for you."

"It's fine. Ryker is Todd's friend. I'm sure Todd wouldn't care that he's there. How is Ryker doing? He got pretty beat up in the river, and those scars on his leg looked bad."

"He's hanging in there, like the rest of us."

Abby leaned against the counter as she waited for the coffee to perk. "Paul really missed Ryker these past several months. He tried to get in touch with him a few times, but he never heard back. I guess Ryker was dealing with problems of his own."

"He mentioned that he had been out of touch and felt bad about it. I do think there's more going on with him than problems with his leg. He seems…haunted."

Abby gazed back at her. "I thought that about Paul, too. He would drift off in the middle of a conversation. He would be miles away from me even when he was sitting two feet away. And he was paranoid, too. He even accused me of having a thing for Colin. How crazy is that?"

"Well, you are close friends," she said carefully.

"That's all we are. I would never cheat on Paul. Never! How could you think that, Savannah?"

"I don't think that," she said quickly, seeing the anger in Abby's eyes. "But I could see that Paul might have been a little jealous of Colin's presence in your life."

"He had no right to be. Colin was there when Paul wasn't. He was in the hospital with me when Tyler got sick. He made me food. He made sure I slept. And he watched Tyler for me when he got better, so I could have a break. Of course, we're close. And, yes, Tyler loves Colin. But why shouldn't he? Colin has been great with him."

"I believe you, Abby. You don't have to defend yourself to me."

"I shouldn't have had to defend myself to my husband. He should have trusted me, but he didn't. Now you're making me think he had a right to be mad at me. Maybe I was blurring the lines."

"Abby, breathe. I'm on your side—one hundred percent. And I don't think Colin was really Paul's problem."

"You're right. Colin was just an excuse for Paul to be angry— as if he needed another one. He loved the army and then he hated it. In some ways, I think he felt the same way about himself." She paused, grabbing mugs out of the cabinet. "Are you still drinking your coffee black?"

"Yes."

Abby filled two mugs and then sat down at the island with her. "I wanted to ask you something, Savannah."

"What's that?"

"You and Ryker."

She almost choked on her coffee. "There's no me and Ryker."

"You've been with him all day. You brought him here. You went to Todd's with him. You seem like you know him, but you only met him this afternoon, right?"

She was surprised that Abby, in all her distraction, had picked up on the connection between them. "Actually, no. I met him five years ago."

"Are you serious? How did I not know that?"

"We had a one-night stand. It was right before I left the army."

Abby's eyes widened in amazement. "Why didn't you say anything?"

"I didn't know his name at the time, and he didn't know mine. It sounds kind of slutty to say that, but it's the truth. It was one of those wild, reckless, impulsive nights. I didn't even realize he was in Paul's unit until two years ago when you showed me a photo of the team."

"I remember that. You asked me his name and you got a funny look on your face. Why didn't you say something then?"

"It was too far in the past by that point. I didn't think I'd see him again. I'd pretty much forgotten about him." Even as she said the words, she knew they weren't completely true. She had thought about Ryker a lot over the years, sometimes comparing other men to him, and they'd always come up short. She wished she'd been able to forget about him, but he'd stuck in her head.

"So you hadn't seen him in five years until today?" Abby asked.

"No. I thought he might come to the funeral, but I wasn't sure he'd remember me."

"How could he forget you? You're a lot of things, Savannah, but forgettable is not one of them. What did he say when he saw you?"

"He was shocked. He had no idea I knew Paul or that I wasn't the dancer he thought I was."

"He thought you were a dancer? This story gets more and more interesting." Abby sipped her coffee. "Why would he think that?"

"We met at a hotel bar in Doha. He was on leave and I was on a layover on my way back to the States. There was a group of Texas cheerleaders staying in the same hotel. They had done a show for the troops in Kuwait. He assumed I was one of them."

"Why didn't you tell him you weren't?"

"It was easier to just be a dancer."

Abby gave her a knowing look. "I thought you got over trying to please people by turning yourself into someone you aren't."

"That night was actually the turning point for that decision. I was so conflicted about whether I wanted to stay in the army or get out, and after that night, I knew. It was so clear. I couldn't be a dancer for Ryker or a soldier for my father or a beauty queen for my aunt. I had to find out who I was."

"That was one of your better decisions. I've hated watching you push the real parts of yourself away. But, wow, I can't believe you had a one-night stand with Ryker. He's…well, he's really good-looking, but Paul said Ryker could also be very cold. He could completely detach from the emotion in any situation."

"I didn't see any sign of coldness that night. In fact, he was pretty irresistible when we met. He was confident and rugged, sexy and charming. He had wit and a killer smile."

"And how was he in bed?"

"Amazing," she admitted. "Hotter than hot. But I have to say he's changed a lot since that night. He's dark and haunted now. He has an uncertainty that wasn't there before, an isolated feeling about him. And maybe now I do see the coldness."

"That ambush changed them all. Only two died that night, but it seems like the rest of them have been dying slowly ever since then." Abby's gaze turned bleak.

"I wish you'd told me how bad things were."

"I kept thinking Paul would get better. I really did love him, Savannah. I just didn't know how to help him, how to reach him. We used to be best friends, but this past year, it felt like we were strangers. It seemed almost deliberate at times, as if he was trying to put a wall between us. He wasn't even that angry when I asked him to leave. He almost seemed relieved, like the other shoe had finally dropped. I thought he would get better when he knew our marriage and our family were on the line. But I was just lying to myself."

She didn't know what to say. No words could change what had happened. "It's not your fault, Abby. You know that. Even if he hadn't left the house, he still could have died. He was over at Todd's all the time. He was drinking all the time."

"I keep telling myself that, but it's so difficult not to feel guilty. I want a do-over, but I'm not going to get one. I have to find a way to move on. I have to be strong for Tyler. I can't let his life be forever ruined by this tragedy. I want him to remember Paul as the good man he was."

"You'll make sure that Tyler knows how good Paul was."

"But I can't begin moving on until we find Todd. I care about him, too, Savannah. He was trying to help me. He was taking care of Paul, even when he was dealing with his own problems."

"Don't give up hope, Abby. Todd is a strong guy."

"It's hard not to give up. I feel like whatever happened to the team nine months ago set off a terrible chain of events, and I'm afraid there's more coming."

"I don't know what more could come."

"I hope we don't have to find out." Abby paused, her lips tightening. "I want to get the elephant out of the room, Savannah."

She gave her friend a commiserating smile. "You don't have to say anything."

"Some people think Paul jumped off the roof, and I'm pretty sure some people believe that Todd drove into that river. You might even be one of those people."

"I might have had that thought," she admitted. "But Ryker doesn't believe either one of them did that—if that makes you feel better. He knew both of them as well as anyone."

"I hope Ryker is right. I also hope he doesn't end up like them, because I saw the changes in him, too, and it felt like the same changes I'd seen in Paul and Todd. I wish he'd come back here tonight instead of staying at Todd's."

Fear ran through her at Abby's foreboding words. She might not ever get back together with Ryker, but she definitely did not want to see him hurt or worse... "It's just for the night," she said. "Hopefully, the morning will bring good news."

"I want to believe that."

"So do I." But she had a bad feeling, and she couldn't seem to shake it.

CHAPTER SIX

RYKER TOSSED and turned on the couch in Todd's living room as the chimes on the grandfather clock rang four times, which meant he'd been trying to sleep for almost five hours. But every hour, just as he managed to drift off, the bells would ring, and trigger his own private ride of noise and terror.

He should have stretched out in one of the bedrooms upstairs and put some distance between himself and the clock, but sleeping in one of his friend's beds had seemed like too much. He had, however, taken a shower and put on some sweatpants and a clean T-shirt that had probably belonged to Paul, since it had an Atlanta Falcons logo on it. He wished now he'd packed an overnight bag, but he'd never expected to spend the night in Dobbs.

Rolling onto his side, he stared out the window. The curtains were wide open. He hadn't bothered to draw them. He hadn't wanted to change anything in the house that was waiting for Todd to come home.

It must have rained because he could see drops of water on the glass lit up by the moonlight. The thought of that river swelling even more with the storm brought forth another wave of despair. Todd had to be out of the river by now. He had to be hunkered down in the woods, waiting for morning, waiting for light. It was the only thought that Ryker could accept.

"Sleep," he muttered, closing his eyes. He had fifty-eight more minutes before the clock rang again. He needed to take advantage of that.

Before the ambush, he'd always been able to sleep on command. But since then, sleep had been his enemy and not his friend. He was lucky, even with total quiet, if he could get a few hours in a row.

He tried to clear his mind, to find a happy place, but he kept seeing Todd and Paul in his mind. He thought about the times the three of them had been together, not just while they were working, or on the battlefield, but the down times: the impromptu soccer games, the bar nights where they'd escaped for a few hours, the life moments they'd celebrated—the birth of a child, a marriage, a death of a family or a friend. They hadn't just been a team; they'd been family. And now his family had lost two more people.

If Todd didn't come back, there would be another funeral. *And who was left to come?*

Neither Mason nor Hank had made it to Paul's funeral. *Would they come for Todd?*

But he was writing off Todd too soon. He would come back. They would talk. He would help him.

He hated himself for not being the man he used to be, for letting down his team. He kept thinking he'd get back to normal and then he'd get back to them. But there hadn't been enough time. Paul was dead. Todd might be, too.

He could only imagine what Savannah thought of him now. He'd seen the questions in her eyes. She'd clearly noticed the changes in him. If they'd met today for the first time, she wouldn't have looked at him twice.

As her pretty image filled his head, his mind went back five years. He could still remember how he'd felt the first time he'd seen her, like he'd been hit in the chest by a fastball. He'd literally lost his breath. Carlos had been with him at the bar. They'd been acting as each other's wingman that night when Savannah had walked in and ordered a double shot of tequila. He hadn't been able to take his eyes off her.

Carlos had laughed and leaned in, saying, "Make your move, dude. She won't be alone long."

He hadn't needed any further encouragement. He'd offered to buy her next shot. She'd given him a long, assessing look and then said, "Why not?"

He didn't remember much after that. They hadn't really talked. They'd drank and danced to some awful band and then made their way out of the bar and up the elevator to his hotel room.

They'd spent the rest of the night making each other very, very happy. He'd drifted off sometime before dawn thinking that he'd buy her breakfast. But she'd been gone when he'd opened his eyes. And he'd felt an unexpected and shocking wave of disappointment.

He'd looked for her in the hotel and at the bar the next night, but she hadn't shown up, and he'd had no idea who she was or where she lived. He'd even tried to track down the dance group, but they'd already checked out of the hotel. He'd thought he'd never see her again.

He certainly hadn't expected her to show up at Paul's funeral, to be tied to Paul's wife, to have a background that was nothing like the one he'd given her in his head. He still didn't completely understand her reason for letting him think she was a dancer instead of a soldier. She certainly hadn't seemed like a soldier that night. And, apparently, she hadn't been one for very much longer after that. Now, she was an FBI agent.

He couldn't quite see her as that, either. He wanted to know more. But that wasn't going to happen. He led a very quiet life on the bay now, and Savannah lived on the other side of the country.

Five years ago, he'd felt like he'd been in the right place at the right time when he'd met her, but now it was not only the wrong place but the worst time.

He wasn't the man she'd slept with. He was damaged, broken, and he couldn't imagine bringing anyone into the hell he lived in. Not that she'd be interested, even if he was willing.

There was also probably a man in her life. *How could there not be?* She was stunning. And she'd kissed like no other woman he'd ever been with…

His body hardened at that memory, and sleep seemed more elusive than ever.

He tried to bring up calming snapshots of the Chesapeake Bay in his head, but his brain fought back, slipping in images from Paul's funeral, from his conversation with Todd on the patio, the crash site, and the empty car. He couldn't stand it. He pushed his brain further back in time trying to find a moment when everyone was happy, but he couldn't get there. Instead he saw the abandoned hotel where they'd conducted their last mission. They'd split up the team, three in the front, two on the side, two in the back. Their point of entry was supposed to be empty, but it wasn't. Flashes of light blinded him. The bangs echoed through his mind. Carlos falling to his knees. Leo disappearing in a burst of fire and smoke. He screamed as he was hit.

As the noise receded, he heard footsteps, a rustle in the bushes, a small bang.

His eyes flew open. He was back in Todd's house. *Had he heard something?* A shadow crossed the window. He blinked twice.

Was someone rattling the door? Was Todd home? Or had the sound come from his turbulent dreams? Why couldn't he trust his brain anymore?

The questions went unanswered as the grandfather clock went off, and his mind shattered.

He jumped to his feet. One chime, and it felt like a knife had gone through his temple… He had to make it stop.

Two…he opened the clock's door and pulled at the chains. Nothing happened.

Three…he grabbed a vase off the table.

Four… he threw the vase against the glass. It shattered and rained down to the floor in a cascade of sharp slivers. He stared at it in bemusement.

Five…the damned clock was still ringing. He hit the vase against the hanging bells, until he couldn't hear them anymore and then he fell to his knees on the floor, staring at the carnage of the clock and the vase that had broken into a dozen pieces.

It was finally quiet again, but there was blood on his hands.

More memories ran through him. *Blood...just like the blood seeping under Carlos's head.*

He stumbled to his feet, to the sink in the kitchen. He ran his hands under the water, scrubbing at his skin until every last staining drop was gone.

And then he found his way back to the couch, exhausted, his body drenched with sweat. He closed his eyes and sleep finally overtook him.

When he awoke, there was sun streaming through the window. It was so bright, it hurt his eyes. He glanced at his watch. It was eight. The morning had finally come, and he'd slept for at least a few hours.

As he swung his feet to the floor, a knock came at the door. He had to ask himself again if it was a real noise or one in his head, but as it came again, he pulled himself together and headed across the room. Maybe there was news of Todd.

He threw open the door and found Savannah on the porch. She'd changed out of her black dress into skinny jeans and a fuzzy dark-green sweater that brought out the green in her eyes and the gold in her hair. She was like a burst of sunshine, and it hurt to look at her, too.

"I brought coffee and bagels." She held up a tray with two cups and a brown paper bag.

"Is there news?"

She shook her head, her gaze somber. "Chief Tanner called Abby this morning. Search and rescue teams started an hour ago. A volunteer search is starting at nine, and they're pulling up the car as we speak. Maybe it will provide some clues. Can I come in?" Not waiting for a response, she brushed past him.

As she entered the living room, her eyes widened.

He followed her gaze to the shattered glass, the broken bells, and the chunks of a once-large ceramic vase and realized that hadn't been a dream.

"Who won?" she asked, giving him a concerned look. "You or the clock?"

"Well, I'm still standing."

Her gaze moved to his shirt. "Is that blood?"

He glanced down at the material tinged with dark spots of red. "Maybe. But I'm fine."

"I seriously doubt that." She set the bag of bagels on the coffee table and handed him one of the coffee cups. "You look like you need this."

"I can't argue with that." He took a sip of coffee, a little surprised that Savannah wasn't reacting in a more hysterical fashion. When he'd first started losing his mind to the bells, the woman he'd been dating at the time had flipped out. She'd become afraid of him. And she'd left very soon after that.

But Savannah didn't seem in a hurry to go. Nor did she seem interested in looking away from him. He was more than a little uncomfortable with her scrutiny.

"Are you thinking it's a good thing you took off five years ago?" he asked finally. "Because you hadn't realized I was a crazy person?"

"Actually, I was wondering why the clock bothered you so much."

"It rang every damn hour. I couldn't sleep."

"So you smashed it."

"It seemed like a good idea at the time."

"Did the pain stop after the clock went quiet?"

He met her gaze. "Yes. But it will come back. It always does."

"Since you were injured?"

"My knee wasn't the only injury I suffered. My brain keeps hearing bells. They drive me crazy. They're not ordinary, soothing bells. They can be jarring, clashing, and grinding. Any sound can set them off."

"What do you do when they go off?"

"I try not to jump out of my skin. I try to find quiet."

"And sometimes you shout at the bells to stop like you did yesterday when I found you by the river."

There was no point in pretending. "Yes, sometimes I shout. But it rarely makes a difference. I can't control when they start or when they stop."

"Is it physical or psychological?"

He shrugged. "No one knows. Apparently, my symptoms are not part of any textbook PTSD diagnosis."

Her gaze filled with sympathy. "I'm sorry, Ryker."

He hated the compassion in her eyes. He didn't want her to look at him like he was wounded. He wanted her to see him the way she had before. But that wasn't going to happen. That man was gone, and he needed to accept that. He took another sip of his coffee, needing the caffeine to kick in fast.

"Did you sleep at all last night?" she asked.

"A few hours. It wasn't just the clock that kept me up. I had a lot on my mind."

"I'm sure. I was thinking about Paul and Todd, too." She paused. "You came into my head as well."

"Oh, yeah?"

"I hadn't let myself think about the night we had together, but suddenly I couldn't stop remembering all the details, from our first drink at the bar to my leaving your hotel room."

"Why hadn't you let yourself think about it?" he asked curiously. "Did you have regrets?"

"No. I just knew it would never happen again. It was better not to think about it, not to drive myself crazy wondering if I should have stuck around to say good morning."

"You could have stayed until I woke up. We could have exchanged names, seen each other another time."

"I don't think that's what you were looking for."

"Or what you were looking for."

"You're right. I had to make a big decision, and it was time to get on with that. But that night was incredible, Ryker. I don't know if it's because we only had the one night, so we didn't have to deal with anything beyond our romantic fantasy, but it was rather extraordinary. At least, that's the way I remember it."

"I remember it that way, too," he admitted, feeling the air

charge around them. They might be different people now, but the attraction was there. Their bodies still wanted each other, even if their brains were on a different page.

"So," she said, drawing in a breath. "Do you want to join the search party?"

He wanted to take her to bed, but he knew that wasn't the right answer. "Yes," he said, forcing himself to focus on what they needed to do, not what he wanted to do.

"It's good that it's not raining and windy anymore. The chopper can go back up. Hopefully, Todd is just lost in the woods and trying to get home."

Her words brought forth another memory from the night before. "I thought he came back last night. I heard something. I saw a shadow outside the window. And then I thought someone was jiggling the door."

"Did you get up to look?"

"I started to, but the clock went off, and my brain shattered. Or maybe the clock went off first and I never heard the other sounds. Sometimes reality and dreams blur together, especially when it comes to noise."

Her gaze narrowed and then she moved over to the window. He came up behind her.

There was a tree outside with long branches that brushed the panes of glass. Below the window were several thick bushes.

"What time did you hear the noise?" Savannah asked.

He tried to remember. "I think it was sometime before five in the morning." He'd barely finished speaking before she headed to the door. "Where are you going?"

"Outside. I want to look around."

"It was probably in my head," he said, as he followed her outside. He was barefoot, and the ground was ice cold, but as she moved around the house and down the side yard, he kept up with her. She stopped by the window, then squatted down to look at the ground. "It wasn't your imagination, Ryker." She pointed to several large footprints in the wet soil.

He was shocked by the sight of them. He'd been almost positive the noises were in his head.

"Someone was standing by this window," she added, straightening. "They could see into the house."

"They would have seen me on the couch," he said, realizing the sofa was in plain view. "And then when I got to my feet."

"They must have left when they saw you."

He thought about that. "Who would have come to Todd's house in the middle of the night? What would they want? And why wouldn't they ring the bell?"

"Maybe someone decided to break in after they heard the news about Todd. They figured the house was empty."

"What are you doing?" he asked, as she pulled out her phone.

"Taking a photo of the print. I'll send it to one of my techs, see if they can tell us more."

"Like what?"

"Size, type of shoe, whether it's male or female. We may get nothing, but you never know."

"You're treating this like a crime scene." The idea bothered him more than a little.

"Maybe it is."

"Nothing happened."

"Because you were in the house."

He could see a mix of emotions flitting through her eyes. "What are you thinking?"

"Maybe Todd's accident wasn't an accident. Perhaps he was run off the road. It's a long shot, and I'm probably wrong, but the fact that someone tried to break into the house after Todd went in the river concerns me."

"I agree. Hell, maybe neither of their accidents were accidents. What if Paul didn't just fall off the roof?"

"But who would have a reason to kill Paul or Todd?"

"I don't know, but it's almost easier to believe that there was someone else involved than to think that one fell off the roof and the other drove off the road. Neither of those actions fits the men I knew."

As they walked through the yard, he could see her looking around for more clues, but there was nothing that stood out. When they came around the front, he looked up and down the street, but he could barely see the nearest house. "If someone was snooping around in the middle of the night, I doubt anyone saw them," he said. "No neighbors to speak of."

"And Todd has no security cameras on the house. Why would he? There's not much crime in Dobbs. At least, not until now."

"We need to find Todd, and we need to look at his car."

"I'm ready whenever you are."

CHAPTER SEVEN

THIRTY MINUTES LATER, they were on the road. Ryker had showered and changed into jeans and a sweatshirt, then downed two bagels before getting into Savannah's car. She'd insisted on driving, since she knew her way around the area, and he'd reluctantly agreed. He liked to be in control of everything, including a car, but he didn't want to waste time getting lost.

When they got to the river, there was a command post set up near the crash site with groups of volunteers walking along the shoreline. The helicopter was back up in the air as well. They checked in at the command post and were told they could start from the crash site, or they could drive themselves to a spot farther down the river and begin there. They opted for the latter. He didn't think Todd would be near his point of entry into the water. He had to have been swept downstream.

As Savannah drove along the river, he realized the water was even higher and faster than it had been the day before. Last night's storm had dumped enough rain to bring the level up several inches. There were lots of people walking along the shore and the road. It felt like the entire town had come out to search for Todd. It was amazing how many people cared about a man who had only been in town a few months.

"There's the car," Savannah said, pulling over to the side. They got out and crossed the road, moving down a steep slope to a flat area where Todd's car had been pulled out of the river.

There were at least a dozen people at the scene. Savannah marched forward, flashing a big smile and her badge at the officer closest to the car. Seeing the dumbstruck look on the man's face as he allowed them to pass, Ryker didn't think she'd even needed the badge.

"All the damage is from where the car broke through the guardrail," Savannah murmured, as they walked around the car, noting the missing front fender and the considerable damage to the hood. "The airbag was deployed. The front window was shattered." She ran her gaze along the driver's side door. "But there's no sign of blood on the airbag, nothing on the seat or the door handle. No personal effects inside the vehicle."

"They could have washed away."

"Possibly." She stopped abruptly as Chief Tanner stomped over to them, anger in his eyes.

"Move away from the car," Tanner ordered, sending a sharp look at the officer who had let them pass. "I told you to keep everyone away."

"She's FBI."

He turned back to Savannah. "This has nothing to do with you or the bureau. Stay out of it."

"I have resources you don't have. You need to use me, not shut me out."

"I don't need your resources or your help. You may think you're a big shot, but in my mind you're the same troublemaker you always were. Now, step away, or you'll find yourself spending another night in my jail."

Ryker was impressed with Savannah's unwillingness to back down, but he didn't think she was going to win this round with the chief, and he didn't want to see them cut out of the investigation completely.

"I wanted to see the car," he cut in. "Todd and I served together. I want to bring him home."

"We all do. You can help by joining the search. I'll deal with the car. Move along."

They walked down to the river's edge where Savannah drew in several deep breaths.

"At least, we had a chance to look at the vehicle before he chased us away," he said.

"Not long enough."

"I wasn't sure you were going to back down."

"I'm not stupid," she retorted. "I know when to retreat."

"I never said you were stupid."

"I'm sorry. I just hate the way Tanner treats me. I have never been my best self in this town. It's why I rarely come back here. People respect me in LA. Actually, they respect me anywhere else but here."

"I get that. When you come back to your childhood home, people tend to see you as you were, not as you are."

"Does that ever happen to you?"

"I rarely go home. Shall we take a walk? We might as well search along this part of the river. It's where the car was found."

"Sure," she said, falling into step with him.

They were farther downstream than he'd gone yesterday, and as they wound their way along the shoreline, they had to weave through tall, thick trees. While the sun was out, there were dark shadows in this part of the woods, and it was quite cold. It was also quiet, only the sound of the river accompanying their walk. He didn't know where the other search parties were, but for the moment, they were completely alone.

They walked in silence for about twenty minutes. Then they ran into a couple coming from the opposite direction. The woman had medium-length, straight blonde hair while the man had dark hair and a thick beard. They appeared to be in their late twenties. The woman stopped abruptly when she saw them, a surprised, unhappy expression crossing her face.

"Savannah, you're still in town," the woman said. "I thought you'd be long gone by now."

"My plans changed."

He could hear the cool tone in Savannah's voice. Whoever this woman was, she wasn't a friend.

"Is this your boyfriend?" the woman continued.

"No. This is Ryker Stone. He served with Paul and Todd. My cousin, Josie Burkett and her boyfriend Dale Howard," Savannah said, clearly struggling to be polite.

"Hello," he said shortly, not really wanting to get into the middle of whatever this was.

"It's nice to meet you, Mr. Stone," Josie said, her gaze assessing and curious. "I'm sorry about your friends. Dale and I have been out here all morning, looking for Todd. We still can't believe what's happened. We were late getting to the funeral. When we arrived, everyone was down by the river. It was shocking."

He nodded, not really caring what she had to say. He just wanted them to move along so Savannah could stop looking like she wanted to hit someone hard, and he suspected that someone was Josie. She had a similar look to Savannah with her blonde hair, but her eyes were a boring brown, and her features weren't nearly as pretty.

"Well, we're heading back now," Josie said, when the silence between the four of them went on too long. "You can keep going, but the river becomes inaccessible in a half mile."

"We'll just walk a little farther," Savannah said.

"Whatever." Josie paused. "Dad said if I saw you to tell you to come by and get some ribs. He has a barbecue truck now in Ridgeview. He parks it by the square. For whatever reason, he seems to actually miss you. He's been having a hard time the last few months, so you should stop by."

"Why is he having a difficult time?"

"Because he quit the law to barbecue, and Mom is less than thrilled. She went to visit her friend, Constance, in Atlanta, and I don't think she's coming back any time soon, or ever. Things aren't good between Mom and Dad. They might even get a divorce."

"I'm sorry to hear that. I can't believe your father actually got a food truck. It was always his dream. He finally did it."

"He doesn't make much money, but he likes it. Of course, he

had to change jobs before my wedding. You did hear Dale and I are getting married, didn't you? You talk to Abby, right? We're friends now."

"She told me. Congratulations." Savannah turned to Dale. "How have you been, Dale? Are you still working at the bar?"

"Always," Dale said. "My dad retired last year. It's my second home, but I enjoy it. Everyone in town comes through there at least once a week."

"Did Todd come into the bar?" Ryker asked.

"All the time and usually with Paul, who was drinking way too much."

"What about Todd's drinking?" he asked.

"Sometimes he'd get a buzz on when he was with Paul, but I never noticed him out of control. He was in bad shape on Saturday night, though. He was reeling from Paul's death, and he'd just come back from seeing Abby and Tyler. He had more than a few drinks that night."

"Was Todd with anyone else that night?"

"No. A few people tried to talk to him, express their condolences, but he was on the phone a lot, texting every other second to someone. He seemed to want to be alone with his drinks and his phone."

"We should go," Josie interrupted, clearly not interested in continuing a conversation that didn't involve her.

"Nice to meet you," Dale said, giving him a nod.

"You, too."

As Josie and Dale moved away, Ryker gave Savannah a thoughtful look. "You and your cousin don't get along."

"Nothing gets by you."

"Why doesn't she like you?"

"Because she's a bitch."

He smiled. "I can't argue with that, since I don't know her, but what's between you?"

"A lot of things. When I first moved in with my aunt and uncle, Josie was thrilled. She was two years younger than me, and she was excited to have someone who could be an older sister to her. But she quickly realized that with me around, she was going to have to share. Things got worse when her mom decided that I should join them on the beauty pageant circuit. That was their thing. They'd been entering pageants since Josie was five. It wasn't something I wanted to do, but if I wanted to fit in with my new family, I had to do it. It worked for a while. We did become closer. We had a lot of car trips together, but then I started winning, and Josie didn't like that. Suddenly, her mother was completely fixated on me. My aunt saw my successes as her successes. When Josie came up short, she lost her mom's attention."

"That must have been rough on Josie."

"I have some sympathy, but she was so hateful to me that it was difficult to feel that sorry for her. She even tried to sabotage me a few times. Anyway, after I won Miss Georgia, and came in third in Miss USA, I quit and went to college, where I joined ROTC."

"From beauty queen to soldier, not the most common path."

"Well, I don't like to be common."

He smiled. "I don't think anyone could accuse you of that. It doesn't sound like you've kept in touch with your cousin or her family."

"I do email and text with my uncle, although I guess it's been a while. I had no idea he'd quit his job and opened a food truck, but he does make fantastic ribs." She paused. "You're probably thinking that since the chief, my dad and my cousin don't like me, that the problem is me, and not them. Right?"

"You do seem to generate some strong emotion," he admitted. "But it seems like they each have a different reason for disliking you, so I'm keeping an open mind."

"Well, you don't have to do that. You can think whatever you want."

"I know, and I don't need your permission to do that."

"True. Do you want to keep walking? The shoreline will be impassable soon."

"We might as well go back. Your cousin and boyfriend already covered this area."

As they reversed direction, she said, "What's your family like? We've been talking a lot about me. Tell me something about Ryker Stone. Was your dad in the service?"

"No. He's the chief financial officer for a venture capital firm that was started by his father. The Stone family business is all about money. But my mother's side is all about service. Her father, my grandfather, went to West Point, and after hearing all his stories, I wanted to go, too."

"Was your mom in the military?"

"No, she was a teacher and then a stay-at-home mom. She spent a lot of time taking care of my sister and me."

"You have a sister?"

"I do. She's married now, with a kid."

"Where does everyone live?"

"My sister and her family are in Connecticut, and my parents are in New York City."

"Do you see them often?"

"I haven't seen anyone since my last surgery seven months ago. They were hovering for a while when I first got back, but I finally got rid of them."

She gave him a speculative look. "Because they were too loud for you?"

"Yes. They were loud. They had a lot of opinions. And I didn't want to hear any of them. I also didn't need them to worry about me."

"Did they know about the problems you were having with the bells?"

"They didn't need to know."

"Your former team members didn't need to know, either. Is that why you stayed away from them, too?"

"We were all dealing with our own problems. They didn't need to carry mine."

"Does anyone help you carry your problems?"

"Like a doctor?"

"Or a friend?" she countered.

"No one can help me, Savannah. I have to solve this on my own."

"What if you can't do it by yourself?"

"I have to. The bells are in my head, no one else's. It's my deal. And I'm beginning to be sorry I told you."

"Well, don't worry, I'm not going to offer to help you."

He was both relieved and a little surprised. "Why not?"

"Because it would be a waste of time. You pushed your family and friends away; I don't think you'll listen to me. But you should, because I'm very smart."

He liked the confident smile that curved her lips. "I have no doubt about that, but I have to handle this my way."

"I have a feeling you only ever handle things your way," she said dryly.

"It's worked so far."

"Has it?"

Thankfully, he didn't have to answer that question since they'd reached the spot where Todd's car had been pulled out of the river. The vehicle was gone now. So were the police. "They got the car out of here fast," he commented.

"I'm sure they want to preserve whatever evidence might be inside. I don't like Chief Tanner, but I'm confident he'll examine the car carefully. However, I'm not confident he'll find anything, unless the brakes were tampered with, or there's clear evidence of a mechanical failure."

"I agree."

"There might be a clue on Todd's phone," she suggested. "According to Dale, he was on it a lot Saturday night. Maybe whoever he was talking to could tell us about his state of mind, what their conversation was about."

"I'm sure he had his phone on him when he went into the river."

"His text history could be on his computer. Did you notice a computer in the house?"

"I didn't pay attention. There might have been one there."

"We should check it out, maybe go through the house more thoroughly, see if we can find anything that would be helpful."

"We can do that." He was happy to have a plan, even if it seemed a bit pointless. "But if Todd drove into the river on impulse, or if it was truly an accident, then there won't be any clues. The only scenario that might leave a trail would be if Todd had planned to take his own life, and that isn't something I want to consider."

"Well, we can do nothing. Just wait and hope that Todd is found alive."

He didn't like that idea, either. "I'm not good at waiting."

"Neither am I," she said, as they got into the car.

"Let's go back to Todd's house and look for a computer or any other clue that might be helpful."

She pulled away from the curb, and for a few minutes, there was nothing but silence. He felt an odd need to break the quiet, which was very unusual. But as he glanced at her beautiful profile, he found himself becoming increasingly more curious about her.

She turned her gaze to meet his, raising a questioning brow. "Something on your mind?"

"You."

"What do you want to know?"

He wanted to know everything. *But what was the point of that? In fact, why had he even told her he was thinking about her?* He couldn't get involved with her. As soon as Todd was found, he'd be on his way back to the bay, to his boat, and to his very solitary life.

"It doesn't sound like you want to know anything," she said, when he remained silent.

"I want to know a lot, but it doesn't seem like a good idea. I'll be leaving soon, so will you."

"Our paths probably won't cross again," she agreed. "But we can still talk now. What's on your mind?"

He really should not say what was on his mind, but somehow the words came out of his mouth. "When I remember you and our night together, three things stand out. How I couldn't catch my breath when I was with you. How easily you smiled and laughed. And how perfectly we fit together."

A flush of red warmed her cheeks. "It was pretty perfect, probably because it was only a night. We didn't deal with each other in the light of day. We didn't get to know our flaws, our weaknesses, or our bad habits. We didn't have time to annoy each other or get bored."

"I doubt you would ever be boring, Savannah."

"You probably wouldn't be, either."

"Oh, I wouldn't say that. I've become quite boring in the past year. It's the only way I can stay sane."

"The bells don't ring when you're alone?"

"Not as often, but they're never completely gone." He paused. "But we were talking about you."

"Were we? I thought you had decided you didn't really want to know anything more about me."

"You said that you saw a photo of me about two years ago. Did you ever think about looking me up?"

"Not really. I was afraid that seeing each other again would ruin a beautiful memory. I also had no idea if you were involved with anyone." She took a breath. "Were you involved with someone when you got hurt?"

"I was seeing someone last year, but she disappeared pretty quickly when she realized I wasn't myself anymore."

"Sounds like she wasn't worth keeping."

"What about you? Is there a man in your life?"

"I've dated a few guys over the past year, but I work a lot and I've made my career my priority. Once I decided to take a path that was completely my own, I wanted to make sure I succeeded, so I put all my energy into being the best FBI agent I could be."

"Is the job what you thought?"

"It's actually better than I thought. No case is the same as the last. I enjoy being part of a team. I formed friendships from my first day at Quantico that have sustained me ever since then. I'm now on a special task force run by one of my former classmates, and it's great. We always have each other's back, and we have the latitude to do what we need to do to get the job done."

"If you've found a way to sidestep bureaucracy, I'm impressed."

"That's all because of Flynn, my boss. He's a brilliant guy, and he brought down some very bad people, making quite a name for himself. His methods are unorthodox, but his results can't be denied, so he was put in charge of his own task force, and we are all reaping the rewards of that."

"I'm glad you found a career that suits you."

"I got some great experience working in Army Intelligence, so it wasn't a bad interim step for me." She turned down Todd's street and pulled into the short driveway in front of the garage.

As he got out of the car, he looked around. The street was as quiet as it had been earlier. He wondered if whoever had come by in the night had returned, but when they reached the front door, it was still locked. That was a good sign.

When he stepped into the living room, he saw the broken vase and shattered glass in front of the grandfather clock. Everything looked exactly as it had when they had left.

"I should probably clean that up," he muttered.

Savannah followed him into the kitchen as he went in search of a broom.

He hadn't paid much attention to the kitchen the night before, but now something felt off. He glanced toward the side door. The dead bolt was not on. And the blinds on the window next to the door seemed askew. *Had someone come into the house?*

Savannah paused by the kitchen table. "Todd has a lot of bills from the Emery Care Center in Jacksonville."

"That's probably where his mom is," he said, barely paying attention to her words. His gut was churning. Something was wrong.

"Some of them say past due. Was Todd having financial problems?"

"I don't know. He has a job with a private security firm. But I have no idea what his mother's care might cost."

As he moved through the kitchen, toward the adjacent laundry room, he heard an odd sound—a tick, tick, tick. There was no clock on the wall or anywhere in view. *Was his brain throwing out some new sound to torture him?*

He pushed open the laundry room door, and the sound got louder. It seemed to be coming from behind the dryer.

Every instinct he had told him to run.

He moved back into the kitchen. "Get out," he told Savannah.

"What?" she asked in surprise.

"Get out," he yelled again. He grabbed her arm and shoved her through the kitchen door leading into the side yard. They were two steps away from the house when an explosion lifted them up and flung them across the grass in a fiery blast of heat and sound.

CHAPTER EIGHT

SAVANNAH FELT an enormous weight on her back. Her ears were ringing, her eyes were watering, her body felt like it was on fire. *Was she on fire?* Smoke filled her nose and lungs as she tried to breathe. She could hear an enormous wave of sound coming from behind her.

As she moved, the weight rolled off her and she stared at Ryker's very still body in shock and horror. She crawled toward him as pieces of plaster and wood fell off her. She could still feel the heat, but the fire was consuming the house, and while she'd probably been hit by some burning embers, she was not on fire.

"Ryker," she yelled, her own voice reverberating in her head as her ears painfully adapted to more sound. When he didn't move, she pressed her fingers to the side of his neck, overwhelmingly relieved when she felt a faint pulse.

"Ryker." She put her hands on his arms, giving him a little shake. Then she leaned forward and put her mouth next to his ear. "Wake up." She prayed that he wasn't slipping away, but his breath barely moved his chest, and there was blood on his shirt. "Please," she begged, feeling a rush of fear as she stared at his face.

His hair was almost white from the specks of plaster and there were small cuts across his cheeks. Every day seemed to bring him more pain, more injury, and her heart ached for him. It wasn't until just this second that she let herself admit how much she liked him —how much she'd always liked him. She'd told him that she'd moved on and left their night in the past, but that hadn't been true. She'd dreamed about him. She'd imagined meeting him again. She'd relived the time they'd spent together so many times.

"Ryker," she said again, and then she impulsively covered his mouth with hers, wanting to give him warmth, breath, comfort, and life.

He suddenly shifted, his lips parting beneath hers.

She pulled back as his eyes flew open, and their gazes caught.

"Savannah," he murmured. "Did you just kiss me?"

"I was trying to see if you were alive."

He stared back at her with his dark-brown eyes. "Let me check." He lifted his hand and put it around the back of her neck, pulling her back in for another kiss, one that he was now completely present for, one that went way out of her comfort zone —into passion, desire, sex. All of her memories came rushing back. She'd thought she'd imagined how good they'd been together, but it was even better than she remembered.

She wanted to keep on kissing him, but the distant sound of sirens brought her head up. "Someone must have called 911." She moved back as he sat up, his gaze moving to the house.

"That was a hell of a blast," he said.

"How did you know it was coming?"

"I heard a ticking sound behind the dryer. I don't know if it was a bomb or a timer or what."

"Then this was deliberate." She frowned, letting that fact sink in.

"Yes. For once, my ears were my friend." His gaze narrowed with concern. "There's blood on your forehead."

"Is there?" She put a hand to her temple, suddenly feeling the sting, and seeing the wet drops of blood on her fingers. But there didn't appear to be too much, and it wasn't dripping down her face, so hopefully that was a good thing. "You're bleeding, too, on your arm," she said.

He glanced down at the shirt sleeve that had been ripped away, exposing a couple of cuts. "If this is the worst of it, I'm fine. I'm more concerned about your head. Are you dizzy?"

"A little, but that might be partly due to what just happened between us."

A faint smile crossed his lips as a gleam entered his eyes. "Yeah, that was something."

"How can you be smiling right now? We almost died."

"But we didn't. And I got you to kiss me again."

"I was trying to make sure you were breathing. We should go out front," she added as the sirens got louder. She got to her feet and Ryker did the same. He swung his arm around her shoulders, and she couldn't bring herself to push him away. She liked the feel of his body next to hers, especially now, after they'd come so close to dying.

They had barely reached the front of the house when the fire truck pulled up.

"Anyone inside?" one of the firefighters asked.

"The house is empty," Ryker replied, still keeping his arm around her.

As the fire commander barked orders to his team, an ambulance pulled up behind the truck and the EMTs came over to check on their injuries. Thankfully, neither one of them was in bad shape, with only superficial cuts that were cleaned and bandaged.

As the medic finished bandaging her head, Savannah noted the gathering crowd on the sidewalk. While the homes on this block were spread out, the raging fire had brought out anyone within a few blocks.

Two police cars came screaming down the street. Two younger cops exited the first vehicle while Chief Tanner got out of the second one. He stormed toward them, a grim line to his mouth.

"What happened?" he asked.

"There was an explosion," Ryker said. "It was centered in the laundry room. Could have been a timer or an explosive device."

"What were you doing in Todd's house?"

"Seriously? That's your question?" she interrupted. "You don't want to ask who would have set fire to this house?"

"Do you know who did this?"

"No."

"Then let's back up," he snapped. "What were you both doing in the house?"

"I spent the night here," Ryker answered. "Todd offered me a place to stay when I came in for Paul's funeral. Savannah came back with me after we finished our search this morning."

Savannah was impressed with Ryker's spin on the story, appreciating the fact that he hadn't mentioned using Abby's key to get inside. She didn't want Abby mixed up in any of this.

"Did you notice anyone hanging around the house?" the chief asked.

"I didn't see anyone today, but I thought I heard someone last night in the yard, and there was a footprint outside the window. From that vantage point, I'm pretty sure someone would have seen me sleeping on the couch as the curtains were open."

"Can you show me?" Tanner asked.

"Sure," Ryker said, leading Tanner down the side of the yard.

She stayed behind, more interested in talking to some of the neighbors than dealing with Chief Tanner. "Hello," she said, approaching two women. "Are you neighbors?"

"We are," the white-haired woman replied. "I'm Amy Gilman. This is my sister Diane. We live at the end of the block. We were just coming back from the market when the fire truck passed us. What happened? Were you in the house? You're all cut up, dear."

"I was nearby. Do you know Todd?"

"We've met him a couple of times," Amy replied. "But we didn't know him as well as Paul. It was so sad what happened to him."

"You're Abby's friend," Diane suddenly interjected. "Savannah, right? The beauty queen?"

"Yes, that's me."

"My son, Richmond, went to school with you."

"Of course, I remember Richmond. How is he?"

"He's a dentist now. And he just got engaged."

"That's nice."

"What are you doing now, Savannah?" Diane asked.

"I'm an FBI agent."

"Oh, my, that's important. Do you know what has happened to Todd? We heard he was missing. Now his house is on fire," Diane continued. "It's very worrying. Is something going on? Should we be concerned?"

"I honestly don't know. I was wondering if either of you have seen anyone lurking around the house or the street."

"Yes," Amy said, nodding her head with certainty. "I saw a car driving slow down the street last night when I was walking the dog. I looked at the driver, and when he saw me staring, he sped up and left."

Savannah straightened at that piece of information. "What did he look like?"

"He had on a ball cap. It was dark, so I couldn't see his features."

"What kind of car was he driving?"

"It was a Prius. I think it was silver," Amy replied.

"About what time did this happen?"

"It was a little after ten."

"You didn't tell me any of this, Amy," Diane complained.

"I didn't think it was important. It's not like he did anything. It just seemed like he was looking for an address and then he left."

"He could have been casing the house," Diane put in. "Should we tell Chief Tanner what Amy saw?"

"You should definitely tell him," she said, as Ryker and the chief came toward them.

As the two ladies called Tanner over, Ryker rejoined her. "The print was destroyed by falling debris," he said.

"I have it on my phone. I can still send it to my team. They'll do more with it than Tanner would have done anyway."

"Did those women have anything to say?" Ryker asked.

"One said she saw a man in a car driving slowly down the street last night, but she didn't get a great look at him. It was about ten last night. When he made eye contact with her, he drove off."

"That's hours before I heard the noise by the window, but that doesn't mean anything. He could have come back."

"Seems like a good possibility. Hopefully the investigators will be able to get some clues once the fire is out. Did Tanner talk to you when you were in the yard?"

"Yes, I'll fill you in, but why don't we get out of here?"

She was a little surprised by his suggestion. "You want to leave now?"

"There's nothing more to do. Since your car is blocked by the fire truck, we can take mine."

She wondered why he was in a hurry to leave the scene, but she didn't see any point in staying now that Tanner had arrived. "All right. We can go to Abby's house," she said, following him to the car. "I'd like to change my clothes and my bag is there."

"I don't know if you should see Abby looking like you do. She'll get upset."

"She's not there. She's in Ridgeview with her parents. She wanted to be with her family and keep Tyler away from the search for Todd."

"I don't blame her. I feel for that kid. I'm glad he has a strong mother."

"They both have support, but they still have to get through this on their own, and it won't be easy."

He gave her a quick look. "I guess you have firsthand experience, don't you?"

"Sadly, yes."

"How did your mom die?"

"Cancer. It was fast. She was only sick for about six months. I was devastated. She was my primary parent. My dad was gone all the time. It was her and me. We were the home team. At least Tyler still has his primary parent with him."

"That's something," he muttered.

"So, why did you want to leave so quickly?" she asked as they got into the car. "Did Tanner say something to you?"

"He did." His mouth drew into a tight line. "He told me that he was glad to have a minute with me alone, because he wanted to say something to me man-to-man, soldier-to-soldier."

"Which was what?"

"The reason he doesn't want you involved in the investigation is because he wants to protect Abby. He believes that Paul's death was suicide, and if the life insurance company finds out, they won't pay her the benefits she'll need to survive. He's afraid that if you dig into Todd's disappearance, that will also put a spotlight on Paul's death. And that could be disastrous."

"Well, I wasn't expecting you to say that," she said with surprise.

"He also told me that Paul had confided in him over the past few months how bad he was feeling, how depressed he was about his inability to find work that would be of value to the family, and apparently there were also financial problems. Paul hadn't just been drinking the past year, he'd also been gambling. Tanner believes that Paul jumped off that roof. I said I couldn't see him doing that, but maybe I'm the one who can't see what's right in front of me."

"It's certainly something we have to consider. But putting Paul's death aside for a minute, I now don't believe Todd killed himself. A suicide wouldn't lead to his house being set on fire. There's something else going on, and we have to figure out what it is, because it might change the circumstances of Paul's death, too. What if neither one of them killed themselves? What if someone else did? What if they pushed Paul off the roof and forced Todd off the road and into the river?"

His gaze narrowed on her face, but he didn't immediately dismiss her suggestions as ludicrous, which they might be.

"Okay, let's say both those things happened," he said. "Why would they come back and set fire to the house? Wouldn't that just draw everyone's attention and make Todd's accident look suspicious?"

She frowned at his undeniable logic. "Yes."

"So…"

"We need more information."

"Tanner did tell me something else. He said they're still going through Todd's vehicle, but there's no sign that there was a problem with the brakes or any other mechanical failure."

"He was certainly more forthcoming with you than with me."

Ryker gave her a faint smile. "He said you'd always been a shit-stirrer, but he wanted me to know that he's doing everything that needs to be done."

"Well, how reassuring," she said, unable to keep the sarcasm out of her voice. "But just because Tanner had his man-to-man, soldier-to-soldier talk with you doesn't mean I'll back off. I'm going to get to the truth. It's what I do. It's actually something I'm really good at."

His smile broadened, crinkling the corners of his mouth, bringing a new light to his eyes and reminding her once again of the man she'd found so completely irresistible five years ago.

"I like your confidence," he said. "And I never thought you would back off. I told him that I have no control over what you're going to do."

"Good answer."

"I also told him that regardless of what happened with Paul, we still need to find Todd. Because if he somehow survived the crash, he's no doubt in some kind of trouble."

"Maybe he didn't come back to his house, because he was afraid someone would come after him again. He could be hiding."

"Agreed."

"Paul and Todd were living together the last three weeks. They could have both gotten into trouble gambling. Perhaps they owed someone money. Although, that wouldn't explain the fire. That seems more like a cover-up or a personal attack or something." She stopped abruptly, a new thought running through her head. "We told the firefighters there was no one in the house, but we didn't go upstairs. What if Todd was there? What if he was unconscious when the fire started?"

Ryker's lips tightened into a grim line. "Damn. I don't want to think that."

"Sorry. My mind is running through all the possible scenarios. But with the explosion, we couldn't have gotten into the house, Ryker. We couldn't have saved anyone."

"Maybe we should go back to the scene."

"They won't know anything yet."

"We still need to let someone know we didn't go upstairs. I'll call Tanner."

She was surprised again. "You have his number?"

"He gave it to me. He said if I find anything out, I should let him know."

"Or if I find anything out, you should let him know," she said.

"I wouldn't betray you, Savannah. But it's not a bad thing for him to want to talk to me. We can use the information channel both ways."

She knew he was right, but she hated the fact that Tanner was trying to play around her. "Fine, but let's call him from Abby's house. I want to make sure everything is all right there and that no one left a similar device in her laundry room. If Todd and Paul are tied together in whatever is going on, I need to make sure she's safe."

At her words, Ryker put the car into drive and pressed his foot down on the gas. The car leapt forward. She braced her hand on the side, but she wasn't afraid of the speed. She was more afraid of what they might find when they got to Abby's house.

CHAPTER NINE

THEY WENT through Abby's home from top to bottom, checking under every sink, in every cabinet, for any sign of an explosive device. Thankfully, they found nothing. But she didn't want Abby to be in the house for another day or two, not until they knew more about what might be going on.

Ryker called Tanner and left him a voice mail to inform him that they hadn't gone upstairs in Todd's house, so they didn't actually know if anyone had been up there when the fire started. Then Ryker headed upstairs to find something of Paul's to change into, and she settled onto the couch in the living room and called Abby.

"Is there any news?" Abby asked, picking up the phone on the first ring.

"They haven't found Todd yet. But something else has happened. Are you with Tyler or your parents?"

"I'm going into the other room. Hang on." Abby went away for a moment and then came back. "All right, I'm on my own. What's happened? No one else is hurt, right?"

"No, but an explosive device was planted at Todd's house, and it went off. The house is completely destroyed."

"Oh, my God! I don't understand. Why would someone put a bomb in Todd's house?"

She could hear the fear and bewilderment in Abby's voice.

"That's what we need to figure out. Ryker and I were actually at the house. But he heard a suspicious ticking sound, and we got out in time."

"You were there? You were almost killed? I can't handle this, Savannah. I can't keep losing people I love."

"I'm fine. I shouldn't have made it sound that close. It wasn't really," she lied.

"Now you're just trying to backtrack. Are you sure you and Ryker are both all right?"

"We are. We're actually at your house now. I wanted to get my bag."

"You're leaving town? I thought you were going to stay a few days. I know I bailed on you today—"

"You did not bail on me. You're exactly where you should be, Abby, and I think you should spend a few more days with your folks. Tyler doesn't need to hear about search parties and bombs. It's too much."

"You're right. Maybe you should come here, too. I can get you a hotel room."

"I will come at some point, but right now I want to see if I can figure out what's going on. Did Todd ever mention any trouble to you? Problems at work or with a coworker?"

"No. He didn't talk much about his job. His work schedule was sporadic. He would be home for a week and then be gone for a few days. He never really said what he was doing or where he was going, but I don't think he liked it all that much." She took a breath. "Todd did tell me the day after Paul died that he'd probably move to Atlanta. With Paul gone, there was no reason for him to stay in Dobbs. I told him we'd miss him, but I understood why he'd want to leave. I just hated the thought of Tyler having to watch another man exit his life. Of course, now it's so much worse. We don't even know if he survived the accident."

"I haven't given up hope."

Abby let out a sigh. "I feel so tired, Savannah."

"I know you do, and I don't want you worrying about all this.

Just be with your son and your parents and let me figure things out."

"Is Ryker staying with you?"

"I think so. He wants answers, too."

"How's it going with him?"

"I don't know. It's crazy around here."

"I'm sure it is. But maybe this is a second chance for you both."

"I doubt that. Although…"

"What? Tell me something interesting, something that doesn't have to do with death or missing friends."

After hearing the shower running upstairs, she said, "Well, we did kiss. It was an impulsive, spontaneous thing after the explosion. It didn't mean anything."

"How was it?"

"It took me back in time," she admitted. "Ryker has changed a lot, but he's still pretty irresistible."

"You should be careful, Savannah."

"I thought you liked him."

"I do, but Paul used to tell me that Ryker would never settle down. He liked his freedom too much. And he was always about the job, the mission. He didn't have time or interest in personal relationships."

"I'm not looking for a relationship. It was just a kiss. Maybe we both just needed to know if it was like we remembered. It won't happen again."

"I can't believe it, but you just made me smile."

"Well, I'm glad I could do that."

"If Ryker is as irresistible to you as you say, then maybe you shouldn't be hanging out with him. I don't want you to get hurt."

"We're helping each other. It's fine. It's nothing."

"If you say so. Feel free to stay at my house, Savannah. Ryker, too. Eat the food that's there. Make yourselves at home."

"Thanks. I'm not sure what the plan is, but I'll be in touch." She ended the call and slipped her phone into the back pocket of her jeans as she stood up. She moved into the kitchen to get some water out of the fridge. It felt really good sliding down her dry, parched throat. She also grabbed another cookie off the plate on the island and ate it in two bites. She was thinking about grabbing another one when Ryker walked in.

Her stomach flipped over at the sight of him. He cleaned up very nicely, his brown hair damp and wavy, his cheeks freshly shaved and full of color, his eyes lit up with more energy than she'd seen in him previously. "You look like you got a new lease on life. Was the shower magical?"

He smiled. "It felt that way. Did you speak to Abby?"

"Yes. She's going to stay in Ridgeview for at least a couple of days."

"Good. That's the best place for her."

"She said we can stay here if we want."

"I'm thinking about taking a drive to Atlanta. I want to stop in at the company where Todd was working, see if anyone knows anything."

She liked that idea a lot. "I'll go with you."

"I don't think so."

"Why not?"

"After you almost died, you have to ask?"

"That's not the first close call I've ever had, Ryker. I'm a trained agent. I can handle myself."

"But you usually work with a team, with backup. Maybe you should bring them in."

"I don't want to do anything official yet. I'll have more latitude if I don't. In the meantime, you can be my backup."

He immediately shook his head. "You shouldn't count on me, Savannah. That would be a mistake. I could be one second away from losing my mind completely."

She saw the somber gleam in his eyes and felt the need to reassure him. "You already saved my life once. I'm not worried."

"You should be worried. You don't know what's going on in my head. I'm not the man you were with five years ago. I barely remember him."

"Really? Because I was with him less than an hour ago, when

he instinctively sprang into action. When he covered my body with his. When he kissed me."

"For a moment, I forgot where I was…who I was… You have a tendency to drive all rational thought from my mind, Savannah."

"You tend to do that to me, too."

"But I have some real problems. The attacks can be overwhelming. You saw what I did to the clock."

"I did, and while I don't know what's going on in your head, Ryker, I trust you. When it counts, you'll be there."

"Putting your trust in me is a big risk."

"I like risk." She just wished she didn't also like him, because that was only going to make everything more complicated.

CHAPTER TEN

THEY TOOK Ryker's rental car on the three-hour drive to Atlanta. It was one o'clock when they got on the road after Savannah had showered and they'd had a quick lunch. It was nice to be driving. He felt comfortable behind the wheel, although he had no doubt that could change in an instant if the bells decided to go off. Since the explosion, they'd been remarkably quiet. He had a desperate, futile hope, that maybe the blast had knocked them out of his head for good. But that was probably just a dream. They'd come back. Until then, he would appreciate the quiet.

Savannah seemed to be caught up in her own thoughts. That was fine with him. It had been a crazy day so far and he had a feeling there was more insanity to come, so it was nice to have a reprieve.

Unfortunately, without conversation to distract him, his mind drifted back to the explosion, to the fire, to waking up with her mouth on his. Out of those three events, the kiss shouldn't have been the one thing sticking in his head, but it was.

For a minute there, he'd felt like he had turned back time. It was just him and Savannah, tangled up in each other. He'd been himself again. And he'd felt an intense attraction to her, the same one that had almost knocked him off his feet five years ago. She'd kissed him like she was feeling the same thing.

But there was nowhere to go from here. He wasn't the man he used to be, and the longer they were together, the clearer that would become. He needed to keep his hands off her. He needed to focus on Todd and the mission at hand, which was to get answers, find the truth, figure out if someone had tried to kill Todd, or if they had in fact succeeded. He also wanted to know if Paul's death was really an accident. Or if it was suicide as Tanner had implied.

The deaths of two more members of his team within days of each other was too much of a coincidence. And the fire raised even more questions.

Why burn Todd's house down? What had they been trying to cover up? And why take such a drastic step? A burglary, vandalism, could have been written off as a crime of opportunity, but not an explosion.

He glanced at Savannah. "I keep adding two plus two and coming up with five."

"I know what you mean. Hopefully, we'll find some answers in Atlanta. What do you know about the company Todd has been working for?"

"Carmack Securities is a private security firm run by Colton Carmack and his younger brother Trent. They specialize in providing personal security for high-level executives and celebrities as well as corporate security. Colton was a Marine. Trent apparently has a lot of cyber-hacking skills." He paused. "I looked the company up online when you were taking a shower."

"Good job. I was going to do that on this drive, but you saved me the trouble."

"I'm sure there's more to learn."

"Probably. I can do more research on the way."

"Can you access your FBI resources from your phone?"

"No. I can, however, call someone to get whatever information we need."

"What's it like being an FBI agent?" he asked curiously.

"It's not all that different from Army Intelligence. There's a lot of fact gathering, puzzle working. But since I joined Flynn's team, I have more opportunities to be in the field, on the front line, and that's something I rarely had the opportunity to do in the army. When I left five years ago, there were still a lot of restrictions on women."

"You wanted to be in combat?"

"I wanted to be a sniper like my dad. Before my mom died, he used to take me to the range to shoot. It was the one thing we did together, and I was really good at it."

He smiled at her candor. He'd liked how direct she'd been the first time they'd met. She hadn't played games. She'd made it clear she wanted him as much as he wanted her.

"But I'm happy with what I'm doing now," she added.

"And there isn't a small part of you that still wants your dad's love and respect?"

"Maybe a small part. He's my father. He's the only parent I have left. And I hate that I can't change his mind about me. But I also can't live my life for him. He certainly doesn't live his life for me."

"How was he with your mother?"

"He was loving and attentive. He wasn't overly affectionate, because that's not his style, but he supported her. He listened to her. He really adored her."

"I can't see your father adoring anyone. Was he closer to you when she was alive?"

"Not really. For a long time, I thought he was, but when I look back now, I realize my mom brought him into our world, but he was there for her, not for me. If he came to anything of mine, it was because she wanted him there."

"What was your mom like?"

"She was very creative. She liked to knit, crochet, and make quilts. She was into decorating. Our house was filled with pillows and paintings and cute knickknacks that she would find at craft fairs. She was sweet and generous. She volunteered at school. She made cookies with me. We had a lot of fun together. She loved me unconditionally. She was my biggest supporter."

Hearing the pain in her voice, he felt the need to apologize. "I'm sorry. I shouldn't have brought her up. It makes you sad to talk about her."

"Actually, I'm glad you brought her up. No one else does. I haven't spoken about her in a long time and that makes me even more sad. I don't want to ever forget her. But as the years pass, sometimes my memories are hazy."

"You'll always remember the love."

"I will remember that." She met his gaze, then grabbed her phone as it began to vibrate. "It's a text from one of the techs on my team. I sent them the photo of the footprint. It came from a hiking boot, size twelve, male."

"That doesn't tell us a lot."

"No, but it's a piece of the puzzle that may make more sense at some point."

"How big is your team?"

"At the moment, we have eight agents, two analysts, a cyber expert and forensic specialist as well as an admin. It's a small enough team to be agile but big enough to cover more complex cases. Our specialty involves cases that usually have an undercover element."

"That sounds fun. What have you gone undercover as?"

"A lot of things. I've been an art dealer, an exporter, a chemist—that one was a little tricky—and I was also pretending to be pregnant at the time, which actually helped. I had a lot of morning sickness whenever I had to do something scientific. I've also been a pharmaceutical sales rep, and one of my favorite covers was as a flight attendant."

"What case required you to be a flight attendant?"

"Smuggling of classified corporate information. I worked on a private jet. It was very posh. Only the best champagne."

He gave her a thoughtful look. "It's funny that you left the military to be yourself, but in your current job, you're a lot of people."

"But not to please anyone. There's a difference. And since I've had a lot of practice being what people want me to be, I'm very good at blending in."

"That surprises me, because I think you stand out in any crowd."

She flushed a little at his comment. "That's a nice thing to say. But I can be very unnoticeable."

"Maybe if you put a bag over your head."

"I have put on some very ugly makeup on occasion. I do whatever it takes to get the job done. Fortunately, I have a great team that helps me make that happen."

"That's important." The pride in her voice reminded him of how he used to feel. "I had a good team, too. We were invincible. We never failed, until the last mission. Before that, our record was unbelievable. I guess we were due for a fall."

"What happened? I know some of it is classified, but can you give me a general explanation?"

"We were supposed to rescue a humanitarian aid worker who had been kidnapped by the Taliban. He was allegedly being held in an abandoned hotel in a town near the Afghan-Pakistan border. But we were set up. The hostage wasn't there. The Taliban were."

"How were you set up?"

"I have no idea. But they were waiting for us."

"Have you tried to find out?"

"Yes, but I got nowhere. And to be honest, I had a lot of other issues to deal with."

"The bells."

"And a couple of surgeries." He paused, thinking about how easily he had dropped his questions. "I don't usually give up on getting to the truth, but I guess I did."

"Maybe it was just bad luck."

"Maybe so." But he couldn't help thinking there was more to it than that.

Carmack Securities was housed in a three-story shiny glass building in midtown Atlanta. They arrived just after four. Ryker parked in the underground garage and then ushered Savannah into the elevator. At the lobby level, they were met by a security guard standing behind a sleek white desk.

"Name?" the guard asked.

"Ryker Stone and Savannah Kane," he replied. "You can tell Mr. Carmack that I have some disturbing news about one of his employees, Todd Davis."

"And you can also tell him that I'm with the FBI," Savannah interjected, showing her badge.

"Hold on." The guard stepped away from the counter and picked up a phone, relating the information they'd just given him. A moment later, he hung up, and said, "You can go on up. Third floor."

"Thanks."

"Have you ever considered joining this kind of firm?" Savannah asked, as they got into another elevator.

"To babysit rich people or celebrities and their kids? No."

"So, you don't like celebrities or rich people."

"I don't dislike them; I just don't want to work for them."

"Fair enough."

The elevator doors opened on the third-floor landing, and they stepped onto a polished white marble floor. In front of them were two glass doors, labeled Executive Offices. As they moved through the doors, their feet sank into thick, shag white carpet.

A young woman greeted them, wearing a slim-fitting black skirt and a silk multi-colored blouse, her dark hair cut in sleek angles, emphasizing her thin, sophisticated features.

"Mr. Carmack is on the phone, but he'll be with you in a moment. You can take a seat." She waved her hand toward the white couches.

"I'm glad we changed out of our smoky clothes before we came here," Savannah said, as she sat down. "It's all very clean. Almost makes you wonder what they're trying to hide."

"Do you think they have something to hide?" he asked, as he took a seat.

"Maybe not relevant to our case, but in my experience, most people are hiding something." Savannah paused as a blonde woman entered the office, wearing black slacks with a matching blazer. She gave them a somewhat worried look and then spoke to the receptionist. "Is there news?"

"I told you I would tell you when there is. You need to go back to your office, Jackie."

"Don't forget to call me."

"I don't forget anything," the receptionist replied.

The woman disappeared through the double doors, giving them one more thoughtful look before she did so. *Had she been asking about Todd?* Perhaps Chief Tanner had already notified Todd's company of his disappearance. He wasn't sure if that was a good or a bad thing. It might save them explanations, but it also eliminated the possibility of surprise.

The office door opened, and he recognized Colton Carmack from the portrait that had been on the website. Colton was built like a linebacker and wore his brown hair short. "Mr. Stone, Agent Kane," he said, as they got to their feet. "How can I help you?"

"We need a few minutes of your time," he said, taking the lead.

"All right. Please come in." Carmack ushered them into his office, which was just as luxurious as the reception area, although the décor in this room was all black, from the leather couch against the wall, to the massive desk and the black leather chairs in front of it. Apparently, at Carmack Securities everything was either black or white. "I'm assuming this has something to do with Todd Davis," Carmack added, as he sat down behind his desk, and they settled into the leather chairs facing him. "I spoke to Chief Tanner earlier today. He filled me in on Todd's disappearance."

"And the explosion at his house?" Ryker asked.

"He did not mention an explosion." Surprise entered his eyes. "What happened?"

"Todd's house blew up."

"Are you serious?"

"Yes. We're trying to figure out why it happened."

"How can I help you?"

"Do you know if Todd was in trouble? Did he make any enemies on the job?"

"To be honest, I don't know Mr. Davis very well. He works part-time and has only been with us a few months. My brother Trent worked more closely with him. Unfortunately, he's out of town. But as soon as I can reach him, I'll certainly ask him if he has any relevant information. I checked with our assignment admin and she said that Mr. Davis had asked for leave until tomorrow, because of the death of his close friend. He hasn't done any jobs for us since a week ago Monday."

"What was that job?"

"Security for a museum event, nothing particularly dangerous and not at all unusual." Colton paused. "The chief I spoke to suggested that Todd might have driven into the river on purpose, that he was perhaps suicidal."

"We don't believe that's what happened, not with the explosion in his house today."

"Perhaps that happened after I spoke to the chief."

"When did that conversation take place?" he asked.

"Around ten this morning."

"That was before the explosion."

"Did Todd have an office here?" Savannah asked. "A filing cabinet, a desk, anything where there might be personal items?"

"He did not have a desk, but I believe he had a locker in the fitness area."

"We'd like to see it," Savannah said.

"Of course. I'll call down and have Kevin give you the number and the key. If there's anything else I can do, please just ask. I consider all my employees to be family, even the ones I don't know well, and I'm very sorry to hear about all this."

"We'll keep that in mind, and we would like to speak to your brother," Savannah added, handing Colton Carmack her card.

"Of course. Is that all for now? I don't want to rush you, but I do have another meeting."

"Thanks for your time," he said, following Savannah out of the room.

When they left Colton's office, the receptionist didn't even look up, her gaze fixed on her computer. They made their way down to the first floor, following directions to the gym. The manager made sure the locker room was clear and then took them both inside and opened the locker. Inside, was a large, thick envelope.

Ryker pulled it out with a sense of foreboding. To his amazement, there were two medals inside, Todd's Bronze Star Medal of Valor and his Purple Heart. There was also a note.

"What does it say?" Savannah asked.

He read the note aloud. "I remember how proud you were of me, Mom, even if you don't. These medals might not mean anything to you now, but at least you'll have them. And you're the only person who should." His stomach churned as he looked back at Savannah. "I think we just found a suicide note."

CHAPTER ELEVEN

SAVANNAH HEARD the pain in Ryker's voice. She wanted to tell him he was wrong, that Todd didn't mean it that way, but she couldn't.

"Ma'am, Agent Kane," the locker room attendant said with an awkward expression on his face. "Some guys want to come in here."

"Sure," she said. "Let's take this with us, Ryker."

He nodded, his jaw so tight she didn't think he could get a word out if he tried. He kept a death grip on the envelope as they walked out of the locker room and took the elevator down to the garage. He didn't speak, but his body was as stiff as a poker, and his breath was coming short and fast. There was a wild light entering his eyes. She could see the panic and knew he was coming under attack from his own brain. She didn't know if he was hearing the echo of his own terrible words, or if the bells were back, but she wanted to get him into the car.

"Give me the keys," she ordered.

He gave her a blank look.

"Keys," she repeated firmly, holding out her hand.

He reached into his pocket and handed her the keys, another sign that all was not well.

Then he walked around the car and got into the passenger seat as she slid behind the wheel. He put the envelope on the console between them and folded his arms in front of his chest as he closed his eyes.

Glancing over at him, he seemed so lonely, so isolated. She could feel a scream rolling around inside him, but he was trying desperately to hold it together. His face was like a statue, nothing moving except the pulse in his neck. He was holding off an army of attackers all by himself, and it hurt her heart to watch his struggle.

Impulsively, she put her hand on his.

He jerked away, but he didn't open his eyes, and he didn't say anything.

She tried again, wrapping her fingers around his, and holding on. She wanted her warmth to seep through the icy cold of his skin. She wanted him to feel support, to know he wasn't alone in the fight. And this time he didn't push her hand away. A long minute passed. She barely breathed, not wanting to make a sound that would disturb him.

Her gaze moved to the envelope on the console. Todd's mother's address was on the front. She hadn't realized that. Maybe Todd hadn't meant to leave the envelope in his locker. He could have been intending to mail the medals to her. In which case, the note might not have been a suicide note at all. It could have just been something he wanted to send to his mother.

She wanted to tell Ryker, but his breath was still coming hard and fast. He was fighting his demons, and she had to give him a chance to win that battle.

Her gaze left the envelope, moving back toward the windshield, and then her heart skipped another beat. There was a piece of paper tucked under the wiper blade, and it didn't look like a sales flyer.

She wanted to jump out of the car and get it, but she couldn't let go of Ryker. She was on this ride with him, even if she was just a silent partner. His fingers tightened around hers, as if he sensed she was distracted, and she turned her attention back to him.

Another minute and he shifted in his seat. A breath swooshed through his now parted lips. He opened his eyes, turned his head, and stared at her with the remnants of incredible pain and raw anger in his brown gaze. She didn't look away. The anger wasn't for her. It was for himself. He hated being a prisoner to his brain, being unable to control the attacks or to vanquish them.

His gaze traveled to her hand still wrapped in his, still tucked against his chest, which seemed to be warming by the minute. In fact, the air in the entire car was heating up. What had started out as comfort was quickly turning into something else, the irresistible pull of desire, attraction, connection. She'd felt it the first second she'd seen him in the bar five years ago, and she was almost overwhelmed by how strong it was now.

But Ryker was fighting the connection. After another hard breath, he let go of her hand.

A chill ran through her. She could almost see his walls going back up. She might have gotten in for a second, but she was out now, all the way out. And this time, she was the one to let out a breath of disappointment. Even though she knew that this wasn't the time or the place for anything more.

As she put her hands back on the wheel, her gaze moved once again to the paper underneath the wiper.

She opened the car door and got out to grab it.

Ryker's gaze narrowed in surprise. "What's that?"

She unfolded the piece of paper. "It's an address—Brittain Park Fountain, six o'clock." She met his gaze. "We have a meet. We just don't know with whom."

"Someone here at Carmack," he muttered. "Let's go."

She hesitated before starting the engine. "Are you sure you don't need another minute?"

"I'm fine."

"All evidence to the contrary."

"The bells are receding," he said.

"Good."

He let out another sigh. "I don't want to talk about it, Savannah."

"I get it, but just tell me, is there anything else you need right now?"

"No. Let's go to the park." He glanced at his watch. "It's five thirty. How far away is it?"

"About fifteen minutes," she said, setting her GPS. "But before we go, take another look at the envelope we found in Todd's locker."

"I don't know if I want to look at it. It didn't go well the first time. It triggered the bells."

"Then I'll just tell you what I noticed. The envelope is addressed to Todd's mother at the facility in Florida. I don't think he left it in his locker as a suicide note. I think he was sending her his medals, but he didn't get a chance to do that."

"Based on the address?"

"Yes. And because if he'd wanted to leave a note telling people what he'd done, he would have left it at his house, not here."

"Why would he send her his medals now?"

"Maybe he thought they would trigger a memory for her. His dad was in the army, right? Perhaps that was part of it."

"His dad never got a medal," Ryker murmured, a new light in his eyes as he looked at her. "Todd was very angry about that. There were two instances where he felt his father had deserved to be honored, but for one reason or another, he didn't receive a medal."

"That makes me even more positive that the medals going to his mother are separate from whatever else is going on. How did he get these medals?"

"The Medal of Valor was from the ambush. The Purple Heart was awarded a few years back. He was shot in the leg, but he was able to recover and return to service."

"How many medals do you have?"

"A few. They don't mean anything to me. I never did the job for a piece of hardware, that's for sure."

She believed that. Ryker wasn't about awards or recognition. His drive came from within, and she hoped that same drive would help him get better.

As she maneuvered through traffic, she felt on edge. It was Tuesday night, and the commute was in full swing. She winced every time there was a horn or a loud muffler or even a car blasting music, hoping none of those sounds would trigger another episode for Ryker. But his body tension eased with each passing minute, and he seemed to be back to normal.

"You don't have to worry about me, Savannah," he said, breaking the silence. "The attacks rarely come back-to-back. I'm probably good for at least another hour."

There was a lighter note in his voice that she was more than happy to hear. "I'm not worrying; I'm just concerned. Can I ask you what happens when the bells ring, when you close your eyes? Does tuning out the world help?"

"It's a trade-off. When I close my eyes, the sounds get softer, but the lights get brighter. All different colors shoot out at me like someone is hitting me with a laser. The lights are so blinding it's painful, but when I open my eyes, the bells get louder, so I have to choose between the sounds or the lights. Usually the lights go away faster than the sounds."

"It's like your brain short-circuits."

"That's the way it feels."

"You felt it come on when you saw what you thought was a suicide note. Was that the trigger?"

"I don't know, probably. I could feel my stress level rising when we walked into the locker room." He shook his head, an angry gleam in his eyes. "It drives me crazy, Savannah. This is not the man I used to be. Before the ambush, I could always control my stress. I could lower my breathing to barely a whisper. I could drop my blood pressure to the lowest numbers imaginable. I could beat a lie detector test with the force of my mind, but now my brain has gone haywire. It has become my enemy. And it's an enemy I don't know how to beat."

She didn't know what to say. She felt his pain down deep in her soul. That's how attuned they were. And it was that feeling of connection that scared her more than his words. She forced her gaze back to the traffic, trying to distract herself.

For a few moments, there was silence, and then Ryker said, "What do you think this meeting is about?"

She was relieved with the change of subject. "Someone wants to talk about Todd out of earshot of Carmack Securities."

"Which probably isn't Colton Carmack."

"Definitely not. He said what he had to say."

"Which wasn't much."

"No, but what he said made sense. Todd did work part-time and has only been with the company a few months. It's certainly believable that Mr. Carmack didn't know him personally."

"I would agree. He didn't appear to have anything to hide."

"I have a hunch it's the blonde woman who came into the office and asked Colton's assistant if there was news."

"That would be my guess," he agreed. "But who was she to Todd? A coworker? A friend? A romantic interest?"

"We'll find out soon enough."

A few minutes later, she parked next to Brittain Park. They got out of the car and walked past a children's playground and a rose garden to a beautiful, flowing fountain surrounded by a circle of stone benches. On one of those benches was the blonde woman they'd seen earlier.

She stood up as they approached, looking more than a little nervous. "Thanks for coming. I—I couldn't talk at the office."

"What's your name?" she asked.

"Jackie Simmonds. And you're an FBI agent, right?"

"Yes, I'm Savannah Kane. This is Ryker Stone."

"I recognize you from one of Todd's photos," Jackie said, her gaze moving to Ryker. "You were his team leader, right?"

"I was," Ryker answered. "I assume you've heard that Todd is missing."

"It's all over the office, how he crashed into the river, and now he's missing. Is there any chance he survived?"

"We don't know," she answered, seeing the fear in Jackie's eyes. "What's your relationship to Todd?"

"I handle the assignments for the security team members. Todd and I have become friends over the past few months. Actually, a

little more than friends," she admitted. "But we haven't been able
to see each other that much, because he lives in Dobbs when he's
not on assignment." Jackie drew in a shaky breath. "I'm so worried.
Do you think he's dead? God, I can't believe I'm saying that out
loud."

"We don't know," she said gently, sensing that Jackie's concern
was very real. "But until he's found, there's always hope."

"I want to believe that. You don't think he killed himself, do
you? I heard it might have been suicide."

She frowned, thinking how that suggestion from Tanner was
taking on a life of its own. "That's just a rumor. Why did you want
to speak to us?"

"I think Todd might have been in some trouble," she said,
worry in her eyes. "Maybe I shouldn't be saying anything, but I
feel like I should tell someone."

"You definitely should tell us why you think that. We're trying
to help Todd."

"Todd and I spent the night together about two weeks ago. He
was texting a lot. I woke up in the middle of the night, and he was
back on his phone. He said it was about an assignment, but I knew
what his assignments were, and he didn't have one. I tried to press
him for more information, and he said that it would be better for
me if I didn't know."

"Know what?"

"That's the thing—he didn't say. I thought it might have to do
with Todd's mom, because he was worried about her. He needed to
move her to another facility, but it was very expensive. I told him I
was sure Colton and Trent would give him more hours, but he said
that wouldn't work because Paul was having a hard time and
needed him to be in Dobbs. But Todd had a guy—Vic—who had
an inside track on some betting thing. I told him to be careful, he
could lose more than he could win and then he'd be worse off. But
he just laughed it off." She paused. "Anyway, the next morning,
when he was in the shower, he got another text, and I read it."

"What did it say?" Ryker asked.

"It said the timetable had been moved up, and he needed to

make a decision. It was time for him to ghost." She paused. "I couldn't ask Todd what it meant, because then I'd have to admit I was snooping. I didn't understand the reference to a timetable, but I was pretty sure the text was suggesting that Todd disappear on me, like so many of my dates like to do," she added bitterly.

"Was there a name on the text?" Savannah asked.

"No, and I didn't recognize the number. It wasn't anyone Todd worked with at our company, nor was it one of his Atlanta or Florida friends. The area code was DC. I looked it up. As you can tell, I'm a little nosy."

She was actually happy that Jackie had been curious. "What happened after that?"

"Things changed over the next week. Todd was distant to me at work and wouldn't text me back. I finally got him on the phone last Tuesday when he was back in Dobbs. I confronted him about our relationship. I asked him if he was ghosting me. He said that I needed to move on with my life, that he wasn't good for me or anybody. And he told me not to tell anyone that we'd been together. He said it might be dangerous. I asked him to explain, but he wouldn't. I could hear fear in his voice, but he wouldn't say what he was afraid of. That was the last time we spoke. When I heard about Paul's death, I tried to reach him, but he never answered or texted back. I've been so worried about him. When the police called Colton today, and the news spread around the office, I got really scared for Todd."

"Were there any other texts or conversations that in retrospect seem troubling?" she asked.

"Isn't what I've told you enough?"

"You could have told us all this at the office," she said. "Why did you need to meet us here? Why couldn't you speak to us there?"

Jackie's tongue darted out, as she gave a nervous swipe of her lips. "Well, okay. Right before you showed up today, Trent came into my office suite and pulled all the files having to do with Todd's assignments. He said the police wanted them, but I don't know. There was something about the way he was acting that seemed weird. And when I asked for information, he told me not to say anything to anybody. He also asked me if Todd had ever left anything at my apartment. I was stunned by the question. I had no idea that Trent knew we'd slept together. I told him no. I asked him what he was looking for, and he said he couldn't tell me."

Savannah glanced at Ryker. "Colton told us Trent was out of town."

"Trent did tell me he was going on a trip, but he didn't say where," Jackie put in. "Anyway, I was afraid to talk to you at the firm after what Trent said to me."

"That was wise. You should always trust your instincts."

"My instincts tell me that Todd is in trouble. I hope he's all right. Even if he doesn't want to be with me, I want him to be alive. I'll do anything to help."

"What kinds of cases was Todd working?" she asked.

"That's the thing; they were nothing unusual. He did some event security. He was a bodyguard for a celebrity who was in Atlanta for a movie premiere. He worked a golf tournament for a bunch of CEOs. The only thing I can think of that might have been in those case files that was at all interesting was when Trent took Todd to talk to a defense contractor who might be interested in using our company. Because Todd was a former Ranger, Trent thought his presence would carry some weight, but it was just a meeting."

"And that meeting was in the files that Trent wanted?"

"Yes. But it was like a page. It was nothing that would cause anyone trouble. I think it's the gambling that's out of control."

"Do you know where we can find Vic?"

"He's a bartender at Maloney's Saloon on Fourth Street."

"We'll talk to him."

"If you find Todd, will you tell him I'm worried about him?"

"Of course," she replied, as she pulled out a card. "If you think of anything else, call me."

"I will." Jackie pulled her jacket more tightly about her and then walked away, hurrying through the dark shadows of the park.

She turned to Ryker. "Looks like we're getting a drink."

"Definitely. What did you make of that?"

"Well, Jackie is in love with Todd. Todd has a gambling problem, which ties in with what we've heard from other people. Trent Carmack grabbing the files...I don't know what to make of that. I should have asked her who the defense contractor was."

"It doesn't feel like there's a connection."

"Except that why did Trent want the files?"

"I can't answer that."

"One thing I thought was a little odd was that while Jackie seemed genuinely upset about Todd, she was also specific in what she wanted to relate to us."

Ryker raised a brow. "As if she was coached to say what she said?"

"Possibly."

He gave her a thoughtful look. "I didn't read her that way, but you could be right. You're a very suspicious person, aren't you, Savannah?"

"It's part of the job. I can't afford to take people at face value. There's often a hidden agenda, even when it has nothing to do with the case. People are always looking out for their own self interests."

"You're not just suspicious; you're also cynical."

She shrugged. "Now that you've discovered some of my negative traits, are you feeling better that we only had one night together?"

His lips curved upward. "Surprisingly, no. I think having witnessed my recent attack, you'd be the one feeling that way."

"Surprisingly, no." She held his gaze for a long moment and then she cleared her throat. "Let's find Vic."

CHAPTER TWELVE

MALONEY'S WAS an Irish sports bar in downtown Atlanta. They had to park across the street and down the block, which gave Ryker a few minutes to mentally prepare himself for the onslaught of sound awaiting him in that bar. The clinking of glasses, the televisions blaring with the latest game, and the cheers from the crowd could all trigger an episode. He could already hear some of those sounds now, and they hadn't even entered the place. He'd been avoiding bars and restaurants for months.

"Ryker?" Savannah asked, giving him a concerned look. "I can do this on my own."

He knew she could do it on her own. But he wanted to be a part of it. He wanted to track down Vic and find out what kind of trouble Todd was in. He wanted to act instead of retreat.

"I can make it." He squared his shoulders and hoped that was the truth.

She handed him his car keys as they paused in front of the bar. "If you need to bail, do it. No questions asked. I'll meet you back at the car."

He both appreciated and hated her compassion. "You must think I'm incredibly weak."

"You're not weak; you're human."

"A weak human."

"More like a wounded warrior."

"Let's get this over with." He opened the door for her and then followed her inside.

He tried not to focus on the conversation, the laughter, or the basketball game on TV. He kept his gaze on Savannah as she moved across the restaurant to the bar. For some reason, focusing on her helped.

There was only one guy working the bar, and they slid onto two open stools, waiting for him to make his way down to them. Hopefully, this was Vic. The bartender appeared to be in his forties, with several tattoos on both arms.

"Do you want me to lead?" Savannah asked.

"Let's save your badge as a last resort. We might get more from him if he thinks we're just Todd's friends."

A moment later, the bartender set two napkins in front of them. "What can I get you?"

"Are you Vic?" he asked.

"Who wants to know?"

"Ryker Stone—I'm a friend of Todd Davis. I heard you might be helping him out."

"What's it to you?"

"Todd is missing. His car was run off the road last night."

Vic's expression changed at that piece of information. "I'm sorry. I didn't know."

"We think Todd might have been in some trouble. Did he ever say anything to you about that?"

"Todd was always looking over his shoulder when he was in here, like someone was following him."

"Was someone following him?"

"Not that I know of. Do you want something to drink? Because that's really all I have to offer."

"I'm sure there's more you can give us," Savannah said, flashing her killer smile at Vic. "We're trying to help Todd. The police are looking into the circumstances of his disappearance, and, well, I'm sure you don't want to have to talk to them, do you?

Wouldn't it be easier just to speak to us?"

Her Southern accent seemed especially thick now, and Ryker wasn't surprised to see Vic's attitude change. He appeared almost bemused, as if he didn't know what had hit him. Ryker knew that feeling well.

"We'd be so happy if you could help us," Savannah added. "We don't want to cause you any trouble, Vic."

"Look, I don't know anything," Vic said. "I made some bets for him. He lost. Our association ended."

"When did it end?" Ryker asked.

"About a week ago. We were supposed to meet. He didn't show up. I haven't seen him since. Judging by how many bets he lost, he might have just run out of cash."

"Did he ever talk to anyone else when he was in here?" Ryker enquired.

Vic hesitated. "He had an intense conversation with a guy named Hank a couple of weeks ago. I didn't recognize him."

"Did you overhear anything they were talking about?"

"I'm not sure. I think Hank wanted Todd to ghost some girl. Todd kept saying he wasn't ready. That's all I got. Now drink or leave. What's it going to be?"

As a cheer lit up the room at the end of a three-point play by the Atlanta Hawks, Ryker decided he'd rather leave. He tipped his head toward the door and Savannah nodded.

"Thanks so much, Vic," she said. "If you hear from Todd again, will you tell him that his friends are worried about him and to come home?"

"I don't expect I'll see him, but sure."

As Vic moved down the bar, Ryker headed for the door, letting out a breath of relief when they got outside. He actually felt a little victorious that he hadn't had another attack. But the cool night air was still welcome. It helped clear his head.

"Are you all right?" Savannah asked.

"Do you know how much I hate that question?"

"I'm guessing a lot."

"You'll know when I'm not okay. So, I'll drive. Are you comfortable with that?"

"I am."

"Good." As they started across the street, a car came racing around the corner on two wheels, heading straight for them. He gave Savannah a hard push, sending her flying into the space between two cars and then he leapt out of the way as the car sped past them. "Stay down," he told Savannah, putting a hand on her shoulder as she started to get up. He looked down the street, but the car was gone.

An older man came running across the street to ask if they were all right.

And for the second time in less than a minute, he had to say he was fine, as he and Savannah got to their feet.

"That car almost hit you," the man said. "He was driving like a maniac."

"You didn't happen to get a license plate, did you?" he asked.

"No, sorry, it was too dark. You should call the police."

"We'll do that. Thanks." He took Savannah's hand and they hurried down the block to his rental car. Once inside, he flipped the locks and gave himself a second to really look at her. Her eyes were wide and bright in the shadowy light, but he didn't see any new injuries.

"I think you saved my life—again," she said.

"That car was out of control. Maybe they were drunk."

She stared back at him, her gaze serious. "They weren't drunk, and they weren't out of control. We need to get out of here, Ryker. You need to drive. Now."

Her tone got him moving. He started the car and drove down the street, keeping an eye behind them. "Where do you want to go?"

"Away from here."

He maneuvered in and out of city streets, until he was sure they weren't being followed. Then he pulled over on a busy street with plenty of traffic and bright lights. "I think we're good."

"Someone followed us to the bar. But the question is where did they pick us up?" she asked. "At Carmack Securities? At Brittain Park? Or did Jackie deliberately send us to the bar?"

He thought about her questions. "Jackie did send us to Vic, and Vic knew Todd. But I don't think she set us up. I could be wrong, but she seemed genuine in her concern for Todd and for finding answers."

"I thought so, too. That means we were followed."

"But why try to run us down?"

"We're asking questions, and someone is getting nervous. That's one possibility."

His gaze narrowed at the odd glint in her eyes. "What's another possibility?"

"You could be a target, Ryker. This might not be about us; it could be about you."

"Why would someone want to kill me?"

"I don't know. But Paul is dead. Todd is missing, possibly also dead. Jackie said Todd was scared, that he mentioned she could be in danger if she was with him. What if someone is taking out your team, one man at a time? It always looks like an accident or suicide. But it's not." She paused, letting her words sink in. "The explosion at Todd's house could have been meant for you. Not to cover anything up but to take you out. And tonight…"

He frowned. "I get it, Savannah, but I can't think of anyone who would want me dead."

"Vic mentioned that Todd had an intense conversation with Hank. That could be the Hank from your unit, right?"

"Probably. But I don't know what he would be doing in Atlanta. He lives in DC."

"DC," she echoed. "The text Jackie read came from a DC number. Why didn't Hank come to Paul's funeral?"

"Todd said Hank couldn't get away from work."

"Not the best reason, considering how close you all were, what you went through together. What's your relationship with Hank?"

"I don't have one anymore. I haven't talked to him since before I had my first knee surgery. Out of everyone on the team, Hank was my least favorite. We butted heads a lot. He liked to second-guess my decisions, but I let it go, because he was tremendously good at his job. I knew I could count on him." He paused. "Vic said they were talking about ghosting a woman. That's not surprising. Hank was never into relationships. He was always telling us not to get tied down. But I can't see how Hank and Todd having a drink together and talking about a woman is of any relevance."

"Well, Hank might know more about Todd's gambling problems."

"True."

"And even if he doesn't, we need to talk to him."

"We also need to speak to Mason," he agreed. "If there's any chance you're right about someone targeting us, they need to know what's going on."

"Where does Mason live?"

"Last I heard he'd moved to Bethesda."

"Which is close to DC." She glanced at her watch. I don't know if we can catch a flight from Atlanta to DC tonight, but we should be able to get one in the morning."

"We? You don't need to go with me, Savannah."

"Yes, I do. I'm following the clues, and that's where they're going."

"If I'm a target, you're not safe. You should stay away from me."

"It's too late for that. We've been a lot of places together already. We're connected and whoever just tried to run us down knows that. Even if I'm not with you, I'll be a loose end. I prefer not to wait for trouble. I'd rather get out in front of it. And we can back each other up."

Her words made sense, but he didn't want her to get hurt because of him. On the other hand, if they stayed together, he might be able to stop that from happening. "All right. Arguing would be a waste of breath, wouldn't it?"

"Yes. I'm as stubborn as I am suspicious and cynical."

He smiled. "Got it."

"Let's go to a hotel by the airport. We can book our flights, and I can contact my team and see if they can tap into the cameras by

Maloney's. If we can find the driver of that car, we'll have a clue. But first, we need to turn off our phones, just in case anyone is tracking us."

"I think we're going to need a phone to find a hotel."

"I've got a burner phone in my bag. It's not traceable."

He met her gaze. "Sometimes I forget who I'm with." He turned off his phone. "Tell me where you want me to go."

Forty minutes later, Savannah checked them into a hotel next to the airport, using her task force-issued fake ID and credit card under the same name. She didn't want anyone to be able to track their location through a card transaction. With their phones off, and after the circuitous route they'd taken to the hotel, she was as sure as she could be that no one knew where they were.

As they took the elevator to the sixth floor, she felt like she was once more stepping back into the past. But five years ago, the elevator ride she and Ryker had taken together had passed in a blur of passionate kisses and hungry touches. She barely remembered how they'd gotten from the bar to Ryker's room, and once he unlocked his door, they'd been all over each other.

Even now, her heart beat faster at the memories.

Ryker was staring straight ahead, but she couldn't help wondering if his mind wasn't going down the same memory lane.

But she wasn't going to ask him. If he wasn't on that path, she didn't need to put him there, not with a long night looming ahead and only one room, because they really did need to stay close to each other for safety reasons. Although she had made sure there were two beds. She had to keep some boundaries. *Didn't she?*

When the elevator doors opened, she peered into the hall before stepping out. Their room was midway down the corridor. She used the keycard to open the lock and then entered the room.

It was a modest room, nothing special: two full-sized beds, a dresser, a television and a small table by the window with two chairs. She moved over to the window, noting that their view was of the airport. She hoped the noise from the planes wouldn't drive Ryker mad, although at the moment she couldn't hear anything. They weren't under the flight path, so that was good.

"Do you ever wear earplugs?" she asked, as Ryker moved next to her. "I'm thinking about airport noise. There are probably some earplugs in the gift shop downstairs."

"I've tried earplugs and noise-canceling headphones. Sometimes they work, but often they don't. I wish I could say there's a pattern, but there's not."

"Well, we could run down and pick some up."

"I'm more interested in food. I'm starving. What about you?"

"I could eat."

"Looks like there's room service." He picked up the menu from the table. "Shall we stay in?"

That meant more time alone with Ryker, but a noisy hotel restaurant would not work for him. "That's perfect." They sat down at the table and perused the menu, and then ordered turkey club sandwiches with fries and salad, with Ryker adding in a slice of apple pie.

"Sweet tooth?" she asked with a smile. "I wouldn't have guessed that."

"Guilty. Especially when it comes to pie. What about you?"

"Chocolate is my kryptonite."

"Damn. We should have ordered the chocolate cake."

"No, it's good that we didn't. But I might steal a bite of your pie."

"You don't have to steal it. I got it to share."

She gave him a smile. "You seem relaxed for the first time all day."

"I feel relaxed. I don't know why considering everything that's going on."

"Maybe it's just that we're back inside a quiet room."

"That could be it."

She pulled the burner phone out of her bag. "I'm going to call my team and see if I can get someone to tap into the cameras by the bar."

"While you do that, I'll run downstairs. I saw a clothing shop off the lobby. I could use a change of clothes for tomorrow. Do you need anything?"

"No, I have clothes in my overnight bag. Should I go with you?"

"I can handle it myself. It's not really a two-person job, Savannah. I may not be a federal agent, but I've got this."

She knew he needed her to see his strength, so she said, "You're right. I'll stay here."

"Put on the dead bolt after I leave. I'll knock three times when I come back."

"Got it." Despite her agreement, she hated the idea of him going out on his own. But she shouldn't be worrying about him. Even with his PTSD issues, the man was a soldier.

After bolting the door behind him, she called Flynn. "It's me. I'm on a burner phone."

"That doesn't sound good," he replied. "How is Dobbs?"

"I'm actually in Atlanta now. Things have gotten complicated."

"With what? The guy who went into the river?"

"Yes. It's looking like someone might have forced that accident to happen. There was an explosion at Todd's house earlier today, which Ryker and I narrowly escaped, by the way."

"What the hell, Savannah? I thought you were just helping a friend."

"That's how it started."

"Were you hurt?"

"A few scratches, no big deal. Then Ryker and I came to Atlanta to speak to Todd's coworkers."

"Ryker is who again?"

"One of Todd's friends. They served together on the same ranger team. Anyway, we were following leads regarding some potential trouble Todd might have been in when someone tried to run us down. Now I need your help tracking down that car. It happened in front of a bar named Maloney's on Fourth Street in Atlanta. We didn't want to hang around to look for security cameras, and the only witness wasn't able to get a license plate."

"What about the police? Did you call them?"

"I didn't want to involve them. It would have taken too much time. And this situation is complicated. This wasn't a random event. Someone came after us, and I think it's because we're asking questions, or because Ryker might be a target. Two guys from his former team die within four days of each other under mysterious circumstances. Now, someone tries to blow up the house Ryker was staying at and then run us down. There are too many odd coincidences at play. I have to figure out what's going on. I just need someone to tap into the security cameras around Maloney's and see if the car and driver can be identified. I can take it from there."

"All right. I can do that. But what's the game plan now? Where are you? Do you need to get to a safe house?"

"No. I'm at a hotel. We're heading into DC tomorrow to talk to the other two members of Ryker's team who are still alive."

"Which makes you a target if you stay with this guy. Why are you staying with him?" Flynn asked curiously. "Is this really just about your friend? It sounds like she's completely out of this now."

"This is still about Abby's husband. If his death wasn't an accident, then I need to find Paul's killer."

"And that's all?"

"That's all you need to know," she said pointedly.

He uttered a small laugh. "Fair enough. If you're headed to DC, why don't you check in with Parisa? Jax is also in DC. He flew in last night to track down a lead in the Bleeker investigation. If you need help on the ground, don't go it alone."

"I won't." She knew she could count on both Parisa and Jax. It was nice to know that she could pull in additional backup if she needed it.

"In the meantime, I'll work on finding that car."

"Great. I may be out all week on this, Flynn."

"Do what you have to."

"Thanks." She ended the call, reminded once again that she'd made a great choice when she'd decided to work for Flynn. She had plenty of autonomy and a boss who respected her enough not to question her decisions. He also understood personal commit-

ment to family and friends. With that thought in mind, she decided
to call Abby. With her other phone off, she needed to make sure
that Abby wasn't trying to reach her.

"Hello?" Abby said, her voice choked up.

"It's me, Savannah."

"This isn't your number."

"I borrowed a phone. What's wrong?"

"You don't know? You haven't heard?"

Her stomach flipped over. "Heard what?"

"Chief Tanner just called me. They found Todd's body. He's
dead, Savannah."

She took a quick breath, more surprised than she probably
should have been. But as long as Todd was missing, there had been
hope. Now there was none. "I'm so sorry. Where are you?"

"I'm still at my parents' house."

"Good. You should stay there for the rest of the week."

"What about Todd's funeral? He has no family besides his
mother, and Chief Tanner said that she didn't understand anything
that he said or that the staff at the hospital tried to tell her.
Someone has to put something together for Todd. He didn't have
any really close friends in Dobbs besides Paul and me. I guess
there's the rest of his team, but it seemed like it was just Paul and
Todd who were staying in touch."

"You need to take a breath, Abby. Nothing has to be done
tonight."

"That's what the chief said. He also said he'd help make any
arrangements."

"Good. I'm sure there will be an autopsy, which will take a day
or two. And I will help you with all this, but just give yourself
some time. As you said, Todd didn't have family. There's no rush to
do a service."

"I don't even know what he would want."

"We'll figure it out. Maybe Ryker has an idea. He knew Todd
very well at one point."

"Are you guys still at my house? I can't believe you didn't hear
about Todd."

"We're not in Dobbs. We came to Atlanta to talk to Todd's employer."

"What did you find out?"

"Not a lot, but we did meet a woman who was in love with Todd. She might want to be part of a memorial service."

"Really? Todd had someone in Atlanta? He never told me that."

"I'm not sure if it was serious on his part, but this woman really cared about him."

"What else did she say?"

"That Todd had money troubles and was gambling."

"With Paul," Abby said. "And they weren't winning, I know that. When are you coming back?"

"I'm not sure. Tomorrow or the next day."

"What aren't you telling me, Savannah? Why stay in Atlanta?" Abby asked suspiciously. "Todd has been found. There's nothing else to know, is there?"

"I just want to make certain there's nothing else to know."

"Because of the explosion at Todd's house."

"Yes. It's the one piece that makes me think Todd's death was not an accident. Until I know for sure, I want you and Tyler to stay in Ridgeview. Promise me you will."

"I will. I'm not that eager to go home. Tyler is doing well with my parents and it helps to have their support."

"Abby, whatever financial issues Paul left you with, I'm going to help you. You should have told me there were problems."

"Are you rich now, Savannah? Because our money problems are too big for you to help with. I might have to declare bankruptcy to get out from under. I told Paul that a few weeks ago, and he had a fit. He said he couldn't do that. He couldn't walk away from his debts. It wasn't honorable. Well, falling off the roof wasn't honorable, either, but that's where we are."

She heard the bitter, angry edge in Abby's voice and couldn't blame her. "We'll talk when I get back, go over all the options. There's life insurance, right?"

"Yes, and I got a letter today from some veterans' fund that said

I might be eligible for compensation. I just had to fill out a form and then they'll get back to me."

"Well, that's good. Hopefully, we can keep the wolves away."

"We got into a lot of debt when Tyler was sick two years ago. That's when we maxed everything out. Paul's injuries just made everything worse. I know I need to get a full-time job now. I just don't know what I'm going to do."

"We'll figure it out. Just let yourself grieve your husband. Paul was a good person. You loved him, and he loved you, and you can't forget that in the midst of everything else."

"You're right. I better go. I hear Tyler calling my name."

"I'll talk to you tomorrow." As she set down the phone, she heard three knocks at the door. She got up to answer it, checking through the peephole first to make sure it was Ryker. Then she opened the door.

He entered with a smile and a large bag in his hand, but as soon as he saw her face, his expression changed. "What's wrong now?"

She closed the door and put on the dead bolt. "I just spoke to Abby. The police found Todd's body. He's dead, Ryker. I'm sorry."

CHAPTER THIRTEEN

RYKER COULD BARELY HEAR what she was saying. The bells had begun to chime as soon as he'd seen the grim look on her face.

"Ryker?" she asked.

It sounded like she was talking underwater. He put his hands over his ears as a chorus of noises echoed through his head. Explosions, bells, screams, squealing tires, garbled shouts…

Terror ran through him. The anxiety that he'd come to expect and yet was never quite ready for was back.

There were hands on his shoulder now—her hands, warm and strong. He stared into her beautiful green eyes and the gold flecks within her gaze shimmered like a waterfall. Her blonde hair was like silk, her lashes a long, beautiful sweep of black, her nose so perfect and straight with just a tilt at the end that seemed to fit her stubborn personality so very well. And then there was her mouth and her full, pink lips, perfect for kissing. He could lose himself in her. He could be who he used to be.

His thoughts shockingly started to drown out the noises in his head.

She wrapped her arms around his neck and moved in closer, her head fitting just under his chin. Her breasts were soft against his chest, and other parts of his mind and body suddenly started demanding attention.

He took his hands off his ears and wrapped his arms around her, holding her close, feeling a connection that he'd been missing the last year—even longer than that. He buried his face in her hair, inhaling her sweet scent, and his mind began to quiet. He no longer heard the bells, but he could hear his heart beating faster, the blood rushing through his veins.

She pulled back slightly, lifting her head, meeting his gaze. "Better?" she murmured, her voice still hushed as if she was afraid of setting him off again.

"Yes. I don't know how you did it. You drove the noise away." He paused. "Actually, I do know. You distracted me. My mind ran away from the bells and straight to you. I started thinking about how much I want to hold you, kiss you."

Her eyes glittered with his words. "You are holding me, Ryker."

"I want more. But…"

"There's a but?" she asked with surprise.

"I don't want you to kiss me because you feel sorry for me or you're trying to comfort me or bring me back to life. I want you to kiss me because you want to. Or not."

Indecision played through her eyes. "I want to. I just don't know if I should."

"I can't blame you for that. I can't imagine what you see when you look at me."

A smile curved her lips. "Sometimes, I see a man in pain, someone who's haunted. But I also see the man who made me want to be reckless, daring, and more impulsive than I'd ever been in my life. You might not believe this, Ryker, but I had never ever picked up a guy in a bar and slept with him the same night—not before you. But it was like you cast a spell over me. I was so caught up in your smile, in your charm, and in your moves…"

A smile crossed his lips. "I had some good moves."

"Really good. And the way you kissed—it was like we were on

fire." She paused. "It was like that earlier today." She licked her lips, and his whole body tightened.

"Man, don't do that; you're killing me," he groaned.

"Then I better do something about that." She pressed her mouth against his.

And just like that, the fire was back. He was lost from the first touch of her mouth, and he wanted to savor every second. He wanted her to feel what he was feeling, so he deepened the kiss, sliding his tongue between her parted lips, feeling like he'd found home in the warm cavern of her mouth.

Sweet Savannah… Sexy Savannah… *His* Savannah.

He hadn't known her name before. Now he wanted to shout it from the rooftop. He'd found her again, and he didn't want to let her go. He wanted to keep this feeling, this moment. He wanted to keep it going forever. And she seemed to feel the same way, as they kissed, then kissed again, their hands roaming as they molded their bodies closer together.

It wasn't enough. He wanted to strip away their clothes and throw her down on the bed. He wanted to give her pleasure and make her crazy, the way he'd done before. And he wanted her to do the same to him.

And then he heard knocking.

For a moment, he thought it was his mind once again flipping out on him.

Then Savannah broke away. "Door," she said breathlessly.

The knock came again, followed by a male voice. "Room service."

"Oh, hell," he muttered.

She laughed. "I thought you were hungry."

"For you."

She flushed. "You'll have to settle for turkey sandwiches and pie." She slid out of his grasp and walked across the room. After checking the peephole, she opened the door.

The waiter pushed in a cart and set up their food on the small table by the window. Savannah signed for the meal, and then they were alone again.

His heart was still racing, and he wanted to take up where they'd left off, but he had a feeling that wasn't going to happen. And maybe it shouldn't happen.

Damn! He'd never thought that before. But this was Savannah, and whatever was between them was more than a little complicated.

"It smells good," she said, lifting the lid on one of the plates. "Ooh, the fries look amazing."

"So, we're really going to eat now?" He had to ask just in case he was misreading her.

"I think we should," she replied, taking a seat, not really meeting his gaze. "We were getting a little carried away."

"A little," he agreed. "But it was…good."

She finally looked at him, desire still written in her eyes, but it was also mixed with determination. "Yes, it was good. But it's over."

"For now."

"Maybe for more than just now."

He could see her slipping away. "Reality is back," he said soberly.

"We have a lot going on, a lot to figure out."

"True."

"Why don't you sit down?"

He moved over to the table and took the chair across from her, leaving his sandwich untouched, as he thought about the terrible news she'd delivered right before he'd flipped out, right before she'd distracted him with a kiss. It was amazing how quickly she'd driven everything else out of his head. "Where did they find Todd?" he asked.

"I don't know. I didn't even ask Abby. She was really upset."

"I'm sure she's devastated."

He felt a wave of anger and sadness run through him. "I knew it was coming, but I just hoped…"

"So did I," she said, meeting his gaze. "We're going to find out what happened, Ryker. And now, more than ever, we need to go to DC and warn the other two guys that they could be in danger."

He nodded. "I still have their numbers. I can text them both now."

She stopped him as he pulled out his phone. "You can't use your phone from here, remember?"

"Right."

"You can use my burner phone."

"I don't know their numbers off the top of my head."

"We'll talk to them tomorrow."

"I hope that's not too late," he said grimly. "I might have let Paul and Todd down, but I won't make the same mistake with Hank and Mason. I have to save the rest of my team, even if it's the last thing I do."

"Let's not make it the last thing. And let's do it together."

"This isn't your fight, Savannah."

"Yes, it is. You're in it for the guys; I'm in it for Abby. If Paul was killed, I need to get justice for her and for Tyler and also for Paul. Plus, you need me. I have resources you don't have. I know you don't like to have help, but you're getting mine, whether you want it or not. Otherwise, we'll both be chasing down the same guys separately and that won't be efficient. You understand the benefit of a team, a partnership. Don't try to shut me out." She picked up a fry and popped it into her mouth. "And you should really eat. We may have some long days ahead of us."

He wanted to tell her he didn't need her help, but he did, and not just because she was an agent. She somehow brought him peace when no one else could. But she could be in danger if she stayed with him, and he didn't trust himself to be able to protect her. On the other hand, she could probably protect herself.

He picked up his turkey sandwich. He wasn't really hungry, but he needed to eat. He needed to be ready for whatever was coming next, and he was quite certain there was something else coming. He just hoped they could figure out what that something was before someone else got hurt.

"I love room service," Savannah said, a short time later, as she finished the last bite of pie, which he had insisted she take. "I don't know why, but it always feels so decadent to have someone deliver food to your room. Of course, my father would say that having room service is about as lazy as anyone can get."

"Well, he's not here, so you don't have to feel guilty."

"Oh, I don't. I feel great." Her expression suddenly shifted. "Now, I feel guilty for saying I feel great after what we learned about Todd."

"You shouldn't. I know you care. In fact, you probably care too much about someone you didn't know that well."

"I didn't know Todd well, but I know how important he was to Abby and Paul, especially Paul. And I was close to Paul. He and Abby started going out our senior year in high school. They were crazy about each other. I wasn't super happy about it at first. I felt like I was losing my best friend to him, but he became a big brother to me, and if it hadn't been for the two of them, I think I might have completely lost it in high school. I was so angry all the time. I hated the pageants by then. Josie was always pissed off at me. My aunt was on me about everything: my skincare, my knowledge of world events, my ability to speak in front of a crowd... You have no idea how much work goes into winning a beauty pageant."

"I really don't. I thought you just had to look good in a bathing suit."

"Even that takes work. And then there were the mind games that I was supposed to play with my fellow competitors. Josie was far better at that part than I was. Anyway, Abby and Paul were what I considered my normal friends. I also liked the way they were together. They had passion, but they were also best friends. I wanted that, too."

"Who was your first love?" he asked curiously.

"Steven Montgomery. He was tall, blond, and the high school quarterback."

"I'm not surprised you got the quarterback."

"I didn't really get him. He was the one who cheated on me."

"Oh, and then you threw the rock at his car and hit the police car instead."

"My aim is usually good, but I was upset that night. I wasn't thinking clearly."

"What about after Steven?" he asked, wanting to know more about her. "Who was the next guy?"

"My next semi-serious relationship was senior year of college, but after I graduated, I went into the army, and he was off to law school. We never saw each other again." She paused. "There were a few other relationships, but none that made me think they were forever, and in retrospect not one of them really knew me, not the real me."

"Why didn't you show your true self?"

She shrugged. "I would probably need a psychiatrist's couch to answer that question."

He didn't believe that for a second. "I think you already know the answer."

"Well, I can give it a shot. Because I was abandoned by my father, I didn't think anyone could really love me," she said. "I do have some self-awareness. But I think it's more complicated than that."

"I'm sure it is."

"It wasn't just about my dad, it was also about my aunt and the pageants, knowing that I had to speak and act a certain way to get approval. It became ingrained in me. I became good at fitting in, just not so good at being myself."

"Until you spent the night with me and then realized you should quit the army and become an FBI agent."

"Yes." She smiled. "I know that probably doesn't make sense to you."

"It doesn't, but as long as it makes sense to you, it doesn't matter." He paused. "I know I made an assumption about you, but I wouldn't have cared if you'd said you weren't a dancer. You could have told me you were an astronaut or a teacher or a farmer, and I would have still wanted you."

"I've never been any of those," she said with a smile.

"You get my point. And maybe you started out being who you thought I wanted you to be, but I don't think that continued once we got to my room. Did it?"

She let out a sigh. "I don't know. Probably not. You kind of made me lose my mind. I don't remember thinking much."

"Do you remember pretending?"

"No." She met his gaze. "I was not pretending anything when we were together."

He was more than a little happy to hear that. "Good. I wasn't pretending, either."

"Well, I know you weren't," she said dryly. "I saw the evidence for myself."

He laughed. "At least three times. Or was it four?"

"We need to stop talking about that night."

"Why?"

"Because we can't go back."

"Are you sure?" He paused at the sound of her phone. "Seriously? First a knock at the door, now a phone call?"

She grinned. "Maybe we should listen to the universe." She opened her text, and her expression changed. "Flynn sent me photos from the cameras near the bar."

He jumped to his feet, moving around the table, so he could see her phone.

"It's a silver Prius, as the witness said. But the driver isn't clearly captured on any of the shots."

"All I see is a baseball cap."

"Todd's neighbor told me the man she saw was also wearing a baseball cap," she murmured, scrolling through the photos to a long text. "Flynn says the car is registered to a Dolores Jamison, an eighty-nine-year-old Atlanta resident, who recently went into a convalescent hospital. Her niece reported that the car was stolen yesterday afternoon." Savannah looked up at him. "I'm sure the driver dumped the car shortly after he almost ran us down, but Flynn says he'll let us know if the vehicle is located. He'll also do some more checking in the morning, look at other traffic cameras in the area that might have picked up a different angle. But for now, we don't have anything."

He nodded, frustrated by their lack of progress. He paced around the room, too restless to sit.

"Are the bells coming back?" she asked.

"No. I'm just thinking about what we need to do tomorrow, how we can get out in front of this."

"Can you tell me more about Hank and Mason?" she asked, as she got to her feet. "I don't know much about either one. It might be helpful." She moved over to the nearest bed and stretched out, resting her back against the headboard.

"Hank is from San Diego, California. His parents divorced when he was young, and then his mom remarried a few years later. She had a daughter after Hank, who was born with special needs, which took up a lot of her time. I know Hank was fiercely devoted to his half-sister, but he didn't get along at all with his stepdad and not too well with his mom, either. From what I heard, he made a lot of trouble for them. One of the problems with Hank is that he has a short fuse. He lives to fight. He is always looking for trouble, and he finds it more frequently than anyone else. I kept hoping his brain would catch up to his physical skills, which were impressive. He's been into fitness his entire life, and since he left the army, he has gotten back into that and apparently works at a gym in DC. He's running some kind of boot camp program."

"And he wasn't injured in the ambush?"

"No. But he decided not to re-up. He said at the time he couldn't stand the thought of joining a new team."

"So he got along with everyone else on the team."

"I'd say so. They weren't in a position where they had to challenge him or criticize him, so there wasn't as much friction between them."

"What about Mason?"

"Mason is the opposite of Hank. He's super smart, always thinking. He got along with everyone. He and I both went to West Point, although Mason was two years behind me. We didn't know each other as cadets, but we had that in common. Mason lost his leg from the knee down after the ambush. He was the most badly wounded of all of us."

"Does he have family support?"

"He has a sister and brother-in-law and a couple of nieces and nephews. His parents divorced years ago. I'm not sure if they've been around much."

"And what does Mason do now? Or is he still rehabbing?"

"I heard he was working for a weapons manufacturing company—Spear Enterprises. In fact, I think your father got him the job."

"My dad?" she echoed with surprise.

"Todd texted me that about a month or two ago when he was trying to get us all together. Apparently, Colonel Vance is also working there, and your father is a consultant or something."

"I didn't know that, but my dad doesn't share much with me. I thought you hadn't been in contact with your team at all, but that's not true."

"I've gotten some texts, but I've rarely texted back," he admitted, feeling guilty about that. "I didn't want to get together. I needed to deal with my problems first."

"So you shut everyone out—your family, your friends, and your team."

"They didn't need to worry about me or get caught up in trying to help me. I didn't want to make their lives more difficult." He paused, seeing an odd look in her eyes. "What?"

"You think that keeping your family and friends away protects them, but sometimes it hurts them."

"Are you talking about me or your dad?"

"Both. I have firsthand experience with being shoved away for my own protection. My father always said he sent me away because it would be better for me. But the truth was that it was better for him. Shutting out people you love is a selfish thing to do. It's not generous, even if you think it is. Your family is worrying about you more, not less, because they're not with you. I'm sorry if that sounds harsh, but that's the way I see it."

Her words stung. Everyone had been treading so carefully around him since he'd gotten hurt. They'd been afraid to make him feel worse, but Savannah had taken a completely different approach with her brutal honesty, and he felt both angry and guilty. *Was she right?*

"I'm sorry if—"

He cut her off with a wave of his hand. "Don't apologize. You spoke your truth. Stand by it."

"I do stand by it. I just probably put a little too much of my own situation onto yours."

"Well, you know what you're talking about, I'll say that."

"I do know, Ryker. You've never been the one who had to stay behind. It's different. I've been in both positions. I've been the person who waited at home and the person who served, and you know what? It's sometimes harder to be the person at home. You're safe, but you're still alone, and you have no control over what might happen."

"You're right. I've never been in that position. Although, at the moment I feel like I have little control over what's happening in my life or in my head, so there's that." He paused. "Have you ever told your father how you felt about his actions?"

"Yes, but he doesn't listen. He always cuts me off or turns the problem back to me. But you're not him, and I shouldn't have suggested you were like him in any way. So, what were we talking about?"

He shook his head. "I don't know. I'm tired."

"Me, too," she said, as she slid down on the bed and rolled onto her side. "The last few days are catching up to me. I'm just going to rest my eyes for a minute."

"You should go to bed."

"I'll change in a second," she said, her eyes drifting closed.

He smiled, as her breath evened out. She was already asleep, but while he was exhausted, he didn't feel sleepy. Still, he kicked off his shoes and stretched out on the other bed. She'd given him something to think about. But as his gaze settled on her, suddenly she was all he could think about.

She didn't think a second night together could be as good as the first, but he thought differently, and he wanted to prove it to her.

But what would happen after that? Would either of them really be satisfied with another one-night stand? On the other hand, what was the alternative?

Their lives were moving in opposite directions, just as they'd been five years ago. Maybe they were destined to only have moments together. Or maybe he was just afraid that wanting Savannah would mean leaving his safety net behind, and for a man who used to be fearless, that was now a frightening thought. He'd gotten used to the isolation. He'd gotten used to the loneliness. Because with those two things came quiet and peace. But neither quiet nor peace were improving his problems.

Perhaps he needed a different approach. Maybe he needed someone besides himself. Maybe he needed her.

But what did she need?

He couldn't imagine it was someone like him, not the man he was now. Maybe the man he used to be...

But was that man ever coming back?

CHAPTER FOURTEEN

SAVANNAH WOKE up to the sound of water running. The hotel room was dark, but there was light coming from under the bathroom door. The digital clock read five fifty-six. She sat up, realizing she'd slept in her clothes. She couldn't quite believe she'd fallen asleep so quickly, but the exhaustion of the day before had done her in.

She got off the bed and moved toward her small suitcase, kneeling on the floor as she unzipped it. She was happy that she'd planned on staying with Abby for a few days. While she hadn't brought a lot of clothes, she had enough to get her through at least another day or two. Hopefully, that would be all it took to get the answers they needed. Because more time with Ryker would only complicate her life.

Already, she was thinking about him way too much. And that needed to stop. There might still be incredible chemistry between them, but they were going in different directions. She couldn't let herself start caring about him, because her life was in California. Her job was her priority. She wasn't living for anyone else anymore; she was living for herself.

Although, that sounded a little lonely now. But she'd get over that. She'd meet someone someday who was the right fit. That wasn't Ryker. *Was it?*

Damn! She hated the little voice inside her head that was always more hopeful, more optimistic than it should be. She couldn't keep yearning for relationships that were completely one-sided. She had to stop thinking about what he needed and focus on what she needed.

But as the bathroom door opened, and he stepped out, looking so handsome, smelling so good, her heart twisted in her chest, and butterflies danced through her stomach. Her hands clenched into fists, as a desire to run across the room and throw herself into his arms swept through her. She forced herself to look at her suitcase, to figure out what she was going to wear.

"Bathroom is all yours," Ryker said.

"Thanks." She grabbed fresh undies, jeans, and a sweater and got to her feet. "I didn't hear an alarm."

"I didn't set one. I still have an internal clock."

As she started to move around him, he stepped in front of her, and her pulse sped up once more as she gave him a questioning look. "What?"

"I just wanted to say one more time that you don't have to come to DC with me. You can go back to Dobbs, spend time with Abby."

Maybe that's what she should do, but it wasn't what she wanted to do. "I need answers, too. Let's not argue about it."

"All right. Then I'll just say thanks."

Her eyebrow shot up. "Now you're thanking me?"

He nodded. "For a lot more than just your decision to continue on to DC. You've gotten me through some bad moments, and you've had to push past my barriers to do that. It made me angry that you could break them down. I thought they were strong. But in the end, I was glad you did. I appreciate you more than I can say."

She was incredibly touched by his unexpected words. Her blood raced through her veins once more as their gazes clung together. She realized then she'd been lying to herself. They didn't just have a physical attraction; they had an emotional connection. And that was scarier than anything. She forced herself to move past him before she did something foolish—like kiss him.

Once in the bathroom, she turned on the shower, opting for a cooler temp. She needed to get her heart rate down and focus on business. But as she showered and dressed, she couldn't stop thinking about his surprising admission. Ryker hadn't let anyone into his life since he'd been hurt, not his family, not his friends, but, somehow, he'd let her in. She was both honored and a little terrified.

What if she wanted to stay in? What then?

Ryker might need her now, but that wouldn't last. He was battling his own private war, but she knew he would win. And she'd help him win, even if that meant he didn't need her anymore.

Hopefully, she wouldn't end up needing him.

———

The flight to DC was uneventful. Savannah rented a car upon landing, using her alias ID, but allowed Ryker to drive, since he seemed to be happier when he was behind the wheel. They decided to see Hank first, so they drove to the H Street NE neighborhood, where his gym was located in a two-story brick building on the corner of an eclectic, busy block filled with cafés and small retail shops. It was eleven in the morning when they arrived, and the gym lobby was fairly empty, as they were a little early for the lunchtime workout crowd.

The desk clerk called for Hank, and he appeared a few minutes later. While she remembered him from the team photo, in person he was much bigger. He was at least six foot four, with dark hair and eyes, and was extremely muscular, his biceps bulging under his short-sleeve T-shirt. There was more than surprise in his eyes when he saw Ryker; there was also wariness. She wondered if that was just because there was always tension between the men or if the stress was coming from somewhere else.

"I can't believe you're here, Stone. I thought you were done with us."

"Not done, just dealing with some of my own problems," Ryker said. "How are you, Hank?"

"All right. Did you go to Paul's funeral?"

"Yes. I wondered why you didn't."

"We had a big event on Monday. I couldn't get away. I didn't think you'd go."

"Well, I did. Todd was there, too."

"He said he'd represent for all of us." Hank's gaze moved to Savannah.

She stepped forward and extended her hand. "I'm Savannah Kane. I grew up with Abby, Paul's wife."

"Oh," Hank said, giving her hand a strong shake. "Why are you both here?"

"Have you heard about Todd?" Ryker asked.

"I spoke to him on Monday morning before the funeral. I haven't heard from him since. Why? What's going on?"

"Todd drove his car into the river Monday afternoon, after the funeral," Ryker said shortly. "He didn't survive."

Savannah watched Hank closely as Ryker delivered the terrible news.

Hank's lips tightened, and his eyes filled with shadows. "I don't understand. Todd is dead? How is that possible?"

"I don't know," Ryker replied. "But I don't think it was an accident."

"If it wasn't an accident…" Hank paused. "Are you saying he killed himself?"

"There's a chance."

"Damn. That's insane." He shook his head in bemusement. "Although, it sounded like that's what Paul did, too. When Todd told me that Paul fell off the roof, I just couldn't believe it. He was as nimble as a mountain goat."

"He was wasted at the time."

"Yeah, that's what Todd said, but there was still a part of me that wondered. Now you're telling me Todd drove into the river, and I'm supposed to think that's an accident, too?"

"Do you think Paul and Todd were suicidal?" Ryker asked.

"They weren't happy. But I wouldn't have thought they'd kill themselves," Hank replied. "I don't know what to say."

"I don't think either one of them killed themselves," Ryker said. "I think someone else had a hand in Todd's death, maybe in Paul's death, too. There's a good chance someone is taking out all the members of our team, which is why I'm here. One of us could be next. We need to have a longer conversation. Can you break away for a bit?"

Hank hesitated, then glanced at his watch. "I have ten minutes before my next session starts. Come with me." He led them into a small adjacent room with a desk and two chairs that was set up to sell memberships. "Have a seat and start at the beginning."

"When I spoke to Todd at Paul's funeral, I thought Todd was extremely agitated. He was angry and ranting about the army, about us all ending up where we are. He was blaming himself for Paul's death. He stormed off, got into his car, and minutes later, we heard a crash. His vehicle had gone into the Dobbs River."

"Ryker jumped in after him," Savannah put in, wanting this man to know that Ryker had done his duty.

"But Todd wasn't in the car," Ryker continued. "They didn't find him for twenty-four hours."

"I can't believe this. But it still sounds to me like he killed himself. What am I missing?" Hank asked.

"There was an explosion at Todd's house yesterday," Ryker replied. "Since Todd was dead, he didn't do that, which means someone else wanted to cover something up. Add that to the fact that someone tried to run me down last night, and there's a pattern emerging. With Paul and Todd gone, there are only three of us left."

Hank sat back in his chair, folding his beefy arms across his broad chest. "Why would someone come after us? We're not doing anything of interest. We're not a threat to anyone."

"I can't figure out a motivation unless it has something to do with our last mission," Ryker said.

"On the other side of the world? I can't see how that would figure into anything."

"Well, if it's not that," Ryker continued, "what else could it be?"

Hank thought for a moment. "I don't know why anyone would be after us, but it's possible that Todd and Paul were gambling and that they might have crossed a line they shouldn't have crossed. I told them to stop looking for the quick fix and just work harder. Todd had a decent job, but he never picked up as many hours as he could. And Paul could have worked there, too, even with his physical limitations. I also said they could come here and work at the gym. Since Paul was having trouble with his wife and wasn't living at home anymore, it seemed like he could make a move if he was that desperate."

"Is that why you texted Todd about moving up the timeline?" she asked.

He shot her a quick, surprised look. "You went through Todd's texts? I don't understand. Do you have his phone?"

"No, I don't have his phone, but someone mentioned they saw a text from you to him."

"Someone? Who?"

"It doesn't matter," Ryker interrupted, drawing Hank's gaze back to him. "You said Paul and Todd might have crossed a line... What line?"

"I think they were both trying to get a loan from a private individual, but I don't know who. Look, unlike you, Ryker, I tried to help them, but, frankly, I have problems of my own. Paul and Todd were spending more time feeling sorry for themselves than anything else. Maybe that sounds cruel, but it's the truth." He checked his watch once more and then stood up. "I have to go."

"We need to keep talking, Hank," Ryker said as he got to his feet.

"Why? We can't bring Paul and Todd back. And I don't even understand why you're suddenly all worked up about them. You abandoned everyone. We haven't heard from you in months."

"I've had a lot of issues to deal with."

"As we all have. Hell, Mason lost his leg, and he stays in touch. You still have yours."

Savannah sucked in a breath as anger raced across Ryker's face. She was sorry to see the conversation disintegrating. Hank had more information than Ryker did, and their brief conversation had only touched on a few small pieces. But now they were bristling like two dogs about to fight.

"You two need to forget about the last few months," she said forcefully. "This is about now. You could both be in danger, as well as your friend Mason. If you each go it alone, you'll be bigger targets. You need to put your pride, your egos, and your pissed-off attitudes aside and sit back down."

They both stared at her with varying degrees of amazement.

"Who the hell are you again?" Hank demanded.

"I told you. I'm Abby's friend. But I'm also an FBI agent, and when I tell you that you're in trouble, you should believe me. This isn't just about Paul and Todd. It's about Ryker, too. And I believe you could also be a target."

"She's right," Ryker said. "We don't have to like each other to work together. God knows, we managed to do that for quite a few years."

Hank frowned but before he could say anything, one of the clerks from the front desk opened the door and said, "Sorry to interrupt, but your noon appointment is here."

"I'll be right there," Hank said. "Look, I have to get back to work. I can't do this now."

"Can we meet later?" Ryker asked.

"How long are you in town?"

"As long as I need to be."

"You really think something else is going on?"

"I do," Ryker replied.

Hank thought for a moment. "All right. I can meet you at seven tonight. There's a bar down the street—Holstein's. If you want to keep talking, we can do it there."

"Great. We'll meet you then."

They followed Hank out to the lobby. He disappeared into the fitness center while they walked out to the car.

"Hank really doesn't like you," she commented, as she slid into the passenger seat.

"No, he doesn't."

"And the feeling is mutual, right?"

"Probably not as much as it should be." He paused, mixed emotions in his eyes. "Behind Hank's anger, there was pain. I let him down. I let them all down."

"Maybe they let you down, too. It's not like anyone drove down to see you, did they?"

"No, but I made it clear I wasn't up for visitors."

"Well, like I said, it's not really about the past, it's about what's next."

"You did a good job of bashing our heads together," he said with a small smile.

"You're welcome."

"I'm running up quite a tab when it comes to thanking you, Savannah."

"I'm keeping track, too. I intend to collect at some point."

"I hope you will. I don't like to be in anyone's debt." He started the car. "Time to track down Mason."

"Maybe we can get him to meet with you and Hank tonight. It would be good to get the team back together."

"At least, what's left of us," he said heavily.

As Ryker drove out of the parking lot, she pulled up the address for the weapons manufacturing company where Mason worked. It was in Bethesda, Maryland, a suburb of DC and about thirty minutes away. Hopefully, Mason would give Ryker a better reception than Hank had. She'd thought Ryker was their beloved leader, but it seemed like the men were all blaming him for abandoning them. *Was it really just that he'd been distant and out of touch since their tragic ambush? Or was there more going on that she didn't understand?*

"Who was your best friend on the team?" she asked Ryker.

He raised a brow. "Why do you want to know that?"

"Just curious."

"As to why everyone hates me?"

"Yes."

He gave her a hard look. "Your honesty is not always appreciated."

"And you haven't answered the question."

"I thought I was close to everyone, except Hank."

"Let me ask it a different way," she continued, as he started the car. "What were the personalities on the team? How did it break down?"

"Carlos was the family man with his wife and four kids. He sometimes felt like the dad in the group, always looking out for us. He was the guy everyone talked to when they had a problem. Mason was super smart. He could calculate patterns, measure distance, assess tactical strategies within seconds. He was also the most computer savvy. Leo was a pilot trapped in a ranger uniform. His head was always in the clouds, and his favorite pastime was making airplanes out of whatever paper he could find. But he never found a way to make it into the sky."

"That's too bad."

"Hank was the warrior," he continued. "Hank was aggressive and competitive. If there was a bar fight, he would be in the middle of it. If you needed someone to have your back in that fight, he'd be there, no questions asked. Paul was the one who made everyone laugh and was the biggest talker. He was almost always upbeat and optimistic. Todd was the worrier, the most pessimistic and nervous, but when it was showtime, he usually pulled it together."

"And how did you fit in?"

"I made the tough calls, the critical decisions. I led and they followed. I thought I had their respect. Now, I'm not so sure."

"Was your isolation only because of the bells in your head? Or did you feel like you'd let them down on your last mission? Was it guilt that kept you from getting in touch?"

He didn't answer immediately, and she thought she might have pushed him too hard. Then he said, "You're right, Savannah. There was guilt in the mix. I let the team down. Carlos and Leo died because I didn't realize our intel was bad. I led us into that ambush, Savannah. It's on me."

"Or it's on the bad intel. I worked in intelligence. I know that sometimes leads are bad, sometimes assumptions are wrong. It happens."

"It's still on me. I was the leader."

She thought he was being too hard on himself, but she also understood why he felt the way he did.

"What did your fellow soldiers think of you?" he asked, changing the subject.

"Me? They probably thought I should have shut my mouth more often and followed orders without question. I had a difficult time doing something I didn't believe was right. And I hated not being able to see the investigations all the way through. I was only allowed to gather intel, not act on it. That was frustrating. I might have complained a bit too much."

"I'm sure you still did a good job."

"I tried. But I'm so happy to be doing what I'm doing now."

"It's good that you found your true calling."

"When I left the military, I had no idea what I was going to do, where I was going to land. For the first time in my life, I was making my decisions only for myself. It was scary and thrilling at the same time."

"You like it when it's scary and thrilling."

She smiled at the knowing gleam in his eyes. "You might be right."

Fifteen minutes later, they arrived at Spear Enterprises. The military weapons defense company sat on a ten-acre campus with two six-story office buildings and two large barn-like, windowless buildings for production and testing. There was a great deal of security at the front gate, and it took them almost thirty minutes to get from the gate to the lobby of the office building. From there, they were told to wait as Mason was in a meeting.

Ryker seemed too restless to sit, getting up, pacing across the room, thumbing through a magazine, then dropping it on the table and walking toward the window. She could feel his tense energy and hoped that Mason would give them a better reception than Hank had.

As the nearby elevator doors opened, she stiffened as a man walked into the lobby. "Damn!" she murmured. "Why is he here?"

CHAPTER FIFTEEN

SAVANNAH COULDN'T BELIEVE her father was at Spear today. He only consulted on a part-time basis. What were the odds that he'd be here now?

Her dad saw her and stopped in surprise. For a split second, she thought he might just walk on by. She could see on his face that he wanted to do just that. But duty made him turn in her direction. She got to her feet as he approached.

"What are you doing here, Savannah?" His gaze moved to Ryker. "And why are you with Stone?"

"We're here to see Mason Wrigley."

"Why? I thought you were in Dobbs, taking care of Abby."

"Did you hear that Todd is dead?"

His lips tightened. "Yes. I can't believe it. I was just speaking to Bill about it. I never thought those boys would take their own lives like that."

"I don't believe either one committed suicide," she said.

"I spoke to Chief Tanner. He's convinced that's exactly what happened."

"Well, I'm not."

He let out a frustrated breath. "Why do you always need to cause trouble?"

"A better question would be why do I need to get to the truth? And I can answer that question. Because the truth matters. It matters to Abby and to Tyler. It matters to Ryker and the other guys on the team. I would think you, of all people, would understand that."

He stared back at her, a glint of what looked like admiration in his eyes. Or maybe that was just wishful thinking.

"Fine. You're going to do what you want to do anyway."

"What are you doing here?" she asked.

"I have meetings this week with the design team."

"This week? You stay here in Bethesda? What about your job at Fort Benning?"

"I've cut that back so that I can spend more time here, developing new weapons that will help our troops."

"And Colonel Vance is involved as well?"

"Yes. He brought me in."

"And then you brought Mason in?"

"I set him up to have a conversation with Vance. They figured out the rest themselves."

"Why didn't Mason ask Vance himself?" Ryker interrupted. "We all worked with Vance in Afghanistan."

"Mason thought my word would carry some weight, and he was desperate. Since his injuries, he'd had difficulty finding a good job. Anyway, it's all working out for everyone involved." He paused. "Are you here to tell Mason about Todd? He already knows. I spoke to him earlier."

"What did he say?" she asked.

"What could he say? He was in shock. He couldn't believe it. Another one of his best friends is dead." His gaze narrowed. "I know you think you're after some hidden truth, but Mason has been struggling a lot, and he has another surgery to go through tomorrow. He doesn't need to get swept up in your crazy theory."

"I'm afraid he doesn't get a choice," she said. "I believe that Mason and Ryker might be in danger, as well as Hank Morgan, the other remaining member of the team."

"You think Paul and Todd were killed?" her father asked, doubt written in every line of his face.

"It's a possibility."

"It's ludicrous. I've always known you have a big imagination, Savannah, but that is a stretch, even for you."

"How would you know anything about my imagination?" she challenged.

"I was there for the early years of your life."

"Well, I'm not imagining anything."

"Savannah, stop," Ryker said sharply.

She looked at him in surprise. "What do you mean?"

"You don't have to defend yourself to him. You know what you're doing. That's all that matters." Ryker turned his anger on her father. "And what the hell is wrong with you? Savannah is your daughter. Why do you talk to her like she's your enemy?"

"You don't know anything—" her father began.

"I know enough," Ryker interrupted. "Savannah is smart, insightful, perceptive, and incredibly determined. She's also a loyal friend. The kind of person you want on your side. She is one hell of a woman, and you should be proud of her. Instead of trying to tear her down every time you see her, you should be building her up. You're her father, not her commander, not her boss. Why don't you act like one for a change?"

Her father was bristling with rage by the time Ryker finished, but he seemed to have lost his ability to speak.

She couldn't believe it. The most intimidating person in her life had been rendered speechless. And Ryker had told her father everything she'd always wanted to tell him and more.

"I don't have to listen to this," her father said, stomping away, his back stiff with anger. He blasted through the front door, letting it slam behind him.

Ryker turned to her. "Sorry if I overstepped."

"Are you kidding? I can't believe what you just said."

"I meant every word."

"I so want to kiss you right now."

His eyes darkened. "You probably picked the worst possible time."

"I know. But I owe you one big kiss."

"I'm going to hold you to that." He paused as the elevator opened once more, and Mason rolled toward them in a wheelchair. "But it will have to be later."

Mason gave Ryker an amazed look. "I couldn't believe it when I was told you were here. It's been too long."

"It has," Ryker agreed, leaning over to give him a hug. "My fault, man."

"And mine. I haven't felt much like talking to my old friends."

Savannah was happy to see that Mason didn't appear to be angry with Ryker. In fact, he seemed to understand.

"I know that feeling," Ryker said. "But I do need to speak to you now."

"Sure. We can go to my office after you introduce me to this beautiful woman."

"Savannah Kane," Ryker said.

Surprise ran through Mason's eyes. "You're Colonel Kane's daughter?"

"Yes, I am. It's nice to meet you."

"You, too. What are you doing with this guy?"

"She's helping me figure things out," Ryker answered for her.

"That sounds interesting. I'm getting the idea this isn't just a catch-up visit." His expression went dark. "It's about Todd and Paul, isn't it? I heard what happened. I'm still in shock. It doesn't seem real."

"Unfortunately, it is real," Ryker said. "And we need to discuss what might be going on."

"All right. Follow me."

Mason led them down a long hallway and through an adjoining courtyard, then used his security card to usher them into one of the windowless buildings.

She could smell burning metal and there was a ricochet of sounds that instantly made Ryker wince. She slid her hand into his as they walked behind Mason.

His fingers tightened around hers as they entered a very small office with a desk, computer, and filing cabinet. She quickly closed the door behind them and could feel Ryker's tension ease in the now quiet room.

There was only one chair in front of the desk and Ryker motioned for her to take it. She let go of his hand and sat down.

"This is where I ended up," Mason said, rolling behind the desk. "I review weapons tests and analyze the results."

"That sounds interesting," Ryker commented.

"It would be a lot more interesting to actually use the weapons, but so far the company seems to think my missing leg makes me unable to shoot a gun," he said, a now brittle edge to his voice. "But it's a job, and I make enough to live on. So, there's that. I heard you're a fisherman now. Can't quite picture that. What do you do with all your energy?"

"I don't have as much energy as I used to."

"I'm right there with you. So, what's on your mind, Ryker?"

"Todd and Paul's deaths could be homicides, not accidents," Ryker said bluntly.

"Whoa. Hold on. I was not expecting you to say that."

"I'm not done. There's a chance someone is targeting our squad. I came to tell you that you might be in danger."

"Why? What would be the reason for that?"

"I have no idea. But someone tried to run me down last night. And after what happened to Todd and Paul, the very suspicious nature of their accidental deaths leads me to believe there's something else at play."

"Do you think it could be tied to our last mission?"

"It's a possibility."

"I've always thought someone sold us out, but I couldn't imagine who. The circle was tight."

"Maybe not tight enough."

"If you hadn't told us to abort, we might have all died," Mason said.

Savannah saw Ryker's face turn to stone and wondered if the bells were coming back. He struggled to draw a breath.

"Are you all right?" Mason asked, echoing the question that was running through her head, but she'd promised Ryker that she wouldn't keep asking him if he was okay.

"Fine," he bit out.

"You should sit down. You look like you're going to fall over," Mason said, his gaze narrowing.

She got out of her chair, but Ryker waved her off.

"I need the restroom," he said.

Mason pulled a key off a hook by his desk and tossed it to him. "Next door."

Ryker blasted out of the room, letting the door slam behind him.

"What the hell is that about?" Mason asked, concern in his gaze.

"I guess he really has to use the restroom."

Mason didn't believe her. "That's not it. What's wrong with him?"

"That's something only he can tell you."

"But you know."

Mason's demanding gaze met hers, and for a moment, she wondered if he could read her mind. He had an intensity about him that made her feel like a liar, even though she wasn't saying a word. "You would have made a good interrogator," she muttered.

"I've done interrogation. And I am good at it. I'm an expert at finding someone's weakness. What's yours?"

"I don't have one."

"Yes, you do." He paused, giving her a long, thoughtful look. "It's Ryker. You're worried about him."

"He's had a rough time this year."

"All of us have."

"I didn't mean to diminish what you've been through. Ryker would say his issues are nothing compared to yours."

"But they're something. I've wondered why he fell off the face of the earth, but he wouldn't talk to me. He wouldn't talk to anyone."

"He's a proud man."

"And that's his weakness," Mason said, rolling his wheelchair around the desk. "I'm going to check on him."

She was happy to see Mason go after Ryker. After the very cold reception Ryker had gotten from Hank, he could probably use a friend right about now.

As Mason left, she got up and moved around his desk, her gaze sweeping the paperwork with practiced ease. The pages revealed weapon test results from a broad range of weaponry, not much of which made sense to her. There were a lot of numbers, but not much text. There were also inventory and packing lists for upcoming shipments and schematics of a weapon that appeared to be a newer version of the AK-47.

She turned her attention to the file cabinet behind the desk. There were some framed photos on the top of the cabinet. One was of Mason and a little girl about five. She wondered who the child was. She hadn't thought that Mason had any children. Maybe it was his niece. There was also a photo of the squad that was not the one she'd seen at Abby's house. This one had been taken on some base somewhere, and they appeared to be in the middle of a football game. Some of them were shirtless. They were all tan. They looked happy, strong, and eager. Those were the good days when they'd been invincible. Each man had the same look in his eyes: anticipation and excitement. Rangers were born to fight. And these men had done just that, over and over again. But now their battles were far more personal and perhaps even more dangerous.

Ryker washed his hands and splashed cold water on his face. The bells were starting to fade, but when the restroom door opened and Mason rolled in, they chimed once more.

"What's going on?" Mason asked, his gaze serious.

"I just needed a minute," he said tersely.

"You never need a minute. You're always ready, even when the rest of us aren't."

"Not anymore. Things change. You know that better than

anyone."

"I do. What's in your head, Ryker?"

"A lot of noise," he admitted. "It comes and goes. I never know what will trigger it."

"Are you getting help?"

"There's nothing to be done. It's not physiological."

"Then go to a shrink."

He shrugged. "Don't worry about it. You have your own problems."

"Doesn't mean I can't think about yours for a minute. I know you don't ask for help, but sometimes you have to take it when it's offered."

"I appreciate what you're saying, but I'm getting a handle on it. I'll be fine. I'm more concerned about you, Mason."

"You really think someone is coming after me?"

"There's a good possibility."

"Did you talk to Hank?"

"I did. We're supposed to meet up at seven tonight to talk further. You could come. It might be good for all of us to put our heads together."

"I don't think I can make it. I have another surgery tomorrow morning, and I have a lot of work to finish before then."

"You should make the time. This is important."

"So is my work. I need to hang on to this job."

"I understand. I just want you to know how serious this is."

"I'll see what I can do. I'll try."

It wasn't a promise, but it was as much as he was going to get. "All right," he said. "Do you see Hank much? You're not too far apart."

"Not really. He's busy with his life, and sometimes I don't think he can stand looking at me in this wheelchair. He gets uncomfortable and awkward, and I don't need that shit. It was easier for him to be around me when I had my prosthesis on, when I looked normal, but I've had some problems with it, so I'm back in the chair until after my surgery."

Mason's words were pragmatic, but Ryker knew there was

deep-buried pain beneath those words. He wasn't completely surprised that Hank was awkward around Mason now. Hank had always had trouble with people who showed a weakness. Even now, he surrounded himself with bodybuilders and gym rats. He was always about building up his physical body, but his mental strength had never been as strong, nor his emotional strength.

"You shouldn't be doing this surgery alone," he said.

"I've been alone for nine months."

"Maybe I should be there for this one."

"I don't need you to be there—not for the surgery anyway. If you want to be a friend again, I'm open to that. Or does seeing me make you feel guilty? I'm fairly certain that's why Hank can't spend more than five minutes with me. He sees me, and he sees failure. But I was just in the wrong place at the wrong time. It was no one's fault."

"Someone put us in the wrong place at the wrong time."

"If they did, I don't believe it was deliberate. It was just bad intel."

He was surprised at Mason's words. "You're able to accept that?"

"What choice do we have? It happened. It's done. It's all about what we do next, right?"

"Right," he agreed, thinking ironically that Mason might be the healthiest one of them all.

"So, how did you hook up with Colonel Kane's daughter?" Mason asked.

"Savannah was at the funeral. She's friends with Abby."

"And she's an FBI agent?"

"Yes."

Mason smiled. "Not your usual kind of woman. Actually, that's not true. You were always a sucker for a hot blonde. But they didn't usually have serious jobs." He paused. "Are you sure you want to mess around with Kane's daughter?"

"I don't care what he thinks. I was never a fan of his. And if I want to mess around with her, that's between us."

"And you do want to," Mason said with a grin.

"I do," he admitted. "But I need to get my head on straight."

"I don't know about that. Sometimes women like a little crazy." Mason pulled out his phone as it began to vibrate.

"Do you need to get that?"

"I'll return the call after I take you and Savannah back to the lobby."

"I know you have a lot of security here at work, but we need to look at the situation at your home."

"My townhouse is very secure. What about you? Are you still living on your boat?"

"Yes, in Chesapeake Beach."

"I can't believe you became a fisherman."

"It's a living."

"What do you think is really going on with your ears?"

"I don't know. I feel like my brain is trying to tell me something, but I have no idea what it is."

He opened the restroom door for Mason and then followed him back into his office. Savannah was standing by the window, but he had a feeling she'd been snooping while they were gone.

"Everything okay?" she asked, with a raised eyebrow.

"Yes," he said.

"It was nice to meet you," Mason told Savannah. "I have to get on with some work, so I'll show you out."

"Of course."

They followed Mason out to the lobby. He shook his friend's hand, and said, "Try to make it tonight."

"I will," Mason promised. "Until then, be careful, Ryker. If you're right about all this, then you're at risk, too."

"I'm very aware of that."

"Good-bye, Mason," Savannah said. "It sounds like I'll see you later."

"I hope so," he replied.

As Mason headed back into the elevator, they walked out to the car. He slid behind the wheel. The bells were gone, and hopefully they'd stay that way.

"What happened in the restroom?" Savannah asked. "Did you

get more information from Mason?"

"Not really. He said Hank has trouble looking at his missing leg. I got the feeling they're not really friends anymore, either. He wanted to beg off from meeting us tonight, but I think I convinced him to come. However, he has another surgery tomorrow, and I guess he has a lot of work to do before then. He said he can't afford to jeopardize his job."

"Well, I hope he can make it. I feel like the three of you need to talk about the past. Maybe you each remember something from that last mission that the other does not."

"It's certainly possible." He started the car, but he wasn't sure where they should go. "What now? It's one twenty. We have hours before we meet Hank at seven."

"I don't know. What are you thinking?"

He didn't want to just drive around the city or go to a coffee-house where there would be people and noise. "Why don't we go to my boat? It's about an hour's drive from here. We can be there by two thirty and spend a few hours on the bay before we have to head back."

"It's a lot of driving, but I'd like to see where you live."

Her words made him wish he'd made any other suggestion but that one. Taking Savannah to his boat was probably a really bad idea. He would only be bringing her deeper into his life. *But wasn't she already there?*

"Ryker?"

He met her questioning gaze. "Are you going to ask me if I'm all right?"

"I wouldn't dare. But I did want to ask you what triggered you today. What made the bells ring?"

"They started chiming when I first saw Mason, but they were soft and bearable. When he told me that we were only alive because I told them to abort the mission, the bells went crazy."

"Why?"

"I think it was because I don't remember telling them to abort the mission." He paused, giving her a troubled look. "If I don't remember that, what the hell else don't I remember?"

CHAPTER SIXTEEN

SAVANNAH THOUGHT about Ryker's question as he drove out of the lot. "Maybe that's it," she said. "The bells are your brain's way of trying to get you to remember something. Let's think about the recent triggers."

"They happen all the time. There's no pattern."

"Let's just see. When we met at the funeral, you swung around like I was going to attack you, like you were about to snap my neck." She saw his profile harden. "You were hearing something then, right?"

"There was an annoying rumbling going on but it wasn't a full-blown attack. I think it was seeing James Lofgren and Colonel Vance in their uniforms that started the bells. They took me back in time."

"That's understandable. Did the bells get louder when you were on the patio speaking to Todd?"

"No. They actually went away when I started talking to Todd. Or maybe I was just distracted. The next attack came after I got out of the river. The rushing water suddenly seemed so loud, like it was going to overwhelm me."

"You were yelling when I showed up."

"I do that sometimes. I don't know what the trigger was then—probably just fear for Todd."

"And the next time the bells came was with the clock at Todd's house."

"Clocks always bother me, even ones that don't chime. If I hear any kind of a tick, it sounds like an explosion in my head. I don't know where you're going with this, Savannah. I told you, there's no pattern."

"I still think there are clues in the triggers. There have to be."

"Why? Sometimes people are just crazy. They hear voices in their head. I hear bells."

She frowned, knowing she was annoying him by stubbornly clinging to her theory, but she couldn't shake the feeling they were missing something. "Let's think about the last attack. It came because you didn't remember telling your team to abort the mission. That makes me think your subconscious is trying to tell you something."

"I don't know," he said wearily. "Can we stop talking about the bells?"

"All right." While she might agree to stop talking about them, she was not going to stop thinking about them.

"Did you snoop around Mason's office while he was with me?" Ryker asked, changing the subject.

"Yes. There was a lot of paperwork: test results, engineering diagrams, inventory, that kind of thing." As Ryker glanced in the rearview mirror, she realized she should probably be paying better attention to their surroundings, to the other cars on the road. "Is someone following us?"

"I haven't noticed anything."

For the next few minutes, she kept a close eye on the sideview mirror, but the flow of traffic seemed normal. Ryker changed lanes a few times. She didn't notice anyone following suit. As they got farther away from DC, she said, "So, how did you decide to live on the Chesapeake Bay?"

"We used to go there when I was a kid. My uncle had a house

on the Maryland side. Every summer, we'd spend a few weeks there, and I always liked it."

"Does your uncle still live there?"

"No, he sold the house a while back."

"Too bad. I would have liked to meet someone from your family. You've already met my father and my cousin. It's not fair."

"Life isn't fair," he said lightly.

"Thanks. I'll make sure to embroider that on my pillow, so I don't forget."

He grinned. "There's no way you embroider."

"I've done some embroidery and I have other sewing skills as well. They're a little rusty now, but when I first started on the pageant circuit, my aunt didn't have a lot of money, so we had to sew our outfits. Eventually, our homemade wear didn't cut it, but a boutique in Ridgeview sponsored Josie and me for a few pageants and paid for our clothes. In exchange, I'd sometimes model for them on the weekends when we weren't competing."

"Was sewing your competition talent?"

"Definitely not. I was a singer. I was pretty good. Not recording label good, but I could hold a tune."

"I think you're being modest."

"Not really. And none of that stuff ever mattered to me. The only thing I liked about the pageant circuit was feeling like I belonged somewhere."

"You found your tribe."

"I thought I had, but then the backstabbing and jealousy drove that good feeling away, and I had to keep looking. It wasn't until I got to Quantico that I really found a group of people I could trust."

"Tell me about your team."

"Flynn MacKenzie is the head of the task force. He's half-American, half-Brit, has a dry sense of humor and reckless streak. As I mentioned before, he ran our training team at Quantico, which included myself, Beck, Caitlyn, Jax and Lucas. All of us are now on Flynn's task force, and we're joined by three of the members from a rival team at Quantico, Wyatt, Bree and Diego. The other two are still working in the FBI. Damon leads the office in LA and Parisa Maxwell, is assigned to the DC office. Flynn actually suggested I look up Parisa if I need some help in this part of the country."

"It's interesting that you've all stayed together since Quantico."

"We were actually spread out the first three years, but the last year and a half we've found our way back onto the same team. Like going through ranger training, you form a bond within your class, and it was the same at Quantico. A lot of the assignments were meant to tear you down, strip you bare, show you what your vulnerabilities were as an agent so that your weaknesses wouldn't defeat you. We all heard very personal and private information about each other, and I think it gave us a trust that we might not have had otherwise."

"And now you're in California. What's that like?"

"Fabulous," she said with a laugh. "The weather is awesome. I have an apartment near the beach. I sometimes bike to work, although probably not as often as I should. It's nice to be in a big, diverse area, with lots of cultures, great restaurants, and amazing entertainment."

"LA is nothing like Dobbs."

"I like Dobbs, but the small town never fit me. And being so close to Fort Benning and my father, it was not a place I was going to stay. I don't know if I'll be in LA forever, but it suits me now. I like the beach."

"So do I. It's just a different kind of beach where I live."

"You already seem more relaxed," she said. "It's like you're leaving your stress behind with each roll of the wheel."

"I am. I can breathe again."

"What do you do for fun, Ryker?"

"Fun?" he echoed. "You don't think fishing is fun?"

"It's a little slow for me. I would think it would be that way for you, too."

"I needed to slow down, and it's easy to keep people quiet so they don't scare the fish."

"Do you go into town on the weekends? Do you have a local bar you hang out at? Any friends? Any women?"

He flung her a smile. "Ah, you want to know about the women. Way to bury the leading question at the end."

She made a face at him. "I'm a little curious."

"There haven't been a lot of women in my life the last several months. I took someone out about six weeks ago, thinking it was time to get back into action, but she was honestly boring as hell. All she could talk about was the drama in her friends' group. Ashley slept with Kenzie's boyfriend, and Melissa posted an unflattering photo on social media of Karen, and that started a huge fight," he said mockingly.

"They sound like a fun group."

"It was not a fun conversation. The only thing I was enjoying was my steak. And then my date's phone went off. It was loud, and it rang, and it rang, because she couldn't find it in her enormous bag, which she proceeded to unpack on the table. There were tampons rolling around by the bread and butter."

She laughed at his words. "That must have been uncomfortable."

"It gets better. It was her ex-boyfriend, and she proceeded to talk to him at the table."

"And your bells weren't ringing then?"

"Oh, yeah, they started going big-time. I ended up throwing a hundred-dollar bill on the table and getting out of there. I'm not sure she noticed I left. She was yelling at Ron about telling Karen all their problems."

"Where did you meet her?"

"At the gym. I was working on rehabbing my knee, and she used to do the elliptical at the same time. I was getting a little tired of my own company. I thought I could try a dinner out. I picked a quiet restaurant. I wasn't counting on her being the noise. And I certainly didn't realize her personality would suck so much. After that, I decided to go back to being on my own."

"Isn't that a little lonely?"

"At times, but I'm happy on the water. You'll see."

She was already beginning to see. His breath came easier the closer they got to the coast. He was starting to look more like the irresistibly sexy man who had first swept her off her feet. It was going to take some work to remember that they weren't on a date. But she had to remember. Both their lives could depend on it.

CHAPTER SEVENTEEN

CHESAPEAKE BAY WAS a large estuary that stretched from Maryland to Virginia and was fed by hundreds of rivers and creeks. Chesapeake Beach, Maryland was only forty-five minutes from DC, but felt like a million miles away. It was a small, charming town with bay views at every turn, as well as seafood cafés touting everything from Maryland blue crabs to fresh-caught rockfish, blue fish and oysters. For a fisherman, it was a good place to set up shop.

Ryker parked at the marina and gave her a happy smile as they got out of the car. "Are you hungry? We can grab some chowder to go over there." He tipped his head to a small shack called Chowder Heaven. "It's good."

"I can smell it from here," she said, following him across the parking lot and into the café.

An older woman gave Ryker a questioning smile as they stepped up to the small counter. "Where have you been?"

"Had to go out of town."

"Well I'm glad you're back. Thought I'd lost my best customer."

"Not a chance. We'll take two large chowders with a loaf of bread."

"You got it."

"Do you want anything else, Savannah? I probably should have let you order for yourself."

"Since the menu basically consists of chowder and bread, I'm good," she said with a smile.

A moment later, the woman handed them a large brown bag. "I threw in some of your favorite oatmeal raisin cookies," she said. "Just in case you or your friend have a sweet tooth."

"You're too good, Lois," Ryker said.

"Oh, I know. That's what everyone tells me when I give them cookies. Don't be a stranger now."

"I won't be. I'll see you later."

As they left the restaurant, she said, "I hope your boat isn't too far away, because my stomach is rumbling."

"It's not far at all."

"So, do you eat here every day?"

"Sometimes I manage every other day. On the off days, I'll cook up whatever fish I've caught on a grill on the boat."

"It really is a simple life, isn't it?"

"Yes. Or at least it was," he said, his tone changing.

She was sorry to see the grin fade from his lips. But, hopefully, the boat would bring back the smile.

Ryker opened a gate and they walked down a long dock to a boat with the name *Escape* scrawled on the side.

"The name is perfect."

"It is. The previous owner named the boat, but when I saw the word *Escape*, it cinched the deal. At that moment, it was all I wanted to do." He helped her on board. "Welcome to my home."

The boat was in great condition. Clearly, Ryker took good care of it. And while there was a lingering smell of fish, it wasn't over-powering. He gave her a quick tour of the boat from the fishing deck that could also be enclosed during cold weather to the cock-pit, which apparently had all the bells and whistles to not only sail but find fish. Downstairs, there was a galley with fridge, microwave, and grill, and a stateroom with attached bathroom.

"It's nicer than I thought," she said, as she stopped by his perfectly made bed. "Can't shake your military training, can you?"

"Nope."

"I like your home. It's cozy."

"It has everything I need. Heat in the winter and air-conditioning in the summer. I can take groups of six to eight out to fish. So, this baby pays her way." He paused. "Do you want to go out on the bay? It's a nice afternoon."

"What about our chowder?"

"We'll take it with us."

"All right." It was probably a good idea to leave the stateroom alone. It was a little too intimate. It would be better if they were up on deck, with the fresh air blowing against their faces.

As they moved through the galley, Ryker grabbed a couple of spoons from a drawer, and then led her upstairs.

She helped Ryker ready the boat and then stood next to him as he motored out of the harbor.

They passed a few boats heading in for the day. One of the skippers gave Ryker a wave. He might have isolated himself, but wasn't completely alone, and she thought that was a good thing.

"Ready to eat?" he asked, when they got out onto the bay.

"I thought you'd never ask." She handed Ryker his soup and then took the seat next to him as she opened her container.

The soup not only smelled wonderful, it tasted heavenly. "Okay, I know why they call it Chowder Heaven," she said.

He laughed. "It's Lois's grandmother's secret recipe," he said, as he put a spoonful of chowder in his mouth.

"It's the best chowder I've ever had. Or maybe it just tastes better out here on the water."

"Everything is better on the water."

She smiled as the wind lifted his thick brown waves and the sun brought a warmth to his face. He caught her gaze and her stomach fluttered. So, she looked back at her soup and tried to ignore the desire building within her.

They finished eating in silence, the quiet continuing as Ryker sailed along the shoreline. She'd never been on the Chesapeake, and she loved all the inlets and coves, and the beach houses with their boat docks. She wouldn't mind having one of those homes, her own deck, her own boat.

"What about those houses?" she asked Ryker. "You could live next to the water instead of on it."

"I'm not looking for roots right now. What about you?"

"I'm also not looking for roots, but those houses sure are pretty. And I like this bay."

"Is it better than the Pacific Ocean? You said you live by the beach."

"It's not better, but it's different. There's a calmer vibe, at least to this part of the bay." She drew in a breath and let it out. She'd been wound up tight ever since she'd gotten the call from Abby about Paul's death last Thursday. It had been one thing after the next since then. And adding Ryker into the mix had completely overwhelmed her.

She could handle the investigation, the search for the truth. She just wasn't as sure she could handle the way she was feeling about him. They were getting closer by the minute, but there was nowhere to go. Their lives were in different places geographically, emotionally and in every other possible way.

She'd slept with him once before, knowing she'd never see him again, but it would be different this time. She knew his name. She knew his wounds. She knew his heart.

And he knew her. They wouldn't be strangers in the night this time around. There had been something so easy about their one-night stand. It had been spontaneous, reckless, and exciting.

Getting together now would be completely different. It couldn't possibly be as good.

But what if it could be?

She knew she was thinking too much, so she tried to force all the *what-ifs* out of her head and just be in the moment. "This is great, Ryker. It's so beautiful out here."

He gave her a warm smile. "I'm glad you think so."

"I kind of hate the idea that we have to go back to DC. It's been a crazy few days."

"It has." He ran a hand through his hair as he gazed out at the water. "I almost didn't come to the funeral, you know. I didn't really decide until I got on the plane. Up until that point, I kept thinking I might bail."

"How did you hear that Paul died?" she asked curiously.

"Abby's mother sent me an email, letting me know about the service, saying Abby would like me to come. Those words rang through my head for the next two days. I didn't want to let her down. But I also didn't want to see anyone until I was normal again."

"Is anyone really normal?"

"You are."

"Are you kidding? With all my family issues? I don't think so. I do know what you mean, though. I just think the problem is bigger in your head than it is to the rest of us. No one looking at you would know you hear bells at odd times."

"Until I start shouting at them to shut up."

"That doesn't happen that often. You mostly just get quiet and stiff and shake a little."

"That must be fun to watch," he said dryly.

"It's not fun. You're in pain. And I want to help you, but I can't."

"You've helped a lot more than you know. You've done more for me than anyone, Savannah."

"Only because I forced you to hold my hand once or twice."

"Sometimes I need a push."

"Or a hard kick in the ass."

"That, too," he admitted. "I hate being less than I should be."

"That's the most difficult part, isn't it? Accepting your limitations."

"It's my new reality. I have to accept it. I have to live with it. But it's rough. I've always had expectations for myself. I never set limits. I always thought I could break through any ceiling above me, any wall in front of me. I liked obstacles. I thrived on challenge. The harder it was, the more I liked it, the more I wanted to win. But I was taken down by a god-damn bell. And that makes me almost as crazy as the wild sounds in my head."

"I still think they mean something, Ryker. Maybe later tonight we can piece things together. Hopefully, we get a few more clues when we meet with Hank and Mason."

"Hopefully. But let's not think about that now." He turned the wheel, suddenly sending them in a new direction.

"Where are we going?" she asked curiously.

"One of my favorite coves."

"You don't think we need to head back?"

"Not yet. As you said, we have plenty of time and this place is too pretty not to share with you."

A few minutes later, they ended up in a quiet cove with low hanging tree branches providing shade and a bounty of colorful flowers along the shoreline. There were no houses nearby. It was wild and beautiful.

"Wow," she murmured. "It kind of takes your breath away. It's so beautiful."

"I agree," he said, but he wasn't looking at the view; he was gazing at her. "I think it's time I got my kiss, Savannah."

"You do, huh?"

"Yep."

She got to her feet. "Okay."

Despite her agreement, neither one of them made a move to breach the two feet of space between them.

"It might be a bad idea," he warned.

"It probably is. I don't think either one of us will want to stop at one kiss."

"No, but it's whatever you want, Savannah. You don't owe me anything. You were joking earlier when you said you owed me a kiss. I don't have to collect."

"I know that. The truth is I've been thinking about kissing you ever since we first saw each other at the church. After the explosion, the kiss felt so good that I couldn't stop thinking about doing it again. But if we try to recreate what we had, it might be disappointing."

"Or incredible." He paused, giving her a serious look. "It

wouldn't be just sex this time, Savannah. I like you. I don't want to hurt you. Which is why I'm still talking…"

She smiled. "I like you, too. You don't have to worry about hurting me. I know what I want."

"That's what you said the first time we met. I liked how direct you were."

"I meant it then. I mean it now. So, are we going to talk all day or—"

He suddenly moved, cutting off her question with a hungry, possessive kiss. Running his hands through her hair, he trapped her in his embrace, and she had no desire to escape. She wanted more kisses, more touches, more of everything.

Today felt a lot like the first time they'd been together, when the passion had exploded—hot, intense, needy, driving every other thought out of her mind.

She pressed her body against his, her nerves jangling, her anticipation building. Wrapping her arms around his back, she pulled him even closer. He might think he was weak, but she could feel the power in his body, the demand in his kiss. And she gave him what he was asking for, because it was exactly what she was asking for.

He broke away, giving her a scorching look as he drew in a ragged breath. "Bed," he said shortly, grabbing her hand and leading her down the stairs to his stateroom.

"It's so neat," she murmured. "I hate to mess it up."

"Are you kidding? I can't wait to mess it up."

"In that case…" She pulled her sweater up and over her head.

He groaned when he saw her breasts spilling out of her lacy black bra. "I missed these beautiful breasts," he said, cupping them with his hands.

She reached behind her back to undo the clasp and he helped her take off her bra, sliding his warm fingers across her nipples.

And then he stepped back.

"Where could you possibly be going?" she asked in surprise.

"One second." He moved into the adjoining bathroom and

came back with two condoms, which he tossed onto the narrow shelf next to the bed. "Now, I'm ready."

She put her hand on the impressive bulge in his pants. "I'd say so."

He laughed. "Let me get these off."

"Do it fast."

"Everything is probably going to be fast," he joked.

She smiled, reminded of the fun they'd had before. She'd forgotten this part—the teasing, the smiles, the laughter. Nothing about that night had been awkward and it felt exactly the same way now.

While he was getting rid of his clothes, she stripped off her jeans and panties and stretched out on the bed, taking a moment to appreciate his very fine male body. But he didn't give her long to look. He was eager to taste and touch, and so was she.

It wasn't just as good as she remembered; it was better. Their hearts were connecting as well as their bodies. Every intimate gaze meant something. Every kiss brought them closer.

When they came together completely, he was looking right at her, and she thought for the first time in her life that he really saw her, really knew her. And she knew him. There was nothing but honesty between them and that made their climax so much more intense and also a little terrifying.

Any rejection that might come later was going to hurt. But she pushed that thought out of her head. She'd deal with the pain if she had to; now it was just going to be about pleasure.

———

Ryker held Savannah's soft, naked, sexy body as they came down from the wild ride they'd just been on. Now, they lay on their sides, face-to-face, their breaths beginning to slow down. Savannah's hair fell over her bare shoulders, and he played with the silky ends, as he gave her a smile that came from way down deep.

He'd almost forgotten what it was like to feel so happy, so complete. And he hoped she felt the same way. Her light eyes were sparkling in the now shadowy light, which brought a new sense of awareness to the passing time. He shifted slightly so he could look at his watch.

"Is my time up?" she asked, humor in her voice.

"It's almost five. We should get back to the dock. We'll need at least an hour to get into DC, maybe more at this time of day."

"I hate to go."

"Me, too," he said, pressing his lips against her forehead. He closed his eyes and inhaled the sweet scent of her, wanting to make it a memory that would never leave him, even if she did. And she would leave. Or he'd make her go, because his life wasn't a life for sharing, not the way he was now. She could handle an afternoon on the boat, but she had her own life to lead, and that life wasn't here.

Her arms tightened around him, and she pulled away slightly so she could look at him. "I just have to say... Second time around, just as spectacular as the first."

"I might need another round before giving my opinion."

"Really? I thought you were in a hurry to get back to DC."

"Well, round three can be later tonight."

"I'm not against that, but we should probably not make promises that we might not be able to keep."

"I hear you," he said, although he didn't really like what he was hearing. But his sense of duty was coming back. As much as he wanted to blow off the rest of the world and make love to Savannah for as long as she'd stay in his bed, he was still on a mission to get to the truth, to find justice for his fallen brothers, and to protect the ones who were still alive. "But I want us to make one promise that we can both keep."

"What's that?"

"No leaving without good-bye."

She met his gaze. "I can do that."

"So can I."

She framed his face with her hands and gave him a long kiss that made him less inclined to want to get out of bed. But then she was rolling off the mattress, grabbing her clothes, and moving into the head.

He slid off the bed and put on his clothes. As his phone fell out of his jeans, he realized it was still off. Savannah probably wouldn't appreciate him turning it on, but he wanted to make sure he didn't have any messages from Mason or Hank.

As the phone came on, there was a text from Mason, and it was more than a little disappointing. He said he couldn't get away from work, but he was taking precautions, and he'd touch base with him tomorrow.

He'd really hoped they could all get together.

Savannah came out of the bathroom. She gave him a pointed look. "Really?"

"I had to check my texts. Mason isn't coming."

"Well, there's still Hank."

"I hope he makes it. I'm going to text him just to make sure. Otherwise, we really don't need to race back to DC."

"Good point."

He sent off a quick text. "I'll just leave the phone on for another minute. I want to throw some clothes into a bag." He grabbed a duffel bag out of his closet and threw in some clothes in case he didn't get back for a few days.

As he finished with that, his phone started vibrating, and he saw Hank's number. "Damn. It's Hank. This doesn't seem like a good sign." He took the call. "Hello? Hank?"

To his surprise, a woman answered. "This is Brenda," she said, her voice kind of choked up. "I'm Hank's girlfriend. I have some really bad news."

His gut tightened. "What happened?"

"Hank went for a run this afternoon, and he was hit by a car."

"Is he all right?" He sank down on the bed, very afraid of her answer.

CHAPTER EIGHTEEN

"HE—HANK DIDN'T MAKE IT," Brenda stuttered.

"What?" Ryker demanded. "What do you mean?" He didn't want to believe what she'd said, but he already knew it was true.

"Hank died on the way to the hospital. The nurse gave me his phone. When I saw your text, I thought I should tell you so you didn't come to your meeting. But I don't even know who you are."

"I served with Hank in the army."

"Oh, that makes sense. I'm sorry I didn't know. We've only been dating a few months and he's not a big talker about his army days. I can't believe he's gone. I think we could have been something, but now I'll never know." At the end of her sentence, Brenda started to cry. "I—I have to go."

"Wait," he said sharply. "Where did it happen?"

"Larimer Park. I can't talk anymore. It's too much. I'm sorry."

The connection ended, and he felt an overwhelming sense of rage. He picked up the phone and threw it against the wall. "Hank is dead."

Savannah stared back at him with concern. "What happened?"

"He went for a run and was hit by a car. Sounds like what almost happened to us."

"Who was on the phone?"

"A woman named Brenda. She said she's his girlfriend. Dammit! I should have stayed with Hank. I should have insisted we meet earlier."

"You tried. I was there. He barely wanted to meet you tonight."

"What about Mason? He could be next."

"Call him," she said, walking over to grab his phone from the floor. "Tell him what happened."

He punched in Mason's number. It went to voice mail after the fourth ring. "No answer," he said tersely.

"He said he was working late."

"Or he could be dead, too." That realization hit him hard, and the phone dropped out of his hand. "I can't be the only one left." He looked at Savannah, feeling a sudden tidal wave of fear and pain. And then the bells went off…

As Ryker covered his ears and fell to his knees, Savannah went down on the floor with him, putting her arms around his shoulders, refusing to let him push her away.

But this time her comfort wasn't enough. He started yelling. "Stop! Stop! Stop!"

Every agonizing word made her cringe. This attack seemed worse than all the rest. And she knew what had triggered it— Hank's death, the possibility that Mason could be gone, too. But hopefully that wasn't true. Mason was just in a meeting; he wasn't answering his phone.

With Hank's death right on the heels of their narrow miss the night before, she had to think about Ryker, about the danger he could be in. Suddenly, their isolated cove didn't seem like a great place to be. They needed to get back to the marina. They needed to go somewhere else, somewhere safe.

She just couldn't go anywhere until Ryker got through this episode. He'd stopped yelling, but his eyes were squeezed tight, every muscle in his face tense, as if he couldn't bear to see what he was seeing or hear what he was hearing.

"Ryker," she said sharply. "Ryker. Open your eyes. Look at me." She paused. "Look at me," she repeated.

His eyes flew open, and his raw gaze almost made her want to turn away.

"Listen to me, not the bells," she ordered. "We have to get out of here. We need to go upstairs, and you need to get us back to the marina. I can't do it without you. I need you, Ryker." She was suddenly terrified that he couldn't come back to her, that his fear that one day he'd go completely crazy and lose his mind might actually be happening now. "I need you to be with me. I need you to protect me," she said, hoping his sense of duty would wake him up.

He stared at her for a long minute, his chest still heaving from his rough breaths, but finally his breathing came easier.

Relief ran through her. She ran her hands up and down his arms, bringing warmth and life with every touch. He blinked again, and his gaze refocused.

"What—what did you say?" he asked in confusion.

"We have to go back to the marina. We need to find somewhere safe to stay. Someone could be coming for you next."

"Right." He scrambled to his feet. "Sorry."

"Don't apologize. You just got horrific news."

"We should leave a message for Mason," she said, picking up his phone once more. "I can do it."

"No. I'll do it."

She handed him his phone. She was happy to see he was pulling himself together.

He called Mason once more. This time, he left a short message saying only that Hank was dead and that he needed to call him as soon as he got the message. Then they went up on deck. He started the engine and took them out of the cove.

It was getting dark, and suddenly the peaceful bay seemed filled with menacing shadows.

Almost ten minutes passed before he said a word, and then it was another apology. "I am sorry, Savannah."

"I told you not to apologize."

"But I have to. I never should have gotten into your car at the river. I never should have let you come with me to Atlanta or to DC or here."

"You didn't let me. I chose to come, and I would have come without you if you'd tried to ditch me."

"You're in danger because of me. You could get hurt."

"I can handle myself."

"Now you sound like Hank."

She frowned at the comparison. "I'm not Hank, and I'm very aware of the danger. But blaming yourself is a waste of time. I'm here. And we're going to finish this together."

He met her gaze. "You should go back to California."

"That's not happening."

"This isn't your battle."

"The reason I got into it still exists. I want to get the truth for Abby, and justice for her and her family. But I have another reason now, too—you. I don't want to see you get hurt, either. And I think you need me."

"I don't want to need you," he grumbled.

"I know. But you do."

He met her gaze. "I know you're right, but it doesn't sit well."

"It doesn't have to sit well. Just don't fight me."

"All right. But there's one more thing—"

"If you apologize for having sex with me, I swear—"

"No. No." He shook his head. "I was not going to say that, because I'm not sorry about us being together."

"Good."

"I was going to ask if you could get my gun out of the locker downstairs."

"I can do that." She went down to the locker and retrieved the gun and ammunition. When she returned to the cockpit, she handed the weapon to Ryker. They were alone on the water for now, but who knew how long that would last?

As Ryker tucked his gun in the waistband of his jeans with ease and agility, she realized he was moving back into warrior mode, which was good, because she needed him to be on his game.

"Where do you want to go?" he asked. "Obviously, we can't stay on the boat."

"Let's go back to DC. I can call my friend in the FBI. Parisa can get us into a safe house. We need time to find some answers. And we need to stay alive while we do that."

His jaw turned hard as stone. "Who the hell is killing my men, Savannah?"

"Maybe whoever set up the ambush wasn't satisfied with only two of you dying. He wants to finish you all off."

"And he waited nine months to do it? Why now?"

"I don't know. We need to find out what happened during that ambush. Is there any way to get our hands on the reports?"

"I certainly don't have access. What about you?"

"Probably not. That would involve a lot of red tape, especially since I'm sure it's classified, and I have no evidence to tie what happened in Afghanistan to what is happening now. We need someone in the military."

"What about your dad? He's in DC. He has a lot of friends in high places. Maybe he could get us the reports."

"Involving my father is a terrible idea."

"Is that the daughter talking or the FBI agent?"

She gave him an annoyed look. "I don't want to answer that."

"Because you already know the answer. But it's fine. We'll figure out another way."

"Maybe my friend Parisa's fiancé could help. He's a CIA agent. Jared might be able to get his hands on the report. The CIA is pretty heavily involved in that part of the world."

"Good idea." He drew in a breath and let it out. "At least we have something to work on. But before we do any of that, we need to get a hold of Mason. We need to get him into a safe house, too."

"I agree. We'll keep calling him, and if we don't hear from him before we get back to DC, we'll go back to Spear or track him down at his house."

She took her gun out of her bag as they neared the marina. As Ryker drove into his slip, everything looked normal and as peaceful as when they'd left. But she couldn't trust that to last.

Everyone knew where Ryker lived. They needed to get off the boat fast.

After tying the boat down, they stepped onto the dock. Ryker took the lead, gun in hand. She stayed close to his back, also ready to shoot if needed. Fortunately, there was no one lurking around the marina. It was dinnertime, and she could see a few people on boats having drinks, but most of the boats were dark.

"I'll drive," Ryker said, as they neared the rental car.

"Sounds good," she murmured, her nerves tightening. She had a bad feeling, but she saw no reason for it. There was no one else in the lot. No one sitting in a car.

She started toward the passenger side of the car as Ryker took out his keys.

"Wait," he said, suddenly putting up a hand.

She froze. "What?"

"Back away from the car."

She took a few steps away. He dropped to his knees and took out his phone, aiming the light at the underbelly of the vehicle. And then he scrambled upright, running toward her.

"Go," he yelled. "Run."

They were twenty feet away when the car exploded, and she was thrown to the ground for the second time that week. Ears ringing, she looked for Ryker. He was on his feet, moving toward her. In the fiery light behind him, she saw a figure running in their direction, a gun in his hand.

"Gun," she yelled.

Ryker dived behind another vehicle as the shot went off. She scrambled toward the same protection, pulling out her gun.

Another shot went off, hitting the window. The glass showered down on her head. She peered around and saw someone behind a car twenty feet away. She took her own shot. It bounced off the fender. As she ducked down, Ryker fired.

Then he looked at her and said, "Cover me."

She nodded, reading his intent. As he ran toward their attacker, she fired off three shots, engaging the shooter.

Ryker was almost to the shooter when the guy took off, running toward the harbor service buildings. She moved from behind the vehicle, following Ryker across the lot. They met up at the corner of one of the buildings. There was a six-foot space between the structures, and they moved down the alleyway, guns drawn, searching for the shooter. It was only when they got to the end that they realized they were trapped by a ten-foot-high chain-link fence.

Whirling around, they started back when one of the building doors flew open.

They instinctively dodged behind the nearest dumpster.

"Come on. This way," a man said, waving at them.

The voice was familiar, frighteningly familiar. She met Ryker's gaze, saw the shocked look in his eyes. He moved around the dumpster, and so did she, wondering if the face would match the voice.

CHAPTER NINETEEN

HER HEART STOPPED. It was Paul, dressed all in black.

"Hurry," Paul said tersely. "We don't have much time."

"You're alive?" Ryker asked, echoing the words running through her head.

Paul stepped into the light, and there was no doubt that it was him.

She sucked in a quick breath. *What the hell was going on?*

"I'll tell you everything," Paul said. "But you have to come now."

Before they could take a step, a shot rang out and Paul fell forward.

Ryker shoved her back behind the dumpster as he took a shot at the figure on the adjacent roof. The guy took off running. And Ryker once again did the same.

She rushed toward Paul, as Ryker sprinted down the alley. She heard sirens in the distance. Someone must have reported the gunshots.

Falling to her knees, she saw blood gushing from Paul's neck. She pulled off her sweater and pressed it against his neck, praying the bullet hadn't hit his carotid artery.

"Sorry," he gasped, his eyes wide and shocked. "Tell Abby."

"You'll tell her yourself," she said fiercely. "You have to hang on, Paul." She pulled out her phone and called 911, reporting their location and the need for an ambulance. She also let the dispatcher know that she was an FBI agent.

"Make sure Abby knows—did it for her and Tyler—better for them."

"You being dead is not better for them. You have to stay with me."

Hearing pounding footsteps, she lifted her head, hoping the shooter had not returned. Thankfully, it was Ryker.

"I lost him," he said, anger in his voice.

"Help is on the way."

Ryker's gaze moved to Paul. "Who shot you, Paul? Who's after me—us?"

"Supposed to—scare you," Paul stuttered. "Not hurt you. Couldn't let them hurt you. Didn't know. Sorry."

"Didn't know what? What's going on?" Ryker asked.

"You're good. Better than everyone else," Paul said, his eyes dazed. "Wouldn't have fallen for the lie."

She wanted Paul to tell them everything, but she also wanted him to stop talking, because he needed to hang on to his strength. If he could survive this, he could go back to Abby. Abby could have her husband back. Tyler could have his father back.

Paul's eyelids started to flutter. "No," she said forcefully. "Fight, Paul. Do it for Abby and for Tyler. They can't bury you again."

He didn't answer her.

"I'll show the ambulance where we are," Ryker said, running back down the alley.

She pressed her sweater harder against Paul's wound, silently praying that he wouldn't bleed out.

A moment later, the paramedics arrived, along with the police and the fire department.

She stood up, as they took over Paul's care.

Ryker put his arm around her as they watched the medics put him on a gurney and run him out to the ambulance.

"He has to make it," she said, feeling desperate to make her words come true. But as she stared down at her bloody hands, she couldn't find much hope to hang on to.

A police officer joined them. "What happened?" he asked. "Dispatch said you're FBI?"

"Agent Kane," she said, showing him her badge. "This is Ryker Stone. We're working a case." She really didn't want to get into it all with a patrol officer, so she gave him just enough information. "The victim is Paul Hawkins. He stepped in front of a bullet to save our lives. The shooter got away."

"Any description?"

She looked at Ryker, wondering if he'd gotten a better look than she had.

He shook his head and said, "It was a male dressed in black with a hoodie over his head. I didn't see his face, his hair, nothing of note."

"Not much to go on. I assume the shooting has something to do with the explosion."

"They're definitely connected," she said.

"Do you want help canvassing the area for witnesses and leads?" he asked.

She gave him a grateful smile. "I do. It will be some time before I can get my team here."

"I'll get the other officers to ask around," he said. "But I'll also need you to talk to my chief, let him know what's happening."

"I'll be at the hospital," she said.

"I'll let him know."

As they moved into the parking lot, she saw that the ambulance had already left, but the firefighters were still there, putting the finishing touches on the fire. They paused for a moment, the skeletal remains of the rental car reminding her of how close they'd come to losing their lives again.

"We're going to need a ride to the hospital," she said.

"Actually, we don't. My truck has been parked here since I took a cab to the airport on Monday. It's in the owners' lot on the other side of Chowder Heaven. I didn't mention it, because I figured we needed to get the rental car back to DC."

"Right. Of course, your vehicle would be here. I wasn't thinking." She paused, seeing his dark-green canvas duffel bag on the ground. "Hey, your bag survived. Unfortunately, my bag was in the car."

"We'll get you some clothes later."

"I'm not worried. I just want to get to the hospital."

"Let's go."

They walked across the lot. When they neared the public restrooms, Ryker paused. "Do you want to wash your hands?"

She looked down at her fingers, still tinged with Paul's blood. "That's a good idea."

He followed her into the restroom. "Just to make sure you're all right," he said at her unspoken question.

She was actually happy to have him there, and no one else was inside. She washed her hands as quickly as she could, but with each drop of blood washing down the drain, she could see the life draining out of Paul. She prayed he would make it. As she dried her hands, she said, "Paul was in bad shape, Ryker."

"I know. You did everything right."

"I hope so. I still can't believe he's alive. How is that possible? There was a cremation. We had a funeral. And he's not dead?"

"If you hadn't seen him, too, I might not have believed my own eyes."

"This just blows me away. I never ever imagined that he wasn't dead. Do you think Todd is alive, too?"

He gave her a bewildered shrug. "I have no idea."

"Paul had to have help faking his death. Maybe it was Todd who did that. Maybe that's why he kept wanting to apologize to Abby."

"It makes sense, but we don't know why Paul did what he did."

"To get out of trouble. He must have felt he was in danger." She frowned. "Is it the same danger that's come after you?"

"You're asking me a lot of questions I can't answer. Let's go to the hospital. Hopefully, Paul survives and tells us everything we need to know."

She nodded and followed him out to his truck. The hospital was about fifteen minutes away, and they didn't speak on the way. Her brain was spinning, and Ryker also seemed to be lost in thought.

Once they reached the hospital, they were sent up to a waiting room on the third floor. Paul was already on his way to surgery. They would have to wait to learn more.

They sat down together on a small couch in the waiting room.

"What did Paul say to you?" Ryker asked. "Before I got back."

She tried to remember exactly what he'd told her. "He said to tell Abby he was sorry. That he'd done it for her and Tyler. You heard the rest."

"Yes. He said they were only supposed to scare me, not hurt me, and he couldn't let that happen."

"But he didn't give a name. He didn't say who *they* were." She paused. "He also said something about you would have never fallen for the lie. What's the lie?"

His jaw tightened. "This whole situation is insane. Paul allegedly fell off the roof of Todd's house. The police department in Dobbs took his body to the morgue." He paused. "Did Abby see her husband? Did she identify his body?"

"I never asked. I never thought I needed to." A painful realization hit her. "I have to call Abby. I have to tell her that Paul is alive." She pulled out her phone.

Ryker put a hand on her arm. "Maybe you should wait, Savannah. What if he doesn't make it?"

"But she'll still have to know he was alive."

"Agreed. But do you want her to have to wait to find out if she's going to have a second chance with her husband?"

His argument made perfect sense, but she knew down deep in her heart that if she didn't tell Abby immediately, her friend would never forgive her. "I have to tell her, Ryker. If it was me, I'd want to know. And it will take her time to get here. If I wait, and she misses an opportunity to see him…"

"I get it. You're right. Call her."

"I just don't know what to say. How do I tell my best friend that her husband wasn't really dead but now he might be dying?"

"You're just going to have to say it."

She drew in a deep breath, turned on her phone, and then punched in Abby's number.

"Hello?" Abby said, a moment later.

"Hi, it's me."

"You don't sound good, Savannah. Where are you? Has something else happened?"

"Yes."

"Please, please don't tell me you or Ryker have been hurt," Abby implored.

"It's not me, or Ryker." She gripped the phone more tightly. "I don't know how to tell you this, Abby. But Paul—Paul is alive."

"What? What did you say?"

"He's not dead, Abby. I just saw him."

"You're crazy, Savannah. Why are you saying this?"

"Because it's true. Did you see his body, Abby? After he fell off the roof? Did you see him at the morgue?"

There was a silence at the other end of the phone and then Abby said, "Chief Tanner told me I shouldn't see Paul, that his face was messed up, and it would haunt me for the rest of my life."

"So, Chief Tanner saw him?"

"And Todd. He agreed that I shouldn't see him."

That meant both Chief Tanner and Todd had helped fake Paul's death. *Why?*

"There must be a mistake," Abby continued. "You just saw someone who looked like him."

"Abby, I know you don't want to believe this, but it was Paul. I talked to him. He told me to tell you he was sorry, that he did it for you and Tyler."

"Sorry?" Abby echoed. "For what? For pretending he was dead? For leaving me and Tyler to grieve him? Is that what you're trying to get me to believe? He wouldn't do that. He wouldn't hurt us like that. How could that be better for us?"

She could hear the bewilderment and pain in Abby's voice, and it broke her heart. "I don't know why he would do what he did. I think he's in a lot of trouble."

"Why didn't you ask him why he did it? Where is he now? I need to see him. I need to talk to him."

Abby's question brought her immediately back to the present. "He was shot, Abby. Ryker and I are at the hospital with him now. Paul is in surgery."

"No. No. That can't be. Now you're telling me he's hurt?"

"Yes, and maybe I should have waited to tell you, Abby, because it's serious. He's in critical condition. I don't honestly know if he's going to make it."

"Oh, God."

"I'm sorry, Abby. I thought you should know."

"What hospital?"

"St. Anne, near Chesapeake Beach."

"That's near where Ryker lives. What are you doing there?"

"It's a long story. I'll text you the address. You can come now, or I can call you when we know more."

"No. I'm coming now. I can't wait, but it's going to take me a few hours. I'll have to get a flight."

"Do you want me to help you figure that out?"

"I'll get my mom to make arrangements. Who shot him, Savannah? Who shot Paul?"

"I don't know, but I think Paul knew him. He tried to save Ryker and me, Abby."

"Save you?" Abby echoed. "I don't understand. I'm so confused."

"You're not alone. We can talk when you get here. Can someone come with you? I don't want you to be alone."

"I can ask my mother. Tyler can stay with my dad. Should I tell Tyler his father is alive?"

"No," she said quickly. "Don't tell him anything."

"You really don't think he's going to make it, do you?"

"I don't know. But I'll be here until you get here. Text me when you figure out your plans."

"He has to live, Savannah. I can't say good-bye to him again. I can't mourn him again, not without knowing what happened, why he did this."

"One step at a time. That's all you can do."

"I'm so scared, Savannah. I thought I was getting a handle on him being gone. Now..."

"I know. I'm sorry."

"Okay, I have to go. I have to figure things out."

"I'll see you soon."

When she ended the call, she let out a breath of frustration and anger and sadness. It wasn't fair for Abby to have to go through this again.

Ryker gave her an empathetic look. "That sounded rough."

"Beyond horrible. Abby is on her way. She didn't believe me at first. Actually, I'm not sure she believes me now."

"That's understandable."

"She never saw Paul's body, but Chief Tanner did, and so did Todd."

"Then they were both in on it."

"Or Tanner was in on it. Then Todd found out, and that's why he was killed."

"Or Todd isn't dead, either," Ryker suggested.

"What about Hank?"

"I don't know. Is he really dead?"

She frowned. "We have to figure out what is going on. We're clearly still missing a crucial piece of information."

"I think we're missing a lot of pieces."

"Remember when Jackie read that text about Hank telling Todd it was time to be a ghost. What if it wasn't about ghosting her but about faking his death?"

"I forgot about that comment."

She thought for another moment, still trying to put the picture together in her head. "If Todd and Paul aren't dead, maybe Hank isn't either. We know you're in the dark. What about Mason? Is he in on this with them? Or is he on the outside, like you?"

"Difficult to say, but since he hasn't been answering my texts tonight, I'm leaning toward him being involved as well. If he was innocent, why wouldn't he react to being told Hank is dead? Even if he's working, he'd have to check his phone sometime."

"So, we have a team of ghosts. Why do they need to be dead?"

He gazed back at her. "They're going to do something that they can't be held accountable for, because technically they're all deceased."

"But what is that something?"

"I wish I knew. I used to be their leader," he said tightly. "Now one or more of them is trying to kill me."

"You don't know that the shooter was one of your teammates. Or that one of them set the explosive."

"But Paul was in on it. He knew enough to come to Chesapeake Beach, and he said he thought they were just going to scare me. Maybe he didn't come to kill me, but he knows who did. He's involved with that person in some way, and the other guys are, too. That makes them just as guilty." His eyes filled with anger. "If we'd gotten in that car, Savannah…"

She didn't need him to finish that statement. "Your instincts saved us once again."

"I don't know how many more times we can get lucky."

"It wasn't luck. It was you. I knew I could count on you, Ryker. I told you that when it counted, you'd be there, and you were."

"You took a big risk. I don't even know what made me look under the car."

"You didn't hear anything?"

"No. Nothing. The bells were quiet. But I just felt like something was off."

"Your gut was right."

"It was too close. You could be dead right now."

"So could you. But we're not. That's what we need to hold on to."

Their gazes met and held. She had so many other things she wanted to say to him. And she thought he had things he wanted to say to her, but where did they even start?

"I'm glad we had this afternoon," he said.

"Me, too. I wish we'd never left that cove. It was so pretty there, so peaceful."

"Peace rarely lasts long. That's why you have to enjoy it when you have it."

"I did enjoy it."

"I could tell."

His words eased some of the tension between them. "Well, I could tell, too."

"I wasn't trying to hide my pleasure," he said with a smile.

"Neither was I." She paused as a nurse walked into the room, but the woman made her way to an elderly man in the corner. "I thought she was coming to tell us something."

"I think it will be a long time, Savannah. Do you want some coffee? I saw a machine down the hall."

"That would probably be a good idea. I need to call Flynn. I took charge of the case without asking anyone if I could do that. But I wanted to avoid having to go down to the station and listen to a lot of questions we couldn't answer."

"I thought it was a good move. Whatever we're dealing with is big."

"Too big for just us. Now that we suspect that the guys are alive, that there's a plan to do something, we need to get help."

"While you make your call, I'll get us some coffee. Cream or sugar?"

"Just black." As he left, she picked up her phone and called Flynn. It was only four on the West Coast, so hopefully he was still in the office. She felt an enormous relief when he answered. She gave him a quick but thorough update on recent events, and finished by saying, "I don't want to put you or our task force in a difficult position, but I need us to handle this case. We have to move fast, and I don't have time to cut through layers of red tape."

"Based on what you've told me, I would agree. We have a group of former Army Rangers, who have faked their deaths in order to do something. It has to be big. They wouldn't go to this much trouble for something small."

"No, they wouldn't. Ryker said that Todd Davis ranted about

how the army owed them, how the country owed them. They deserved more than they got. A lot of them were released because of their injuries in an ambush that also seems to have taken place under suspicious circumstances."

"I'm going to bring Beck in on this. He's former military. He might have some insights. And I'll talk to the local police," he added. "I'll confirm that we're handling the case and set up security for the man in surgery. I'll also call Jax. He's in DC, getting an expensive thank-you dinner from Senator Wickham. He can get to you in an hour."

"I don't need him to break away from that." Jax had saved Senator Wickham's college-age daughter from a trafficking operation that had been targeting young women at his daughter's private school.

"He won't care, and I'll get Parisa involved as well. In fact, we might want to pull in Jared."

"I had the same thought. If he can pull any information from the CIA files on Ryker's last mission, we might find a clue. That's where everything started." She paused. "I really appreciate this, Flynn."

"We're a team. When someone has a need, we all step up; you know that. I just wish you'd gotten us involved sooner."

"Everything has been happening very quickly."

"Stay safe until I can get you backup."

"Believe me, I'm not going anywhere."

She set down the phone as Ryker returned to the waiting room and handed her a coffee.

"Machine was broken, so I went to the cafeteria," he said.

"I'm sure this will be better than anything out of a machine."

"Did you reach your boss?" he asked, as he sat back down.

"Yes. The cavalry is on the way. We should have some help within the hour."

"Good."

"My boss will also set up security for Paul here at the hospital and for Abby when she arrives."

"He sounds like a man who gets things done."

"He is definitely that." She paused, realizing that she'd been so personally caught up in what had been going on that she hadn't done what she needed to do. "Paul's personal effects," she said, getting to her feet. "He probably had a phone on him, maybe some other clue. I should have taken his phone at the scene. I need to get whatever he had on him. I'm going to check with the nurse."

After showing her badge to the nurse, she was given a large plastic bag containing Paul's belongings. She took it back into the waiting room. Sitting down next to Ryker, she removed Paul's wallet and handed it to him. Then she pulled out Paul's phone. It appeared to be a cheap burner phone, probably bought with cash somewhere, but hopefully they could still trace where it had been.

"Look at this," Ryker said, handing her a driver's license.

The photo wasn't exactly Paul, but close. The name on the ID was Walter Rogers. The address was Atlanta. "This looks like Paul but with altered features. The nose is thicker, the brows darker, the hair almost black and the glasses distort his eyes."

"He clearly wanted to disappear and become someone else. There are no credit cards, but there is a receipt for a dozen bagels and three coffees from Bagel Mania in DC."

"That's great," she said with excitement. "The order is clearly for more than one person. Maybe we can pull security footage from the bagel shop. This could be huge."

"What about this? There appears to be about two-thousand dollars in cash." He pulled out a thick stack of hundreds. "I thought Paul allegedly died in debt."

"He did say his death was supposed to be better for Abby. Maybe he died so Abby would get the insurance money."

"Then how did he get this cash? There's another plan in play besides insurance, although that could be a factor. Every time someone died, their heirs would get a payoff. That could be the reason for becoming ghosts."

"It's actually very clever. Who would come up with that?"

He thought for a moment. "Out of the four of them, I'd say Mason or Hank. I don't think Paul or Todd were the ringleaders.

Paul obviously didn't want to take me out. And Todd was always the most nervous, the biggest worrier. This doesn't feel like him."

"Plus, we know Todd was being persuaded to become a ghost. And someone told him the timeline had been moved up. Maybe he had to fake his death earlier than he had thought. Perhaps that's why his house was set on fire. He didn't have time to remove some piece of evidence. I know it's all speculation, but we have to start somewhere."

"Well, Hank works at a gym, doesn't have a lot of money, but he does have a lot of confidence in his abilities. I can see him being the new ringleader. He was always after my job. But Mason is smarter."

"Mason works for a weapons manufacturer, a job my father and Colonel Vance helped him get. Is that a clue?"

"It might be."

"Well, while we ponder that, I'm going to text my team with Paul's number and the information about the bagel shop," she said.

Ryker took out his phone. "I'm going to text Mason again, too."

"Maybe you should be careful what you say. You don't know which side he's on."

"If he is involved, by now he's heard about Paul's injuries and my escape. I'm going to tell him I know what's going on, that Paul told me everything. I'll say I want in. That I've been hurt just as badly as everyone else. I want a payday, too."

Her gut tightened at his words. "He won't believe you. There's a reason they didn't ask you in already. They know who you are. They know you won't do what they're doing."

"Maybe that's not the reason. Maybe it was just that I wasn't responding to their texts."

"I don't think so, Ryker. You wouldn't have joined them in doing something illegal or even in faking the deaths. That's not the kind of man you are. And they know that."

"They knew who I was. I can convince them I've changed."

"It's a bold move," she said, seeing the determination in his eyes.

"I don't know how to move any other way."

His cocky words reminded her of the Ryker from five years ago, and while she appreciated his return, she also worried that this Ryker might be a little too reckless. But she couldn't blame him. Finding out that Paul was alive, that he'd faked his own death, had rattled her, too.

"Done," he said, sending his text. "We'll see if Mason takes the bait."

"Or if he comes back asking you what you're talking about."

"Either way, we'll find out something."

CHAPTER TWENTY

AN HOUR LATER, Ryker was beginning to think his bold move was a big bust. There had been no answer from Mason. Either he hadn't gotten the text, wasn't interested in the offer, wasn't in on the plan, or someone had killed him. The latter idea painted a more sobering picture.

Despite the fact that Paul was miraculously alive, the attacks on himself and Savannah had been very, very real. There had been nothing fake about the explosions or the bullets that had come their way. There was a chance that Paul had escaped whatever danger had been tracking them and had faked his death to stay safe.

"We might be wrong," he said aloud.

Savannah, who had been pacing around the waiting room for the last ten minutes, came back to the couch. "About which part?"

"A team of ghosts. We've been starting to think that everyone is alive, that they all faked their deaths, but the danger to us has been real, right?"

"That's true. If you and I had died last night, there wouldn't have been anything fake about it."

"What if Paul realized he was in danger, and he set up his death so that he could stay safe and protect his family?"

"Interesting point. And if Paul convinced Todd that he was also at risk, that could have started the bigger plan in motion. But if they were faking their deaths, why wouldn't Todd have just done it at the same time as Paul? Why wait and go through the funeral—somehow get his car into the river? It's more complicated."

"Unless two accidental deaths at the same time was too much," he said. "I keep going back to how nervous Todd was at the service. I attributed his agitation and anger to Paul's passing, but it could have been that he knew Paul wasn't dead and seeing the hell his wife and kid were going through was too much. Then Todd decided to disappear himself. Or he really was forced off the road by whoever had been after Paul, and his death was real. Did you follow any of my twisted logic?"

"I followed it all. Unfortunately, until we actually see a dead body, I'm not sure we're going to have an answer."

"We might be able to get at least one answer from Chief Tanner. He responded to Paul's fall. He told Abby not to see her husband. He allegedly got Paul's body through the medical examiner and the mortuary. Did he do all that alone without Todd's help? It seems doubtful. Then he's the one who discovers Todd's body, and I'm betting no one else has seen it but him."

"Tanner does run that town. I think anything is possible." She paused. "I'm so angry with Paul. If he wasn't close to death, I'd want to kill him myself," she said darkly.

He understood exactly where she was coming from, especially because she was so close to Abby. She was feeling her best friend's pain with every breath she took. "He did hurt his wife and child. No doubt about that."

"The trauma that they might have to live through again if he dies could break Abby. And how is Tyler ever going to understand any of this? He's a little boy. His father chose to leave him by faking his death. Now he might die again…this is horrible. Abby is just the sweetest, kindest person on this earth, and I can't stand that she has to deal with this."

"I feel exactly the same way."

"I just want to help her, but I honestly don't know what to do. I can't imagine anything I could say would help her."

"Probably not." He paused. "Did you two become friends when you moved to Dobbs?"

"Yes. She was my thirteen-year-old lifeline. The first day at my new school, I sat next to her in math, and she must have seen my terrified, lost look and decided I was a stray puppy who needed a home. She introduced me to her friends. She invited me over to her house the next day. Abby helped me survive that first year after losing my mom and having to move to a new family. If I hadn't had her, I feel like I would have spiraled out of control."

"I don't think that would have happened," he said quietly. "You are made of steel, Savannah, which doesn't mean you can't also be incredibly soft and caring and have deep, deep emotions, but there's a core of strength in you that makes you a survivor."

She drew in a shaky breath. "That's a very nice thing to say. I just wish I could give Abby some of my strength."

"You will. You'll be there for her the way she was there for you. And it won't be about this one night, it will be about tomorrow and next week and next year. Whatever happens with Paul, she won't lose you."

"No, she won't." She let out a sigh. "I feel so restless. I don't know what to do with myself."

"How about some food? Not more coffee, because you are clearly wired, but we haven't eaten since the chowder hours ago."

"I'm not hungry, but you should go down to the cafeteria and get something."

"Maybe later. I'll hang with you."

She sat down next to him. "One thing I thought was interesting was that the explosion and the gunshots didn't trigger your bells. You jumped into action both times."

"That's a good point," he said thoughtfully. "I didn't have time to think; I just acted. I guess I didn't give my brain a chance to flip out."

"Or your brain wants action and when you take it, it thinks you're going down the right track."

"Are we back to the bells trying to tell me something?"

"I do still believe that."

"You could be right," he conceded. "Maybe the missing clue is stuck in my head."

"Eventually, it will come out."

"It has been nine months."

"But you've been running from the bells. Maybe you have to find a way to stop and listen."

"It's not always bells or noises; sometimes it's light—blinding light—like a flash bang, an explosion, a burst of gunfire."

She stared back at him. "Is that what you saw that night? Blinding light?"

"I don't remember the light, but I remember the gunfire, the explosions, the sight of Carlos falling right in front of me." As soon as he saw the image in his head, a dull beat began to sound in his ears. He wanted to run away. He wanted to block it out. But maybe Savannah was right. He had to stand his ground.

But as a trio of people entered the waiting room, the noises faded. Savannah was on her feet, hugging each one of them. The cavalry had arrived.

And with them, the noise in his head receded.

Savannah introduced him to Parisa first, a beautiful brunette with long dark-brown hair, olive skin, and brown eyes. She'd brought along an overnight bag for Savannah, saying she wasn't sure if she had a change of clothes, but if not, she could at least get through the night with what she'd brought.

Next was Parisa's fiancé Jared MacIntyre. Jared was a stocky guy with rugged features, brown hair, and green eyes. And the third man was Jax Kenin, a tall, blond man, with penetrating blue eyes, who wore a very expensive suit. They looked more like a group of friends than FBI and CIA agents.

But then it was on to business.

Parisa had found a conference room on the second floor for them to gather, so they went downstairs to discuss their next moves. Parisa was bringing in security, working with the hospital and local police to ensure Paul's continuing safety if he made it through surgery. The security would also include Abby and her mother when they arrived. Flynn and someone named Wyatt were checking cameras near the bagel shop and attempting to track the path of Paul's phone over the last few days.

And then Savannah took over, filling the others in on all the information they had so far.

Hearing her lay it all out in a pragmatic, logical fashion wasn't easy. This was just another case for her team, but for him, it was extremely personal. These men they were talking about were his friends, his brothers, men he'd spent years with. At one time, he'd known everything about them. Now they seemed like strangers.

But they were definitely not acting like the men he'd once known. Those men had been loyal, fierce patriots. They'd fought for their country. They'd been heroes.

What were they now? Three more of them were either dead or ghosts, and Mason was still a question mark.

As the discussion continued, he could see that the team was starting to buy into the idea that all the men had become ghosts to carry out some plan that Paul had finally realized was a lie. They were putting a lot of stock into the pain-addled comment that had come out of his mouth. With that assumption came the idea that these men were planning to do something so bad that they'd had to leave their families, their friends, their homes and become ghosts in order to do it. Since they were all very well-trained soldiers, that plan could be horrifically bad. Unfortunately, while there were a lot of wild theories, they really had no idea what the men might be thinking, and it bothered him that he couldn't figure it out. Because he knew them the best. He should be able to get inside their heads and see the plan.

But he was still at a loss. Maybe it was good there were more people involved now, people who would not be swayed by emotion and personal history. He had to admit he was impressed with the speed and dedication at which Savannah's team had jumped in. They were covering all the angles, throwing out possible scenarios and then examining those possibilities with sharp precision. Jared was even texting back and forth with a CIA source who was trying to get information on the ambush. And then there was Jax.

Jax had taken a secondary role in the meeting, but he had the sharp, watchful gaze of a man who didn't miss a thing. In fact, Jax had given him quite an assessing look, as if he wasn't quite sure he was a victim or if he had some hidden agenda. He didn't know if he looked suspicious or if Jax was being protective toward Savannah. Savannah seemed to share a closer bond with Jax than the other two. He wondered if they'd ever been more than friends and partners. Not that it was his business. Savannah had a history that didn't include him. He had a history that didn't include her.

But they also had history together. Even more importantly, they had a present. He could hardly believe how fast things had changed since they'd made love on the boat. They should have had more than two hours together. They should have had at least the night or a few more days, several more weeks, maybe longer…

He sucked in a breath as he realized there might not be another moment. And if that were the case, he should have taken more time. He should have memorized her face. He should have breathed in her scent. He should have made her laugh or cry out with pleasure more times than he had. There should have been more of everything.

But he couldn't go back in time.

He'd told himself the same thing the last time he'd woken up alone.

They were still together now, but the distance was already growing between them, and he didn't know how to bridge it, or even if he should bridge it. He'd almost gotten her killed a couple of times. She was safer now that there were others involved.

"Jared and I will go back to DC now," Parisa said, drawing his attention back to their conversation. "Jax will hang here with you until you can leave."

"We don't need a bodyguard," he said sharply.

Jax flung him a short look. "Considering you both almost died, I'd say you need someone watching your backs."

Jax might be right, but he didn't want this man taking the job of watching Savannah's back. Since he couldn't say that, he decided to take a minute. "I'm going to get some coffee," he said, getting to his feet. He didn't really need coffee, but he did need some space.

It wasn't just that he needed to wrap his head around the information Jared had provided, it was also that he needed to find a way to tamp down the unexpected jealous anger brewing inside him.

***

"What's his problem?" Jax asked as Ryker left the room.

Savannah was surprised by Ryker's abrupt exit, and the anger she'd seen in his eyes. "He has a lot to deal with," she murmured. "There's a good chance one of his best friends just tried to kill him."

"And you," Jax put in.

"Ryker saved my life. And not just tonight, earlier, too. His instincts are good."

"But he is the odd man out," Parisa said. "If there's a plan, he's not in on it, which is odd, since he was the leader of the team."

"Ryker would never do anything illegal or anything that would betray his country, so if that's the plan, it makes sense that they left him out. Todd told him right before he allegedly died that they didn't speak the same language anymore, that they weren't on the same page. In retrospect, I think he took that one last opportunity at the funeral to make sure that Ryker should be left out. Todd ranted about the army, about how they deserved more than they'd gotten, how they were shadows of their former selves. He wanted more than a thank-you for your service. But Ryker told him that that's not why any of them joined. It was never about a reward. It was always about fighting for their country."

"So, now they want to kill him?" Jax asked, a doubtful gleam in his eyes.

"Paul didn't want to kill him. As I told you, he tried to save us, but they took him out instead. He thought there was just a plan to scare Ryker away, probably because we were going around town asking a lot of questions."

"They have to be worried now about what Paul will say when he wakes up," Jared interjected.

"That's why we have to keep him safe."

"We will," Parisa promised. "Jared and I will head back. With any luck, we can find the bagel shop and wherever these guys have been hiding out. Although, it's doubtful we'll get to speak to anyone tonight. But first thing in the morning, we're on it."

"And since you don't need a babysitter," Jax said with a smile, "I'll head down to Dobbs later tonight. Tomorrow, I'll talk to the chief there, go by the morgue and the mortuary and see how this fake death might have occurred."

"Chief Tanner won't crack easily," she said.

"I'm not worried," Jax said with complete confidence.

"I really appreciate the help," she said, her gaze encompassing all of them. "But I don't want any of you to jeopardize your own work for me. Parisa, if there's a conflict with your office—"

"Don't worry," Parisa said, cutting her off. "I already spoke to my boss. He's agreed to let me help. Apparently, Flynn's reputation has once again preceded him. I made it sound like this was for Flynn's unit, which it actually is now, so it's all good."

"And I'm happy to help off book," Jared added, giving her a smile. "Parisa misses working with you guys, and since that's because I'm holding her hostage in DC, it's the least I can do."

Parisa put her arm around Jared's waist. "You're not holding me hostage. I'm where I want to be."

"But still…" he said, giving her a knowing smile.

"It is nice to be back in the loop," Parisa admitted.

"Well, your assistance is invaluable," she said, giving them both a hug before they left.

As they departed, Jax stayed behind. "What's his deal, Savannah?"

"Are you talking about Ryker again?" she asked, not sure she liked the gleam in Jax's blue eyes.

"Yeah. What's he to you?"

"He's a friend of Paul's, and I'm a friend of Paul's wife. That's how we started working on this together. I thought I explained all that."

"You did, but it's a load of crap. That man wants you. He didn't leave to get coffee. He left because he was pissed off at me for wanting to stay with you. So, what's really going on?"

"Nothing."

"Savannah, come on. You know what I do. I watch and I listen. There was a lot going on between you and Stone that was not being spoken aloud."

She could see that her story was quickly falling apart, so she opted for the truth. "We met five years ago. We had a one-night stand. I didn't know who he was. He didn't know who I was. It was before I joined the FBI."

"And the first time you saw him again—"

"Was at the funeral. I had learned by then he was in Paul's unit, but our paths had never crossed."

"Hell of a way to reunite. And now? What's going on?"

"We've gotten closer," she admitted. "How could we not? We've been tied together the last couple of days. When this is over, he'll go his way and I'll go mine. No regrets."

"You sure about that?"

"Pretty sure. My job is on the other side of the country."

"What about his job? He's a fisherman, isn't he? We have fish in California."

She shrugged. "We're not making plans. And I don't think he left because he was jealous of you, Jax. He's dealing with the betrayal of his friends and that's rough."

"It is rough. But at least one of his friends didn't betray him. He saved him—and you."

"I'm relieved that Paul didn't go completely bad. I always liked him. And my friend loves him. I don't want him to have done anything really horrible. I hope he hasn't, but I don't know."

"We'll get answers."

"Flynn told you to stay and help me, didn't he?"

"He didn't have to tell me. As soon as I heard what was going on, I volunteered." He paused. "I have to admit I kind of like that Stone is jealous of me."

"He is not jealous of you. And you have never been interested in me."

"Only because I don't like to get in line."

"Very funny. But getting back to business, what do you think about all this, Jax? You have fantastic instincts. And you're objective."

"It's complicated," he said, a serious note in his voice. "These guys have gone to a lot of trouble to disappear. Whatever they're up to must have a big payoff." He paused. "I'm going to need some food before I find my way to Georgia. Why don't you join me in the cafeteria? I'm starving. You must be hungry, too."

She laughed. For a man with not an ounce of fat, Jax could eat like no one else. "You are always hungry, Jax."

"Food fuels the mind. You should remember that."

"I need to find Ryker first." She paused, wondering if she should tell Jax about Ryker's issues with noise.

Jax gave her a thoughtful look. "Something you want to tell me about Stone before we meet up with him?"

She debated one more second and then said, "No. We're good. Let's find him and then we'll get some food."

CHAPTER TWENTY-ONE

RYKER DIDN'T FEEL MUCH like eating but after Savannah and Jax had tracked him down in the waiting room, he'd felt compelled to join them in the cafeteria. He'd managed a few bites of turkey chili, but the thought of anything else turned his stomach. The longer the surgery took, the more he worried that Paul would never wake up, that he'd die for real this time. He couldn't stand that thought. Not just because what he knew would die with him, but because he'd be gone, and that wasn't right.

He didn't know what Paul and the others were up to, and maybe he shouldn't feel one ounce of sympathy or worry for them, especially since at least one of them had wanted him dead. But until he knew who was behind the attacks on him and Savannah, he had to hope it wasn't one of his guys, that it was someone else, someone who didn't know him personally, who hadn't been such an important person in his life.

"Ryker?"

Savannah's voice finally penetrated. He saw both her and Jax giving him quizzical looks.

"Sorry? What did you ask me?"

He could see that she wanted to ask him if he was all right, but she was trying very hard not to do that. "I'm fine, just thinking," he told her.

"I'm going to get some ice cream," Jax said. "Anyone need anything?"

He shook his head.

"No, thanks," Savannah said.

Once Jax had left the table, he added, "The bells are quiet. You don't have to worry."

"I'm glad. What are you thinking about?"

"Everything," he said with a shrug.

"The surgery should be over soon."

"It will probably be tomorrow before we can talk to him."

"At least we'll know if he's going to make it until tomorrow."

"That's true."

She licked her lips, giving him a hesitant look. Then she said, "Does Jax bother you?"

"No. Why?"

"You haven't had much to say since he got here."

"I don't think we need a babysitter, but he's your friend and coworker, so if he wants to make sure you're protected, I have nothing to say. I'm sure you feel safer with him here."

"Really?" she asked. "That's what you have to say?"

"What?" he challenged.

"Why don't you like him? You don't even know him."

"Who said I don't like him?"

"I'm saying it now."

"He's fine. Can we drop it?"

"Yes," she said. "But just for the record, we don't need a babysitter, and Jax is heading down to Dobbs later tonight."

"Oh."

"He's going to shake down Tanner and see what else he can find out. We need someone to do that."

"We do." His gaze moved over to the ice cream station where Jax was making a hell of a sundae. "Did you two ever hook up?" The question came out before he could stop it. "Forget it. You don't have to answer that."

"I know I don't," she said, drawing his attention back to her. "But I will. No. We've never been anything but friends. Jax is not my type, and I'm not his."

"Are you kidding me, Savannah? You are every man's type."

"Well, I'll take that as a compliment but my answer still stands. Not that you had a right to ask the question."

"That's why I said you didn't have to answer it."

"I wanted to be honest with you. It's the way I live my life now. No more pretending. No more lies. So, if I say something, you should believe me."

"All right. I believe you."

She flashed him her high-voltage smile, and his body warmed more than a few degrees. He couldn't imagine how cold his life would be without that smile in it.

"I like you being jealous," she said.

"I wasn't jealous."

"Yes, you were." As she finished speaking, her gaze moved to her phone, where she'd just received a text. Her smile disappeared. "Abby is on her way upstairs to the waiting room."

She stood up and motioned to Jax, who hurried across the room.

"What's up?" he asked.

"My friend has arrived."

"Let's go," he said, taking the bowl of ice cream topped with whipped cream, nuts, and chocolate sauce into the elevator with them.

By the time the doors opened, he was halfway done, but as Savannah ran down the hall to embrace a bewildered and terrified Abby, Jax hung back, and so did Ryker. Abby and Savannah needed this moment to themselves.

"I can't imagine what that woman is going through," Jax murmured. "She buries her husband and then finds out he's alive, but he might be dying. That's a hellish roller coaster to be on."

"It amazes me that Paul would have done that to her. Todd didn't have any family left, just a mother with Alzheimer's, who doesn't know who he is anymore. But Paul had Abby and a son. He had a life that he chose to give up, and for what?"

"Cash? Revenge?"

"Neither motivation seems worth it. I know Paul was in a lot of debt. He must have felt that he was better for Abby dead than alive, but I still don't understand how he could do that to her. It was unbelievably cruel, and he wasn't a cruel man. But he was injured on our last mission, and he had nerve damage in his arm. He couldn't continue to serve. And he didn't know what to do next. At least, that's what Todd told me. I haven't actually heard Paul's side of the story." He paused. "I could have heard it, but I didn't keep in touch with anyone. Maybe if I had, I could have stopped this."

"It doesn't sound like they wanted to give you that chance." Jax tossed his empty ice cream container into a nearby trash can. "By the way, I'm not interested in Savannah, just in case you were wondering."

"I wasn't," he lied, realizing that his poker face was apparently nowhere as good as it used to be.

Jax gave him a knowing look. "Something you might want to know about me, Stone. I see everything."

"You think very highly of yourself."

He laughed. "Guilty. But I'm good at what I do. I don't pretend otherwise."

He used to be a lot like Jax, and for the first time, he actually started to like the guy.

"This looks like our security team," Jax added, moving toward two men in uniform who were coming down the hall.

Leaving Jax to deal with that, he went to join Abby and Savannah in the waiting room.

———————

Abby finally let go of her and sank into a nearby chair. Savannah was happy that they had the waiting room to themselves. But then, it was almost ten and most surgeries were probably done for the day. Paul's surgery was now past the three-hour mark. She couldn't imagine what was taking so long. But she hoped it was a good sign that it was still going. That had to mean he was still alive.

She took the seat next to Abby as Ryker entered the room. He sat down across from them, resting his arms on his legs.

"Why would he do this, Ryker?" Abby asked. "Why would Paul fake his death?"

"We're going to need him to tell us that," Ryker answered.

"If he wakes up," Abby said darkly.

"When he wakes up," she corrected. "Don't give up, Abby."

"Give up? I don't even know how I feel. All the way down here, I felt like I was in a dream, that none of this could possibly be real."

"How did you get here so fast?" she asked.

"My dad's friend is a pilot for a charter service. He flew me here. First time I've ever been in a private plane, but I couldn't enjoy it. I spent most of the trip crying or trying not to cry."

"I thought you were bringing your mom."

"I did. She's downstairs. She wanted to get something from the cafeteria before it closes."

"We were just there. I'm surprised I didn't see her."

"You must have just missed her. Do you have any idea what Paul has been up to, where he's been living, how he'd been living?" Abby asked. "He doesn't have any credit cards or money. Is he on the street?"

"We're trying to figure that out, but it looks like he's been in DC the past few days."

"What about Todd? Is he alive, too?"

She'd been expecting that question. "We don't have evidence that he is, but it's possible."

"Chief Tanner told me they found Todd's body. I believed him. But I also believed him when he told me Paul was dead. Why would he lie? He's the chief of police. He has known me my whole life. He plays cards with my dad. How could he do this?"

She wished she had an answer, but all she could do was offer an unhelpful shrug.

"Chief Tanner can't just break the law like this," Abby continued.

"Who would turn him in?" Ryker interjected. "He controls the investigation. He must have also had someone at the morgue and mortuary working with him."

"More people who lied to my face," Abby said bitterly. "I want to scream at each and every one of them. Tell me again what Paul said tonight when you saw him."

"He said he was sorry," Savannah replied. "That he thought what he'd done would be better for you in the long run."

"How could he think that?"

"Maybe he thought the insurance money would make your life easier." She stopped abruptly, remembering something else Abby had told her. "The other day you said something about a veteran's fund that might pay you additional money. Do you have that information?"

"It's in my email. Why?"

"I'm curious where that money comes from."

"Well, I haven't gotten any of it yet. I haven't even had time to fill out the form. Now that Paul is alive, I'm sure I won't be getting anything. And if he dies today, maybe the insurance won't come either, because of the suspicious circumstances. Not that I care about the money. I mean, I have to care a little, because I have to support Tyler. But I really just want Paul to wake up and tell me that everything will be all right. He has to do that, Savannah. He has to."

Every word tore at her heart. "He will," she said, hoping she wasn't lying.

"I need to use the restroom. Is there one nearby?" Abby asked.

"Across the hall. I'll come with you."

"Just give me a minute. I need to be alone."

As Abby left the waiting room, she let out a breath, turning to Ryker. "This is killing me. She's in so much pain. And even if Paul wakes up, I don't know that they can ever have what they had."

"It seems unlikely," he said quietly. "But at least he won't be dead. And she'll know the truth, whatever it is."

"I don't know how she'll explain it to Tyler." She drew in a breath and slowly let it out. "That fund that Abby was talking about bothers me. I've been wondering how Paul's death could benefit her besides the life insurance, and I'm wondering if that special fund is somehow a part of this. I need to get that information from her."

"That would make sense. There has to be some payoff. But she's right. With everything that's going on, if Paul dies now, her circumstances could be even worse. The life insurance will get held up. There will be an investigation."

"It will be a huge mess," she agreed.

Jax stepped back into the room, and they both stood up.

"The security team is here," Jax said. "I have a man stationed outside the operating room. He'll stay with Paul wherever he goes next. The other security guard will stay with Abby. He's outside the restroom as we speak. He'll stay with Abby while she's here in the hospital. Parisa also arranged for a room at the hotel across the street if Abby and her mother want to get some rest, the guard will accompany them whenever they're ready to go.

"Parisa thinks of everything."

"She's very good that way," he agreed. "I'm going to take off, unless you need anything else."

"No, we're good."

"I'll let you know what I find out in Dobbs. It's going to be interesting to see your hometown."

"Trust me, it will be anything but interesting."

He smiled. "Somehow, I doubt that."

Jax had no sooner left when Abby returned, and her mom was now with her. Jeanette set down a plastic grocery bag and opened her arms to Savannah.

She was touched by the gesture and gave her a hug. Jeanette had always made her feel a part of their family.

"Thank you for doing all this, Savannah," Jeanette said. "You've always been a good friend to Abby."

Guilt ran through her at that comment. She didn't think she'd been a very good friend at all, but hopefully she was making up for it now. Before she could say anything, a man in scrubs walked into the room.

"You're all here for Mr. Hawkins?" he asked.

"I'm his wife," Abby said.

"I'm Dr. Nicholson. I operated on your husband. The carotid artery was nicked by a bullet. It took some time to repair it."

"But you did?" Abby asked. "Does that mean Paul will be all right?"

"We're cautiously optimistic. He's stable, but his condition is still critical. He lost a lot of blood. We'll know more tomorrow. He's going to be sleeping for hours. You should all get some rest. We won't know any more tonight."

"When can I see him?" Abby asked.

"Tomorrow," the doctor replied.

"I can't just sit with him now?" she begged.

The doctor hesitated. "All right. You can see him for a few minutes. The nurse will take you to him shortly."

"Thank you," Abby said. "For saving his life."

The doctor gave them a brief smile and then left the room.

"He's alive," Abby said, the tears spilling out of her eyes. She crossed the room and gave Savannah another long hug. Then she turned to her mother, and they embraced as they cried.

Savannah's gaze moved to Ryker. He hadn't said a word, but she could see the relief in his eyes. There was still anger there, too, but Paul had saved their lives, and that meant something.

"Abby," she said, as her friend pulled out a tissue and blew her nose. "I hate to leave you, but I need to get to DC. I need to find out what's going on."

"Don't you want to stay and ask Paul?"

"He won't be awake until tomorrow. There are things I need to do before then. There's a hotel across the street where you can spend the night. We have a security guard who will stay with you here at the hospital and will accompany you to the hotel when you're ready to go."

"That's the guy outside?"

"Yes."

"Why do we need security?"

"I don't know. I just want you to have it. Paul will also have security. He'll never be alone."

"I hate that any of us needs this," Abby said. "But thank you. And you should go, Savannah. Find out what Paul has been up to and how we can fix it."

She nodded, really hoping they could fix it.

CHAPTER TWENTY-TWO

THEY ARRIVED in DC around midnight. Parisa had texted them on the way that there were two Bagel Mania cafés in the city, and they were still trying to open Paul's phone to see if they could narrow down a location. They decided to split up in the morning and each take one of the cafés. Parisa and Jared would visit the one in Georgetown, that was near their townhouse, and she and Ryker would hit up the other one, which was located in Logan Circle.

They found a hotel about a mile away from the bagel shop with a secure underground parking garage. They had been vigilant on the drive from Chesapeake Beach, especially once they'd gotten into DC, doing everything to ensure they were not being followed.

When they got to their room, Savannah put the overnight bag that Parisa had thoughtfully packed for her on the dresser and then moved to the window to close the curtains. She paused in front of the glass for a moment, looking at all the bright city lights.

Ryker came up behind her, sliding his arms around her waist, and pulling her back against his chest. With his strong, warm embrace, she felt the tension seep out of her.

"What are you thinking?" he murmured. "You haven't said much the last hour."

"Right now, I'm thinking about how many views we've seen

today. We've been all over; Hank's gym, Spear Enterprises, the boat, the beautiful bay, and now we're back here. So much has happened. My head is spinning." She turned in his arms to face him. "But I have to say that out of all the views I've had today, this is the best one."

He gave her a smile. "I would have to agree. But it's after midnight now, so it's actually a new day."

"We need to be ready for it."

"We will be. Failure is not an option. I'm going to find out what my team is up to, and I'm going to stop them."

She liked the steel glint of determination in his brown eyes. "We're going to stop them," she corrected.

"That's right—we. And your team will help."

"They will. We can count on them."

And just like that, his smile dimmed. "I used to feel that way about my guys." He cleared his throat. "But I'm not going to think about the way we used to be. It's all about the present and the future. Did Parisa pack you something to wear to bed? Otherwise, you can have one of my shirts?" He waved his hand toward his duffel bag.

"That's a nice offer. I'm sure Parisa packed something for me."

"Good. I want you to be comfortable."

She gazed into his eyes. "What if I just wear you instead?"

Sparkling lights of desire filled his gaze. "Even better. But I know you're tired, Savannah. We can just…sleep."

"I'm exhausted but also wired. And, to be honest, after we almost died earlier, I had this thought that I can't seem to let go of."

"What's that?"

"I didn't want the last time we were together to be the last time."

"I was thinking the same thing," he murmured.

"So, it won't be the last time."

She put her hands on either side of his face, feeling the stubble of his beard under her hands, loving the way the waves of his hair fell over his brow. His lips parted and she could feel his warm breath and that little bit of heat spread all the way through her.

"Are you going to kiss me any time soon?" he teased.

"I'm getting to it. I like looking at you, Ryker."

"I like looking at you. But I love doing more than looking."

She pressed onto her toes and gave him the kiss they both wanted. It set off the explosive sparks it always did, which made it really difficult to go as slow as she wanted. But she had this feeling down deep in her gut that this time might be the last time, and she wanted to remember every second of it.

So she fought the feelings of impatience and need and took her time tasting his mouth, molding her body to his, letting the anticipation build higher and hotter.

But Ryker wasn't on the same page, his eager hands running up under her top, his mouth demanding more. She might have been able to resist his mouth, his hands, but when he lifted his head, when he looked into her eyes, when he said, "Savannah," in a husky, rough voice, her heart melted. And when he added, "I need you," she was completely lost.

"I need you, too," she admitted. "It's scary."

"Terrifying," he murmured. "I'll protect you if you protect me."

It was the most honest, most vulnerable, most amazing thing he could have said to her. He'd made them equal. He'd respected her in a way no one else had. She did the only thing she could do—she pushed him toward the bed. When the back of his legs hit the mattress, he sat down, and she moved onto his lap, straddling his legs, taking another long, deep kiss.

And then he shifted, tossing her onto her back, pulling up her shirt, and pressing his mouth against her stomach, lighting every nerve on fire. Then he lifted his head and said, "You're going to remember this."

"So are you," she said with a promising smile.

He grinned, then undid the button on her jeans and slid them down her hips, taking her panties along with them.

They made love twice, which was the number of condoms he had in his bag. He really should have brought more, Ryker thought as he held Savannah in his arms, Thursday morning, watching the light break through the slit in the curtains. It had been a great night. They hadn't gotten a lot of sleep, but he wasn't complaining. They'd made every touch, every kiss, every time they'd lost themselves in each other completely memorable. He wasn't worried about forgetting anything about her anymore.

He was now more concerned with not being able to forget her. In the crazy world that he was living in, Savannah had become an island of truth in a sea of lies. He trusted her. She might be the only one he could trust.

His mind drifted to Paul, to the moment when Paul had looked into his eyes and said he wasn't supposed to get hurt. That he would have never fallen for the lie.

What was the lie? What had made Paul do what he'd done?

It had to be a huge lie, an incredible but obviously believable fabrication.

And Paul had thought his wife and kid would be better because of the lie.

What about the other guys?

Did they know someone had gone to Chesapeake Beach to kill him? Or, like Paul, had they thought someone was just going to scare him? Scare him away from what? Investigating? Searching for the truth? Had his questions to Mason and Hank worried someone—perhaps even one of them?

He wanted to believe that if Todd or Hank or Mason had known he was going to die that they also would have stepped in and tried to stop it. But Paul had been alone.

The buzzing of a phone took his gaze to the nightstand. It was Savannah's burner phone that was vibrating. He was about to give her a nudge when she woke up, her eyes flying open, as she rolled out of his arms. Her long blonde hair tumbled down her bare back as she reached for the phone.

"Hello?" she said, her voice breathless. She listened for a moment and then said, "What? All right. I guess I shouldn't be surprised." She paused. "I'll ask Ryker and text it to you."

She set down her phone and turned toward him, giving him a sleepy look as she ran her fingers through her tangled hair. "That was Parisa. They checked all the hospitals in the DC area and talked to the police near Larimer Square where Hank was allegedly struck by a car."

"But there's no evidence that that happened. He's not dead, either."

"It doesn't appear so." She paused. "By the way, good morning."

He smiled, loving the look of her in his bed. "This is what I missed the first time we were together."

"A phone call from an FBI agent?" she teased.

"A beautiful woman tangled up in my sheets."

She scooted forward and gave him a kiss. Then she said, "I didn't actually miss this sight. I gave you a long, long look before I left that morning. But this is better."

"I'll say." He kissed her again, wishing they had more time, but the room was getting brighter by the minute.

She gave him a helpless look as she sat back. "I'd love to keep this going, but..."

"We need to get to the bagel shop."

"Yes." She slid out of bed, then hesitated. "We could shower together, save time."

He grinned. "Do you really think that will save time?"

"No, but it will be fun, and it might be our last chance for a while to have some fun."

"Say no more. I'm in, and I know just what to do to relieve that stress." He scrambled out of bed and proceeded to show her exactly what he meant.

CHAPTER TWENTY-THREE

RYKER WAS DISAPPOINTED to see a long line when they arrived at Bagel Mania a little before eight. The café offered up sixteen varieties of bagels as well as bagel breakfast sandwiches and a wide assortment of spreads. There was also coffee, tea and cold-pressed juices. A half-dozen small tables filled the room in front of the counter, with additional tables outside. But since it was February in DC, those tables were empty. The sun was out, but the temperature was still in the forties.

He shifted his feet restlessly as they waited their turn, keeping his eye on the door and also the sidewalk outside the café. He wanted to be alert just in case one of his other teammates decided to get a bagel for breakfast. He doubted Hank would eat anything but a protein bar, if that. He was probably fasting until noon and then downing a vegetable smoothie. The man was insane about fitness.

Todd would be a good candidate for a bagel, though. He'd always had a weakness for food. When they'd been stuck in the desert for days on end, he'd literally dreamed about chocolate bars and triple-decker chili burgers. And then he'd felt compelled to talk about food for hours on end until they'd told him they were going to make him eat some dirt if he didn't shut up.

As he thought about Todd, he couldn't help wondering if Todd knew about the attack on him, if he had any idea what had happened to Paul. The shooter hadn't stuck around to assess Paul's condition, but he might have been able to get information from the hospital or one of the first responders. *But would the shooter relay that information to the rest of the team?* He would, only if they were in on it, too, if they were on the same page as him. He was really hoping for some dissension in the ranks. But these guys were military men. They followed orders. If they'd pledged loyalty to a leader, it would take a lot for them to abandon that person.

His gaze swept the café once more, then settled on Savannah. "You look beautiful today, Savannah. In case I don't get a chance to tell you that later."

She flushed at his words. "Parisa put some expensive makeup in the bag."

"It's not the makeup."

"Well, thank you. You don't look so bad yourself. I wish we could have just had the day together to get some bagels, go for a walk, hit up a museum, take a bike ride…"

"Is that your idea of a perfect day?"

"I don't know about perfect, but it sounds nice, doesn't it?"

"It does. Although, I'm not really a museum guy."

"Really? Museums are wonderful. I love wandering around centuries-old art and thinking about the people who made it, who lived in that time. I'm a little bit of a history buff."

"It sounds like it." He couldn't help thinking that the more he got to know Savannah, the more he appreciated how unique and individual she was.

"Looks like we're next," she said, as the line moved. "I'm going to order breakfast sandwiches along with information."

"Get me two. And coffee as well."

Savannah stepped up to the counter and gave the teenage boy with the glasses and bad case of acne a smile that probably blinded him. His jaw literally dropped open, and Ryker bit back a grin. He knew exactly how that kid felt.

After Savannah finished ordering and handed her credit card to the boy, she also showed him her badge, and then pulled out her phone and showed him a photo of Paul. "Have you seen this man?"

"Uh, yeah, sure. He's been coming in every day the last couple of days," the kid said. "Always gets a bunch of bagels and coffees."

"Does he ever come in with anyone else?"

"No. Why? What did he do?"

"Do you think he lives around here?"

"I don't know. Probably."

"You ever talk to him?" Ryker interjected. "Did he tell you his name?"

"I just sell him bagels."

"Thanks," Savannah said. They slid down the counter toward the pick-up window.

"At least we know this is the right bagel shop," he said.

"And we know Paul was always buying more bagels and coffees than he could eat or drink himself. Whoever he is working with has to be nearby, Ryker."

"That narrows it down, but maybe not enough."

"I'll let Parisa know that it's this shop. After we eat, we can walk around the neighborhood."

He nodded, his gaze moving back to the window. There was an apartment building directly across the street. "We can start there."

She nodded. "We'll check out all the possibilities. There was also a motel down the street. I noticed it when we were looking for parking. That's a better bet for a hideout. They could probably pay in cash. No trail."

"Good point."

When their order was up, Savannah showed Paul's photo to the female server.

"Sure, I've seen him," she said. "He always orders extra spreads. He didn't come in today, though. Maybe he left town."

He frowned at the server's words. "Did he say he might be leaving town?"

"He said DC was too cold for him. He couldn't wait to get

somewhere warmer. I guess I assumed he was going somewhere. I didn't ask."

"Thanks," he said.

They took their food to a nearby table and sat down.

"Paul picked a good place to eat," Savannah said, biting into her scrambled egg bagel with green onions and cheddar cheese. "This is delicious."

"You know who always orders extra cream cheese—Todd."

She met his gaze. "It would make sense they were together. Hank, too, probably. Perhaps Mason."

"I still haven't heard a word from Mason," he said, as he ate his bagel and washed each bite down with a swig of coffee.

"I don't think you will, Ryker."

"We still don't know if he's involved. He's supposed to have surgery today. That doesn't sound like a man who's caught up in some big plan, does it?"

"Maybe not. I know you don't want him to be involved, but his silence is damning."

She was right. Maybe he was just sticking his head in the sand, desperate to find one man on his team who didn't want to kill him or fake their death. But it was time to stop speculating and get on with finding some answers. He finished the last of his coffee. "Let's go."

His truck was parked down the street, in the direction of the motel that Savannah had noticed earlier. Along the way, he scanned the block for a familiar face. To his utter shock, he finally found one. Todd came out of a newsstand with a pack of cigarettes in his hand. "There he is."

"I see him," Savannah said.

Todd had stopped walking, his head down as he paused to light his cigarette.

"I'm going to cross the street and come up behind him," she murmured. "Just in case he runs."

He barely heard her. He was completely focused on Todd. He slowly crept forward and was about twenty feet away when Todd looked up and saw him. Todd froze, then tossed his cigarette on the ground and took off running in the other direction.

He ran after him, wishing his knee was a hundred percent, but he was determined not to let Todd get away. Ignoring the pain in his leg, he sprinted down the street. He didn't know where Savannah had gone, but maybe she could cut him off.

Todd made an abrupt turn, dashing through the alley between two buildings.

He followed, picking up the pace as Todd paused to throw a couple of trash cans out of his way, allowing him to close the gap between them.

With one last extra burst of speed, he tackled Todd, throwing him to the ground.

Todd scrambled away, taking a swing at his face. He ducked, and Todd's fist only landed a glancing blow. He swung left, then right, connecting to Todd's cheekbone, his shoulder. Then he shoved him back against the wall. Todd's head bounced off the stucco, and he gave him a dazed look.

Ryker pulled the gun out from under his jacket. "Don't move."

Todd stared back at him, his left hand moving toward his waistband.

"Don't do it," Ryker warned.

"You won't shoot me," Todd said, but there was doubt in his voice.

"He might not, but I will," Savannah said, coming from the opposite direction, her gun trained on Todd.

"Take out your weapon and put it on the ground and kick it over here," Ryker ordered.

"You don't understand what's going on," Todd said.

"Do what I said."

Todd hesitated, then took out his gun, dropped it on the ground and kicked it in his direction. "It's not what you think," he said.

"You don't have any idea what I think. I know you faked your death, as did Paul. Why?"

"Money," Todd said shortly. "My mother needs better care than

I can afford. The job I had wasn't cutting it. Paul was having the same struggles."

"So how are you going to get money? What's the plan?"

"How do you know about Paul?" Todd asked.

Seeing the question in his eyes, Ryker knew that Todd had no idea what had happened last night. "I saw him last night," he said. "Right after someone blew up my car and tried to kill me. Paul stepped in front of a bullet, by the way. He's fighting for his life in a hospital in Chesapeake Beach."

Todd turned white. "That's not true."

"Trying to pretend you don't know someone wanted to kill me?" he asked scornfully. "Or did you also think I was just supposed to be scared off? How the fuck could you believe I'd ever be scared off? Do you not know me at all?"

"I swear I didn't know anyone was trying to kill you. I didn't. You've just been asking so many questions everywhere. We had to find a way to slow you down. We were just going to scare you."

"Well, Paul knew it would be more than that. He saved me. But he might not make it, Todd. He might actually die this time."

Todd swallowed hard.

"By the way, Abby is with him," Ryker continued. "She's wondering how her dead husband could be dying again. You might want to think about the very special hell she's going through right now."

Todd immediately shook his head, disbelief in his eyes. "No way!"

"It's true. And before he passed out, Paul told me that he found out someone was trying to kill me. He said he was sorry that he had believed the lie. What's the lie, Todd?"

"You could be lying right now. Paul could be fine."

"He's not fine, but, hopefully, he will live. And if he does, he will talk. Because he knows what he did was wrong. It's over, Todd. Whatever you're involved in won't work. You have one chance to save yourself, and that opportunity is now. I know you're not the ringleader. This is not your plan. Do you really want to go down for it?"

"The team goes down together," Todd said dully, repeating the mantra they'd all lived by.

"The team isn't together. Not without me. I'm the leader. Why did you leave me out?"

"You abandoned everyone."

"You can be pissed off about that. But I didn't try to kill anyone. I didn't fake my own death. I didn't hurt everyone around me. Tell me what's going on."

"We just wanted to take care of the families. Carlos's wife and his four kids are struggling. Hank's stepsister has special needs. Paul was going to have to declare bankruptcy. He and Abby were losing their house. My mother will have to be moved into this awful place run by the county, because I can't pay for the facility where she is. I can't let that happen to her. She may not know me, but I know her. I'm her son. I have to take care of her the way she took care of me, and I can't earn enough money to do that."

He tried not to be taken in by Todd's noble words, although some of them rang very true. "How are you getting the money?" he asked.

Todd stared back at him, a plea in his gaze. "It can still work, Ryker. You just have to walk away and let it happen. Don't you want everyone to be all right?"

"At what cost? And I don't believe it's just about money. Someone tried to kill me and Savannah. That wasn't for the families. Who's running the show? Is it Hank? Mason? Someone else?"

"Hank was just supposed to scare you. That was it," Todd said, desperate to believe in the lie he was telling himself.

"You should tell Paul that when he wakes up. The bullet tore into his carotid artery. He could have bled out on the street if we hadn't been there. Even if he survives, he'll have a hellish recovery. He may never be the man he was. Now tell me what's going on."

"Why should I?"

"Because maybe I can help you. But you have one second to decide."

Todd finally blew out a breath of defeat. "We're going to intercept a truck filled with weapons, and we're going to sell them."

"To our enemies? How can you do that? How can you betray your country like that?" He was beginning to wonder if he'd ever known any of the men in his unit.

"No. No," Todd said more strongly. "We're going to sell them back to the company we steal them from—Spear. They'll have to buy them back or risk their weapons ending up in the wrong hands. And if they don't want to pay, we'll threaten to leak that the weapons were stolen. Then they'll lose their government contracts. The company will be destroyed. They won't let that happen, so they'll pay up. We'll have enough cash to take care of everyone. We've already set up a fund. As soon as we get the money, it will go in there. It will be a win for everyone. And the military will still get their guns." Todd paused. "Come on, Ryker, you have to admit it's a brilliant plan. We're only taking what's ours. Carlos and Leo died because those rebels had our guns, our explosives. Why shouldn't we take care of the people they left behind?"

He felt a little relief that they weren't planning to sell the weapons to terrorists, but what they were doing was still wrong. He also didn't think Todd had the whole story. "Paul said it's a lie. Are you sure it's going down the way you say?"

"Yes," Todd said, but he didn't sound quite as confident as he had earlier.

"Where are the others? Where is Mason?"

"He's in surgery. It was part of his cover. He couldn't be at Spear today."

His heart sank as he realized Mason was involved, too, and that their entire conversation the day before had been a lie. Hell, Mason was probably the one who had sent Hank to kill him. He had to be the brains of this operation.

"That's why Mason got the job at Spear," he said, as more pieces of the puzzle fell into place. "He wanted access to security, to shipping, to everything. When's the intercept happening?"

"This afternoon. We're waiting for an exact time."

"Waiting to hear from who? You just said Mason is in surgery."

"Hank is driving the truck. He's at Spear now."

They'd thought of almost everything. Except they probably

hadn't counted on Todd to stumble into him and tell all. Which brought up another question. "Why are you alone, Todd? Are you sure you're still in this?"

"Of course I am. Why would you ask that?"

"Because things are changing fast, and you don't seem to be in the loop."

"Ryker?" Savannah interrupted. "I know you and Todd have a lot to talk about, but we need to take Todd in. We need to notify Spear. We need to get agents out to the intercept site."

He knew she was right, but he wanted to finish this himself, not have a bunch of feds do it for him. Before he could reply, a black SUV turned down the alley. "You texted Parisa," he said, irritated by that fact.

"As soon as I got to the alley," she admitted.

He wished she hadn't done that. He wanted more time to talk to Todd alone. They still didn't have enough details. But the agents were already getting out of the car.

"You gotta help me," Todd said, as the agents handcuffed him and led him to the SUV. "You said you would, Ryker. You owe me. I'm not going to give out any more information until someone makes me a deal."

The door slammed on Todd's words, and he was more than happy about that, because anger was raging within him, not just with Todd, but with all of his team. And he had a little left over for Savannah. But that was going to have to stew for a while as Parisa came back to speak to them.

"What did Todd tell you?" Parisa asked, shooting them both a quizzical look.

"The plan is to hijack a weapons shipment from Spear and hold it for ransom," Savannah replied. "It's supposed to happen today, but we didn't get the details on when or where that's going to happen. Apparently, Hank Morgan will be driving the vehicle from Spear to wherever it's going."

As Savannah filled Parisa in on the rest of what Todd said, Ryker's stomach continued to churn. They had Todd in custody, but that wouldn't stop Hank and Mason from carrying out their plan. It was actually a clever idea, and it was difficult to deny that he didn't understand their desire for money. While he didn't have the same needs, he knew that all of the guys had been struggling since they'd left the service. Hell, Mason had lost a leg.

And taking care of the families of the fallen, there was something honorable about that, but not the way they were going about it. He also didn't know if he bought the fact that all the money was going to this family fund. There was no way they were giving it all away. Even Todd had admitted that Hank wanted to start a chain of gyms. Where was the nobility in that? No, there was greed involved here, too.

What else?

Paul's words rang through his head once more: *I fell for the lie.*

Were Mason and Hank working some other plan that Paul and Todd knew nothing about?

After Paul had been shot, Hank and Mason might have decided Todd was a liability. They might not trust that Todd would continue to be loyal if he heard what had happened to Paul, what had almost happened to him and Savannah. They might have changed the plan since last night's events.

He paced around the alley, feeling the sounds beginning to build in his head. He couldn't let them in. He couldn't afford an attack now. He had to keep it together.

"Ryker."

Savannah's sharp voice cut through the fog building in his head.

"What?" he snapped back.

"Are you all right?"

"I told you to stop asking me that."

"I'll take that as a no," she said, annoyance in her gaze now. "Here's what's happening. Parisa is calling Spear right now." She tipped her head toward Parisa, who had stepped away to make her call. "We'll stop any shipments from leaving the facility today."

"Good."

"Then Parisa will head back to the office with Todd, where he'll be interrogated. You and I are going across the street to check out the motel and see if the guys left anything behind."

Her calm, logical words drove away the creeping wave of incoming bells. She had a plan, and he needed to take action, to keep moving forward. "Fine," he said shortly.

"Savannah," Parisa said, rejoining them. "I spoke to the CEO of Spear, Randy Jepsen. He says one of their trucks left the building thirty-eight minutes ago. According to the GPS tracker, it's exactly where it should be, heading toward the Baltimore shipyard. Highway patrol and agents are heading that way now. With any luck, we'll have the truck and its contents in our custody within the hour. Spear is putting the building on lockdown. No other vehicles will be leaving their facilities today."

"Great," Savannah said. "We'll meet you at the office as soon as we check out the motel."

"Great."

As Parisa got into the SUV, they walked down the alley.

"So, on a scale of one to ten," Savannah began. "With ten being so angry you're seeing fiery-red dragons in your head, how mad are you at me?"

"About a thousand."

"Okay, that's more than I was hoping for. You're angry that I brought Parisa in before you had a chance to get all the information from Todd."

"It wasn't the best timing." He paused as they reached the end of the alley.

"When I sent the text, I didn't know what we were walking into, Ryker. I had to play it the way I've been trained, and that's to call for backup, to let my team know where I am, what I'm doing, how they can help."

"I get it, Savannah. But I wish I'd had more time alone with Todd. Now there will be lawyers and federal agents involved. We missed the perfect opportunity to find out how the plan was going to be executed and who else is involved."

"We know the players—Mason and Hank."

"There could be others. Chief Tanner was involved. Who knows who else they've recruited?"

"True." She gave him a thoughtful look. "But here's what I really want to know... Do you wish you had more time alone with Todd, because you think you could have gotten Todd to call it off? Are you trying to stop your former team, or are you trying to save them?"

CHAPTER TWENTY-FOUR

SAVANNAH'S QUESTION rolled around in his head. It would be stupid to try to save the people who were trying to kill him. But there was a voice in his head that kept reminding him that these guys had once been his best friends, his brothers, the men who had always had his back, who had saved his life on more than one occasion. And Paul had done that last night.

Were they all bad? Or was just one of them pushing his own agenda?

"Maybe I do want to see if any of them can be saved," he said finally.

"Well, Todd might have a chance. He can't move forward on the plan now. He didn't seem to be aware of the attack on us. Maybe he hasn't done anything more illegal than fake his own death."

"He's still involved in the conspiracy."

"If he turns on the others, he'll get a deal. And if he can prove that he had nothing to do with the attacks on us or on Paul, he might still have a life to save. Maybe the motivation behind the plan will also play in his favor—if they were truly trying to just take care of the families."

He heard the doubt in her voice. "You don't believe that?"

"Not entirely. I think it might have been the lie that Paul was talking about."

"I had the same thought."

"Todd sold it well, though. He believed it."

"I thought he did, but I'm not sure I can trust my gut anymore, because I could have never imagined any of them doing any of this."

"There could be levels of knowledge—not everyone is in on the entire scheme. I can't imagine Paul doing any of this, either. Yet he is. Maybe I'm too naïve. God knows, I've seen a lot of shitty people in my line of work. Perhaps I'm not cynical enough."

"Don't let the shitty people change you, Savannah."

She gave him a small smile. "Can I just say that while the take-down might not have gone the way you wanted, I'm really glad you're all right."

"You were worried that Todd was going to take me down?" he scoffed.

Her smile broadened. "That was stupid, wasn't it?"

"I'll say. Todd has never taken me down in his life."

"So, on a scale of one to a thousand..."

He couldn't help but smile back at her. "I'm no longer seeing fiery-red dragons. Come on, let's check out the motel."

They crossed the street and walked down the block to the Happy Days Motel, a two-story, run-down building that probably rented rooms by the hour. The older male desk clerk was eating a bag of chips while the television blasted a game show in the background. The lobby smelled like cigarettes and stale coffee.

He let Savannah take the lead, using her badge to cut through any resistance, but there was none to speak of. The clerk took one look at Paul's photo and immediately handed over the key card and a room number.

"There were three of them," the man said. "They've been here since Sunday. Paid me in cash. But both their vehicles are gone. Saw 'em leave last night. Never came back."

"Did you get a license plate on either vehicle?" Savannah asked.

"No, we don't do that here. No cameras in the lot, either. Our guests like privacy. But one was driving a big gray truck. The other was in a silver sedan, looked like a rental car."

"Thanks," Savannah said.

"I wish we'd gotten license numbers," he said, as they left the office.

"That would have been helpful, but we can check traffic cameras in the area to see if we can pick up either vehicle."

"You're always thinking."

"It's what I do."

"You're good at it."

"I have to be. Otherwise, I don't catch the bad guys," she said lightly.

He had to admit as pissed off as he'd been about her calling in Parisa before he had a chance to really talk to Todd, Savannah was a damned good partner.

They made their way up to the second floor and paused on either side of the door, guns drawn.

Savannah knocked on the door and said, "Room service."

There was no answer. She used the hotel key to open the door, and they moved into the room in perfect sync. There were two double beds and a pullout couch, all of which were unmade. There was a pile of junk food wrappers and bags on the table and empty beer bottles and energy drink cans on the dresser.

"Your friends are slobs," Savannah commented, as she tucked her gun into the back of her jeans. "Apparently, unlike you, they forgot their military training." She walked over to the table and moved a bag from Big Fat Taco to the side. "Wait a second." She pulled a piece of paper from under a taco wrapper. "Look what we have here."

He was at her side in an instant, peering over her shoulder at a road map. "That looks like a service road off the main highway." He studied the map with a critical eye. There were several Xs marked in various locations along the road. "They're setting up a perimeter. This is the intercept site."

"But how will they get the truck off the highway and onto the service road?"

"They'll block the highway in some way—a vehicle fire or a broken-down truck blocking all lanes. The only way out will be this road." He felt like he was back in the military again, assessing a target, calculating different scenarios, weighing the risks, the opportunities for success or failure.

"That makes sense. But the truck would certainly have other armed security besides Hank on board."

"That person could be in on it, too. If Hank is driving the truck, he could take the service road because of said blockage, which will make sense if someone checks the GPS. He could even radio in that he's taking a different route. He stops the truck. The rest of the team moves out at least some of the weapons, maybe not all. Maybe just enough to escape immediate notice."

"Or Mason will just tamper with the inventory. I saw inventory sheets on his desk. That's his job."

"Exactly."

"I need to call this in."

As Savannah got on the phone, he looked around the room, hoping for more clues, but there wasn't much else to see. There was one duffel bag on the floor. He guessed that belonged to Todd. He put it on the bed and riffled through it, pausing at two framed photos. The first one was of the team, taken probably three or four years ago.

He sucked in a quick breath at the sight of the seven of them, looking so young, so alive, so invincible. They'd been deployed to Afghanistan and even in the hot desert, they'd thrived as a team. It hurt to look at them now, to know that the dark-haired, dark-eyed Leo who had dreamt of being a pilot would never see that dream come true, that Carlos with his olive skin and laughing eyes would never laugh again, would never see his wife or his four young children, the oldest only eight, the twins only two.

And then there was Hank, bare-chested, as he always preferred to be, sporting a thick dark beard and sunglasses, Paul with his sandy-brown hair and boyish charm, Todd, with his dirty-blond hair, dragging on a cigarette.

His gaze came to rest on himself, on the warrior he'd once been: courageous, fearless, unwilling to look at any obstacle as anything but a challenge. He'd been their leader, their friend, their brother, their confidant. But maybe that's the way he'd seen it, and not the way they'd seen it. Because he realized now that he was a bit removed from the group, a foot of space between him and the next guy.

Had he always been just that little bit separate? Had he had his walls up even before his injuries, before the bells began to chime?

Frowning at that question, he moved on to the next photo and found himself looking at a very young Todd. He was probably ten in the photo, and he was sitting next to his mother in front of a very tall Christmas tree. She had her arms wrapped around him and was planting a kiss on his cheek. She was young, blonde, pretty, her face lit up with happiness.

This was the woman Todd had done this for—the mother he'd already lost to Alzheimer's but still felt a desperate need to take care of.

Ryker drew in a deep breath, feeling like he'd just taken a punch to the gut.

"What did you find?" Savannah asked, moving next to him.

"Some photos." He handed her the one of Todd and his mother. "That's Rebecca, Todd's mom, before she got sick."

"She's pretty. Did you ever meet her?"

"About a year before she got sick. She was devoted to Todd. And she used to write him long letters. She'd tell him about every detail of her day, whether it was not being able to find the canned tomatoes she wanted or if she had a cavity at the dentist or if she'd run into some old friend of his. And she always had gossip about the neighbors. Mr. Pearson who was painting pornographic art in his garage studio while his wife thought he was doing sunsets and Mrs. Richardson who would sneak into her neighbor's garden and steal their vegetables. At least, they thought it was Mrs. Richardson. It could have been Mrs. Draeger. There was going to be a sting one day to see who it was." He smiled at the memory. "Todd used to read us the letters when we were passing long hours of boredom. I remember we were all amped up trying to figure out which neighbor was stealing the tomatoes."

Savannah gave him a soft smile. "It reminded you of a normal life back home."

"I guess it did." He looked back at the photo. "Todd adored his mom. After his dad died, it was just the two of them. He was the light of her life, and she was his."

"I'm sorry. It sucks what happened to her."

"It does suck. I understand why Todd needs to take care of her in the right way."

"But does the end justify the means?"

"Well, that's the question, isn't it?"

"What's the other photo?"

He handed it to her. "The team—in much better days."

"This is the one I saw a couple of years ago, when I realized you were in Paul's unit. Carlos was with you at the bar the night we met. He was your wingman."

"He didn't think you'd even noticed him."

"Well, I was pretty wrapped up in you," she admitted.

He put the photos back into the bag, wishing he'd never looked at them.

Savannah put a hand on his arm. "I know this is difficult for you, Ryker."

"It doesn't matter if it's hard. It is what it is," he said tersely. "What did Parisa say?"

"That the map we found is good news, because they located the GPS tracker, and as you may have guessed, it was placed on another vehicle."

"Then they're off the grid."

"Hopefully not for long."

"They could have changed the hijack point. Or they could have already taken the weapons. It looks like they moved up the time, so who knows? Clearly, Todd was left out."

"Speaking of Todd, Parisa said that Todd is requesting to speak to you and only you."

"All right. Let's hope he has more to say."

He led the way to the door, and they walked briskly back to his truck. As soon as they got there, he had second thoughts. He didn't want to waste time looking for an explosive device, but he also didn't want to take the chance that someone had seen them go into the bagel shop and into the motel. "Let's take a cab."

She met his gaze. "Good idea."

Ryker was quiet on the cab ride to the DC FBI field office, and since Savannah didn't want to say much in front of the driver, she remained silent. She knew that Ryker had been moved by the photos he'd found in Todd's bag. She had been touched as well. *How could she not be?* She might not know the rest of the guys, but she knew Paul. She knew the people Paul had been doing this for, and seeing Todd with his mom had definitely put a more human face on his actions.

As she thought about her friend, she took out her phone. "I'm going to call Abby. It's weird that I haven't heard from her this morning."

Abby didn't pick up the phone, so she left a short voicemail. She'd barely finished doing that when her phone buzzed, but it wasn't Abby; it was Jax.

"What's up, Jax?"

"I just left the mortuary in Dobbs. After applying some pressure, I got the truth. There were no bodies brought into the mortuary. No one was cremated. Chief Tanner asked them to provide an urn with ashes. They were not the physical remains of anyone. The ashes were from a fireplace."

"I can't believe the chief did that."

"I got the feeling from the staff at the mortuary that Tanner runs Dobbs like his own personal business. He's the boss. They do whatever he says."

"I don't doubt that. But what was in it for him?"

"I'm trying to figure that out. However, when I stopped in at the police station, I was told Chief Tanner had had a family emergency and left town last night. I checked with his family, which includes a sister in Omaha and a brother in Des Moines. Both said there was no emergency they were aware of and that they hadn't spoken to Tanner in days. In fact, his sister hadn't spoken to him in a couple of years. She didn't seem to like him much. She said he was controlling and egotistical and sometimes a little creepy where women were concerned. Apparently, when his first wife left him years ago, she confided in Tanner's sister that the chief had a porn addiction."

"Bingo."

"Addiction is always a weakness to exploit. And an addiction to porn when you're the chief of police could be very upsetting to the local community. Especially if that porn extended to underage girls. Anyway, that's it on my end. I just spoke to Parisa before I called you. She filled me in on the weapons grab. It's quite a plan. She says she has one of the guys in custody."

"Yes. Todd Davis. He seems to be out in the cold now, so he's definitely not the mastermind, but hopefully when he realizes he has a chance to make his sentence easier, he'll start talking."

"That's usually the way it works. First one to talk gets the deal."

"That's what we told him."

"I should be back in DC tonight, depending on when I can get a flight. I don't think there's much more to find here in Dobbs."

"I would agree. In fact, if you want to just head back to LA, you can do that, too. Parisa is getting her entire team involved in this."

"Well, if you're covered, then I will head back to Los Angeles. Although, it might be fun to come to DC just to annoy your new boyfriend," he said with a laugh. "Damn. I'm not on speaker, am I?"

"No, you're not. And I'm hanging up now. Thanks again for your help."

"Good luck with the rest of it."

"I'll see you back in LA." She ended the call.

"Want to fill me in?" Ryker asked.

"I'll give you the details when we get to the office, but there were no bodies at the mortuary, and it looks like Tanner was involved in the coverup. He's now disappeared."

A gleam entered Ryker's eyes. "Interesting."

"Well, at least Tanner's reign is over now. My dad always thought Tanner was such a wonderful guy. He used to rave about his discipline, his control, his unwillingness to bend the rules just because he was watching over a small town and not a big city. It gives me a little pleasure to know my father was wrong. I'm sure I'll never hear him admit it, but it's true."

"Your father was wrong about Mason, too. Didn't he get him the job at Spear? Didn't your dad put Mason in a position to steal from the company? From what I know, he talked Colonel Vance into giving Mason a shot."

"That's right. Another check mark against him." She paused, frowning at the reminder that her father was involved with Spear. But there was no way he could have had anything to do with this. She forced that thought out of her head as the cab pulled up in front of the FBI office.

CHAPTER TWENTY-FIVE

AFTER THEY WERE CLEARED to enter the offices, Ryker was escorted into an interrogation room where Todd was waiting, while Parisa took Savannah into the room next door where they could monitor the interview through the one-way mirror. Todd was hand-cuffed to the desk and he looked bad. His hair was wild. His eye was swelling from his fight with Ryker, but it was his nervous tension that was really noticeable. He was tapping his fingers on the desktop and his feet on the ground, shifting in his seat every other second.

"I wonder if he's high," she muttered.

"Seems like it," Parisa said. "He's been begging for a cigarette since he got here. But he wouldn't talk to any of us. Hasn't asked for a lawyer, though. That's something."

"I don't know what he thinks Ryker can do for him."

"Maybe he just needs to look into the eyes of someone he trusts."

"Does he trust Ryker? Who knows? Their relationship has gotten very complicated." She paused as Ryker started to speak.

"We found the road map," he told Todd. "This will all be over today. As soon as everyone else is rounded up, your opportunity to talk isn't going to be worth that much."

"The map won't help you. You're seriously underestimating your former team."

"Then talk to me."

"They're listening, aren't they?"

Ryker shrugged. "You've never been stupid. Look, Todd, the shipment left earlier. This plan is already being executed, and you're on the outs. Your team has moved on without you. They clearly consider you a liability. In fact, you should count yourself lucky that you're in custody, because you might be targeted if you weren't. You know too much. You're a loose end."

"They're my team. You stepped away, I didn't."

"Paul didn't abandon anyone, but he's in the hospital. Are you sure you know who you're working for?"

Hearing the coldness in Ryker's voice made Savannah understand why he'd so often been called Stone Cold. He'd just never talked to her that way. But now his anger, his feeling of betrayal, was making him heartless. And Todd was getting nervous.

"I'm working with my team—our team," Todd said.

"It's not *our* team anymore."

"We knew we couldn't count on you. That's why we didn't bring you in. You always thought you were better than us because you went to West Point."

"Mason went to West Point, too."

"Mason got there through a lot of hard work. You had family connections. And Mason has little support now. His medical expenses are beyond belief. You have no idea what it's like to have money problems. You've always had it easier than the rest of us. You don't know what it feels like to be desperate. But I do. And so do the others. We're doing this for the right reasons."

"Is Ryker rich?" Parisa asked, drawing her attention away from the interview.

"I don't know. I don't think so," she said. "He lives on a boat on the Chesapeake Bay. He drives a ten-year-old truck. If he has money, I don't know where it is." She frowned as she realized there was probably a lot about Ryker she still didn't know. She turned her attention back to him.

"Once again," Ryker continued. "I have to remind you that Paul is in the hospital after he stopped someone from trying to kill me. The team is shattered. It's done."

"I told you I don't know what happened there. You're trying to get me to turn on my team. I don't do that. You should know that about me."

"Who else is involved besides Hank and Mason? Is Chief Tanner part of this plan? How did you get him involved?"

"Paul knew some shit about him. Tanner cooperated to keep us quiet, but he only helped fake our deaths. He didn't know anything else." Todd paused. "But he got nervous when he realized you were staying at my house. He thought you might find the evidence we'd told him we had on his porn problems. I guess he decided to blow up the house, which was stupid. Mason was really pissed about that."

"It made everything look suspicious," he agreed.

"Yeah. The whole thing was harder than I thought it would be. I wish I'd died first. Having to see Abby's face, Tyler's tears..." Todd shook his head. "That was rough."

"It's too bad Paul didn't get to see what he was putting his family through," he said sharply. "Did you tell him the pain his wife and child were in?"

"I couldn't. He was having too many second thoughts. I had to tell him they were okay. I even said Colin was there. He thought Colin was better for Abby, so it made him more comfortable."

"It made him comfortable to know another man was going to take care of his wife?"

"He felt like a failure. He was trying to make it legitimately, but he couldn't find work."

"He could have found work. He could have joined your company. Are they a part of this? Because after you left, they were grabbing up your files like there was some big secret in them."

Todd had no reaction to that beyond a simple frown. "I don't know why they'd do that. They weren't a part of anything. Those jobs were stupid. I was a babysitter, and they didn't pay me well. Colton and Trent were raking it in, but not the rest of us."

"How's it going down today? Who's working the intercept? Where are the guns going? How is the ransom going to happen?" The questions shot out of his mouth, one after the other.

"Before I say anything more, you have to promise to help me."

"I'm not FBI. I can't do anything to help you."

"You seem tight with Savannah. Can you get her in here? She loves Paul. She'll want to help me."

"Will she? After what you guys did to Abby?"

"It was for her own good. And for Tyler, too."

"Whatever you say to me, you're saying to the FBI. You know that. If you want a deal, show them you have something to sell. Give us information that we can use."

There was a long moment of silence. Savannah watched as the two men stared at each other with so many emotions she couldn't begin to decipher them.

Then Todd sat back in his chair. "I'm not talking until I get a promise in writing." He looked past Ryker to the mirror. "Do you hear that, Savannah? Make me a deal or get me a lawyer. That's all I have to say."

"You're a fool, Todd," Ryker said. "We carried you for years, covering up your mistakes, making excuses for your lack of abilities, for the way your nerves got in the way of executing your missions. I can't carry you anymore. I'm done."

Ryker pushed back his chair and stood up, leaving the room without a backward glance.

"That was cold," Parisa commented.

"Yes," she said, feeling a chill in her bones. When Ryker didn't immediately enter the room where they were, she wondered if he'd left so abruptly because he was truly pissed at Todd or because the bells had started going off. "I thought he'd come in here when he was done. I should find him."

"Give him a minute to cool off. And while you're doing that, you can tell me what's going on between you two," Parisa said, giving her a speculative look.

"We're working together."

"I'm not blind, Savannah. I've seen you work with plenty of

men, but there is a hell of a lot of tension between you and Ryker. It feels like romantic, sexual tension to me."

"Fine. We had a very brief fling a long time ago, and since we saw each other at the funeral, it got going again."

"I knew it."

"Yes, you're very insightful," she said dryly.

"You should be careful, Savannah."

"Why? Because hanging around with him almost got me killed?"

"No. Because he looks like the kind of man who could break your heart."

She let out a sigh. "He probably is that kind of man. But as much as I tell myself that there is no future and I should keep my guard up, I can't do it. I can't seem to back away from him. It's like there's this invisible rope between us, always trying to pull us together."

Parisa gave her an understanding smile. "You have it bad. And I know exactly what you mean."

"It was that way with you and Jared?"

"Yes, and like you and Ryker, we met under extreme circumstances. That only heightened everything."

"But you guys made it last. That's impressive."

"Do you see a future with Ryker?"

"I don't know. Our lives are in very different places. He has issues he's dealing with that stem from the attack on his team. I think that's why he's having trouble handling Todd. He knows how much the guys have suffered since leaving the service, because he has suffered, too. And he appreciates their desire to take care of their families, even though he hates what they've chosen to do."

"The road to hell is paved with good intentions. That's what my stepfather always says. We've both seen a lot of people do terrible things for what they think are good reasons. But you can't get caught up in their motivation, not with a multi-million-dollar cache of weapons on the line."

"You don't have to worry. I won't compromise myself."

"Not even for Ryker?"

"He would never ask me to do that." Her gaze flew to the door as it opened, but it wasn't Ryker; it was the special agent in charge of the DC office, Lloyd Paxton, a fifty-something man, with twenty years of experience at the bureau. She'd met him briefly on her way into the office, and he hadn't seemed too thrilled with the fact that she'd delayed bringing them into the case until this point. He also didn't seem to like having Ryker in the mix, but so far, he had let Parisa run the show.

"I have an update," he said. "Agents Ball and Lukowski found the Spear truck on the service road. However, the truck was empty."

"The weapons were gone," she murmured, feeling a wave of disappointment.

"Yes. Two members of Spear's security team were found unconscious in the truck. They appear to have been drugged. One was in the cab, the other in the back of the truck. The driver was not at the scene. Spear gave us the details on the driver: Roland Walker." Agent Paxton handed them a copy of a driver's license.

Savannah took a quick breath. "That's not Roland Walker. That's Hank Morgan. He's part of Ryker's former ranger unit."

"That makes sense. The address on the ID led to a car wash."

"So, Hank Morgan was driving the truck. What about Mason Wrigley?"

"I checked with the hospital earlier," Parisa answered. "He's expected to be in surgery for another hour at least."

"He's really having surgery."

"Yes, he is."

"Get a warrant for his house," Agent Paxton said.

"Already working on it," Parisa confirmed.

"Good." His gaze moved to Savannah. "We appreciate your help, Agent Kane, and that of Mr. Stone. But we need you to step back now. We'll take it from here."

"I'm not stepping back," she said quietly. "I'm going to see this through. I know the players better than anyone else in this office. You need me."

"But I don't need Mr. Stone. He didn't get anywhere with Mr. Davis. Send him home. If you don't, I will."

As Paxton left the room, she muttered, "Ass."

Parisa smiled. "He's territorial. You know how it goes. Or maybe you've forgotten, because you have Flynn in your corner."

"You could have Flynn as your boss, too. He'd love to have you on the team. We all would."

"Right now, Jared needs to be here. But we are talking about making some changes in the next year, so we'll see."

"Ryker is not going home."

"I know, but he doesn't have to be here in the office."

"He'd probably rather not be here," she admitted, wondering again where he was.

Her phone buzzed and she pulled it out of her bag. "Oh, my God," she said.

"Bad news?"

"It usually is when my dad texts me. He says he needs to see me immediately, that it's urgent and has to do with Spear. Maybe he's found out something."

"Do you want me to go with you?"

"He specifically asked me to come alone."

"Why would he do that?" Parisa asked. "Does he have something to hide? You don't think he's involved in this, do you?"

"I can't imagine that he would be. He prides himself on his honesty, integrity, loyalty to country. He's so righteous in being right."

"I've seen people who are very righteous and they're very wrong."

"My dad is a lot of things that aren't wonderful. He's emotionless and hard. He can be ruthless and a little cruel. But he's not a traitor."

"What are you going to do?"

"My job. I'm going to talk to him. I'll take Ryker with me."

"I thought you were supposed to go alone."

"He can wait out front, but I want to get him out of Paxton's hair." They walked out of the room and down a short hall to the operations center. There were a dozen agents working on their computers but no sign of Ryker.

Parisa stopped to ask one of the agents if they'd see him, and the woman pointed to the elevator.

They went down to the lobby, stopping at the front desk. The security guard confirmed that Ryker had left ten minutes earlier.

"I can't believe he just left," she said, feeling shockingly surprised and disappointed by his actions. "Why would he do that?"

"Maybe he just went out to get some air, take a walk around the block," Parisa suggested.

She pushed through the revolving door and walked into the afternoon sunshine. The street was crowded, and she scanned both directions with a sinking heart. "I don't see him anywhere."

She pulled out her phone and texted him: *Where are you?*

There was no immediate reply. "Damn him. Why does he have to be so stubborn and independent?"

"Because he's a man," Parisa said with a soft smile. "Not that you aren't exactly the same, Savannah. You stood up to Paxton, and not many people in our office are willing to do that. It seems like Ryker is cut from the same cloth."

"He was angry that I called you to the alley. He thought he could have gotten more out of Todd if you hadn't shown up."

"It was the right play."

"I know it was. And I thought we'd gotten past it. We'd agreed that we'd work off the same page in the future, but now he's gone, and I don't know where. Should I be worried? Could he be in trouble?" She wasn't normally a worrier. She didn't blow things out of proportion. She attacked problems one at a time. But now she found herself lost in a haze of concern. "What if the other guys have come after him? They tried to kill him last night."

"He left the building under his own steam," Parisa reminded her. "Maybe he ran into Paxton, who told him thank-you for your service, and it made him angry."

"That's possible."

"You said he's been dealing with his own issues, and the

betrayal of his friends has to be hitting him hard. Maybe he needed a minute."

"I hope you're right. But I can't wait around here. I have to go to my dad's place. I really need a car."

"You can have mine," Parisa said, pulling out her keys. "Let's go back inside. It's in the underground garage."

She took one last look around and then headed to the garage. After hopping into Parisa's car, she texted Ryker again: *Going to my dad's. He has information. Where are you? Text me.*

Once again there was no immediate reply, so she put the car in drive and pulled out of the garage.

CHAPTER TWENTY-SIX

I⊤ WAS two o'clock in the afternoon when Savannah parked in front of a duplex about two miles from Spear Enterprises. She was still surprised that her dad had gone so far as to get a place in Bethesda to stay in. Before she got out of the car, she sent Ryker another text: *I hope you're all right. Your silence is alarming.* She sent the message and then added: *If Agent Paxton said something to you about not needing your help, don't worry about that. You're still in the loop. You and I are a team. Don't forget that.*

She sent the text and then got out of the car, not just feeling worried but also angry. She and Ryker had gotten so close. They'd been incredibly honest with each other, and he knew how important it was to her to be trusted, to be respected for who she was. Cutting her out now was making her feel like he didn't need her for anything. She couldn't stand that thought. But she might have to accept that he didn't need her, that whatever fantasy relationship future she'd been building in her head was just that—a fantasy.

Ryker hadn't made her any promises, and she hadn't made him any. But there had been so much more between them than just sex. There'd been an emotional connection. *Had it all been in her head?*

Damn him for making her doubt herself.

She pushed him out of her head and pulled herself together, because she had another man to deal with who had always made her doubt herself. And the only reason she was dealing with him at all was because he might have knowledge that would help her figure out where the weapons were and who else was involved. Otherwise, she would have told him flat out that just because he said jump didn't mean she had to jump. She was done racing to see him whenever he wanted to throw her a crumb of attention.

But this was work. And she was good at her job. She did what she had to do to be successful, even if that meant talking to him.

She walked up the steps and rang the bell. Her father opened the door a moment later, waving her in with a somber expression on his face. He was dressed in uniform, as always. She couldn't remember the last time she'd seen him in casual clothes.

The living room was sparsely furnished, with a couch and an armchair surrounding a coffee table laden with books. There was no television in the room. When her father wasn't working or keeping himself in impeccable shape, he read.

There was a round table with two chairs next to the kitchen, and there appeared to be two bedrooms, accessed by a short hallway.

They stood in the middle of the room. She didn't want to sit down. She didn't plan on being there that long.

She folded her arms in front of her chest. "What did you want to talk to me about?"

"What's going on at Spear. I was with the CEO, Randy Jepsen, when the FBI called. I understand someone has stolen a shipment of weapons."

"That's correct. It doesn't sound like you need to talk to me at all."

"Are there suspects?"

"Yes."

"Well?"

She debated whether or not she wanted to tell him more. She doubted Parisa had told the CEO of Spear about Todd's arrest. But she was more than a little curious to get her father's reaction. He knew Todd and Paul. In fact, he knew Ryker's entire team. He'd trained them. He'd helped Mason get the job at Spear. He was tied up in this in a lot of ways, which also concerned her. *Was he looking for information that might help him protect himself?*

But he couldn't be involved. It wouldn't make sense.

On the other hand, very little of this made sense.

"Jepsen seems to think Mason might have sold us out," her father continued. "If he did, that's going to be on me, because I helped him get the job. I convinced Vance to take him on, to give him a chance."

"Why does the CEO think Mason sold out the company?"

"He's heavily involved with the details of our shipping program. And he's conveniently gone the day the shipment goes missing."

"He's having surgery. That's not exactly convenient."

"Are you saying he's not involved?"

"No. Look, I really can't tell you anything."

Anger ran through his eyes. "This is bigger than our relationship. I understand you blame me for everything that went wrong in your life, but this is about weapons going to the enemy, innocent lives being lost. This is about your country."

"Don't lecture me about patriotism. I know exactly what this is about. I was a soldier, Dad. And now I'm an FBI agent. I am just as dedicated to protecting the innocent and serving justice as you are."

He seemed taken aback by her response.

"And I'm not petty enough to withhold information because you shipped me off to live with my aunt and uncle when I was thirteen years old."

"It always comes back to that," he said heavily.

"It does, doesn't it? Funny how something so simple as abandoning your daughter would keep coming up." As soon as she heard the bitterness in her voice, she got mad at herself. *Why was she letting him rile her up?* She was making a mockery of what she'd just told him about being professional.

"I didn't abandon you. I thought you would be better off with

Stephanie. You needed a woman in your life, and you got a sister, too."

"But I lost my father. Look, we don't need to talk about this. We don't need to talk about anything. I have moved on."

"It doesn't sound like you have."

She was shocked to see a small smile cross his lips. "You find this funny?"

"Not funny. You just remind me of your mother. She was the only one who would call me on my bullshit. Everyone else was afraid of me."

"You wanted everyone to be afraid of you."

His smile faded. "I didn't want you to be afraid of me. I just didn't know how to be your father, Savannah. I'm not good with kids, especially girls. Your mom understood you. She knew what you needed. I didn't."

"You didn't try."

"You're right. I was devastated when your mother died. The bottom fell out of my world."

"Mine, too."

"I buried myself in work. I told myself I was doing my duty by you and that you were better off. But by the time I realized you weren't happy, you were so angry with me, and you were acting out every other second."

"I wanted your attention. And when I was in trouble, you usually showed up. Until you didn't. And then I tried something else. I joined the army. I thought we could connect if I was a soldier, too. But that didn't work, either. You were angry with my choice."

"Because I didn't want you to go to war. I wanted you to be safe. I knew I couldn't protect you once you joined up."

"But you did try. That's why I got into Army Intelligence, why I got great posts every time I made a move. That was you working behind the scenes, wasn't it? I thought it was because you didn't trust me to be a good soldier."

"It wasn't that. I couldn't stand the thought of something happening to you. I owed that to your mother." He paused. "I have to admit I was glad when you got out. But then you joined the FBI. Why can't you do something…normal?"

"Because I'm not normal. Because, ironically, I'm a lot like you. I can't stand it, but it's true. I'm not like Mom. I'm not creative or nurturing. I can't bring plants back to life. I'm a terrible cook, but I am a good agent."

He gave her a long look. "Do you think I have something to do with the missing shipment, Savannah? Is that why you don't want to talk to me?"

She thought about his question. "I don't think you do, no. But this is an ongoing investigation. And you don't have a need to know."

"Fair enough. Then I'll tell you why I really asked you here."

Her stomach fluttered with his somber tone. "Go ahead."

"I'm concerned that Bill may be involved, too."

"Bill Vance? Why would you say that?"

"Because I've known him for thirty years, and since his wife, Doris, died five years ago, he has changed. I've tried to ignore it, telling myself I'm imagining things. But I don't have a big imagination. I've always dealt in facts, and here are the facts. Bill quit the army after the mission that killed two members of Stone's team. After that, he seemed like a different person. He was angry. He was guilty. He was conflicted. I could see it, even if he wouldn't admit it. When Mason came to me asking for my help in getting a job at Spear, I thought Bill might feel better if he could help Mason get back on his feet."

"Okay, but why do you think Colonel Vance is involved?" she asked, still not sure where he was going with their conversation.

"Since Paul died, he's been cagey, and when I told him Todd was dead, too, he almost jumped out of his skin. He knew something I didn't; that was clear. Then we were informed about the possible intercept of a weapons shipment, and he started sweating like a pig. He was on his phone constantly. He kept disappearing into the bathroom. After the truck went missing, he suddenly had an appointment out of the office. He was so squirrely I knew something was going on, so I followed him."

"You followed him?"

"Yes."

"Well, where did he go?"

"The Ambassador Hotel. He met a man in the bar there, and it was not a man I wanted to see him with."

"Who was it?"

"His name is Rajeesh Buthanu. Mr. Buthanu is an arms dealer, and one who is believed to play all sides. He sells to whoever will pay the most money. I couldn't believe he was in the States or that he was meeting with Vance, right after a shipment of weapons went missing."

"Did they see you?"

"No. I've been trying to get a hold of Vance since then, but he's not answering my calls. I know he didn't go back to Spear, because I talked to his assistant. I went by his house, but there was no answer."

"Then he's in the wind. Why didn't you just call the FBI and tell them what you told me?"

"Well, here's the tricky part."

She could see the answer in his eyes. "You want to try to save Vance."

"Yes."

She shook her head at his surprising optimism. "You want to save Vance, and Ryker wants to save his guys, but neither of you can do that. This has gone too far."

"What do you mean Ryker wants to save his guys?"

She frowned, realizing her mistake. "Never mind."

"Mason is involved, too? Damn. Are he and Vance working together?"

"I have no idea."

"Come on, Savannah. Tell me what's happening. Maybe I can help."

"All right, I'll tell you this much. Paul and Todd are not dead. They faked their deaths. And it looks like Ryker's former team decided to steal the weapons to take care of the families they were leaving behind."

Her father shook his head in amazement. "That is a crazy plan. You're telling me this team of Army Rangers, who I trained, stole the weapons?"

"Yes. They claim they're going to sell them back to Spear."

"I talked to Jepsen right before you came. There hasn't been a demand for payment."

"It's probably coming. Or…maybe the demand is going directly to Vance, if he's involved." She paused as the truth hit her. "That's it. It's all starting to make sense."

"Is it? What am I missing?"

"Ryker said they always thought that someone in intelligence set them up for their last mission ending in ambush. Maybe Vance was the one who did that. Mason or someone else figured it out. Perhaps the team doesn't want just the money. They want to make Vance pay. But can he get the cash out of Spear without anyone else knowing? Does he have that much power within the company?"

"He might not need to. His wife inherited a great deal of money right before she died, and then it went to Vance. He made three trips to the Cayman Islands in the past year."

"He has an offshore account? We have to find him. Where would he be if he's not at home?"

"He could be anywhere."

"I need to call this in. I'm sorry, but I can't protect him. We need to track his phone, his car, and find his location. If he's going to buy the weapons, and he was meeting a shady arms dealer this morning, then I think the only way he makes his money back is to sell the shipment to the enemy."

"Spear will take the hit, but not Vance," her father said grimly.

"Exactly."

"Do what you need to do. You're right. He's too far gone."

As she reached into her bag, she saw a shadow by the window. Instead of grabbing her phone, she pulled out her gun, tipping her head toward the window.

Her father immediately crossed the room, taking a gun out of the desk drawer.

They might be overreacting, but the hairs on the back of her neck were standing straight up, and her gut told her that Vance might have realized that her father was onto him. Her dad waved her back toward the hallway bedroom. She took a few steps into the hall, but she was more than ready to cover him.

The shadow shifted. And then the door blasted open. As a man in black burst into the room, her father jumped, bringing the butt of his gun down on the man's head.

Savannah started forward, freezing when the front door flew open with a violent noise. A second gunman entered, and as he took aim at her father, she shot him. He fell back in stunned surprise, the weapon falling from his hand.

She ran forward, grabbing his discarded gun, while her father disarmed the now unconscious man.

"Nice shot," he said, joining her. "Right in the shoulder. Not life-threatening. "

"We need him to talk." But the man wasn't talking. He was rolling around on the floor in pain. She hadn't seen either guy before, and she didn't know who they were attached to, but it was probably Vance.

Her father positioned himself over the gunman while she called 911, requesting an ambulance. Her next call was to Parisa. She gave her a brief recap and then hung up, moving next to her dad. "Help is on the way."

He looked at her, and for the first time she thought he actually saw her for who she was.

"You didn't hesitate," he said, pride in his eyes. "Not for a second."

"If I had, you might have been shot. But thanks for taking out the other guy."

"This is very odd, Savannah."

"It is. We're definitely never going to have a normal father and daughter relationship."

"Probably not." A long pause followed, and then he added, "But I wouldn't mind talking to you more often."

A wave of emotion ran through her at the words she'd wanted to hear for a very long time. "I wouldn't mind that, either."

"Okay then."

"Okay," she echoed. They still had a long way to go in their ability to communicate, but maybe this was a start.

The ambulance arrived moments later, followed by Parisa and two other FBI agents as well as the local police, who had been alerted to the shooting by 911 calls from the neighbors.

She made a short statement to the police, and then while her father was being interviewed, she told Parisa everything she had learned.

"This is a new twist," Parisa said, a gleam in her brown eyes. "We need to find Colonel Vance. We also need to see if we can get anything out of that guy." She tipped her head toward the man who had regained consciousness, only to find himself in handcuffs.

"I don't think these men know anything. They look like hired guns. They probably don't even know who hired them, but it had to be Vance. He must have realized my father had followed him to his meeting with Rajeesh Buthanu, and he decided to take him out."

"That's a good assumption. We can put your father into a safe house until this is over."

"I doubt he'll agree."

"You should try to convince him." Parisa gave her a thoughtful look. "I know I should tell you to come into the office and talk to Paxton, but between you and me, I think he'll bench you and bury you in paperwork, and you don't want that."

"I really don't."

"I'll tell him you're staying with your father, until we can get him to a safe place, that your dad is shaken by the events that occurred here—even though he's not."

"It takes a lot to rattle my father. I think staying away from the office is a good plan. I'd like to help you find Vance, but I can't be benched."

"Understood. Don't worry. We'll pull out all the stops to find him."

"Did Ryker come back to the office while I was gone?"

"No. You never heard from him?"

She looked back at her phone, realizing she had gotten a text. "Wait, I did." She read the text with a deepening frown and then repeated it aloud. "Need a little time, will get back to you. Don't worry." She looked at Parisa. "That's an awesome text. Men suck."

Parisa smiled in commiseration. "At least you know he's all right."

"And pushing me away. I've known all along it was coming. I just didn't think it would be so soon." She drew in a breath and pulled herself together. "Well, I can't worry about him now."

"No, you can't. I'm going back to the office. Talk to your dad. Let me know what he wants to do. In the meantime, we're going to track down Colonel Vance and, hopefully, those stolen weapons."

As Parisa left, she debated for a moment and then sent Ryker another text: *New developments. Call me. It's important.*

Then she put down her phone and joined her father. He'd finished making his statement, so they stepped onto the back patio while the investigators went through the crime scene.

"We'd like to put you in a safe house," she said.

"I can take care of myself. Didn't I just prove that?"

"Vance may not stop with this attack."

"I suspect he'll be occupied with more pressing matters than trying to take me out. Once he realizes this failed, he'll disappear. He has a lot of money and connections all over the world. You need to find him before he leaves the States."

As her father spoke so pragmatically and coldly, she couldn't help but wonder what he was really feeling. "This must be difficult for you. Colonel Vance was one of your best friends."

His expression hardened. "I obviously did not know him as well as I thought I did. He wasn't worth saving. I don't care what happens to him now."

She believed him. Her father certainly had the ability to cut someone from his life and move on, but despite his words she had to believe that Vance's betrayal had hurt him. Not that he'd accept her sympathy. Or that he'd even want to acknowledge that emotion in front of her. So, she changed the subject. "If you won't do a safe house, maybe you should go back to Fort Benning."

"I might do that," he conceded. "By the way, you never told me how Paul and Todd faked their deaths. They had to have had help."

"They did, and you're not going to like my answer."

CHAPTER TWENTY-SEVEN

RYKER HEARD HIS PHONE BUZZ, and he suspected it was Savannah again. She was probably pissed that he'd bailed on her, but after his meeting with Todd, and an irritating run-in with Agent Paxton, he'd needed to get out of the FBI office. Once he'd left the building, he'd just kept walking. He'd finally found his way back to his truck and after searching for an explosive device, he had found the courage to open the door and turn on the engine. Thankfully, nothing had happened, and he had been more than happy to get behind the wheel. He'd needed to exert some control over his life and that was the first step.

Then he'd driven to Mason's townhouse and had found getting inside surprisingly easy. For a smart man, who was probably involved in weapons smuggling, Mason had taken very few precautions with his personal living situation. Ryker had been able to guess the code in less than ten minutes. Of course, that was also because he knew the six lottery numbers that Mason had played repetitively for the seven years they'd served together.

As he stepped into the entry, he paused to listen for a moment. According to the FBI, Mason was in surgery, so there shouldn't be anyone in the house. He was a little surprised the FBI wasn't here yet, but when he'd left the building, they'd been talking about getting a search warrant. Hopefully, that would take a little more time, and he could complete the search on his own.

With his weapon in his hand, he made his way through the two-story, two-bedroom home, noting the cleanliness of every room, and the neat organization of the shelves in both the living room and the kitchen. Some adjustments had been made to the house to accommodate Mason's injuries. The doors allowed for a wheelchair. The bathroom shower had been modified. And the lower shelves in the kitchen were all filled while the upper ones were empty. He knew that Mason was a renter, not an owner, but for a man who allegedly had financial problems, Mason was living quite well.

As he wandered around the house, he found little in the way of personal items. Mason had no photos on the walls, no reminders of his past life in the army. The bills on the desk in the living room were all from medical providers and the usual array of utility companies.

With a sigh, he stood in the middle of the room and wondered what the hell he was going to do next. And why he'd come here alone.

He'd been ignoring his phone ever since he'd gotten the first text from Savannah. He knew she was angry that he'd left the building without telling her where he was going. But he was still glad he'd left. With Parisa's team taking over the case, he and Savannah were going to be sidelined. Or at least, he'd be put on ice. She might be able to stay in the thick of things, but they wouldn't want a former Army Ranger and a former teammate of their group of suspects around to muck things up. However, he was starting to regret leaving Savannah behind.

Being alone wasn't really getting him anywhere. He was missing the hell out of Savannah and feeling like crap, because he knew he'd probably worried her and disappointed her. She would think he didn't respect her, that he didn't think she could handle herself, that she wasn't capable of helping him, and that wasn't it at all.

He'd never respected anyone more. He also cared about her.

He might even love her...

That thought caught his breath and sent his heart racing. He'd cared about women, but he didn't think he'd ever really been in love.

But Savannah... *Damn!* She was everything he'd ever wanted and more.

He'd let her go the first time. *Was he really going to push her away the second time?*

He knew the answer to that question, because he'd already done it. He'd left her behind so he could be alone. He'd made up a lot of excuses in his head. He needed air. The bells were ringing. Todd and the others had betrayed him, so he needed to think. The FBI didn't want to work with him. *Why should he work with them?*

But it was all bullshit. He'd left because that's what he always did. Todd had been right about that. Ever since he'd gotten hurt, he'd been running away. And he'd never run away before. He'd always stood his ground, even in the face of unspeakable fear. It wasn't an enemy that had brought him down; it was his own mind.

And now he wasn't just running from friends, he was running from the most incredible woman, who for some unimaginable reason wasn't at all scared off by his issues or the fact that every time they were together, she was fighting for her life.

He had to do better. Not just with her, with everyone and everything else. No more running. No more standing alone.

But first, he had to get those weapons back. He knew the guys better than anyone. He should be able to figure out their plan, where they would go, what they would do next. He just needed to think. He couldn't stand the thought of those weapons ending up in enemy hands. So, he'd take one more pass through Mason's house to make sure he wasn't missing anything. Then he'd call Savannah back, plead for forgiveness, and hope she hadn't finally decided she was done with him.

As he returned to the living room, his gaze landed on the small trash can by the bookcase. There were two coffee cups tossed in the garbage. His pulse leapt. Maybe they could get some DNA off the cups. One or both of them might reveal who else had been in

Mason's house. But as he took the cups out of the trash, and set them on the floor, his heart began to race even faster at the sight of the piece of folded paper in the bin. It was a paper airplane.

His head spun with images of Leo making those airplanes out of any piece of paper he could find. *Had Mason taken up that hobby? Or was Leo...* He couldn't finish the thought.

His ears started to ring. *Not now*, he silently pleaded. But the bells were chiming, and Leo's name was echoing off each ring. He put his hands over his ears and closed his eyes, wincing at the strobe lights going off in his head. He was losing touch with reality. He was going into his head. And he wasn't sure if, this time, he would come back out.

The bells had never been this loud, this painfully piercing. They were followed by explosions, flashes of light, and images from his past: the guys were playing soccer to while away the time; wading through knee-deep water on a night raid; patrolling some small desert town, trying to talk to the locals who didn't want them there. He could see that village square, the coffee stand where they'd grab a cup before heading back to the barracks.

The bells rang louder—church bells.

Another memory came into his head.

Every week Leo asked them to stop by the church so he could say a prayer. They'd always agreed, respecting his faith, and it never took longer than a few minutes. But one day, Leo had been gone a lot longer, and the locals near the church had been getting restless with their military presence. They needed to go.

He went into the church, but Leo wasn't there.

He walked out the back door and saw Leo talking to a man. When Leo saw him, he broke away from the conversation and rushed toward him.

"Sorry it took so long," Leo said. "I was just trying to make the locals feel like they're being heard."

"We need to get back to the team," he replied, thinking something was off. Leo was acting strange.

Why hadn't he asked him what was wrong?

The images moved forward in time: the mission to rescue an aid worker; listening to the ops team outline the plan; waiting for the helo to spin them up; creeping through the dark of the night toward the abandoned hotel.

And then the nearby church bells rang twelve times—midnight. They were happy for the noise to cover up their presence.

He positioned himself in the front with Leo and Carlos. Mason and Hank were at the side door. Todd and Paul went around the back.

When his three-man group hit the lobby, shots rang out. The lights blinded him again. Flash bangs. Explosions. Smoke. Heat. His brain felt like it was on fire.

Figures were shooting, others were running, the building was collapsing. He yelled into the radio to abort the mission.

And then there was Leo, standing over Carlos's body. He should have been dragging Carlos to safety, but he was backing away. Leo ran into the shadows toward another man.

He strained to see the man's face. Was it one of his team?

The smoke cleared for one second, and he caught his breath. It was the man from the church, the one he'd seen Leo talking to the week before. It was Rajeesh Buthanu, an arms smuggler and terrorist who was on the CIA watch list.

Leo knew him. Leo knew one of the men who'd just killed Carlos!

They both disappeared into the smoke as more bullets rang out.

He dodged for cover, but he was too late, feeling a horrendous shredding pain in his leg. As he rolled behind a wall, he wasn't sure his leg was even there anymore. He needed to get away. He needed to save his team, but he couldn't wake up. He couldn't move. He couldn't see anything.

Then the light began to prick at his eyes. He finally found the strength to open them.

He wasn't in the hotel anymore. He was at Mason's house. His gaze lit on the paper airplane.

Leo! He scrambled to his feet and grabbed his phone. He saw the text from Savannah and wondered what the new developments were. But he was more interested in telling her what he'd just realized. She'd been right all along. The bells had been trying to make him remember what he'd seen at the church and at the hotel. Leo had been working with an arms dealer. And if that were true then, it had to be true now. Leo had to be alive. He had to be running the show.

He punched in Savannah's number. It went to voice mail.

Dammit! He needed to talk to her.

Checking his watch, he realized at least thirty minutes had passed since he'd arrived at the townhouse. He needed to get out before anyone else arrived, including the FBI, who would only stop him from acting on what he knew.

After leaving the house, he jogged down the street to his truck and hopped in. As he drove away, he called Savannah again, this time leaving a message.

"I just left Mason's house," he said. "I saw a paper airplane in the trash and the bells went wild. I finally listened to what they had to say, what they had to show me. Leo is alive, and I think I know where the guys are, where they've taken the weapons. Call me back." He paused. "And I'm sorry, Savannah." There was a lot more that he wanted to say, but this wasn't the time. He ended the call without giving her the address of where he was going. He knew the FBI wanted him off the case. Paxton had told him as much. If he pulled Savannah into this or took the FBI on some wild-goose chase, he could be jeopardizing her job, and he knew how much it meant to her.

He set his phone in the drink holder next to his seat. He'd call her back when he got to the scene, as soon as he knew if he was really on to something. Then she could call in whatever teams she wanted.

She might think he wanted to save the guys, but what he really wanted was answers, and his best shot at getting those answers would be if he went in alone.

Although, there was a good chance he'd get no answers and end up dead. He couldn't forget how far his team had strayed. He wanted to believe that they didn't all know the end game, but he couldn't be sure. What he was sure of was that if Leo was alive, and he was controlling this plan, then those weapons weren't going back to Spear. They were going to the enemy, and he couldn't let that happen.

————————

After filling her father in on Chief Tanner's involvement with the faked deaths of Paul and Todd, Savannah got back into the car Parisa had lent her and pulled out her phone. She was surprised to see she'd missed a call from Ryker. But she'd been caught up in having one of the first real conversations she'd ever had with her father. Their relationship had definitely taken a huge turn. She hoped that would continue once this was all over.

Her dad had agreed to head back to Fort Benning as soon as he got someone over to put a temporary fix on the broken doors leading into his home. She would have preferred he leave immediately, but he was his own man and he always had been.

As she listened to Ryker's message, her heart sped up once more. *Leo was alive?*

Maybe no one was dead. Maybe Carlos was alive, too.

She wondered what else Ryker had remembered and where he was going now. Clearly, he hadn't chosen to give her any details, but that wasn't going to work for her.

She called him back, and to her surprise, he answered.

"It's about time," she snapped. "What is going on? Where are you?"

"I'm headed to a horse farm near Silver Springs. Did you listen to my message?"

"Yes. You think Leo is alive?"

"I do, and I know where he is. He used to spend Christmas at his grandfather's farm. It's about halfway between DC and Baltimore. It's the perfect place to stash a truckload of weapons. And no one is looking for Leo, because he's dead."

"What's the address?"

"I'll tell you when I get there."

She did not like his answer. "You can't do this alone, Ryker.

You have no idea how many men you'll be up against. Stop pushing me away. I'm in this, too, and you need me." He didn't reply for a moment, and the silence made her nervous. "Ryker, I know you hate to ask for help, but this is me."

"It's not just about asking for help. I want answers."

"And you think they'll talk to you?"

"If I'm alone, there's a chance."

"No there's not. They tried to kill you, Ryker. You're not one of them anymore. They won't listen to you. They won't follow you. They're in too deep. You know that, even if you don't want to admit it." As she was talking, she started the car, leaving the phone on speaker as she headed toward the expressway. She might not have an address yet, but she knew the direction she needed to go.

"You're probably right," he admitted. "But there's a chance that Leo is calling the shots. They may not even know he's alive."

"At least one of them does."

"Has Mason come out of surgery yet?"

"No, but there are agents at the hospital. He'll be arrested as soon as he wakes up. Now the team's focus is on finding Vance."

"Vance?" he asked with surprise. "Why? Did he get a ransom call?"

"No. It's a long story, but my father got suspicious of Vance and followed him to a meeting with an arms dealer by the name of Rajeesh Buthanu."

"That's the same guy Leo met with in Afghanistan. That's what I remembered. Buthanu is in DC?"

"Yes. And you're saying that Leo met with him while you were deployed?"

"When we did our weekly patrols, Leo always wanted to stop in at this particular church. He'd be gone a minute, maybe two. It was always quick. We didn't think much of it. His faith was important to him. But one day he was missing for almost ten minutes. There was action in the village. It felt like something was going on. We needed to get out of there, so I went looking for Leo, and I saw him talking to some guy in the back of the church. I didn't get the greatest look at him, and Leo brushed me off, saying it was just a local complaining about us being there. A week later, I saw a CIA watch list and the man's face was on it, but I didn't have a chance to ask Leo about it before we were sent on our last mission." He took a breath. "What I remembered today was that that man was at the hotel. Leo had a chance to kill him, but he didn't take the shot, and then Carlos went down, and my knee was ripped apart and the building exploded."

"You're saying this arms dealer was involved in your ambush?"

"Yes, and I think Leo was, too."

"Maybe he set you all up."

"Or someone set Leo up. He could have been involved in smuggling guns, and they wanted to take him out of the game. While he never had weapons on him, he could have been an intermediary, a money collector."

"For someone like Colonel Vance. Vance might have set up the entire team just to get rid of Leo."

"Why would he get rid of someone who was helping him?"

"What if Leo was blackmailing him?" she suggested. "What if he wanted a bigger cut? Vance might have found him to be a threat. But it doesn't matter. We need to find both men and then figure it out."

"You were right, Savannah. The bells were trying to tell me something. I should have listened to them long before this. They were trying to remind me of what I knew, but it was buried in my subconscious."

"Well, you know now. I need the address, Ryker. If you won't give it to me, I'll just get Parisa to track it down."

"I could be on the wrong track, Savannah."

"I'm sure you're at least fifteen or twenty minutes ahead of me. If you get there, and there's nothing to see, then I'll call everyone off. You know it's the right play. If Leo is in charge, he's clearly very dangerous, and he won't have any loyalty to you. I know that's probably hard to hear, but you have to hear it."

"You don't pull any punches, Savannah."

"We said we'd be honest with each other."

"There's another reason I don't want you there. I don't want you to get hurt. And it's not that I don't think you can't take care of yourself. You've become very important to me."

Her heart squeezed with love at his words. "I feel the same way. But we're better together. You know we are."

Silence followed her words, and then he said, "Twenty-three Morning Glory Way."

"Thank you. Will you wait for me to get there?"

"I can't make that promise. I know you've seen me debilitated by the bells, but my head is clear now. You want me to trust you, and in return you need to trust me."

"I do, Ryker. I'll text you when I'm close. And you better answer."

"If I can, I will."

That answer didn't make her feel good at all. But she needed to get to the farm and fast.

Contrary to what she'd told Ryker, she didn't call Parisa right away. She had no interest in saving any of the guys, not after multiple attempts on her life and the hell they'd put Abby through. But she did want to save Ryker, and coming in quiet would be the best way to do that.

CHAPTER TWENTY-EIGHT

THE FARM WAS LOCATED in a heavily wooded area, with the nearest neighbor a mile away. As Ryker drove down a lonely two-lane road, he remembered hearing Leo talk about the place, the trails that ran around the property and along the creek that led into town. When he was almost there, he pulled off the road, driving into the trees, and hiding his truck in the woods. He would go the rest of the way on foot.

He texted Savannah the location of his truck and said he was going to take a closer look at the property. He didn't wait for a reply as he grabbed his gun and got out. He found the creek and followed it toward the farm.

He knew that Leo's grandfather had died eighteen months ago, and that Leo had inherited the property but hadn't been that excited about it because it needed a lot of work. He'd said that his granddad hadn't done any improvements or had horses there in over a decade, so he'd probably have to fix the place up before he could sell it. Leo would have rather had cash. But now Ryker suspected that the farm had come in very handy. In fact, it was probably where Leo had been hiding out since he'd faked his death and somehow been able to slip out of Afghanistan and get back to the States without anyone knowing. He must have had help for that, too.

When he drew near to the two-story home and the adjacent horse barn, he paused, sliding back into the shadow of the trees. There was a black Jeep in the driveway and the back door to the barn was partially ajar. He couldn't see the front of the barn from his location, but there certainly had to be another entrance from the driveway.

His brain quickly computed the facts. Since the Spear truck had been left empty, he was guessing they'd loaded the weapons into a smaller van and brought it here. It had to be in the barn. There were two ways into that structure—front and back.

There was no sign of movement in the house. The shades were drawn in front of almost every window, except a bedroom at the back.

His phone buzzed. Savannah had arrived and parked next to his truck. He told her to follow the creek, and she'd find him in the trees before she got to the house.

He wasn't sure he'd made the right call in telling her where he was, but he did trust her, and she was very good at her job. They'd also been in this together from the beginning, and they needed to finish it together. He just hoped he could keep her safe. Because at the end of the day, he didn't care about anything more than he cared about her.

He saw her coming down the shadowy trail a moment later. He moved back toward a natural rock barrier and motioned her over. They squatted down behind the rocks.

"Anything happening?" she asked.

"I haven't seen any movement. There's a Jeep in the driveway. Is the FBI on the way?"

"I didn't call Parisa until I was almost here. She's on her way, but it will be close to a half hour before she can get here. Oh, and they think they have a beat on Vance. They're sending a team to check out a warehouse in Bethesda. It's only about five miles from Spear. There's a chance the exchange is going on there."

He could see the hope in her eyes, but he didn't buy it. Even though he hadn't seen anyone yet, every instinct he had said this was the right place. "This is a better spot. It's remote. It's controllable. No witnesses nearby. No cameras."

"I don't disagree, just telling you what's going on." She pulled a pair of binoculars from a small duffel bag. "I found these in Parisa's car. She lent it to me earlier today when I went to meet my father."

"I do want to hear about that sometime."

"I have a lot to tell you." She peered through the binoculars. "There's movement now. I see someone."

She handed him the glasses. A man came around the corner of the barn with a semi-automatic in his hands. He was alone. As he walked back and forth, he checked his watch, pulled out his phone, and then walked toward the front.

"He's waiting for someone," he murmured, looking at Savannah now.

"Probably Vance. You're right. The weapons have to be in the barn."

"Along with Leo and Hank and God knows who else," he said grimly.

"What's the play? This is your show. Make the call."

He appreciated the respect she was giving him, and that trust gave him even more determination. "We need to get that guy's attention, draw him away from the barn, take him out quietly."

She nodded. "I'll be the decoy."

"I'll set up over there," he said, waving toward a line of trees near the barn. "Savannah, if this goes south, run like hell. Do not come after me."

She stared back at him with her amazing green eyes and said, "You know I won't do that."

"I want you to. I've made a lot of mistakes the past nine months. I don't want to make the biggest one now by putting you in danger." He grabbed her by the shoulders. "I love you, Savannah."

Her lips parted in shock.

"I need you to stay alive," he continued. "I do not want you to die for me. I want you to live for me. Do you understand?"

"No one is going to die. We're going to do this together," she said, a desperate note in her voice.

"You're not hearing me."

"I am hearing you. But you can't tell someone you love them and push them away."

"I can when their life is on the line. If you can't make that promise, then we'll both walk away. We'll wait for the team."

"No. Let's do this now," she said. "We may have only a small window of opportunity to get into that barn before everyone arrives."

"Do you promise?"

"You're going to have to trust me to do the right thing, Ryker." She opened the duffel bag, pulled out a zip tie and handed it to him. "Take that guy out."

He took the tie and then gave her a hard, emotion-filled kiss, hoping it wouldn't be the last. He moved into the shadow of trees that was only twenty feet from the side of the barn. The guard was walking toward him, but he was more interested in checking what was on his phone than his surroundings. And then a cascade of rocks drew his head up. The man looked in Savannah's direction. He walked straight toward the trees where Ryker was waiting.

As soon as the man moved in front of him, he crept up behind him and put him in a chokehold before he could react. A second later, the man slid to the ground. He tied the guard's hands behind his back and pulled him into the woods. Then he grabbed the semi-automatic, sliding his own gun into the waistband of his jeans.

He saw no further movement in the area, so he motioned Savannah forward. She joined him in the cover of the trees.

"I'm going through the back door of the barn," he told her.

"I'll cover you. And then I'll be right behind you."

He didn't waste time arguing. He ran toward the open door and slid inside. He could hear two men talking. They were arguing. He moved down the hall, past a stable office and around a corner. And there in the middle of the barn was a green van. Next to it were two men he used to know as well as he knew himself.

"Why didn't you tell us you were alive, Leo?" Hank demanded. "I thought Mason was running the show. I thought his surgery was just a fake-out. But it's been you all along, hasn't it?"

An odd sense of relief ran through him. He wasn't the only one who hadn't known that Leo was alive.

"Mason and I needed to keep the circle small. He's having surgery so he couldn't be implicated, and we can continue to use his connections."

"You said this was a one-time thing. Then we disappear. We start over in new lives."

"You won't want to stop after you get the cash," Leo told Hank.

"I don't like this. Where have you been? What have you been doing? How the hell did you get out of Afghanistan?"

Ryker wanted to know the answers to those questions, too, but before Leo could say a word, they heard the sound of an engine.

"That's Vance," Leo said. "Keep it together, Morgan. Everything goes as planned, and we walk away rich men."

Ryker moved behind the wall of a stall as Vance entered the barn. He was accompanied by a heavily armed younger man, but he waved him toward the door once he saw Hank and Leo in the barn. In Vance's hand was a laptop computer. The payment was going to be a wire transfer, Ryker realized, and probably untraceable.

"Open the van," Vance told Leo, not acting at all surprised that Leo was alive or in charge.

Leo motioned for Hank to do the honors.

"Half of the shipment is there," Leo said. "The other half will be yours when the transfer goes through."

"I need it all now or no deal," Vance said, anger in his voice. "Don't fuck with me, Leo."

"You're not in charge anymore," Leo replied. "I'm not your errand boy. This is my deal. And I've been waiting a long time to collect."

"You won't get away with this."

"Of course I will. I'm already dead. No one can touch me. And it's all because of you. You tried to take me out and you failed. But in doing so, you gave me great cover."

"Wait a second," Hank interrupted. "Vance took us out?"

"He sold us out to the insurgents," Leo said. "Did you really just figure that out, Morgan? I forgot how stupid you can be."

"You set us up?" Hank turned on Vance. "You killed Carlos?"

"He was collateral damage. The target was Leo," Vance said, without a trace of remorse in his voice. "He was trying to blackmail me to get a bigger cut. I had to take him out."

"Carlos was a hell of a lot more than collateral damage." Hank turned to Leo. "Does Mason know that Vance is the reason he lost his leg?"

"He didn't need to know. Keep your eye on the prize. This is how we take care of everyone, remember?"

"Carlos is dead because of you," Hank repeated. "Everything that happened to us is because of you."

"Because of him," Leo said, tipping his head to Vance. "I wasn't the mole; he was."

"But you were working with him in Afghanistan."

"That doesn't matter. Let's do this. Make the transfer, Vance."

Ryker moved slightly to get a better view of the unfolding scene.

Hank was shifting from one foot to the other, fury stiffening every muscle in his body. He was going to blow, but he was clearly waiting for the transfer to go through. He wanted that cash. But he also didn't want to let Vance walk away.

Vance must have sensed the changing mood, his gaze moving back and forth between Leo and Hank.

"No," Vance said suddenly, closing his computer. "This isn't happening."

"It's happening. Make the transfer," Leo bit out. "Do it now."

Vance started to back away and Hank snapped. He took one shot, hitting Vance square in the chest. Vance fell backward, blood spurting out of his chest, shock in his eyes. His guard ran in, but Hank was too quick for him, sending him face-first into the ground with a bullet to the head. Then he swung his gun toward Leo. Before Hank could shoot again, a bullet hit him in the leg, and he squealed as he crumbled.

The shot had come from the loft, and he knew who had taken it —*Savannah!*

Leo ran toward the back of the barn, and Ryker stepped out in front of him, taking his own shot, hitting Leo in the arm. The gun slipped out of Leo's hand as he fell to his knees.

"That was for Carlos," Ryker said coldly.

Leo stared back at him, no trace of surprise in his gaze. "I knew you would get in the way. How did you figure it out?"

"You're not as clever as you thought."

"What are you going to do—kill me? I'm already dead."

"Dying the second time might be more painful." He saw Savannah moving up behind Leo, but she held back, letting him play this out.

"Carlos's death was on Vance," Leo said. "He set up the ambush."

"Because of you. And you knew it. That's why you disappeared."

"I played dead, because I thought he might try again. It was self-preservation."

"How did you get Mason involved in this?"

"I showed him how we could take care of Carlos's family and the rest of the team. He bought it."

"But Paul found out, didn't he? You shot him."

"I didn't even know he was in Chesapeake Beach until he stepped in front of you."

"And you shot him."

"That bullet was meant for you, but he got in the way."

"Why did you want to kill me?"

"You were asking too many questions and you got the FBI involved. I had no choice."

There was no remorse in Leo's voice or in his eyes. "How did you turn into this?" he asked in bewilderment. "How did you become a monster, a man willing to betray his brothers, his country?"

"How? You don't know? You were there for every minute. We were the ones doing the dirty work while people like Vance were making millions. Why shouldn't we have had some of it? The guns he was selling were the same weapons that were taking out our troops."

"You could have stopped him, but instead you decided to profit from him."

"So, kill me. It's what you want to do." Leo gave him a scornful look. "But you've never been as cold as everyone thought you were. You like to believe in people. You saw me at the church with Buthanu, but you let it go. You bought my explanation, because you wanted to."

"Because you were my brother. But you used all of us."

"And I'll keep using you. I'll take everyone down with me. Or you can shoot me and call it self-defense. No one would blame you."

For a split second, he was tempted, more than he'd ever been tempted in his life. There was a blinding rage running through him. He wanted revenge for Carlos, for Paul, even for Mason and Hank and Todd, who had been blinded by Leo's evil. But he couldn't pull the trigger. He couldn't cross that line.

He heard engines roaring, the pounding of feet. Savannah went out front to meet her team.

"You're lucky," he told Leo. "You're not going to die today."

"You call that luck?" Leo asked, finally defeated. "I was so close to having it all."

"And then what? You would have only wanted more. It would have never been enough."

"I could have gotten more. You never appreciated how good I was."

"Or how bad." He stepped back as the agents came down the hall. It gave him great satisfaction to see Leo cuffed and led away. He might be going to the hospital first, but then he'd be headed to jail, where he would hopefully stay for a very long time.

As he moved back into the main part of the barn, he saw Hank being loaded onto a stretcher. Hank asked the paramedics to give him one second and waved Ryker over.

"I'm sorry," Hank said. "I didn't know about Leo. I swear I didn't know about him and Vance. I didn't know they were the reason Carlos died. You have to believe me, Ryker."

"Why does it matter?"

"Because I'm not like Leo. I was doing this to help the families. I shot Vance because he's the reason Carlos's kids don't have a father. I just wish Leo was dead, too. He did all this. I don't believe Mason knew the whole story, either. Leo suckered us all. You have to help us, Ryker. Get Savannah to use her connections. Please."

"We need to go," the paramedic interrupted.

"Then go." He didn't have anything else to say to Hank. He'd gotten the answers he'd come for, but they didn't make him feel better. Leo and Vance were traitors and probably Mason, too. He supposed it was good to know that Hank, Todd, and Paul had not known about Leo or Vance. They had bought into a plan that didn't involve selling weapons to the enemy, but they had still been incredibly stupid, and they would pay heavily for what they'd done.

As Savannah walked toward him, he realized he was happy about something. She was alive. She was safe. And that was the most important thing of all. He wanted to put his arms around her and hold her tight, but the FBI, police and agents from the ATF were swarming the barn.

She gave him a searching look. "What did Hank say?"

"He was sorry. He didn't know about Leo and Vance."

"That was pretty clear from their exchange." She paused. "I'm not going to ask if you're all right, but how do you feel?"

"I don't know yet. I'm processing everything. Nice shooting, by the way. I don't even know how you got into the loft."

"I was very quiet, and once Hank and Leo started arguing, no one was paying me much attention. I was, however, surprised when Hank shot Vance."

"I knew he was about to blow. I just didn't know who he was going to take out first."

"I only shot Hank because—"

"You had to," he said, cutting her off. "It was the right move. And your shot sent Leo running straight toward me. There was a part of me that wanted to kill him, Savannah."

"But you didn't. That's not who you are."

"I just hope he gets a life sentence."

"We'll do everything we can to make that happen. Unfortunately, some of the other guys will probably go to prison, too."

"I know. They faked their deaths to take care of their families, and now their families will see them go to jail. It's hard to see the justice, even though I know it's there. At one time, they were good men, Savannah. They were patriots."

"Maybe they'll have a chance to do something good with the rest of their lives, even if they are in jail."

"I hope so. I hope this wasn't all for nothing, but I'm afraid it was."

———

Ryker's statement rang through Savannah's head for hours, but she had no chance to talk to him about it. After returning to the DC field office, they were separated for a more thorough debriefing. It was almost eight o'clock at night before she was done. She walked back into the now almost-empty operations center. Most of the agents had gone home for the night, but Parisa was still at her desk.

"I hope you didn't stay for me," she told her, sinking into the chair next to her desk.

"I had a lot of reports to do. Ryker just finished talking to Paxton. He's in the restroom now."

"He must be exhausted."

"I'm sure. You look tired, too."

"The adrenaline rush has finally receded. Have I missed anything while I've been going over and over the same facts for the past hour?"

"A few things. Mason Wrigley was officially arrested at the hospital and informed of the failed plan. He's not talking. He requested a lawyer."

"He's going to need a good one. He was right in the middle of this."

"Hank Morgan will spend the night in the hospital and then go to jail. He's facing homicide charges for Vance and his security guard."

"I'm sure he thinks the killings were justified, because of what Vance did in Afghanistan."

"Well, he'll get to tell his story to a jury," Parisa said. "Todd Davis is talking up a storm now. Once he realized Leo Romano was alive, and he'd been sold a false narrative, he was much more interested in making a deal. He was probably lucky that they decided to cut him out at the last minute. He wasn't involved in the theft of the weapons or the shootings, and he'll probably face much less severe charges for his part in the conspiracy."

"I hope the same will be true for Paul."

"I also checked in with your friend Abby. Paul is awake and he's also talking. We sent an agent down to Chesapeake Beach to take his statement and to officially put him under arrest."

"That must have been difficult for Abby to see," she said, her heart going out once more to her friend.

"She told me that she understands Paul could be in trouble, but she's glad he's going to live. Beyond that, she isn't sure what's happening with their relationship, although he's very apologetic and remorseful."

"She doesn't owe Paul anything. I hope she takes her time in deciding what she wants to do."

"So do I. By the way, I also removed her security. I don't believe she's in any further danger, and she was fine with that."

"Thank you for taking care of all these details, Parisa. I know there's a lot to sort out."

"This case has a lot of layers to it," Parisa said. "I suspect Ryker will be riding an emotional roller coaster for a while. Are you going to be riding with him?"

She wished she knew the answer to that question. Ryker had told her he loved her, but that had been in the heat of the moment. *How could she hold him to it? How could she even believe it?*

But she wanted to believe it. She wanted to believe there was a chance for them. But she just didn't know what would happen when everything settled.

"Savannah?" Parisa gently prodded.

She shrugged. "I don't know. We'll see."

"If I can just give you one word of advice?"

"Can you really stop at one word?" she asked lightly.

"Geography. That's the word. But you're right, I can't stop. Don't let geography be the deciding factor. You could work closer to the Chesapeake Bay. You could work here."

"Oh, yeah, Agent Paxton is my greatest fan."

"He's not so bad when you get to know him. At the end of the day, you made a big case. You kept a truckload of weapons from being sold to terrorists. You helped unravel an illegal arms network. Trust me, by the time he's done telling his bosses about it, you will have been his secret weapon."

"I can live with that. I'm not looking for praise or a promotion. I got into this because I wanted answers for Abby. Unfortunately, those answers are going to make her lose her husband for the second time."

"Well, maybe she can take solace in the fact that he wanted to provide for her."

"Maybe." She paused, wondering why Ryker was taking so long and hoping he hadn't pulled another vanishing act on her. "Ryker is still in the building, isn't he?"

"I'm here," Ryker said, coming up behind her.

Relief ran through her. "Oh, good. I was afraid you'd bailed again."

"Nope. Not this time."

"Do you guys want to stay at my place?" Parisa asked. "I have an extra room and a couch, if that was to be needed."

"I don't want to put you out," she replied. "But thanks for the offer."

"You wouldn't be putting me out. But if you want a little more privacy, I get it."

Her cheeks warmed at the gleam in Parisa's eyes. "Thank you for everything," she said, getting to her feet.

"Any time, Savannah. And remember what I said."

"I will," she promised. Then she turned to Ryker. "Are you ready to go?"

"More than ready."

They took the elevator down to the garage and got into Ryker's truck. "Where do you want to go?" she asked, as she fastened her seat belt.

"Let's find the nearest hotel and order room service."

She liked the sound of that. She was not ready to say good-bye to him yet.

Fifteen minutes later, they walked into a beautiful and luxurious suite at the Carmichael Hotel, a five-star property. Ryker had insisted on picking up this room, since there was no longer any need for them to be staying under an alias. She had to admit she was impressed with his choice, especially with the king-sized bed in the over-sized suite that included a love seat, a dining table, and an antique desk. There was also a large flat-screen television along one wall. But it was the bath that really took her breath away: white marble floors, and a deep Jacuzzi tub, big enough for two.

"Good enough?" Ryker asked, as they returned to the room.

"More than good. This is really expensive, Ryker."

"Don't you think we deserve it?"

"We do."

He walked over to her and pulled her into his arms. She happily went into the embrace, resting her head against his solid chest. It felt like it had been years since they'd made love, but it had only been twenty-four hours ago. So much had happened, and she was thrilled to have a moment to just hold on to Ryker and to have him hold on to her.

"So," he began.

She lifted her head. "You have something you want to say?"

"I'm hoping you have something to say," he replied, with a gleam in his eyes.

She knew exactly what he was talking about. "I love you, too, Ryker."

"Well, it took you long enough."

"You didn't give me a chance before. And there was a part of me that wasn't sure you didn't say it just to keep me from following you into the barn."

"That wasn't the reason. I wanted to say it in case I didn't get a chance. I wanted you to know how I feel about you."

"It's crazy fast."

"It's been five years."

She smiled. "I don't think all those years in between count since you didn't even know my name."

"I still missed you. More than I ever would have expected. Probably more than you would ever believe. But you would pop into my mind at random moments, and I would often see you in my dreams."

Her heart twisted with pleasure at his words. "I thought about you, too. But then I'd tell myself it couldn't possibly have been as good as I remembered. I had to convince myself of that so I wouldn't try to find you, so I'd be able to move on." She took a breath. "But what now? I know that's the question every man hates, but I have to ask it."

"I don't hate the question; I'm just not sure of the answer."

"You don't have to know the answer," she said quickly. "We don't have to decide anything tonight."

"That's true." He drew in a breath, as his gaze darkened. "I need to apologize for what I did earlier, leaving you without a word, not answering your texts, not treating you with the respect you deserve."

"Why did you do it?" she asked, genuinely curious to know the answer. "I thought we were on the same page."

"It was a combination of things. I was angry after my talk with

Todd. And then Agent Paxton got in my face, making it clear I was not part of whatever was going to happen next. It pissed me off, and I had to get out of there. I wasn't really intending to stay away, but one thing led to another. I figured I might as well get the truck, and then I wanted to check out Mason's house."

"The truck could have been rigged with explosives. You took a big chance."

"I checked it out before I got in. Anyway, you know the rest."

"Well, I'm glad you finally called me."

"I didn't leave you out because I don't respect you, Savannah. It wasn't really about you at all. I know that sounds selfish. I've been so focused on myself, on my issues with the bells, that I stopped seeing anyone else. I was completely self-absorbed. I put up huge walls to keep everyone out. Maybe that's the way things would have gone on if I hadn't met you again, if you hadn't broken down my walls, pushed past my defenses, forced me to let you see the pain I was in. I hated you seeing me so weak, half the man I used to be, the one you fell for that night in the bar."

"Oh, Ryker, you are not weak. You are one of the strongest men I know. You not only had to face your demons to get to the truth, you had to deal with the betrayal of close friends. I know you must be in pain, even though you won't admit it."

"You're starting to know me a little too well."

"I don't think I'm even close to knowing you too well, but I'd like to get there."

"I'd like to get to know you better, too. You're an amazing woman, Savannah—smart, brave, generous, and beautiful."

Moisture blurred her eyes.

"Hey," he said gently. "I didn't mean to make you cry."

"It's what you said. You put beautiful at the end. It's always been the first and often the only thing anyone saw in me."

"You are so much more than a pretty face. Although, you still take my breath away every time I look at you."

"You're not so bad yourself."

He grinned. "I'm glad you think so."

"And I'm happy you see me—the real me. To be honest, Ryker,

I don't think I've ever shown my true self to anyone else. I was brave about a lot of other things, but not that, not the personal stuff. My father's desertion did a real number on my head."

"Hey, you never told me what happened with your dad."

"We can hash that out later. But I can tell you this; we spoke our truths, and for the first time I think we actually heard each other. And then we bonded over taking out the two gunmen who had come to kill my dad."

He frowned. "Wait a second. I think you glossed over that before."

"The important thing is we survived the hit, my dad trusted me enough to tell me what Vance was up to, and we put our past behind us. He's even willing to talk more often in the future."

"Do you want that?"

"I think so. We'll see how it goes. I know it won't be easy or perfect, but I understand him better, and I think he understands me. Only time will tell." She paused. "Getting back to us, I just want you to know that you broke down my walls, too—walls I didn't even know I had up. So, we're even."

"Then let's see where this thing goes."

"Well, I have to go back to LA," she said, bringing some reality back into the conversation. "I really like my job, Ryker. And after having a glimpse into Parisa's work life, I appreciate mine even more."

"I get it. And I have no problem with California. They have fishing boats there."

"Really? You wouldn't mind moving?" She had to admit even after everything they'd just said to each other, she was surprised.

"I'm done hiding on the Chesapeake Bay. Not that I don't like it there. But I need more. And I need you. I don't want to say good-bye to you, Savannah. And I don't want you to say good-bye to me. If you're in LA, I'm there, too."

Her heart swelled with love. "I'm the luckiest woman in the world."

"I'm the lucky one." His arms tightened around her as he gazed into her eyes. "I'm going to do everything I can to make you happy."

"If I have you, I'll be happy." She pressed her mouth against his, savoring his taste, his heat, and relishing the fact that there was no longer a ticking clock on their relationship. This kiss was just the beginning of a lifetime of kisses, a lifetime of loving each other.

"Now how about that bath?"

EPILOGUE

THREE MONTHS LATER...

Savannah couldn't believe her father was walking barefoot on Santa Monica Beach with Ryker, that Abby was playing in the surf with Tyler, or that Parisa was sitting next to her on a blanket, sharing an afternoon picnic. So much had changed and all for the better.

"I can't believe how warm it is," Parisa said. "I'm not going to miss the DC winters."

"I'm so glad you're joining our task force. You're going to be a tremendous asset."

"I hope so. I'm looking forward to working together, Savannah. Actually, I'm looking forward to being back with everyone. I think when you came to DC, I realized how much I had missed everybody."

"Now, you'll just get sick of us."

"I doubt that. And I have to thank you for the opportunity. The only reason I can make the move is because of what Ryker is doing. I never thought Jared would leave the CIA, but Ryker's new company got him excited for the first time in a long time. He's doing a good thing, Savannah."

She nodded. She was more than a little proud of Ryker. "He

couldn't get past the idea that the families weren't going to be taken care of after the weapons deal went bust. And he blamed himself for not having considered the toll his teammates were suffering. He decided to do something about it. When he first told me he wanted to take care of everyone, I had no idea how he could actually do it. I had no clue that he was wealthy."

"Well, at least he knows you didn't fall for him because he was rich."

"I definitely did not. I knew very little about his family, least of all the fact that his grandfather had left him a huge trust fund. I guess the guys in his unit knew and that was partly why they didn't involve him and maybe why they resented him a little because they were struggling. He was struggling, too, just not with money."

"Well, he's using the money for a great cause."

She nodded. Ryker had decided to create a foundation that would help support the families of fallen soldiers. In addition to his trust, he was going to fund it by running his own private security company. He'd be hiring soldiers who needed to move on to the next chapter in their lives. Jared was going to come on board as Ryker's second-in-command. They'd become good friends in the past three months, and Jared was ready to use his agency and international experience in a different way, one that would give him more autonomy.

"Is your father also joining the company?" Parisa asked.

"I think so. He has really warmed up to Ryker and vice versa. How they're going to work together is still to be determined, but my dad will be making more trips to Southern California."

"I'm sure you're part of the draw."

"Maybe. It's still baby steps with us. We can really annoy the hell out of each other, but there's something building." She paused as Abby came running back to the blanket and sat down, her cheeks red from exertion.

"Tyler is having so much fun," Abby said. "He adores Ryker, by the way."

She smiled, seeing Ryker and her dad throwing a football

around with Tyler. "I'm glad he's having a good time, and that you are, too."

"I really am."

"I just got a text from Jared and Jax," Parisa interrupted. "They need a hand bringing food down from the parking lot. I'll be right back."

"Do they need our help, too?" she asked.

"I think we can handle it," Parisa answered, as she got up. "If not, I'll text you."

"She's nice," Abby said. "It's fun to see you here in your world with your friends and coworkers."

"I'm so happy you came."

"The trip was a great idea. Tyler has been doing better, but I think we both needed a break from home."

"Has he seen Paul?" She knew that Abby had been hesitant to take Tyler to the jail where Paul was being held. Out of all the guys, he was facing the least amount of charges, but he would serve time for what he'd done.

"No, but Tyler has written to him, and Paul has written back. Tyler doesn't understand what happened. How could he? It's difficult for me to understand. But I told him that even though his father has done some things that were wrong, he still loves him very much. That seems to work for now."

"How are you feeling about Paul?"

"Like I need to let him go."

"Really?" she asked, a little surprised.

"It's not that I can't understand or even that I can't forgive him. I just don't think I love him the way I used to, the way I should if I'm going to stay married to him. To be honest, I think our love ended a long time ago. Paul realized it before I did. That's why he was drinking so much, why he was floundering. I'm always going to have feelings for him. He's the father of my son. But I don't want to be his wife anymore. Is it horrible that I don't want to support him through this? That I don't want to wait for him?"

"No, it's not horrible; it's how you feel. And you're entitled to feel any way you want. Paul hurt you in a terrible way. Frankly, I don't know if I can forgive him for what he did to you and Tyler. But, on the other hand, I am grateful to him for saving Ryker's life and mine as well."

"He realized that he'd made a horrible mistake. When he found out Leo was alive, he knew there was a hidden agenda."

"Well, Leo will be going to jail for a very long time."

"I hope so. He's the reason we all ended up where we are. Although, I still don't know how the guys drifted so far from their moral compasses. They say war changes people. It must have changed them."

"I think it did."

"But Ryker would have never fallen for that scheme. And not because he has money, but because he has such a strong sense of right and wrong. I admire that about him."

"So do I. But he did feel bad for abandoning his guys for so long. He wants to make it right."

"I already got a check from the foundation he started. It was very generous. I hope one day when Paul gets out, maybe he can also give back. I think it would be good for him. Not that Ryker would probably want his help."

"He's open to it."

"Well, it's a long way off." Abby paused. "It looks like our party is getting bigger."

Savannah jumped to her feet as Jared, Jax, and Parisa came back, joined by Flynn and his now fiancée Callie. They'd gotten engaged a month ago and were planning a summer wedding. They'd also brought two large coolers with them as well as bags of food.

"This is amazing," she said.

"We were hungry," Jax told her with a laugh.

"You're always hungry," she reminded him.

"I work hard."

"And he plays hard," Flynn put in.

"You're just jealous cuz you can't play anymore," Jax retorted.

"That's right, he can't," Callie said.

"Hey, Stone, you want a beer?" Jax asked, as Ryker joined them, while her dad continued to entertain Tyler.

"Definitely," Ryker said. He took the beer out of Jax's hand and then put his arm around her shoulders and gave her a loving look. "How are you doing?"

"Great," she said, smiling back at him. "I like having everyone together. I spent so much of my life thinking I didn't really fit in anywhere, but this is where I fit."

"Your team loves you. I love you. Hell, even your dad loves you."

She laughed. "We're still a work in progress."

"I love you, too," Abby put in, as she got to her feet. "And you better be good to her, Ryker, because she is my oldest and best friend, and I will hunt you down if you don't treat her right."

"I will definitely treat her right," he promised.

"I'm going to rescue your dad," Abby said to Savannah.

As Abby left, she turned back to Ryker. "You fit in well, too. I'm so glad that this move worked out for you. As grateful as I was that you were willing to come here, I didn't want you to be unhappy."

"Are you kidding? I couldn't be happier. I have you and a new purpose in life, and I can finally put some of my family money to good use. I talked to Carlos's wife earlier today. She's doing well. They're going to move into a bigger apartment now. She'll only have two kids in a room, instead of three."

"You are going to do a lot of good with your foundation, and I think the work side of it, the security firm, will give you that excitement and adrenaline rush you might be missing."

He laughed. "Are you kidding? Living with you, loving you, is more than a little exciting." He gave her a hot kiss. "Later tonight I'll show you."

Her heart filled with love. "I can't wait."

# # #

Have you missed any books in the series?

OFF THE GRID: FBI SERIES

PERILOUS TRUST #1
RECKLESS WHISPER #2
DESPERATE PLAY #3
ELUSIVE PROMISE #4
DANGEROUS CHOICE #5
RUTHLESS CROSS #6
CRITICAL DOUBT #7

More Thrilling Romantic Suspense

Lightning Strikes Trilogy
BEAUTIFUL STORM
LIGHTNING LINGERS
SUMMER RAIN

Sanders Brothers Duo
SILENT RUN
SILENT FALL

Deception Duo
TAKEN
PLAYED

For a complete list of books, visit Barbara Freethy's website at
www.barbarafreethy.com

Barbara Freethy is a #1 New York Times Bestselling Author of 68 novels ranging from contemporary romance to romantic suspense and women's fiction. With over 14 million copies sold, twenty-three of Barbara's books have appeared on the New York Times and USA Today Bestseller Lists, including SUMMER SECRETS which hit #1 on the New York Times and DON'T SAY A WORD, which spent 12 weeks on the list!

Known for her emotional and compelling stories of love, family, mystery and romance, Barbara enjoys writing about ordinary people caught up in extraordinary adventures.

She is currently writing two ongoing series: The romantic suspense series OFF THE GRID: FBI SERIES and the contemporary romance series WHISPER LAKE.

For more information on Barbara's books, visit her website at
www.barbarafreethy.com

You can also follow Barbara on Facebook at www.
facebook.com/barbarafreethybooks

CPSIA information can be obtained
at www.ICGtesting.com
Printed in the USA
LVHW111603140820
663221LV00003B/618

9 781951 656003